MOMENTS IN TIME
BOOKS 1-3

KAREN STIVALI

DREAMSPINNER PRESS

Published by
DREAMSPINNER PRESS

5032 Capital Circle SW, Suite 2, PMB# 279, Tallahassee, FL 32305-7886 USA
http://www.dreamspinnerpress.com/

This is a work of fiction. Names, characters, places, and incidents either are the product of author imagination or are used fictitiously, and any resemblance to actual persons, living or dead, business establishments, events, or locales is entirely coincidental.

Moments in Time
© 2015 Karen Stivali.

Cover Art
© 2015 Anna Sikorska.
Cover content is for illustrative purposes only and any person depicted on the cover is a model.

All rights reserved. This book is licensed to the original purchaser only. Duplication or distribution via any means is illegal and a violation of international copyright law, subject to criminal prosecution and upon conviction, fines, and/or imprisonment. Any eBook format cannot be legally loaned or given to others. No part of this book may be reproduced or transmitted in any form or by any means, electronic or mechanical, including photocopying, recording, or by any information storage and retrieval system, without the written permission of the Publisher, except where permitted by law. To request permission and all other inquiries, contact Dreamspinner Press, 5032 Capital Circle SW, Suite 2, PMB# 279, Tallahassee, FL 32305-7886, USA, or http://www.dreamspinnerpress.com/.

ISBN: 978-1-63216-957-0
Library of Congress Control Number: 2014920196
First Edition May 2015

Printed in the United States of America
∞
This paper meets the requirements of
ANSI/NISO Z39.48-1992 (Permanence of Paper).

Table of Contents

Moment of Impact 1

Moment of Truth 87

Moment of Clarity 185

Moment of Impact

This book is dedicated to Karen Booth, my awesome critique partner,
for always supporting me and my ideas,
even when I think they're crazy.

Acknowledgments

Many thanks to KD Wood for encouraging me to follow my heart, to Mandy Pennington, Kira Decker, and Amanda Usen for being beta readers extraordinaire, to Kim Pearson for giving me her expert opinion and an enthusiastic thumbs-up, to Saritza Hernandez for loving Collin and Tanner and believing in me, to Sue Adams for being a joy to work with and making my words shine, and to Elizabeth North and her amazing staff at Dreamspinner Press for giving me the opportunity to share this story with the world.

Special thanks to Damon Suede for giving me the best possible advice at the precise moment I needed to hear it.

Chapter One

I DIDN'T mean to see Tanner D'Amico's cock. I really didn't. When I heard his key in the door, I assumed he'd be coming in with Wendy. She stayed over Monday nights because Tuesday mornings she had class in the building right next to our dorm. That meant every Monday I'd pretend to be asleep and try not to hear them fucking. Not that that ever worked. The more he'd whisper to her that she should be quiet, the more noise she'd make. Which probably wouldn't have bothered me if it didn't make me so fucking jealous.

As soon as the keys jangled in the hallway, I flipped off the bedside lamp and sprawled on the bed. Since it was earlier than usual, I wasn't under the covers yet, and in my haste I wound up on my stomach, facing Tanner's half of the room. That was never the plan. On my side, turned toward the wall, was the optimum position—the easiest for closing my eyes, focusing on something random, and trying to forget what I was hearing.

Light from the hall filled the room for a few seconds, then faded back to semidarkness. No room that faced the courtyard was ever completely dark at night. I kept my eyes shut and wondered if I could get away with rolling over without giving away that I was still awake.

Tanner left the lights off. His backpack thudded onto the carpet. His shoes knocked into the dresser when he kicked them off. Clothing rustled, and his back cracked like it always did when he took off his shirt. The sound of his zipper lowering made the base of my cock tingle. He flopped onto his bed with enough force, the springs moaned in protest. I closed my eyes tighter and thought about my Econ exam. That was enough to kill any form of boner. Usually.

This time it worked until I realized I hadn't heard a single sound from Wendy and made the mistake of opening my eyes.

Wendy was nowhere in sight. But there it was. His cock. Pointing at the ceiling like a goddamn arrow. At first I thought it was wishful thinking. In the seven months we'd been roommates, I'd had more fantasies about Tanner's cock than I could count, many of which started with him flat on his back and his dick straight in the air. Just like this. My pulse rate skyrocketed. My mouth went dry. I must have blinked a dozen times, thinking if I opened my eyes one more time, the image would be gone, replaced by the unwanted sight of Wendy on top of him. But this time he was alone, and no matter how much I blinked, nothing changed.

Until he started to move.

Mother of God.

I knew I shouldn't watch. Somehow it felt like an even bigger invasion of privacy to be looking at him alone than it had been to listen to him in bed with Wendy.

Econ. Econ. Econ. Jesus, he's touching himself.

I couldn't have gotten harder any faster if his hand had been stroking my cock instead of his own. Only it wasn't *stroking* exactly. I'd always imagined what he'd look like with his fist wrapped around himself, but that wasn't what he was doing. His hand was open, his fingertips gliding up and down the underside in total silence. Any blood left in the part of my brain that told me to look away headed straight to my groin. My stomach contracted as I pressed into the mattress, desperate to feel any kind of friction.

Tanner shifted, rustling the covers. *Please don't get under the blankets.* I swallowed hard, hoping he couldn't hear the boulder-sized lump moving around in my throat. He ran a hand through his hair, then slowly trailed it down to his shoulder, across his collarbone, over his chest. I took inventory as he went, wishing the glow from the streetlights would make the room a little brighter. Tanner flicked a nipple back and forth, and my own rasped against my T-shirt with every breath I took. *Fuck.* My dick was now poking out past the waistband of my shorts, leaving both the comforter and my stomach slick. Moving terrified me, but I couldn't help it. I raised and lowered my hips the tiniest bit and nearly choked on the sigh I couldn't let out.

By the time his hand made it back to his cock, mine was ready to explode. Every muscle in my lower body was tense, primed, begging for release. *Don't come. You can't come. He'll hear you. There's no way you can be quiet enough that he won't hear you.*

Not looking seemed like the best idea. I closed my eyes. Tight. So tight, I saw colors instead of darkness. Swirls of blues and purples danced behind my eyelids, and I watched each one, hoping for distraction.

Then he moaned. It wasn't loud or anything. Just a small gasp, really. Just the most erotic fucking sound I'd ever heard. My cock heard it too and throbbed in silent reply. At least I think it was silent. My pulse hammered in so many places, it wouldn't have surprised me if Tanner had sat up in bed and told me to quiet the fuck down. He seemed too busy to notice. The second I opened my eyes, my gaze zoomed straight back to his cock. He'd started stroking. Two fingers or maybe three, still massaging the underside but focusing on the sweet spot just below the head. When I moved, that was the same spot that slid back and forth against my now wet comforter. I'd have given anything to trade the sensation of damp cotton-poly blend for the touch of his fingertips.

His hips pitched, and his thigh flexed out to the side. *Shit. He's getting close.* My eyes raked over him. His neck arched as his head pressed back, his dark hair splayed across the pale pillowcase. The ridges of his tanned abs bunched as his hand moved faster. The lack of sound amazed me. Had he done this before, in complete silence, with me right there? Had I simply missed it? I'd have watched every night if I'd known it was an option.

Heat filled my face. *Fucking voyeur. He doesn't want you watching. He thinks you're asleep.* Shame flooded through me, making my stomach roll over. Didn't stop me from watching. Those fingers—up and down, up and down, swooping across the head every third stroke. He sucked in a soft breath. *This is it. Oh Jesus. He's gonna come.*

My balls pulled up so tight they practically disappeared into my body. I squeezed my legs together, trying to hold still. I trembled with the need to move, to feel something against the impossible hardness that consumed my thoughts.

Tanner's hips jerked up off the mattress, his head rose off the pillow, and he finally fisted his cock, jacking hard and fast. With three final strokes that seemed like the most important movements I'd ever witnessed, he came. I didn't see the first blast, but I heard it *thwack* against the poster hanging behind his bed. *Fuck.* The next two splattered across his chest. He kept pumping, and the white streaks continued to coat him. Four. Five. Six.

My hips were moving of their own accord, rubbing my dick against the bedsheets. *Shit. I need to stop, or I'll come. I'll come and cry out, and he'll know.* I clenched the blanket so hard my hands ached, trying to get some semblance of control, but I still couldn't force myself to look away from Tanner. Perfect. Beautiful. Peaceful. Still except for the gentle rise and fall of his chest. I wondered if maybe he'd fallen asleep.

Then he turned toward me and opened his eyes.

Chapter Two

I FROZE, which seemed appropriate since my body had gone cold from head to toe. *He can't be looking at me. His eyes probably aren't adjusted to the dark. I bet he can't even focus after that orgasm.* My heart pounded against the bed so hard and fast, I thought I might throw up.

Tanner tilted his head, and his eyes flashed in the light filtering through the window. He grabbed the T-shirt on the edge of his bed and wiped his chest and cock, then swiped it across the poster.

He tossed the shirt to the floor and propped himself on his elbow. "Did you come yet?"

If the bed could have opened up and swallowed me whole, I'd have been ecstatic. *Fuck me. He knew I was awake. Knew I'd been watching. Knew I was on the verge of coming just from looking at him.* Humiliation burned through me so fast, I wouldn't have been surprised if the entire room had burst into flames. Then it hit me—he hadn't stopped. He'd jerked off knowing he had an audience. An audience with one very rapt member. Me.

Tanner drew in a deep breath and exhaled slowly, continuing to stare at me through the semidarkness. "I know you're awake, Collin. I saw you humping the bed. It's okay."

Okay? What part of this is he okay with? The part where I spontaneously combust, or the part where I die of shame and have to be buried in an extra-tall coffin because I can't get my erection to subside no matter how many bar graphs I call to mind? I opened my mouth, but no words came out. I pressed my forehead into the pillow, hoping somehow I'd wake up and this would all have been some strange dream induced by too much late-night pizza and not enough anytime sex.

Tanner's bed squeaked, and his feet hit the floor. "Dude. You need to say something. You're starting to freak me out."

Starting to freak him out? There wasn't a word in existence to describe how freaked-out I felt. "I'm sorry."

"Sorry for what?" He didn't sound angry or upset, just curious.

My jaw ached from clenching it so hard. "For everything. I should have made some noise to let you know I was awake or left the room or something."

Tanner scrubbed his hand through his hair, pushing it off his forehead. It fell right back across his face the second he let go. *Did he just chuckle?*

"I knew you were awake."

My eyes bugged. "How?"

"For one thing, it's only ten thirty. You never go to bed before midnight, not even on the nights Wendy stays over. And while we're on that topic, I know you're not usually asleep when she's here either."

Fuck.

"For another thing, I saw the light on in our room when I crossed the quad, so I'm pretty sure you turned it off when you heard me coming in."

Dammit. Could I have been more obvious? I closed my eyes again, wishing the colors would come back so I could see or feel anything other than my own stupidity.

"All I couldn't figure out was why you were facing my side of the room. You're always hugging the wall when you pretend to be asleep, so I thought...." Tanner paused and brushed his hair out of the way again. "I don't know. I thought maybe this time you wanted to watch. So I went for it."

Went for it? "Did you want me to watch?"

"If it turned you on, then, yeah." He looked down at the floor, then over at me. "Did it?"

My hands and feet tingled. "Yeah."

His lips curled into a crooked smile. He studied me a second longer, then stood up, crossed the five feet that separated our beds, and sat down on the edge of mine. He was still naked, his body tightly muscled but lean, his cock still long and thick.

No part of us was touching, but heat radiated off him. "It turned me on too. A lot."

He must have been able to hear my heart at that point. I couldn't hear anything else. It drummed in my ears like the bass at a dance club, impossible to ignore. *Focus. This is ridiculous. He can't be saying what you're hearing.* "I thought you were straight."

"Bi." He inched closer to the head of the bed. "I thought you were straight."

"Not exactly." My cheeks burned again, partly from embarrassment and partly because having him so close was making my temperature rise at an alarming rate.

His dark eyes narrowed. "What exactly, then? I know you've been with women."

"Two women. And let's just say neither was the kind of experience anyone rushed home to write in their diary about."

He chuckled. The rumbling sound vibrated through me, making me even more aware my cock was still hard as a rock. "And guys?"

"No." I answered louder than I'd intended. "I mean, not yet. I mean... I didn't think I wanted that."

"Oh, okay." Tanner braced his arm on the bed to stand up.

Don't blow this. Not now. Not when he's right here. So close. So... Forcing myself to move, I reached out and clutched at his shoulder. His skin was smooth, warm. I pressed my fingers into his flesh with enough force, he flinched. His gaze darted to mine, wary.

Swallowing hard, I willed myself to maintain eye contact. "I didn't think I wanted that, until I met you."

Tanner's gaze raced back and forth between my hand, which was still gripping his shoulder, and my eyes, which felt like they were about to bulge out of my skull. I couldn't blink. Couldn't breathe. Couldn't think. *Do something. Say something.*

Then his mouth crashed into mine.

I like kissing. I always have. Even though I wasn't super into any of the girls I'd been with, kissing was the one thing I still enjoyed. Warm mouths, wet tongues, moving together. It felt good. I seriously thought I'd done some decent kissing in my life.

I was wrong. Tanner's mouth on mine for one fucking second proved to me that what I'd done before might have looked like kissing, might have felt like kissing, but was like the frozen french bread pizza version of kissing. Nothing like the real thing.

Nothing like this.

His tongue swept into my mouth, hot and velvety. His hand gripped the back of my neck, tugging me upright. Everything fell away. Disappeared. The whole world was this one kiss. I could have drowned in it and died happy.

Tanner pulled away, breathing hard, his forehead pressed to mine. The room spun like a carnival ride.

"You okay?"

His voice sounded lower than usual. Deep and gravelly. I gave a shaky nod, and he tipped his head back, looking at me.

"You sure?"

"Yeah." My heart beat double time as I realized he still had his hands on me. And he was still naked. And I was probably harder than I'd ever been in my entire life. *Jesus.*

"We can stop."

"No." That wasn't what I wanted. Not at all. "I just... I mean... we're roommates. What if this doesn't work out?"

Tanner's lips pulled into a grin so sexy my brain turned to oatmeal. He rubbed the back of my neck. "So, one kiss and you're already thinking about what happens if we break up?"

I shook my head. "I don't know."

"Let's see how we feel after another kiss." His face moved toward mine in what felt like slow motion. My mouth watered, and I trembled. If it had taken any longer, I might well have passed right the fuck out. He stopped a breath away from my lips, and I couldn't wait any longer. I slammed my mouth into his with enough force he almost lost his balance.

I'd always imagined his thick dark hair would feel coarse, but it didn't. It was like silk… rabbit fur. I wove my fingers through the strands, stroking again and again. I couldn't get enough of the softness, of the scent of his shampoo—some coconut-lime shit that made me think of the beach.

The closer he pulled me, the closer I wanted to get. He held my neck so hard I was pretty sure I'd have bruises. I didn't care. It felt too good to care. I'd never felt so wanted by anyone. I fisted his hair, trying to steady myself. My other hand was shaking, but I needed to touch him.

It landed on his chest. Firm. Solid. Warm, smooth skin stretched taut over muscles. I grazed his nipple and he groaned, low in his throat. Sexy as fuck. I felt the vibration in my mouth and had to remember to keep breathing. It would have been so easy not to. To just keep kissing him until I passed out or died.

Tanner broke away again, panting hard this time. His forehead stayed pressed against mine, his breath warm and fast on my lips. He tugged at my shirt, and I reached behind myself and yanked it off, tossing it to the ground.

I shivered, but it had nothing to do with being cold. Tanner ran his hand down my chest, and my abs bunched so tight they nearly cramped. My hips arched up of their own accord, and the tip of my cock bumped against his wrist. I almost came right then. Just from that little bit of contact. He wrapped his hand around me and stroked all the way down, slow and deliberate, putting just enough pressure at the base that I was able to focus. As I closed my eyes, I forced myself to breathe. *Don't come. Not yet.* All the times I'd wanted this swirled through my head like a storm of erotic images. A pornado of fantasies. And not once did that fantasy include me blowing my load after a single stroke.

Tanner made a tentative pass up my cock with his thumb, sending my blood straight back to the boiling point. "Christ, you're hard."

I'd never heard his voice so low. Thick and rumbly. Like I needed anything to turn me on more than I already was. I tried to think of something to say in response, but before my brain could kick into gear, Tanner's mouth was back on mine and thoughts weren't even a possibility. *Tongue.* That was the only word I could remember, and even that one blurred as his rolled around mine.

He tugged at my shorts, and I helped shove them far enough down my legs that I could kick them off. I don't remember lying down, but I must have, because the cool sheets were bunching under my back as Tanner's body pressed me against the bed. Sound seemed layered—hearts pounding, breaths rasping, Tanner's low groans. Sticky wetness echoed with each movement. Somewhere beneath it all, the faint squeak of the bed kept time with us.

Tanner ground his cock alongside mine, pressing into my stomach as I bucked against him. Hard thighs bracketed my hips, and he rolled us onto our sides, still thrusting.

"Fuck, Collin. You feel so fucking good." His mouth moved to my neck as his hand slipped between us, wrapping around both of us. Our cocks rubbed together, surrounded by the warmth of his hand. Up and down and up and down, all that heat sliding back and forth. His teeth grazed my throat.

I wanted to touch him. Wanted to kiss him. Wanted to do anything, but I was lost in the sensations. My breath huffed out in giant wordless puffs. I ground my head against the pillow, fighting for air or control or anything I could find, but there was nothing. Nothing besides Tanner's cock and mouth and hand.

Coming wasn't an option—it was an imperative. A need. I tried to hold back, but the pressure was too great. I crested past the point of no return, not even wanting to look back, aching for release. The first shot pulsed out of me so hard and fast, I wasn't even sure it had really happened, and then the feeling crashed over me. Waves of pleasure knocked me sideways, then swept me under as the rest unleashed.

Hot, thick bursts painted my chest, running down my ribs as Tanner continued to pump. My head jerked up with the final burst, and I caught my first glimpse of what was happening. Tanner's dark hair swung low over his face. He was watching too. Watching me come. Watching our cocks move together as he stroked them. He uncurled his hand for a second, letting my cock slip free as he gripped his own, increasing the speed and thrusting into his fist.

The moan that rumbled through him made my balls clench again.

"Fuck," he whispered, throwing me a look so full of lust and desperation, I grabbed his head and pulled it toward me.

My mouth crashed against his, and I felt his body tense as the first shot blasted out of him. I kissed him, hard, swallowing his groans as he emptied himself all over us. The tension ebbed from him, and he leaned into the kiss, tongue deeper in my mouth, spirals slower, exploring. He broke away once, twice, but each time he came back, like when you're full but the food's so damn good you want just one more bite. For the first time in my life, I wanted to be food. I wanted to be a goddamned *buffet*.

And I wanted him to devour me.

Chapter Three

Tanner rolled onto his back, and reality started to sink in. *Fuck. What just happened?* Without the heat of Tanner's body pressed against me, I could feel the cool air of the room drying out the come covering my chest. My come. His come. The blissed-out feeling gave way to something that felt a lot more like… panic.

"Shit," Tanner said, shifting up onto his elbow. "Good thing tomorrow's laundry day. We got your bed pretty good."

He's worried about my sheets? I opened my mouth to say something, but I had no words. None that made any sense to me, at least. Nothing made sense.

Tanner leaned across me and grabbed my shorts, mopping at his abs, then mine. I tensed when he touched me. "Dude. You all right?"

"Yeah." I wasn't sure I believed it, and I guess I didn't sell it very well either, because his hand stilled, and then he tossed the shorts onto the floor and sat up. "Are you?"

He scrubbed his hand through his hair, then cracked his back again. I was scared shitless he was going to say no. Or worse, not say anything, go back to his side of the room and act like none of this even happened.

"Actually," he said, and my heart froze, "I'm fucking starving. Have we got any food?"

Seriously? Food? I still couldn't move, but I managed to nod. "There's a chicken parm sub in the fridge."

"Really?"

"Yeah. Some lady ordered one without cheese, but they made it with, so she didn't want it."

"What's the point of a chicken parm sub without cheese?"

Tanner climbed over me and walked to the microwave-fridge in the corner of our room. *Still naked. Jesus. So am I. Do I put on clothes? Do I wait for him to put on clothes?* He pulled the sub out of the fridge and set it down on the desk.

"Want half?"

"No, thanks."

The foil crinkled as he unwrapped it. He took a bite and groaned. My cock gave a nod of approval as it recognized the sound. *Jesus.*

"You sure you don't want the other half? This is fucking awesome."

"I ate at work." *And I can barely swallow my own spit right now, let alone consider eating something.*

"You're so fucking lucky. There's never any food at the bookstore unless the manager brings in muffins. And she doesn't bake very well. I should have applied at Gino's when you did."

"I think a few people are gonna leave soon. I'll let you know if they're hiring." A flash of Tanner shoving me up against the wall at Gino's—his tongue in my mouth, his hands undoing my pants—raced through my mind, and I shuddered from head to toe. That could never happen. Didn't stop the image from replaying.

"Cool." He'd already finished half the sub. "Last chance." He held out the other half in my direction.

I shook my head.

"Your loss."

My arm was starting to fall asleep, so I shifted. The second I moved, I felt the cold wet spot on the bed. "Uh...."

"Yeah, sorry about that. I've got an extra blanket if you want it."

"It's okay." I sat up, still not knowing what the fuck I was supposed to do or say. The dark spot in the center of my bed stared up at me, and heat prickled through me as I remembered how it got there. I pulled the covers down, wadded them into a ball and shoved them inside my laundry bag along with the soggy shorts at the foot of the bed. "I just need to make sure I do laundry before my mom stops by tomorrow."

"Your mom's coming?"

My stomach churned at the thought. What if she knows? What if she walks into the room and *knows* the second she looks at me? I sorted through my bottom drawer, looking for another pair of shorts. I didn't feel any less naked after I had them on.

Tanner crumpled the foil and tossed it into the trash can next to the fridge. "You're starting to freak me out again. You sure you're okay?"

"I don't know." The words left my mouth before I could stop them, then there they were, hanging in the air between us.

"Okay."

Tanner stood up, and my heart made a mad dash for my throat. He was three feet away from me. If I'd taken one step forward and reached out, I could have touched him. I wanted to touch him. He took a step back, and disappointment washed over me in a cold wave. He plucked a pair of shorts off the back of his desk chair and tugged them on, then opened the fridge again.

"You want a drink?"

"Snapple?"

He handed me an iced tea, and my hand shook as I took it from him. The *pop* of the lid made me jump. Calm down. I forced myself to take a gulp and focused on the sweet, tangy taste. I hadn't realized how thirsty I was until that first swallow. The bottle was half-empty by the time I stopped drinking.

Tanner sat on the edge of his bed, picking at the plastic label on his Coke bottle. He lifted it to his lips, took a sip, and—God help me—all I could think about was his mouth. On mine. On anything. My cock shared my thoughts. *Christ.* I was getting hard again. From watching my roommate drink a fucking soda. I sat down on my bed. The sheets felt cool against my legs, and I tried to concentrate on that.

"So why's your mom coming over?"

I could tell Tanner was trying to keep his voice as normal as possible, but it sounded different. Worried? Or maybe that was just me. Maybe he'd already forgotten what we did.

"She's dropping off my suit. My niece's first communion is this weekend."

"Oh. Cool."

"You've never been to a first communion before, have you?"

Tanner shook his head and took another swig of Coke. "Nope. But I kind of assume that's the type of thing where there's food after, right?"

"Jesus, is that all you ever think about?"

He swiped his hand through his hair, and it fell right back across his face. "No. Sometimes I think about sex."

Laughter snorted from me, quickly giving way to full-blown cackling when I realized Tanner was laughing too. The sound filled the room, lifting all the heaviness that had been crushing me since Tanner left my bed.

Tanner fell back on his mattress, rubbing his side but still howling. "Oh, man, stitch. Ow."

All I could think about now was his hand moving over his abs. "Sorry."

I wasn't sure what I was apologizing for, but I was sure there should be something.

Tanner breathed out a combination groan-chuckle. "Is that why you're freaked-out? The Catholic thing?"

"Yes." I hadn't actually thought about that, but now that he mentioned it, the answer was obvious. "I mean, I think that's part of it."

"What's the other part?"

I tried desperately to read his voice. It sounded just like it had when he'd asked if I'd come yet after I watched him jerk off. Not mad... curious. "It's... I mean... I don't know. It's kind of all connected. My family's like the opposite of yours."

Tanner chuckled again. "Pretty sure that's a good thing in most ways. My family's pretty fucked up. Last time I checked, my dad was dating some chick who's around my age. And my mom's having some guru dude read her tea leaves or some sort of shit, so she can decide what her next life path should be."

He air quoted the words "life path" and rolled his eyes.

"Okay," I said. "Different kind of fucked up. Still, I don't think either of them will disown you for... anything."

Tanner propped himself on his elbow, and his eyes flashed as he studied me from across the room. "And you think yours would?"

"In a heartbeat."

"For what?"

Sitting up felt like a monumental effort. I rested my elbows on my knees and rubbed my forehead with both hands, trying to think of a way to explain. "You know about my brothers, right?"

"I know one's got kids and the other one's gonna be a priest, right?"

"Right. You know why?"

"Nope. Well, actually now that you mentioned it, I think it crossed my mind that maybe the one in the priesthood might be gay."

My mouth fell open. That thought hadn't crossed my mind. Not once. *Is he?* I shook my head. Not what I needed to be thinking about right now. "I don't... I can't even.... Okay, let me start over. When I was twelve, my mom caught Quinn jerking off. He was fifteen. We'd all been out shopping and he'd... taken advantage of having the house to himself. He must not have heard us come home."

"Yikes. So I'm guessing your mom freaked?"

"She didn't scream or yell. She stood there, made him put his clothes on, loaded us all back into the car, and drove him over to the church for him to go to confession."

"Wait, I'm not Catholic, but I thought you were only supposed to confess shit you were sorry for and didn't plan to do again."

"Yeah, well, in my mom's eyes that wasn't something he should ever do again."

Tanner snorted. "That's not realistic."

"Yeah, well, I don't know what the fuck the priest said to Quinn. He never wanted to talk about it. That night before dinner, she sat all three of us down at the kitchen table and said 'she wouldn't have that behavior in her house.' The next day she changed every doorknob to every room in the house, so none of them locked."

"Fuck."

"Quinn must have taken what she said, or what the priest said, totally to heart. Or he was so embarrassed he couldn't even think straight. I don't know. Whatever happened, he was different after that. So was my mom. She wouldn't even look at him anymore, until the day he announced he wanted to enter the seminary program. Then it was like he could do no wrong in her eyes."

"No offense, but that's kinda fucked up. I mean, if that's what he really wants to do, that's great, but if his reasons are based on that one event...."

"Right. Then it's totally fucked up. Anyway, Sean had a slightly different reaction. He got a girlfriend a few months later and got her pregnant. Married her. Now they've got three kids."

"And he's how much older than you?"

"Only three years. He turned twenty-three last month. He was sixteen when he got married."

Tanner plucked at a stray string on his comforter. "Shit. That's crazy. How old's Quinn?"

"Twenty-four. My mom had him and Sean less than a year apart. She had two miscarriages after that, then me. The doctor told her no more pregnancies, but she got pregnant again, had another miscarriage so bad she needed a hysterectomy. Otherwise I'd probably be one of fifteen kids."

Tanner blew out a breath. "Remind me not to bitch about being an only child."

I smiled. "I'll remind you."

"What about your dad? He didn't weigh in on any of this?"

"My dad wasn't around much when I was little. He worked a lot. He died when I was ten."

"Jesus, I'm sorry. I didn't realize that."

I shrugged. "I don't talk about it. Truth is, I don't remember a ton about him. My mom was always the more hands-on parent. Once he was gone, she called all the shots—she's not the kind of person a lot of people argue with."

"So it seems." Tanner paused, and I wondered if he thought my family was completely crazy. "Okay. So one brother chose celibacy, the other one chose crazy-young marriage... what about you? You don't seem to have done anything that dramatic."

"I opted for a different interpretation of 'not under my roof.'"

"What do you mean?"

"There was a big shed way at the back of our property, and I convinced my mom to let me turn it into a garage so I could fix up old cars. Said it was a great way for me to earn money for college. And it was. I bought these piece-of-shit cars and worked on them until I could sell them. By my senior year, half the teachers at the school were paying me to do their oil changes and replace their mufflers."

"I knew you were good with cars. Yours is like the fucking Batmobile. What does this have to do with anything?"

"I didn't jerk off in the house...."

"The shed?"

I felt heat creeping over my face. I'd never told anyone this. "The cars."

"No shit. Other people's cars?"

"Yeah. Until I got my own."

Tanner's eyes were round as he stared at me, and then he burst into laughter.

Great. I sound like the world's biggest dork. Why did I tell him?

"Sorry." He choked the words out. "I just can't stop thinking that the Batmobile is really the *Bate*-mobile."

Batemobile? Oh. Mastur-bate. Duh. Okay. I guess that is *kinda funny.* "Yeah, well, don't expect me to get that as a vanity plate anytime soon."

Then we were both laughing, and it felt good.

Tanner rubbed his eyes and raked his fingers through his hair. "I've never really been into cars. Not a lot of New Yorkers have them. But I have a whole new appreciation for the automotive industry now."

"Oh yeah?"

"Uh, yeah. The thought of you getting off in all those cars? That's fucking hot."

My cheeks prickled. "You like thinking about that?"

"What's not to like?"

I shrugged.

"I'm a little worried I'll get a boner every time there's a carjacking announced on the news." Tanner grinned and drained the rest of his Coke, and my cock and I watched, envying the bottle. He set it down on his desk. "What about you?"

Something in his voice made the boulder reappear in my throat. "What about me?"

"Do you like thinking about me that way? Because if you don't, it's cool. If this was a one-off, I'll get over it."

My mouth was so dry, I wasn't sure I could speak. "You'd get over it?"

"If that's what you need, then, yeah. Dude, you're my roommate. You're my friend. I'd—"

"That's not what I meant. I meant… it would require getting over?"

"Well, yeah. I'm bi, but I don't just go around humping anything with a pulse."

That seemed true enough. I knew he hooked up with Wendy for whatever their weekly arrangement involved, and I'd seen him date a few different girls the past couple of years when we lived on the same floor. I didn't even know he'd ever been with a guy. We didn't talk about stuff like that. Until now.

"Can I ask you a question?"

"Shoot."

The image of come pumping out of his cock hit me like a ton of bricks. My cock had crept down the leg of my shorts and was pressing into my thigh, leaving another very wet spot. I didn't know how to phrase what I wanted to ask.

"You've, like, been with guys?"

"Yes."

"Plural?"

"Two."

The thought turned me on and made me jealous in equal measure, but I couldn't even tell what I was jealous about—the fact that he'd done this before or the fact that it had been with someone other than me.

"Here?"

"No. No one at school. Last summer, when I worked at that restaurant on Fire Island, there was another waiter. He was a few years older than me, and I guess he saw what I'd been afraid to admit. We were closing one night, and no one else was there. One minute we were covering the salad dressings in the walk-in, and the next he was kissing me with my dick in his hand."

The feeling returned. A pang, deep in my stomach, twisting and burning. What he was describing wasn't much different from what I'd pictured when Tanner mentioned getting a job with me at Gino's. Only this was him and some other dude. An older guy, who probably had way more experience.

"Obviously you liked it."

"Yeah. And it scared the crap out of me. So I get it, you know? If you're not sure, or you're over there losing your shit about this, I understand."

"Who was the second guy?"

Tanner planted his hand in his hair and scratched the back of his head. I wanted to feel his hair under my fingers again. "I went back to my mom's place in the city, for a week between when the summer job ended and I was due to move in here. There was this guy in her building. Our age. He was home for break too, and we hooked up one night."

Hooked up? What does that even mean? I felt like an idiot not knowing. My blood was back to whooshing in my ears so fast I couldn't concentrate. I had questions. So many questions they all jumbled together.

"How come you never said anything?"

"Like I said, I thought you were straight."

"You still could have told me."

"You could have told me too."

Touché. My fingers ran along the edge of my pillowcase, playing with the trim as I screwed up the courage to say what was playing on an endless loop in my brain. "Tanner?"

"Yeah?"

"I'm gay."

Chapter Four

I DIDN'T think it was possible for any two words to mean as much as it felt like those two meant. Heat and cold flooded my body at the same time. Sure, I'd thought it was possible I was gay. More than possible. But somehow, even though I'd already known, I never in a million years thought I'd ever tell anyone else. Saying it out loud, to someone else, to Tanner, my roommate, whom I'd been trying not to fantasize about since we met, blew my mind.

"I'm glad." Tanner's voice startled me.

"What?"

He sat up and shrugged. "I'm glad you're gay. I'm glad you told me."

Of all the reactions I could have gotten to announcing I was gay, that had to be one of the best-case scenarios. *Shit. Did I just come out?* I grabbed my Snapple and took a big gulp. I needed something normal, something familiar to focus on so I wouldn't give in to the panic I felt. The weird thing was, as much as it terrified me to think about what I'd just said, what we'd just done, another part of me was more at peace than I think I've ever been in my life. Like I was caught up in a huge storm, but a small part of me was at the eye, where everything was calm. I took another deep swallow, concentrating on the way the cold liquid felt spiraling down my throat.

My vocabulary had reduced to almost nothing, but I managed a "Thanks."

Tanner smiled. "Tonight would have been pretty fucking awkward if you weren't."

"Yeah, I guess so."

"Shit, it's cold." Tanner shifted around until he was under the covers. "You sure you don't want a blanket?"

"I'm sure." I drained the rest of my drink and tossed the bottle into the recycling bin. When I glanced back at Tanner, he was looking straight at me.

"You could sleep here."

Did he just ask me to sleep in his bed? With him? My heart forgot it was supposed to keep to a certain rhythm and ping-ponged around my chest. Tanner scooted over a tiny bit, and his gaze darted down to the bed. He looked a little nervous, and that made me feel more at ease.

My feet didn't even feel the floor as I took the few steps toward him and sat down, half expecting him to say he'd changed his mind or that he'd meant something else, but he just held up the covers so I could get under them with him. Lying back against his pillow, I couldn't contain the thoughts swirling in my brain. I hadn't been in bed with another person in ages, and even then it had only been a few times. The only times it was with a guy was when my brother Sean and I had to share a bed when we stayed at our grandmother's house for a week each summer. And that hadn't happened in years.

"You tired?" Tanner's voice was soft and low, almost a whisper, like he was afraid he'd wake me if I was already dozing off.

Fat chance. The way my body was buzzing, I wasn't sure I'd ever sleep again. "Nope. You?"

"Not really."

Did he move closer, or is he just rolling over? I wriggled to try to give him more room in case I was taking up too much space. Then I felt it. His cock bumped against my hip. *He's hard. Again. For me?* My cock liked the idea of that enough, it propelled me onto my side so we were face-to-face, dick to dick. Tanner's breath smelled like Coke. His side of the room was brighter than mine. I could see his features more clearly—his eyes dark as night, his lips parted just enough that I could imagine slipping my tongue between them. I'd never noticed how thick his eyelashes were, or at least I'd never thought about it, but with his face so close, they looked like dark wings as his eyelids drifted shut, his body drawing closer… and then his mouth was on mine.

As intense as the other kisses were, this was somehow more. Slower, less frantic, deeper. His tongue explored my mouth with long, slow passes, like we had all the time in the world and nothing to do or think about other than kissing. Tanner's lips were sweet, but his tongue was vaguely spicy. He tasted fucking incredible. His hand cupped the back of my neck again, and I sighed so deep in my throat that I felt it vibrate all the way into my chest.

Tanner's cock flexed against my stomach, and I strained to be closer to him. This wasn't some heated spontaneous act of passion. This was… this was… real. His hips moved, and I bucked against him. God he felt good—hard cock, lean body, warm tongue. My brain spun from the mix of sensations.

His mouth slid from my lips to my neck. "It's okay to touch me, you know."

I struggled to swallow. *Touch him.* "Okay."

It wasn't cold anymore, but I shivered. His breath heated my neck. Silky hair swept across my chin as he moved to my collarbone, his teeth grazing my skin. My hand shook as I brought it to his waist. He sucked in a breath as his muscles bunched beneath my fingers. Taking that as a positive sign, I inched my hand between us. His shorts were soft cotton, like a T-shirt, and I could feel every ridge, every contour of his erection as I palmed it through the thin fabric.

Tanner hissed the second I started to stroke. Knowing I'd made him make that sound turned me on more than I could have thought possible. Do. Not. Come. I didn't know what to focus on. I didn't want to fuck up what I was doing, but if I thought about his cock too much, I was going to explode. If I thought about my cock, forget it. Then his hand wrapped around me and I couldn't think at all. *Fuck.*

He gave a few slow strokes through my shorts, then slipped his hand inside. I whimpered at the feel of his skin against mine. His cock expanded in response. *I guess he likes sounds.* I couldn't remember a time when I'd done anything sexual and made so much noise. Usually silence was essential, part of the deal, so parents or roommates wouldn't hear. *Not tonight.*

Tanner let go of me and tugged at my shorts. As soon as I started to push them down, he rolled onto his back and took his own off, kicking them away under the covers before rolling toward me. This time when I touched him, I felt him. Smooth, hot skin slid beneath my fingers, gliding up and down his length. He was uncut, like me, and I was grateful. I'd heard cut guys talk about how it hurt to jerk off without lube. I already felt like I didn't know what the fuck I was doing, at least this felt… familiar.

My palm grew slick with precome as the sound of stroking filled the room. Was there any sound sexier? I couldn't think of one. I couldn't think past how amazing it felt to have him in my hand. Pulling his skin taut, I lightly stroked his balls and was rewarded with a deep groan as his hips started to pump into my fist.

"Fuck, yes."

Hearing his voice all choked and strained made me even harder. His breaths grew faster, fierce puffs that let me know he was getting close. Nothing in the world seemed more important than making him come. I wanted it. Wanted to know I'd made it happen. Nudging his head away, I found his lips with mine and kissed him, hard. This time he whimpered. The sound shot through me like it was electric, sending goose bumps scattering all over my body.

Feeling bold, I shoved him onto his back. With girls I'd always been so gentle, moved with so much care, not wanting to hurt them or scare them. With Tanner? He was my size, almost exactly, and probably a little stronger. I wasn't worried about being too rough—I wasn't worried about anything. I just wanted to keep touching him. Stroking his cock felt amazing. Like stroking my own but different. Mesmerizing.

Gauging his response, I varied my grip, my speed. He moaned into my mouth, and his tongue could no longer keep the rhythm of our kiss. I pulled my head away, wanting to watch, needing to see that this was actually happening. Tanner must have needed the same thing because his head lifted off his pillow as he shoved the blankets out of the way.

The sight of his cock thrusting into my fist nearly undid me. Each pump made my cock throb. Beads of precome ran down my length.

"Fuck, Collin. So good. Don't stop."

Stop? I couldn't have stopped if my life depended on it.

Tanner groaned and arched back, his head pressing hard into the pillow. His cock got even thicker, and I felt the pulse travel up through him. *Jesus.* Come splattered on his chest and abs, coating my hand. I slowed my stroke, not wanting to stop before he was ready. He grabbed my wrist to let me know he'd had enough.

I let go, reluctantly, my body still humming from the thrill. Tanner reached under the covers and came up with his shorts. He swiped them over himself, then handed them to me. I wiped my hand, amazed at how much he'd shot, considering it was his third orgasm in probably less than two hours.

His breathing slowed, and he turned to look at me. "Guess now we both need to do some laundry."

Laughter snorted out of me, but only for a second, because then a mouth covered mine. This kiss was slow and deep like the other one, and I leaned into it. He pulled back slowly, his hand running up and down my back, then curving around my side, then around my cock. I flinched from pleasure. I was so full of need, my eyes were swimming in it. Tanner's lips slid to my neck again. A slow, lazy slide. He was all loose limbed from his climax, while I was so tight I could have snapped in two at any moment. He let go of my cock, and I had to stop myself from begging him to put his hand back where it had been.

"Tell me what you like."

His voice was low and soft and rippled through me like a breeze. I opened my mouth but realized I didn't have an answer. "I don't know."

Shit, I felt stupid. How could I not know what I liked? What I wanted? Tanner didn't seem to care about my answer one way or another, he just kept rubbing his hand over me, up my back, down my chest, over the length of my thigh—everywhere but my cock.

"You want to show me?"

Show? As in jerk off while he watched? My stomach clenched with equal parts desire and abject terror. I shook my head. "I can't."

I closed my eyes, feeling lame and even dumber.

His mouth moved over my ear. "How about if we go down to your car?"

I laughed even though I felt like crying. "Very funny."

"I take that as a no. Guess I'll just have to figure out something to do here."

His hair tickled my neck as he placed a kiss on my chest. Warm breath spread across me as he shifted in the bed, kissing lower. *Jesus God.* His hand slid back and forth, up and down my thigh, grazing my balls but still not touching my cock.

Tanner lifted his head and glanced up at me with a crooked smile. Our eyes locked. I couldn't breathe. My heartbeat drummed in my ears, behind my eyes, deep inside my belly. Tanner's gaze held mine as his lips parted. I couldn't even blink. *Please. Oh, please.* Then his mouth was on me. His hot, wet tongue swirled around my swollen head, then slid down my length as he took me deep into his throat.

A cross between a sigh and a growl tumbled out of me, and Tanner's eyes closed with what I recognized as pleasure. He was enjoying this too. He liked having my cock in his mouth. The thought in itself was almost enough to push me over the edge, but I didn't want this to stop. Not yet. Not ever. His tongue swirled over me as his head moved up and down. I'd only ever had two blowjobs before, and, to be blunt, I hadn't understood what all the fuss was about. Now I got it.

Tanner sucked my cock like there was nothing in the world he'd rather be doing. Strong fingers dug into my hip, holding me still as he worked me over, lips and tongue moving over me in ways I didn't know were even possible. I hit the back of his throat, but somehow he didn't gag, he just sucked harder, took me deeper. His hand slipped around, cupping my balls, tickling just below them so close to my ass that my whole body tensed. I sniffed in a breath so hard my brain tingled like I'd breathed under water.

My cock begged for release. I felt myself cresting past the point of no return. *Oh God. Oh yes. Please.* I tried to find the words to warn him. "Tanner… I… fuck…."

He pressed his hand firmer against my balls, fingering that same spot in front of my hole. This time when I tensed, it was all over. Come rose through my length so white-hot and fast I thought I might black out. Stars streaked before my eyes, and Tanner swallowed all around me, the pull of his mouth drawing everything out of me—come, breath, and sounds I didn't know I was capable of making. My abs clenched so hard I rose up off the bed, then fell back against it, my body convulsing.

Tanner slowed but continued to suck, gentle licks replacing the heated swirls. My brain felt warm and staticky, like a blanket fresh from the dryer. My eyes wouldn't open. I felt Tanner shift in the bed until he was alongside me again. He leaned toward me, and my head turned on instinct so our lips met for a brief kiss.

The last thing I remembered was his arm tugging me closer as I slipped into the darkness.

Chapter Five

WARM. BRIGHT. My brain woke up before the rest of my body. My eyelids were still shut, but everything was practically glowing yellow and orange. *What the hell?* I blinked, squinting into the light, disoriented by the stream of sunshine pouring through the window. Why is the window on the other side of the bed?

Then it hit me. *I'm in Tanner's bed.* Memories of the night before came back in a rush. Trying to process it, I rolled onto my back. *I'm alone.* Tanner wasn't in the bed or anywhere else in the room. The bathroom door was open, and it was dark inside. My stomach went cold. Tanner was even less of a morning person than me, if that was possible. And he didn't have class on Tuesday mornings. He never got up early if he didn't have class.

I scrubbed my hands through my hair and sat up. The sheets dragged across my body, making me instantly aware I had no clothes on. A mix of fear and pleasure tumbled through me as more flashes appeared in my head. *Jesus. What did we do?*

My heart pounded as I crawled out of bed. I grabbed my phone to check for messages. Nada. But I did catch the time. Almost noon. Fuck. I'd forgotten to set my alarm. That's what I'd been about to do when Tanner had come home. Damn good excuse for forgetting, but it didn't change the fact that I was late.

Working the screen with my thumb, I called Gino's. Marissa answered.

"It's Collin. I'll be there in fifteen minutes. I promise."

"Shit, Collin. You'd better get here faster than that, Gino's head's about to explode. We're slammed today."

"Sorry. Be there as soon as I can."

Fuck. Fuck. Fuck.

I flipped on the bathroom light and one bulb over the sink sizzled, then went out. *Great.* Turning on the shower with one hand, I grabbed my toothbrush with the other. I brushed fast and furious, spitting mouthfuls of blue into the sink and shoving the brush back into the stand. The shower was still cold, but I didn't have time to be picky. As it was, I'd be lucky if I didn't get my ass fired.

The second I ran my hand over my stomach, the slippery, slick feeling made me forget about my job. The water had reactivated the leftover come, and all I could think about was how I wondered if it was mine or Tanner's.

My cock seemed to be contemplating the same thing. I didn't have time for speculation or an erection. I shampooed, soaped, and rinsed in record time, willing my dick to cooperate and settle down.

Not caring that I was still half-wet, I pulled on jeans and my Gino's polo, shoved my phone in my pocket, and flew out the door. I was halfway down the hall before I realized my keys were still on my desk. *Fucking hell.*

A headache started behind my eyes. There was no one at the front desk—of course. Was this God punishing me? *Whoa. Where did that come from?* That sounded like something my mother would say. My mother. *Holy shit.* She was coming tonight, and I hadn't done laundry. God knew what condition the bed was in—mine or Tanner's.

I pushed the door open, thankful for the smack of cold air on my wet hair to give me something else to think about for a second. My car was twenty yards away but totally useless without keys. The sound of the campus bus echoed in my head, and I saw it pulling up to the stop.

"Wait! Hold the bus!"

The driver closed the door and started to pull away as I barreled toward it, still yelling. "Stop!"

Like some sort of miracle, the bus screeched to a halt, letting out a puff of exhaust that made me cough as I raced through it toward the now open door.

"Thanks, man."

"Don't thank me, thank her." The driver pointed over his shoulder as he pulled away from the curb.

I stumbled from the jerky movement and sat down before I fell over.

Looking up, I saw who he'd pointed to. Wendy sat in the seat across from mine.

"You're lucky I saw you running."

"You asked him to stop?"

"Yeah."

"Thanks."

Blonde curls bounced around her cheeks as she shook her head. "No worries. How come you're taking the bus? Car broken?"

"Locked my keys in my room."

"That sucks. Couldn't the RA let you in?"

"Didn't have time. I'm late for work."

She took a pack of gum out of her purse and held it toward me. "You're having a shit day."

I pulled a stick out, unwrapped it, and popped it into my mouth. "Thanks."

She crumpled the wrapper from her piece, studying me. "You look different."

She narrowed her eyes. *Holy fuck, can she tell?* I looked down at my shirt, making sure I hadn't thrown on one of the ones we'd used as a rag last night. No, clean. My ears felt like they were on fire.

"It's your hair," she said. "I've never seen it wet. It looks so much darker."

I could have cried, I was so relieved. "Oh, yeah."

She ran her fingers through her curls. "That doesn't happen as much with us bottle blondes. Your hair's so light. You must have looked like an angel when you were little."

I sure as hell don't feel like one now. "Hey, this is my stop. Thanks again for holding the bus."

She smiled and waved. She was so nice that I felt guilty for all the times I wished I'd never see her again. Tanner popped into my head as I jogged down the street toward Gino's. Did he just leave to go to class? Or had he not wanted to be around when I woke up? I hadn't seen a note. There was no message on my phone. *Shit. I'm acting like a goddamn girl. He probably had shit to do. Unless he woke up with buyer's regret.* My stomach rolled over as I yanked open the back door of Gino's.

I grabbed the last apron on the rack and quickly tied it at my waist. The cheese bin at the prep counter was low, so I went straight to the walk-in fridge. There were only two bins left, which meant they'd already gone through three. They really were getting slammed. *Gino's gonna kill me.*

I strode up to the counter and dumped the remaining shredded cheese into the new container, then pushed it back into place. Gino glared at me as he ladled deep-red sauce onto a circle of pizza dough. I watched as the bottom of the ladle made concentric spirals across the pale dough.

"You want to tell me what was more important than your job?"

"I'm sorry, Gino. My alarm didn't go off."

"You need an alarm to get up and be here for 11:00 a.m.? What the fuck were you doing last night that made you so tired at 11:00 a.m.?"

My face burned so hot, I'm guessing it was redder than the sauce.

Gino started laughing, then knocked his shoulder into mine. "It's about time, kid."

What? "I don't, I mean, I...."

"Hey, relax. She must be some piece of ass to have you so rattled. I'm just glad you finally got yourself a girl."

Oh. "Uh, yeah."

"Next time tell her you need to be at work on time. Now go work the sandwich side. Let Marissa get back out on the floor and take some tables."

"Sure." I was glad he didn't want me to help him with the pizzas. I didn't think I could fake my way through a convo about my hot night with some nonexistent chick. *Is this what it's going to be like all the time?* I'd never thought about it. I mean, sure, I'd thought about what it would be like to have a night like I had last night with Tanner, but I sure as hell never thought past it. Probably because it never occurred to me that it would actually happen.

I pulled a paper ticket off the spinner. Two Italian subs, one turkey with Swiss, lettuce, and mayo, and one tuna salad with hot peppers. I split four long rolls and laid them out on the counter. Layering sandwiches was something I could practically do in my sleep after seven months at Gino's. Oil and vinegar squirted onto the bread as I grabbed the sliced provolone with my other hand. My phone stayed silent in my pocket.

Is he as confused as I am? Is he somewhere having a conversation with someone who's assuming he spent last night with a girl? And what about Wendy? Where did she fit into all this? They'd been doing their once-a-week thing for months. Would that stop now? My head pounded. Ham, salami, *capicola*, tomato, shredded lettuce, slippery strips of roasted red peppers, oregano, salt, pepper, and another squirt of oil and vinegar. I wrapped both sandwiches in thick deli paper and taped them shut, then scribbled "Ital" on both and shoved them into the window above the counter.

I hadn't eaten since dinner the night before, but I wasn't hungry. All I wanted was answers. The big clock over the stove said it wasn't even one o'clock yet. That meant three more hours before I could get out of here. Maybe then Tanner would be home and we could talk. Then... oh, fuck. My mother. She'd said she'd be over between four and five. I was so screwed.

Chapter Six

THE BUS was late, and I was certain I felt an ulcer eating away at my stomach. That was the only thing that could possibly explain the burning and twisting behind my ribs. There was no way I'd get back to the dorm before my mother arrived, which meant she'd either have to watch me beg my RA to key into my room for me or Tanner would have already let her in, which would mean she'd see God knows what on my side of the room. I desperately tried to remember what condition the sheets were in, but I didn't have a clue. For all I knew, there were come stains on the pillow. The pain moved between my shoulder blades as I half jogged in the direction of the dorms.

By the time a bus came by, I only needed to ride it for one stop, but it was probably still faster than walking. My mother's car was right there in the parking lot alongside the building. I held my breath as I scanned the lobby, but there was no sign of her. She must have gone straight upstairs. *Dammit.*

Taking the stairs two at a time, I tried to figure out what I was going to say. As I neared the door, I saw it was propped open. I heard laughter as I pushed it open. My mom was perched on the side of my bed—my *completely made bed.*

What the hell? Did she do my laundry? My hands went cold at the thought of her pulling crusty blankets and shorts out of my laundry bag. I could already hear her telling me quietly to get in the car so we could go talk to Father Thomas. It was a good thing I hadn't eaten, or I'd have thrown up right there in the doorway.

Mom turned to look at me with what seemed to be a normal smile. "Oh, there you are, honey. I was just having a chat with Tanner and his lovely girlfriend."

Wait, what? Glancing around the room, I saw that not only was my bed made, so was Tanner's, and the rest of the room was straightened as well. Trash cans empty. No clothes strewn around. And Tanner and Wendy sat cross-legged on his bed, grinning like talking to my mom was some frigging amusement park ride.

"Thanks, Mrs. Fitzpatrick," Wendy said. "These cookies are amazing."

"They're Collin's favorite, but I know Tanner likes them too, so I always bring double. I know the cafeteria's not like home cooking."

She reached for the enormous tin on my desk and held it out to me. Oatmeal chocolate chip. She was right. They were my favorite.

And I couldn't have eaten a bite if she'd paid me.

"Thanks. I ate at work, so I'm full."

Liar. I didn't like to think of myself as a liar, but I couldn't deny I was one. A pretty damned good one, judging by how quickly she shrugged and set the tin down.

"What's in the bag?" she asked.

I'd forgotten I was carrying one. "Just sandwiches from work. My boss is really good about letting me take food home. It's subs. Anyone want one?"

Tanner's eyes darkened when they met mine, but I couldn't tell why. Was he hungry? Pissed that he'd had to entertain my mom? Trying to forget about last night? Wishing we'd leave so he could be alone with Wendy? Or was he like me, having flashbacks no matter what else he tried to think about? I hoped I didn't look as freaked-out as I felt.

No one wanted a sandwich, so I stuck them in the fridge. Mom stood up and handed me a garment bag. "Your suit's in here, along with a shirt and tie, and your dress shoes are in that bag."

I hadn't even seen the shopping bag at the foot of my bed.

"Thanks."

"Just make sure you're at the church on time. I e-mailed you all the details." She turned toward Tanner and Wendy. "You two are welcome to come if you'd like. We're having food at our house afterward."

Wendy smiled. "I wish I could, but I go home most weekends. Thanks for inviting me."

"Tanner?" Mom asked.

His brow furrowed. "I'll have to check my schedule. I'm not sure I'm free on Sunday. If I can, I'll be there."

He will? I didn't know which option weirded me out more—the thought of him there with me or the thought that he wouldn't want to go anywhere with me.

"Okay, honey." Mom put her hand on my arm and pulled me lower, then planted a kiss on my cheek. "I wish I could stay, but I promised your brother I'd babysit tonight."

"Oh, all right. Thanks for the cookies. And the suit."

"No problem." She picked her purse off my bed and smoothed the covers where she'd been sitting. Where Tanner had sat less than twenty-four hours before. Naked. "It's so nice to see your room all clean. I'm glad you got such a good roommate this year."

Tanner smiled and shot me a look that surely took at least five years off my life. I'd have traded my left nut to know what he was thinking. "Thanks, Mrs. Fitz," he said.

"See you Sunday." Mom walked out the door.

"Bye," Wendy called in a singsong voice that set my teeth on edge. She leaned past Tanner and grabbed another cookie from the tin on the desk. "These are, like, the best cookies ever. I wish my mom could bake like this."

She rested against Tanner like he was a human pillow. I didn't know what to think about anything, but I did know that I couldn't spend another minute in the room with the two of them all cozy on Tanner's bed.

I hoisted my backpack off the floor and slung it onto my shoulder. I hadn't even changed out of my work shirt yet, but I didn't care. Leaving was all that mattered. The sooner the better.

"I've gotta hit the library. See you later."

Tanner sat up fast enough that Wendy lost her balance a little and smacked him.

"Collin, wait," he said.

His eyes were dark, his brows pinched together. His lips parted like he was going to say something else, but he didn't. What could he possibly say with Wendy sitting right there? Nothing that mattered. Nothing I wanted to hear.

"Gotta go," I said and strode out the door.

Chapter Seven

I'D BEEN at the library for six hours and accomplished next to nothing. I tried to read, but the words blurred together on the page. Writing was no better. I'd get a paragraph into a paper, and my mind would wander. My back ached from the combination of uncomfortable library chairs and the fact that I was so tense, I was about to shatter.

I dug around in my pocket and fished out enough change for a soda. Food still wasn't appealing, but I figured the sugar might help clear my head. Making my way through the stacks, I hoped the machines weren't empty. Everyone hit the library midweek so they could have their weekends free, and even though it was pretty empty now, it had been packed when I arrived.

Only one light was lit. The one next to the Sprite. Of course. No caffeine. Oh, well, at least it had sugar. The can tumbled down through the machine, sounding ridiculously loud in the quiet of the hallway. I popped the top and drained half of it. You weren't really supposed to take drinks into the main part of the library, but no one enforced or followed that rule.

My phone vibrated, and I pulled it out of my pocket just in time to see the low battery symbol flash and the screen turn black. *Shit.* When I'd forgotten to set my alarm the night before, I'd also forgotten to charge my phone. I wondered who'd texted me, and when. The back area where I'd been sitting all evening had shit reception. The call that buzzed right then could have come in hours ago. I tried to turn the phone back on to see if it had enough juice left to at least show me who'd called. No such luck.

I was still fiddling with the power button when I saw Tanner. Well, I saw his shoes. Before I rounded the corner, I spotted them through the empty row on the bottom bookcase. Navy blue Chucks, no laces, crossed over each other. My heart beat double time as he came into full view. He was half leaning, half sitting on the edge of my table, arms behind him in a way that made every vein and muscle in his forearms stand out. I could barely swallow my mouthful of Sprite.

"Hey," I whispered, even though there was no one at any of the nearby tables.

"Hey."

"What's up?"

He shrugged, shoulders bunching up to his ears, hair falling over one eye. "Had to return a book. Figured you'd be up here."

"Yeah. I've got—" *What? What have I got?* No reason whatsoever to have spent half the night in the library other than the fact that I was avoiding going home. "—stuff due soon."

Tanner nodded.

I tried to keep my voice casual. "I thought you and Wendy might have wanted some time alone too."

One dark brow popped high on his forehead. "Why'd you think that?"

My cheeks heated—I'd blushed more in the past day than in the past six months. "She didn't come over last night. You know… every Monday… I figured since you skipped a night you might want to, I don't know, make up for it."

Tanner raked a hand through his hair, then braced his arm behind himself again. "She left a few minutes after you did."

"She did?"

"Yep. The only reason she came over was to help me get the room clean for your mom."

My jaw dropped. "What do you mean?"

"She stopped by the book store and said she'd run into you on the bus and that you looked frazzled. Her word."

"Wait, you worked today?"

"Yeah, we all switched our shifts around because of midterms last week."

"Oh." So he hadn't left our room to avoid me. I felt like an ass.

"Anyway, she said you'd locked your keys in the room, and I remembered you said your mom was coming. Then I got home, and the place was still trashed, so I called for backup. I threw all the laundry in the wash, and she helped me straighten up."

"You did my laundry?"

"Just the bed stuff."

"Wow." *I can't believe he did all that.*

"After the stuff you told me last night, I figured it was probably kind of important to you."

"It was. It is. Thank you."

"I owe you at least a load of laundry for all the food you bring me."

A smile tugged at my lips, but something still nagged at me. "What about Wendy?"

"She said it was worth it for those cookies."

"No, I mean did she, like, ask anything? Like why…." I was too scared to complete the question.

"Don't freak out, okay?" Tanner's eyes scanned mine.

Of course I started freaking out. My heart drummed in my ears again. "What?"

"Wendy kind of knows what happened. With us."

Every bit of oxygen left my body. If there hadn't been a bookcase for me to lean on, I probably would've fallen over. "Knows...."

Tanner looked at the floor for what felt like a decade, then looked up at me through his dark hair. "She didn't come over last night because I'd told her I was into someone else."

He might as well have punched me in the gut. *Someone else? So it's not Wendy I have to worry about, it's someone else?* "You are?"

His eyes met mine, and I forced myself not to look away. "You. I told her I was into you."

"But you didn't even know if anything would happen at that point."

"Yeah. Didn't matter. Even if nothing had, I thought I should tell her."

"Why?"

Tanner gave a long blink, and I watched those black wings cover his eyes for a moment. *Fuck, he's gorgeous.* "It felt important. Turns out she already knew before I'd even said anything."

My eyes were so buggy, I didn't even think I could manage a blink if a sandstorm hit the library. "She did? How did? I mean when did...?"

"I don't know. She's a girl, and we've been friends since we were fifteen. She knows me pretty fucking well."

"I'll say."

"We were never really a thing, you know. I mean, Monday nights, that was just a hookup. She's got a boyfriend at school in the city. That's why she goes home as many weekends as she can afford. It's to see him."

"She has a boyfriend?"

"Yeah. They've both done the long-distance thing before, and it didn't work out, so they made a pact that they can do the friends-with-benefits thing with someone nearby. To keep them from meeting someone new and having the new person turn into a relationship. I don't know. It works for them."

I struggled to wrap my head around everything he was telling me. I knew he and Wendy had been friends since high school, but I had no idea they were doing this friends-with-benefits thing in an official capacity. Honestly, I'd figured she was in love with him. "So you're not into her?"

"Not the way I think you mean." His lips twitched in a smile.

"Yeah, I know you've literally been into her. I'm not deaf."

His grin got broader, and God help me, my stomach flipped over just from watching his mouth. My cock noticed too and seemed to be having a flashback of that mouth wrapped around it. I shifted—as if there was a pose I could strike that would make it more comfortable to have a hard-on in jeans.

"And she's okay with you not being into her?"

"It was just sex, Collin. I mean, we love each other as friends, but really, that's it. She's cool."

I still hadn't had one question answered, though. I took a deep breath. "What did she say? About us?"

"She's glad I finally got my head out of my ass and manned up—her words. She thought I should have told you when we first moved in."

"You knew back then?"

"That I was interested? Shit, yeah. I kinda knew since we first met."

"Two years ago?"

Tanner nodded. I wanted to touch him so badly, my fingers burned with need. "That night you and I were the only ones who didn't go to that big party and we got drunk on the roof? I'd never wanted to kiss a guy so bad in my life."

That night flashed back into my head. I'd wanted the same thing. So much. "Me too."

"Really?"

"Yes. I'd never had feelings that strong before. Like I almost couldn't control them. I convinced myself it was because I drank so much. And I didn't have a clue you felt the same way."

"Took me by surprise too. And I sure wasn't ready to admit it. I think Wendy started noticing way back then, though. She didn't say anything, but I bet she picked up on it. Once we moved in together, though, she definitely thought I should tell you. She gave me some shit about it when I didn't."

"But she still hooked up with you."

"I was pretty adamant about staying quiet. I told her guys don't just tell each other shit like that if they think the other guy's straight. She forgets sometimes that I'm not out at school."

"But you are at home?"

"Well, yeah, sort of. I mean, my parents know. And most of the people I worked with over the summer. Bi isn't exactly a tragedy down there the way it is in smaller towns. Or, I'm guessing, at your house."

I stared at my shoes. "Thanks for doing all that. With the room and everything. I was really scared she'd show up and... know."

"It's okay. I get it. And so does Wendy. That's why she stayed and chatted up your mom. Your nice hetero roommate and his pretty girlfriend...."

"Worked like a charm. I bet you anything she gives me a lecture about how I should find a girl just like Wendy."

Tanner chuckled. "Well, you know, she does have Monday nights free now...."

I laughed, way louder than I'd intended, earning a sharp hiss from the woman wheeling a cart of books down the center aisle. Tanner grabbed my arm and pulled me between the stacks. With his hand gripping my arm and his smiling face that much closer to mine, suddenly nothing seemed funny anymore. He gave me a playful shove up against the books. My gaze darted from his eyes to his lips, then back again. Then his mouth was on mine.

It was such a relief, I didn't even think about where we were or who might see us. I just kissed him, hard. The shelves bit into my shoulders and ass as he pressed up against me. Even through our jeans, I could feel how hard he was. My cock rubbed against his through the thick fabric, making me dizzy. His warm tongue swept inside my mouth, filling me with want. I needed more—more tongue, more friction... more Tanner.

He pulled away and took a step back. The cool library air made my wet lips tingle. Only then did I think to look around. No one was in sight. Relief mixed with need, and I forced myself to breathe.

Tanner adjusted his jeans. The thick outline of his erection created a long sideways bulge. My cock strained to get closer. I cleared my throat. "I think we need to head home."

"Good idea." Tanner handed me my backpack.

I couldn't get my laptop and notebooks into it fast enough. Everything felt slow-motion, like running in waist-deep water. All I wanted was to get to our room.

The walk from the library to our door had never seemed longer. Tanner's hand bumped mine several times, and each time I could have sworn sparks flew off our bodies. More than once I had crazy thoughts of pushing him down in the bushes between buildings or shoving him up against the brick pillars along the darkened alley behind the student center. That wasn't me. I didn't even kiss my girlfriends good night if anyone was watching. Public stuff wasn't my thing. Was it? My cock seemed to think maybe it was. I was so hard, I could barely see straight enough to make it up the stairs to our room.

Our room. It had been our room for all these months, but now that had a different meaning. Now it was the place where we could be together. Really together. Tanner fumbled with the keys, and I wondered if he was as shaky inside as I was. Nervous anticipation had me vibrating from head to toe.

The door next to ours flew open, and Tim and Eric stumbled into the hall, laughing.

"Hey," Tim said. "We were just gonna knock on your door. We're heading to The Coop for food. You wanna come?"

I froze with paranoia. Could they tell? Could they see the desperation? Could they sense how aroused we were? *Fuck, did they hear us last night?*

Tanner's voice was smooth as glass. "Nah. We just ate."

"'Kay," Eric said.

"See ya." Tim gave a quick wave, and they disappeared into the stairwell.

Tanner opened our door and stepped inside. I followed, still shaken. Tanner took my backpack and set it in the closet as our door clicked shut. He reached up and turned the lock, then slammed me up against the door so hard it knocked the breath out of me. His mouth was back on mine before I could speak. Hot. Demanding. Exactly what I needed.

The door rattled behind me as Tanner bucked his hips against mine. *So good.* How could it possibly feel so good? The tingling at the base of my cock radiated outward like a starburst of pleasure. This was what all the fuss was about when people talked about how hot sex was. I finally got it. And I didn't want it to stop.

Another door opened and closed in the hallway. Footsteps echoed as they trailed past our room. Could people walking by our room hear us? Would they know? Tanner sucked my lower lip into his mouth, taking all my concerns along with it.

He leaned back, still pressing his groin against mine, and tugged off his shirt. I would never get tired of looking at him. Golden brown skin, smooth muscular chest—not pumped up like some gym rat, just firm definition. Warm hands inched under my shirt, shoving it up. I raised my arms, and he yanked it over my head.

The magnetism between us pulled me toward him with irresistible force. I had to touch him. Smoothing my palm across his chest, I felt his nipple harden at my touch. My cock flexed against his, struggling in the confines of too much fabric. My hand trailed lower, over the silky dark hair that disappeared into his jeans. I popped the button and inched down the zipper.

Surreal. I kept expecting him to stop me. To tell me to get off him. Instead he shivered with what I realized was need.

His cock sprung out the minute I spread his fly open. No underwear. He must have noticed my surprise, because he laughed.

"I had time to do your laundry, not all the laundry."

"Not complaining. Trust me." I wrapped my fingers around him, and he thrust into my fist. Silky heat glided across my palm. Stroking him made my cock throb, but I focused on him. Turning to the side, I gave his shoulder a push until he was up against the wall. His hands went for my zipper, but I pushed them away, continuing to stroke. His head thumped against the wall, and pleasure surged through me, knowing he was this turned-on. Because of me. Because of what I was doing to him.

My mouth watered, and I knew if I stopped to think, I'd get caught up in my own thoughts. I dropped to my knees, dragging his pants down as I went. My pulse jackhammered throughout my body—my ears, my fingertips, my throat. I slid my hand around him again, feeling him swell in response. The head of his cock was right there. Right in front of me. Dark red, skin so smooth it shone.

I swallowed the lump in my throat and risked a glance up at Tanner. His eyes were dark and serious. He barely seemed to be breathing, as if he worried that any sudden movement might break the spell and I'd change my mind. That wasn't about to happen.

Moving with slow deliberation, I stroked up to his swollen crown, then down to his balls, holding his skin taut, then slipped him into my mouth. Even against my tongue, his skin felt hot. I curled my tongue around him like he'd done to me. At least I hoped that was what this felt like. That good. That sexy.

Tanner's breaths puffed out, hard. Labored. So I guessed I was doing something right. I eased him farther into my mouth, wanting to take him as deep as possible, but I gagged. My cheeks heated from embarrassment and frustration. I sucked. And not in a good way. I tried again, but before I got to where I gagged, Tanner's hand wrapped around mine. My lips bumped against his thumb. *Is he stopping me? Is it that bad?* Worries spiraled inside me. *I'm wrecking this.*

The feel of Tanner's fingers sinking into my hair pulled me out of my thoughts.

"Just like that," he said, lightly gripping my neck, urging my head back and forth. "That's perfect."

He kept his fingers over mine for half-a-dozen slow strokes as my mouth moved over him, and then he let his hand fall away. His other hand stayed on my neck, fingers pressing in just like they had the night before. Firm. Possessive. And even better than it had felt the first time. The pressure of his grip touched something deep inside me. Something I didn't know was there. I just knew that whatever it was, I wanted more of that feeling.

Flattening my tongue against the underside of his cock, I sucked harder, tasting salt. His balls puckered, and I cupped them with my free hand, gratified when I heard a low moan. More saltiness leaked from him as he grew thicker, harder. His thigh muscles tensed and shook, and I could tell he was pressing his back against the wall to stay upright. Having this effect on him gave me a new level of determination. Licking, sucking, stroking, I did everything in my power to keep him feeling whatever was making him quiver like he was about to lose control.

My own body was on fire. Every inch of me tingled with anticipation of his orgasm. Every rasped breath of his felt like it drew from my lungs. A loud noise in the hallway startled us, and I nearly lost my balance, but I grabbed his hip, steadying myself, keeping the rhythm.

Pounding on the door sounded inches away from my ear, followed by Tim's booming voice. "We got takeout instead. You guys wanna watch a movie?"

My gaze darted up to Tanner. His face was contorted, a mix of fear and lust, exactly what battled inside me. Going as slowly as I could, I slid him deeper into my mouth. His eyelids fluttered as his fingers tightened on my neck.

Faint muttering came from the other side of the door.

"They must have gone out."

"Yeah, whatever."

Then their door slammed.

Relief mixed with need, and I sucked Tanner hard and fast. A low gasp left him, thrilling me as much as the bruising fingers desperately clinging to my neck. *Come. Please come.* I silently willed him as I worked hands, tongue, lips, focusing all my energy on nothing but his cock.

Tanner's body jerked, then froze, but I kept moving, bobbing my head in a steady tempo until I felt the first burst inside my mouth. It hit the back of my throat, staggering me with its force, but I made myself hold still. Pulse after pulse pumped out of him, pooling in my mouth. I pulled back just enough to swallow, then slid him deep.

"Fuck," he whispered, abs clenching and unclenching as he continued to twitch against my tongue.

When he stopped convulsing, I let him slip out of my mouth. I was breathing at least as hard as he was. The room swam, and I braced my arm against the door.

Tanner grabbed me by the shoulders and hauled me up. I tried to read his expression. Eyes glazed and heavy lidded, lips parted, face flushed. His hand slid around my torso, and he dragged me toward him.

"*That* was fucking awesome."

The lazy smile on his face grew blurry as he moved closer. Warm lips touched mine. He moaned as his tongue swept into my mouth, and I knew he could taste himself on me.

And he liked it.

Chapter Eight

WE LEFT the lights off and stumbled around the room, kicking off shoes, stepping out of pants, tugging off socks until we were both completely naked. I wasn't comfortable being naked. Not even by myself, let alone standing there with another person looking right at me. I didn't know how to stand or where to put my hands or where to look. It was stupid to feel like that with Tanner. He'd never had an issue with nudity in the entire time we'd lived together. But I'd turned the act of keeping my eyes averted into an art form.

Then Tanner did the unthinkable. He turned on the lamp on his desk. The low-watt bulb felt like a spotlight compared to the glow from the street lamps. Heat flooded my cheeks.

Tanner chuckled. "You know, it's really fucking hot when you blush like that."

My face flamed, and Tanner stepped closer.

His thumb brushed across my cheek, and I shivered. "So hot." His voice was thick, like melted candy. I wanted to kiss him. To feel his lips on mine and have a reason for us to close our eyes. Tanner just kept looking. The more his gaze raked over me, the deeper I flushed. My neck and chest prickled as if I'd spent a day in the sun.

Tanner trailed his fingers down the midline of my chest, and I watched as they passed over my stomach. My abs clenched, and he paused, tracing the divots. My cock strained, straight up, like it was trying to get Tanner's attention or leap into his hand. He bypassed it completely, sweeping his hand down my thigh, then up between my legs to stroke my balls.

"You okay?" Tanner asked.

I nodded.

"Collin, open your eyes."

I hadn't realized I'd closed them.

Tanner continued to ignore my cock as he massaged. I looked down just in time to see a bead of precome land on Tanner's wrist. I swallowed hard.

"You can look at me, you know."

My eyes darted to his.

"Not just my face. All of me. You know, like porn, only live and in person."

Laughter snorted out of me.

"What? Now you're going to tell me you don't like porn?"

Stupid didn't begin to cover how I felt. "I don't really know. I mean, I've never really...."

"Jesus, Collin. No Internet? Not even a magazine?"

"The house rule was that computers all needed to be used in one place. Just for homework. I had to actually show my mom the letter from the school about how 'students greatly benefit from having a laptop they can take to class' before she agreed to let me get one."

"Well, what about then? The first thing I'd have done was look up porn."

I shrugged.

"What about your phone?"

"I figured it might show up on the statement somehow."

"Fuck. No wonder you're so wound up all the time."

It's that obvious? That only made me feel worse. "I'm sorry."

Tanner's eyes popped wide. "Don't be sorry. Shit. It's not your fault. You just have to, like, tell me if I do stuff that makes you uncomfortable. And for fuck's sake, tell me if you need some recommendations for good porn sites."

I breathed out a laugh. It was hard to imagine needing porn when I had a living, breathing person willing to have sex with me, who at the moment was brushing his knuckles against the base of my cock.

"Okay."

"This'll give you some idea of how different our families are. My dad went through my browser history when I was in maybe seventh grade, and he must have seen that I'd hit a few of the free sex sites. The next day I came home and found a box of condoms on my desk and a note that said 'If you do anything with anyone besides yourself, promise me you'll wear a condom. Don't catch anything and don't knock anyone up. And stop looking at that free shit.'"

I couldn't have closed my jaw if I'd needed to. "Your dad said that?"

"Yup. Left me an account number and a log-in name. Told me not to give out any personal info. Said I should stay safe and have fun and let him know if I had any questions."

"I can't even...."

Tanner nodded. "I know, right? It felt a little weird at first, that my dad knew, but he was so cool about it and I wasn't about to look gift porn in the mouth, so to speak, so I went to the site. Now that I think about it, that was a great gift. I learned a fuckload of stuff."

"Like what?"

"All sorts of stuff. Up 'til then I pretty much thought sex was ramming your dick in and out of a woman or humping your fist as fast as you could. Watching the people on that site? Shit. I had twenty new ways of jerking off by the end of the day."

My cock approved of that by twitching enough that it slapped against Tanner's arm. He smiled and finally curled his hands around the base, giving a slow stroke up, then down. Mesmerizing. I growled. Right now humping a fist as fast as possible seemed like a very viable option for getting off.

Tanner stepped closer. Coconut lime mixed with the heat radiating off him and made my mouth water with desire. His lips brushed my neck as he took another slow-motion pass up and down my erection.

"You wanna show me? What you like?"

"I like that." I trembled as his fingers returned to my balls, leaving my cock desperate for attention.

"What else?" His voice was warm against my neck. "Show me."

Show him! my cock demanded. *Don't leave me here all alone. Stroke. Pump. Anything. Let's go.* But I couldn't do it. I tried. I went to reach for my cock, but it was like some invisible force field surrounded my crotch. My hand dropped to my side.

"I can't."

This is ridiculous. I suck.

"It's okay."

Why did he have to be so understanding? There must be a million other guys who'd give their left nut to be where I am right now, with Tanner naked and touching and asking to be shown what they want.

All I can do is say "I can't," which is stupid because it's not like I've never jerked off before. It's not like he hasn't seen me have an orgasm. It's not like I haven't come on his hand and stomach and in his mouth. It's not like I can't still taste him on my tongue.

But I still can't. "I'm sorry."

"Dude, stop with the sorrys. I mean, yeah, I'd like to watch, but it's not like I can't figure stuff out on my own." He trailed a hand down the center of my back, and I swear it felt almost as good as if he'd just stroked my cock. His erection nudged mine, and that felt even better.

Goddamn. He bent his knees a little, raising and lowering himself so that his dick rubbed back and forth against mine, leaving wet streaks across my stomach. I loved that we were the same height. Our bodies matched up so well, like mirror images. Light and dark. My hands finally figured out how to move, and I slid them up and down his back, feeling every muscle. Firm. Solid. I hoped what I was doing to him felt as good as what he was doing to me.

Tanner anchored a hand on the back of my neck, and my heart sped with anticipation because I knew that meant he was going to kiss me. With the lights on, I could see his face so clearly. Pupils wide and dark, forehead slightly furrowed like he was trying hard to control himself, mouth—that fucking perfect mouth—open just enough to make me think about sliding inside it.

His head tilted and drew closer, hovering a breath away, but I couldn't take it anymore. I closed the gap between us, slamming my lips into his with enough force he had to take a step back to steady himself. He answered by shoving me against the wall so hard, the lamp nearly fell off the desk. Shadows danced behind my eyes as the light shook with every thrust he made against me.

If I wasn't careful, I was going to come just from this. Just from him rubbing up against me, with his tongue in my mouth and his fingers digging into my neck and hip. He nipped at my lower lip hard enough that I yelped, which seemed to turn him on even more. My stomach was slick from both of us, making our cocks slide against each other that much easier. I wanted to come so badly my eyes swam, but I didn't want us to stop. I didn't ever want this to stop.

He pulled away, breathing fast, eyes heavy lidded. "Tell me what you want."

Was that a trick question? I swallowed and choked out, "You."

Tanner chuckled, and I felt his laughter vibrate straight through me. "Good answer."

He maneuvered us toward his bed and pushed me down onto it, then walked away. I sat up, about to protest, but he threw me a smile. "Hold that thought." He rummaged in the closet, rustled a paper bag, and returned holding a towel. "Let's try to keep from having to do laundry every day."

I helped him spread the towel across the center of the bed. He climbed on, sprawling alongside me. My heart thudded with anticipation. I didn't know it could feel like this—being with someone, wanting them so much you couldn't breathe.

Tanner put something down on the bed beside me, but before I could see what it was, his mouth was back on mine. I groaned the second his tongue touched mine, and he smiled against my lips. Strong hands smoothed their way over my body, up my torso, down my chest. My brain raced to keep up with the sensations. It was pointless. I couldn't catch up. They surrounded me, drowning me, pulling me under. And I didn't care. I just didn't want it to stop.

Breathless, Tanner pulled back. "Is there anything you want to try? Or, like, anything you don't want to do?"

Like what? I hated that I didn't have an answer either way. "I don't know."

"Okay." He kissed me again as his hand moved along my thigh, cupping my balls and kneading. He wrapped his hand around me and gave a painstakingly slow stroke all the way up, then all the way down, pulling my skin so taut I hissed. "Good?"

I nodded, breathing out a "Yes."

I caught the hint of a smile before his mouth moved over mine again. Tanner shifted, making room for his other hand to slip between us. He stroked with one while the other patted the bed in search of whatever he'd tossed aside. The snapping sound of a lid popping open made me suck in my breath.

"You ever used lube before?"

"No."

The grin returned to his face. "Never too soon to start."

Cold liquid rained down on my cock, heating almost instantly under the stroke of his hand. "Fuck."

Tanner chuckled, continuing to drizzle it over me. It dripped into the crease of my thigh, tickling its way over my balls. I shuddered as he slicked it over my skin, kneading and caressing. He leaned forward and gave me a kiss, long and deep, then sat up.

"If you don't like something, tell me and I'll stop. Okay?"

My hair rustled against the pillow as I nodded. I couldn't imagine anything he'd do to me that I wouldn't like. I tingled from head to toe and tried not to quiver with anticipation. It didn't work. I shook as if I had a fever.

Tanner straddled my thigh, and I focused on the weight of him. His balls rested against my skin, plump and full. His thick cock jutted straight up, hard and shiny. Firm hands massaged up to my rib cage, then back down, trailing around hips before they settled back between my legs. He pumped slow and steady and rolled his palm around my head on each upstroke until I thought I might pass out.

Remembering that not long before Tim had been in the hall and we'd been able to hear every word he was saying, I tried to keep quiet, but whimpers hummed out of me. Tanner's other hand rubbed across my balls, then below. He pressed a finger firmly against me, then slid it along my ass crack.

My stomach clenched, lifting my ass up off the bed. *Jesus God.* Every nerve ending in my body lit on fire. Tanner swirled his finger in the crease of my thigh, coating it in the now warm lube, then slipped it between the cheeks of my ass, running his fingertip right past my hole.

"Nuh."

A smile lifted the corner of his perfect lips, and he bent forward, pressing his dick into my hip as he kissed my chest. Hot breath eased over me as he nipped at my ribs, his finger still circling.

"Good?"

"Yuh-huh." I clutched at the sheets, my ass tensed so tight I thought it might cramp, but Tanner managed to keep moving, pressing in a little more with each pass. Shimmering waves of pleasure raced up my cock, and he kneaded them deep into me with every stroke.

He's inside me. His finger's inside me. Nothing's ever been inside me. Nothing. I wanted to fight it. Wanted to push him away or hold myself tight enough to make it impossible, but it felt so good all I could do was spread my legs wider, opening to him.

"Good," he said, easing his finger in so far I yelped. Pressure and a faint burn were replaced by… by…. Stars swam before my eyes as his fingertip stroked and massaged a spot inside me. *Holy fuck.* No words. Just sensations. Fullness. Like my entire body was about to burst.

I managed a fleeting glance at Tanner. His eyes were narrowed, focused on my cock. His lower lip hung open, his breaths came fast. The intensity of his expression heightened all the things I felt—the need, the desire, the pleasure. All of it doubled and tripled as he worked me over. I didn't want to come, but I couldn't wait a second longer.

The first blast of wetness hit my chest before I even realized I was coming, then the full impact washed over me. Come pulsed out of me as Tanner continued to stroke in and outside my body, drawing out every drop. My head pressed into the pillow so hard it muffled my moans.

Tanner eased out of me and continued to massage my balls and shaft. My eyes fluttered open just in time to see him stroking himself, his hand still coated white from my load. The wet slapping sound made my cock twitch as I realized he was jerking off with my come as lube. He came hard and fast, shooting onto my stomach, then collapsed alongside me, panting.

The air in the room seemed to settle over us, cool and welcoming. I still felt like I was set to vibrate. Tanner pulled up the edge of the towel and wiped his hand, but quickly gave up and let it drop.

"That's not gonna cut it. You wanna take a shower?"

With him? Hell yeah. I wanted to do everything with him. I answered the only way I could, with a kiss.

Chapter Nine

For the past eight years, I'd spent most of my waking hours trying not to think about sex. The past few days, I'd been able to think about little else. Everything I heard, saw, smelled, or touched somehow reminded me of Tanner. And all it took was him passing through my mind for the rest of my body to respond with a vengeance. In less than one week, I'd had more orgasms with him than I'd ever had with any other person.

Daytime was pretty much as it always had been. I went to work. I went to class. Then I came home, and the second the door clicked shut, Tanner and I were in our own world. A world I liked. A lot.

When Tanner said he wanted to come with me to the Communion, I thought he was kidding. Why anyone would subject themselves to that was beyond me. I mean, being at the church would be awkward enough, given how Tanner and I had spent nearly every free moment of our time together. But my parents' house? Full of relatives and neighbors? Everyone asking questions about who he was and when was I going to come home with a girlfriend? I wasn't sure I could deal with that. I also wasn't sure what it would be like to be around Tanner for that amount of time when we couldn't touch one another. And touching was something that definitely couldn't happen with anyone from my family around.

I still hadn't given him an answer by Saturday night, so he asked again. While we were in bed. Foul play. There hadn't been a single thing he'd asked with his hands on my body that I'd been able to say no to. Not one damned thing.

"Well," he asked in between kisses, his breath warm as he nipped my neck, "are we both going?"

I closed my eyes, trying to think straight, but the rhythm of his hand rubbing back and forth against my arm made that impossible. "Do you have any clue how boring this will be? Not to mention that my family isn't exactly laid-back. You'll hate it."

"So? You have to go."

"Right. Have to. I don't have a choice. You do."

"Well, I choose to get to know your family better. Unless you don't want that."

The underlying hurt in his voice made my stomach roll. It was so much more complicated than he made it seem. "I just don't want things to be...."

"What?" He slowed his hand and pulled back enough to look at me. Those dark eyes didn't do anything to make it easier for me to focus. "What are you worried about?"

Loaded question. What wasn't I worried about? "I don't know. Questions. Them doing or saying something stupid. Arguing. Someone... noticing."

"Noticing what?"

"You know. Us. The way we are now."

Tanner grinned. "Don't worry. I think I can play the role of roommate and manage to keep my hands off you for a few hours of a religious family event."

My face tingled. "I know. I'm sorry. I just...."

"I know." The stroking resumed, and this time he moved to my back. Kneading tension out of my shoulder as he spooned behind me. "I do get it, you know, but trust me. People can't tell by looking. I'm your roommate. That's all you need to tell anyone. I promise I won't embarrass you."

"I'm not worried about you doing anything. I'm worried about them. My mom may seem nice, but she can be a nutcase."

"All moms can."

"Maybe. But you have no idea what it was like growing up at our house. Do you know how it feels to explain to your friends why your parents don't allow locks on the doors, even to the bathroom?"

"I can imagine. But look, I already know about that. And you know your mom likes me. I'd like to meet your brothers. See where you grew up. That's all. If you don't want me to, I'll stay here."

I knew he meant it. If I said no, he wouldn't go. But he wanted to, and I didn't want to say no to him. A part of me wanted him to meet my brothers. And an even bigger part of me didn't want to be away from him even for a few hours. Shit. When had that happened? When had I become the type of person who couldn't be away from their... my heart did a funny beat and seemed unable to get back on track. What was Tanner? Definitely more than a friend. The word "boyfriend" rolled around in my brain, but I couldn't grab hold of it. Not yet. Besides, even if I thought of him that way, which I wasn't sure I did, did he think of me the same way?

His lips were back on my neck, right below my ear, making my body press against his. "You can come if you want to," I said, hoping that was the right decision.

I could feel him smiling against my skin. "I love it when you say those words."

I laughed as he pulled me on top of him. "I'm serious."

"So am I."

He kissed me hard and deep. I didn't care if we spent tomorrow in jail or on a trip to the moon. All I could think about was right now and getting more of Tanner.

Chapter Ten

The service was typically long, and it didn't help that the sight of Tanner in his black suit and gray dress shirt had my body on high alert. It seemed like this idea was even worse than I'd anticipated. Even something as simple as standing up had become a danger—a challenge. I'd gotten boners in church before, but never like this. Never raging ones where my cock seemed to be attempting to do anything necessary to attract someone's attention. Tanner's attention. I shifted in my seat and saw the smirk play at Tanner's mouth. He knew. That wasn't helping. How would I make it through a few hours at my house?

"Doing okay?" he whispered into my ear, and every hair on my arms stood at attention, just like my cock.

"Sort of." I could tell the priest was almost done. We'd be heading home soon. *Home. Not our home. My family home.* I must have lost my mind.

When everything wrapped up at the church, Tanner followed me out to my car. He swung into the passenger seat, as relaxed as if we were going on a goddamned picnic. "How long's the ride to your mom's place?"

"About two minutes. Mom always said that was her favorite thing about the house. Being able to be at the church any time you needed."

I could tell Tanner had a wiseass comment, but he didn't make it. "So, anything I need to know before we get there? I mean other than the obvious—knock before you enter the bathroom and if any animalistic urges hit, make tracks to the shed."

I closed my eyes, not knowing if I should laugh or get annoyed or turn the car around, head back to our dorm, and make up some off-the-wall excuse about why we didn't show up. Herd of escaped zoo animals? Extremely localized tornado? Cops locked down the street due to suspicion of alien invasion?

"That ought to do."

Tanner put his hand on my leg, and I jumped.

"You have got to calm down. It's just us in the car. Jesus, I really didn't mean to make you this jumpy. You want me to call a cab or something and just go back to the dorm?"

My gut twisted. Because a part of me would have been relieved if he'd done just that. The rest of me would have felt like shit, though. "No. I'm sorry. I'm just nervous."

"I know you are. And it'll get easier the more times we do shit."

"I guess."

Tanner shifted in his seat, and I had the feeling it wasn't the suit that was making him uncomfortable. "Do you think you'll ever tell them?"

My stomach had advanced from twisting to some form of elaborate knotting. Macrame. Sailing. Knots I wasn't sure would ever come undone. "I don't know."

Tanner stayed quiet for what seemed like a long time but was probably only a few seconds. I glanced over but couldn't read his face. Serious but not pissed. At least I hoped not. "Okay," he said, "one thing at a time. One more question."

"Shoot."

"Is there cake at this thing?"

I managed a laugh as we pulled up to the house, and then nothing seemed funny anymore.

"Surreal" didn't begin to describe what it was like to watch Tanner socializing with my family. I heard him talking baseball stats with Sean, which shouldn't have surprised me. He charmed every woman in sight from my mother to my sister-in-law to my six-year-old niece. I don't know why that surprised me either. It's not like I hadn't seen him do it before with every female student, teacher, cashier, or waitress we'd ever encountered. Whatever he had, he should try bottling it. He'd be rich. Particularly considering that it seemed to be equally enchanting to certain guys. Like me. Keeping a safe distance from him was making me crazy. More than anything, I wanted us to get home, close our door, and be alone. Together.

Sean handed me a piece of cake. Yellow with a thick layer of bright white frosting and a tiny white chocolate cross on the top. "It's good. It's from Carmine's."

We'd gotten all our cakes there since I could remember. They were amazing. But that didn't make me feel any less weird about eating virginal white cake in a room with two priests, my entire family, and the guy I'd been naked with every day the past week.

"Thanks."

"You're still working at Gino's, right?"

"Yep." Gino was Carmine's brother. That's part of the reason I'd been able to get a job with him back in freshman year. They'd both gone to the same Catholic school as my family, although they lived on the Italian side of town, while we were on the Irish side. Didn't matter. Loyalty to our small town was a big thing with the locals. My brothers had both worked at Carmine's while they were in high school, so it only seemed fitting that I got a job at Gino's when I moved three towns away for college. It also made it that much more important that I was a good employee. And that I kept my private life… private. Anything

Gino knew would undoubtedly make it to my hometown in record time. My stomach twitched again. "The service was nice."

"Thanks." He made eye contact just long enough for me to know what he was thinking.

"It made you miss Dad?"

Sean nodded and looked down. Even though he was only slightly older than me, he had more memories of our father. As happy as he'd been after each of his kids had been born, I remembered him telling me every time that it made him sad that Dad wasn't around. It always made me wonder if I'd feel that way if I had big news to share some day. Would I miss him more then too?

"I'm sorry."

Sean shrugged. "It's okay. I'm just glad the baby didn't cry the whole time. He's teething."

I'd babysat the older two when they were teething. That was the opposite of fun. "That sucks."

"It's all right. Besides, sometimes it's easier to deal with Mom when you're delirious from lack of sleep." He gave me a playful elbow in the ribs.

I knew exactly what he meant. "How's she been doing lately? Anything nutty?"

"Nothing out of the ordinary. She leaving you alone?"

"Yeah. Just phone calls telling me I should go to Mass."

Sean chuckled. "You're in college. You must have some awesome sins to confess."

My face burned, and I tried to shove the biggest possible bite of cake in my mouth to make it look like maybe I was just having a sugar rush.

Sean's eyes widened. "Well, look at you. You do have something to confess. Good for you. At least one of us does."

Would he be so happy if he knew what I'd been doing? Sean wasn't fanatical like Quinn and my mom, but still… how would he feel about a brother with… and there it was again. That missing word.

Sean cleared his throat. "You're not gonna tell me, are you?"

I shook my head. "Not yet."

"Well, when you're ready, I'm all ears."

When I'm ready. I didn't have a clue when that might be.

Chapter Eleven

I HADN'T seen Tanner in at least a half hour, so I went in search of him. I found him in the kitchen, chatting with my mom. *Oh God.*

Mom's eyes were round as she listened to whatever Tanner was telling her. Panic stirred in my chest, making me wonder if I could make it across the room to them without keeling over. Or if I even wanted to. *Please don't let him be talking to her about sex. Or politics. Or religion....*

"Yeah, I never went to church growing up. My dad's half-Jewish and wasn't really raised religious at all, and my mom's sort of a free spirit...."

"Oh." Mom nodded, but I could tell she didn't approve. "So where were your parents married?"

Tanner chuckled. "They got married on Broadway, on stage."

Her jaw dropped. "Really?"

"They met doing a play. My dad was the director, and my mom was one of the makeup artists. One of their friends from the production had gotten ordained to do weddings on things like cruise ships and stuff, and the night the show closed, they decided to turn the wrap party into their wedding celebration."

"That's certainly an interesting wedding story."

"It's pretty romantic, I guess. Would be a better story if they'd actually stayed together, but they're both happy, so it all worked out."

"I'm sorry. Collin's told me you're from New York, and I just assumed with a last name like D'Amico that you'd be Catholic and you'd be from some big Italian family."

Tanner gave her his trademark grin. "No, ma'am. No big family here. Just my mom and dad and me. The D'Amico comes from the Italian side of my dad's family, but the other half is Jewish. I know bits and pieces of all the different traditions. I just wasn't raised in any of them formally. I really enjoyed the service this morning, though."

Her eyes brightened. "Did you?"

"Yeah. The formal ceremony was cool, and it's great to celebrate stuff as a family. My family's nice and all, but we don't do a ton of stuff together anymore."

She smiled. "Well, I'm glad you could join us. I'm sure Collin could bring you with him to Mass at school."

Oh, that would be priceless. Yeah, I'll get right on that. "Tanner's usually working when I go to Mass."

"There you are," she said. "I'm packing up leftovers for you two to take with you."

"Your mom's awesome." Tanner gave me a small wink as he shoved another bite of cake into his mouth. "And this cake is insane."

Mom beamed. "That cake is a family tradition. We've had the same one at every baptism and Communion in our family for decades."

Tanner's tongue flicked a bit of frosting off the corner of his lip. Watching that with my mom in the room nearly made my brain shatter.

"Don't worry, Mom. Whatever you pack for us, we'll eat. Thanks."

"That whole stack there is yours." She pointed to a pile of Tupperware containers. "Put them in a grocery bag so they're easier to carry."

I bent and searched under the sink for a paper bag, then started loading the plastic tubs into it.

Mom snapped another lid closed and handed it to me. "Quinn said to tell you he was sorry he missed you. He had some emergency he had to attend to. They've got him on call at the hospital for some sort of spiritual crisis counseling."

"That sounds intense."

"I guess we have to get used to him having bigger responsibilities than us." She sounded wistful, but I knew she was proud. Her son, the almost priest. For her that was way more meaningful and impressive than "my son the lawyer" or "my son the doctor." I wondered if she'd ever even mention me. Somehow "my son the gay social worker" didn't seem to have quite the ring I thought she was hoping for.

"Tanner tells me he won an award from the university." Mom gave me her infamous "when am I going to get news like this out of you" look.

I nodded. "It was a great project. His team came up with an awesome charity campaign."

Tanner shoved his hands in his pockets. He didn't like when people made a fuss over him. "It was a group effort. I'm just glad we raised money for the clean water fund. That was the cool part."

My mom tsk-tsked at him. "I don't know. The grant money sure sounds nice to me. Not to mention that's a wonderful thing for a resume. I'm still not sure how my son intends to support himself with a social work degree."

Before I could get a word in, Tanner answered. "There's always a need for social workers. Not to mention that Collin's professors all gush over him. I'm just another business major. For all I know, I'll wind up managing a Starbucks or something."

I bit my tongue to keep from laughing. Tanner hated Starbucks, and every one of his professors adored him. But I appreciated him standing up for me. "I'm sure we'll both be just fine, Mom."

She handed me the last container. "I hope so. I just worry. Do you have a summer internship lined up, Tanner? I know Collin didn't get one."

"I didn't apply. I'll be heading down to Fire Island like I did last year. There's good money working the upscale restaurants out there."

My mother's eyes grew wide as saucers. "Aren't all the people on Fire Island, you know…"

Tanner gave her the blankest stare ever. "All what?"

"You know." She dropped her voice to a whisper. "Isn't the whole island *gay*?"

She breathed out the last word so softly you'd think she was saying "cancer" or "prison."

"No, ma'am." Tanner managed to keep a straight face. "Only two of the towns on the island are known for being predominantly gay. The other dozen or so cater to the NY elite—some celebrities, wealthy couples, families with young kids who've been going to the family beach houses for generations. I live with a bunch of people my dad knows from the theater set. Musicians, dancers—it's a fun bunch. And we earn a ton at the restaurant."

"Sounds like a nice way to spend the summer."

"It is. I'm trying to convince Collin to join me. Way better money than at Gino's. Besides, it's dead in the summertime with so many less people on campus." He gave me his cheekiest grin. "You should come."

Maybe I will. But I'm not going to decide with my mom giving me the stink eye about any choice I make. I'll decide later. Right now I just want to leave.

The bag crinkled as Tanner lifted it off the floor and passed it to me. "You carry the leftover cake, so I don't eat it before we get to the car."

My mom reached up and hugged me and gave me a kiss on the cheek. "Be careful going home."

"I will. Don't worry."

"Thanks again for having me, Mrs. Fitz."

"Anytime, Tanner. You be sure to tell that pretty girlfriend of yours I said hello."

I shook my head as I followed Tanner out into the cool night air, feeling for the first time all day as if I could finally breathe.

Chapter Twelve

WITH THE big family gathering out of the way, it seemed like smooth sailing. Tanner and I went about our daily routines, and at night we had each other. I lived for the nights. And the mornings. Waking up with him pressed against me made every day the best fucking day I could imagine. All day long I'd count the minutes, savor every cryptic text, and try to control the raging hard-ons that plagued me anytime he crossed my mind. All of it was one big delicious secret we shared.

Then worlds collided.

I took an extra shift at Gino's. More money was always a good thing, plus Gino had always been more than fair to me, so I wanted to help him out whenever he needed. I'd just cleaned up from the lunch rush and was about to take a quick break when Tanner strolled in.

My heart leapt into my throat with excitement, but my stomach churned too. My response to him was so strong it always felt like a goddamned neon sign flashing over my head, like everyone who even glanced at me could tell instantly—gay. And I wasn't ready for that. Sometimes I wondered if I'd ever be ready. Certainly not yet.

Tanner threw me his lopsided grin, and my body warred with itself. Half of me melted, and the other half went rigid—and not the good kind. Fear prickled through me.

Gino saw him right away. Tanner was one of his favorite customers, and I knew Gino wanted to entice him to work at the shop next year. "Hey, it's Bottomless Pit Roommate. Long time no see."

"They've been keeping me busy with extra shifts at the bookstore." Tanner scanned the pans of pizza behind the glass enclosure, then made eye contact with me in a way I felt down to my fucking toes. Hunger burned bright in him, and not just for food.

I swallowed hard.

Gino swished his hand over the food. "What can I get you? Or you want me to try out one of my new specials on you?"

Tanner grinned. "I'll try anything you want. I'm starving."

"That's what I like to hear. You come work for me someday, kid. I may lose a little money on what you eat, but I'll make it back with you smiling at the ladies."

"Sounds good to me." Tanner hadn't taken his eyes off me, and I shifted, throwing a look over my shoulder to make sure Gino was back in the kitchen before I moved closer.

"You want a Coke?"

"Sure." Tanner headed over to one of the low booths on the side of the room.

The soda fountain bubbled and spurted as I filled two cups.

I set the drinks on the table and slid into the booth across from him. "I just went on break. I've only got about ten minutes."

Tanner took a deep pull from his straw, and my cock responded by stiffening and snaking up my belly under my cargo shorts. Thank God for aprons.

"What time do you get off tonight?" he asked, a smile playing at that perfect mouth.

My cheeks heated. "Ten, I think. Someone else is supposed to come in to close."

"Long day."

"Yeah, but it's good money. What are you up to?"

"I'll probably hit the library. I can get a paper out of the way, then I'll have the weekend free."

Gino yelled from the kitchen. "Order up!"

"Be right back."

I slid the tray from the window, grabbed silverware from under the counter, and brought the food over to Tanner. "Sheesh. He must really like you. I haven't even seen this yet."

Tanner inhaled and groaned. The sound shivered through me, and I quickly sat down and took a gulp of soda. "This looks fucking amazing. Want some?"

"No, thanks." It did look good, though. A sub roll, split open, layered with chicken tenders, mushrooms, peppers, tomato sauce, cheese, pepperoni, and topped off with mixed greens tossed in balsamic dressing with fresh parmesan curls.

Tanner made happy noises as he chewed, and I tried not to picture him naked and on top of me. It didn't work. "Fuck, that's good," he said, then turned and yelled. "Gino, you're a genius."

"That's what I keep telling everyone," Gino called from the kitchen with a laugh.

"Don't tell him I said this, but he most definitely would lose money on me if I worked here. Which I'm thinking I'd fucking love to do. Jesus. How do you not eat stuff constantly?"

I shrugged. "I eat plenty. Just not as much as you."

Tanner twirled his tongue to get an errant string of cheese off his fork, and my cock strained against my waistband. *Christ.* If he worked there, would

I feel like this all the time? I'd never survive. I was about to say something, but every thought slid right out of my head as the door jingled and Angela DeMoula headed straight for Tanner.

She swung into the booth right beside him, draped her long-nailed, thin fingers over his shoulder, and purred like a sex-starved cat, "Oooh, I thought I saw something delicious when I walked by."

My eyes rolled before I could stop them, and I knew Tanner noticed.

"Hey, Ange. What's up?"

"Nothing." If she shifted any closer to him, she'd be on his fucking lap. "I just haven't seen you in a while. You never hang out in the lounge anymore. Where've you been at night?"

The pouty look on her face made me feel like retching. So did the answer. He'd been with me. Would he say that? A part of me wanted him to, which shocked the hell out of me. Possessiveness washed over me as I watched her hand on his arm, saw the way she eyed him, and waited to see what he'd tell her.

"Just been busy." Tanner threw me a look that made my face heat again.

"Well, you've been too busy. You need to come hang with me."

As much as I didn't want to leave her there alone with Tanner, my break was over. I stood and picked up my drink. "You want anything to eat, Angela?"

"I'll take a Diet Coke."

Of course. "Sure thing."

I got her soda, hating the way she practically nuzzled Tanner's neck as she whispered to him about God knows what and giggled like he was the wittiest guy in the world. *What's wrong with me?* I never thought of myself as a jealous person, but seeing her there, hanging all over him, had me completely inside out. *Does he like her? Does he want her?* If the tables had been turned, he'd have had nothing to worry about. No woman had ever turned me on the way he had. But he liked girls. *Not past tense. Likes.* My stomach hurt.

I placed the drink and a straw in front of Angela.

"Thanks." She smiled, but the look in her eyes said, "You can go now."

Tanner had polished off nearly the whole platter of food. "You really have to go back to work? There's no one here."

Was that his way of saying he wanted me to hang around with them? My heart stuttered. *Maybe he doesn't want to be alone with her.*

I tried to keep from grinning like a doofus at the thought. "I have to go do the prep work for the dinner rush."

Before Tanner could answer, the doorbells jingled again, and this time Wendy swept inside.

"So this is the place to be," she said, slinging her backpack into the side of the booth where I'd been sitting. "Hey, boys. Ange. Mmm, that looks good." She plucked a cheese-covered mushroom off what was left on Tanner's plate and popped it into her mouth.

"Hey, get your own." Tanner threw a crumpled napkin at her, and she laughed.

"Good idea, what was that?"

I didn't know if it made me feel better or worse to have Wendy there. Now Tanner had two women with him, one of whom he'd slept with and who happened to be the only person on campus who knew about us. My stomach couldn't take much more of this kind of stress.

"I'll have Gino make you one. It's not on the menu."

"Yet," Tanner said. "It better be soon. It's fucking awesome."

"Thanks, Collin." Wendy gave me a smile that didn't comfort me. Would she say anything? Make an inappropriate comment? Worry filled me as I went and placed her order. Torn between wanting to know and not wanting to know, I busied myself in the kitchen until her food was up.

By the time I came back out with her order, Angela was gone. Somewhat relieved, I neared the table. I slid the metal pizza pan in front of her. "Careful, the tray's hot."

"Thanks." She grabbed the fork off Collin's empty plate and stabbed some of the greens. The level of closeness and familiarity she had with him tugged at my stomach again. "Anyway, as I was saying, if you want, there's room in the car."

"Room for what?" I asked.

Wendy chewed and swallowed. "I'm grabbing a ride to New York this weekend with my roommate and her boyfriend. They've got room for one more, so if Tanner wants to go home for a visit, we can squeeze him in."

She winked at Tanner, then shoved another forkful of salad into her mouth.

"You going?" I didn't particularly feel like spending a weekend without Tanner, but I knew he hadn't been home in two months.

"Probably not." He smiled at me, then dumped some of the ice from his soda into his mouth and crunched.

Wendy rolled her eyes. "That's right. You two are still in the honeymoon phase."

My stomach nearly fell out. I whipped my head around so fast my neck spasmed. Gino was still back in the kitchen, and the other server hadn't come in yet. No one had heard her. I willed my heart to slow down. Wendy must have seen the look of panic on my face.

"Sorry," she said, lowering her voice. "There's no one here but us."

I reached for the empty platter in front of Tanner, desperate to make it seem like I was busy working, needing to do something that seemed normal. Tanner's hand knocked against mine, and he briefly passed his fingers over mine.

My gaze met his, and the look in his eyes wrapped around me like a blanket. Dark. Soothing. "It's okay."

When he said it, I could almost believe it. Almost.

"Yeah," Wendy piped in, throwing me a wink. "Don't worry."

She dug into her food again, shoving a giant forkful into her mouth.

Sure. Don't worry. Easy for her to say.

Chapter Thirteen

My favorite thing in the world had become lounging in bed, watching TV. With Tanner as my backrest. I'd never been much of a hugger or a cuddler, but something about lying there, pressed up against him, made me want to stay there forever. I loved the feel of his body, warm and firm. I loved how our breathing would sync after a while, how his laughter would shake through me. And I really loved how I could reach up and stroke his hair anytime I felt like it.

I ran my fingers through the dark, silky strands, and he tugged on my hair until I tipped my head back. Gazing up at him like that made my heart swell like a balloon. He kissed me, and our tongues rolled around together for just a second, then he shifted, settling his head back on the pillow and pulling me closer. I leaned back against him again and closed my eyes, thinking that I could be happy even if we never left our twelve-by-twelve room again.

Tanner chuckled at Jon Stewart's closing remarks, then turned off the TV. "You studying more or going to sleep?"

We'd already showered, postsex, and I was limp, content, and half drifting off. "Sleep."

He reached up and flipped off the light, then eased himself down behind me. It wasn't even a question anymore about whether or not I wanted to stay in his bed. I did. Nightly. Thinking about it made me warm from head to toe, but woke me up a little. I turned enough to be able to look at him. I loved looking at him, especially from this close where I could study the curve of his strong cheekbones and those crazy thick eyelashes. He probably didn't know it, but sometimes I watched him while he slept, memorizing his face. I'd read about people doing shit like that, but honestly it had never occurred to me before. With Tanner I could have done it all day and night.

His eyes fluttered open, and he looked right at me. "What?"

"Nothing." There wasn't really a thought in my head. At least not one I could put into words.

"You okay?"

"Yep. Happy."

Tanner's perfect lips curved, and he put his hand on my arm, which was enough to send tremors up and down my spine. "Good. Hey, I forgot to ask. Did you get your laptop working?"

"Yeah. Whatever was up seemed to stop after I reinstalled a few things. I don't need to borrow yours."

"Okay. Cool. You can if you ever need to, though. I use my tablet for most shit now anyway." He paused, his hand still idly stroking my arm. "I thought maybe you wanted to borrow mine to check out my porn stash."

My face heated. Even with all we'd done together, he could still make me blush without even trying. "Why do I need porn when I've got you?"

He laughed and nipped at my ear. "Because it's still fun, that's why. You don't care, right? I mean, that I look at it."

I shook my head. I didn't.

"Good. It's just porn. And I still say you should check it out. You could, you know, tell me stuff you like or want to try."

I rolled onto my side to be able to look at him easier. "Is there stuff you want to try?"

"Hell, yeah. I told you, I learned half my repertoire from watching that shit."

That did make it sound more tempting. I wanted to know more, especially if it was stuff he wanted to do. I didn't mind him teaching me things, but it would be nice to be the one to surprise him once in a while.

"Maybe I'll take a look someday."

"Okay. If you want." He paused again, and I could tell he wanted to say something else.

"What?"

"Can I ask you a question?"

"You mean besides that one?"

"Asshole." He knocked me onto my back. As much as I wanted to hear the question, another part of me just wanted him to climb on top of me and stop talking.

"You still jerk off?"

The heat returned, spreading up to my ears and along my collarbone. "Not lately."

"Do you just not want to?"

I didn't know how to explain. It's not like I wasn't aroused enough. All I had to do was think about Tanner, and it didn't matter where I was—insta-boner. Worse than middle school, because now I had the memories to go along with the fantasies and it made it that much harder to fight what I was feeling.

"I don't know. I mean, I guess I'd just rather be with you."

"You can do both, you know?"

I nodded. I knew what he was saying. He didn't care. No, not the right word. He didn't *mind*. It wasn't like he hadn't been clear on the fact that he'd be more than happy to watch too. I just couldn't do it. Not yet, at least. I'd spent a lifetime feeling guilty about jerking off, and now I felt guilty about *not* jerking off. Beyond weird.

"How about this," he said, settling himself alongside me again. I could feel him half-hard against my hip, and that didn't make it any easier to think about his words. "You do what you want, but if you ever do check out the sites or find something you want us to do, tell me. Okay?"

I nodded again, easing my thigh up so it rubbed against his balls.

He slid his hand across my stomach and over the bulge in my shorts. "Again?"

I couldn't keep the grin off my face as he stroked and squeezed through the fabric. "Is that a problem?"

His hair tickled against my cheek as he shook his head back and forth, his lips brushing mine. "No problem at all."

Chapter Fourteen

Movie night hadn't sounded like an awful idea. The student center was showing a double feature. Tanner loved both movies, and we hadn't been out to do much of anything in weeks. I knew he was restless, so when Tim and Eric suggested we go, I said okay. It was packed, and we wound up with seats in the back.

"Perfect," Tim said.

"The screen looks smaller than my laptop from here."

"Yeah." He grinned and put his backpack between his legs as he sat. "But no one will see that I've got these."

Tim opened his bag and pulled out a six-pack of beer.

Shit. None of us were twenty-one yet, and alcohol wasn't allowed at school-sponsored events anyway. They looked the other way at house parties and in the dorms but not at big gatherings. That wasn't what scared me most either.

"Here," Tim said, keeping his voice low as he passed me one. "Just hold it below the seat level until after the movie starts. No one's going to see it."

He reached past me and handed a bottle to Tanner.

"Thanks, man," Tanner said, smiling at me. He leaned in and whispered, "You don't have to if you don't want, but it might help you relax."

Relaxing sounded great. I just wasn't sure that was possible under these circumstances. If I didn't, it made me look even more like I had a stick up my butt, so I waited until the lights were off, eased open the bottle cap as quietly as possible, and took a drink.

I'd had beer lots of times, among other things. You didn't grow up in an Irish household without plenty of opportunity to sneak drinks. Honestly, we barely had to sneak them. It was the one thing no one seemed to bother keeping tabs on.

The beer was colder than I'd expected. Tim must have had them in his freezer. The cool bubbles felt good working their way down my throat. By the time I'd finished the bottle, I did feel a little more relaxed. Tanner's shoulder bumped mine, and I turned toward him. I recognized the look on his face—crooked grin, eyes heavy lidded and lusty. It was my absolute favorite expression to see on his face, apart from his O face. But not here—not in a room with four hundred other students and Tim and Eric not six inches away on my other side. My heart hammered. I knew drinking made Tanner more amorous. I'd seen him all over girls at more parties than I cared to recall. I didn't know what to do.

Tanner leaned back in his seat, and I silently thanked God. Then I felt his shoe rub against mine. Any contact with Tanner—even his fucking Chuck brushing mine—was enough to get me going. My dick plumped, pressing against my fly. But that was the last thing I wanted. Not now. Not here. His foot continued to move. Up and down. Tiny movements, probably not even noticeable to anyone but me, but it felt like he was stroking my entire body.

I shifted, moving my foot forward, but that just gave Tanner room to slide his leg under mine. Now his shoe rubbed my instep and his calf brushed mine. Fire rushed through me—arousal and fear. Someone could see us. My cock clearly didn't care, but my mind did. At least, the functioning part of it.

Not wanting to do anything too obvious, I turned to face him. I'd planned to tell him to cut it out, but the second I looked at him, I saw that expression—that "holy shit I want to fuck him when he looks at me like that" expression—and I froze. Tanner didn't. He was downright fluid as he slipped closer and put his lips on mine. His lips. On mine. In a room full of people.

I lost it.

I jumped up so fast, my bottle clattered to the ground and a bunch of people started shushing and barking "Quiet!" Panic overtook me.

"I gotta go." I squeezed past Tim and Eric, headed straight for the door to the auditorium, and didn't look back.

A light rain was coming down, and I didn't have a jacket. I didn't care. I was already chilled from head to toe with a mix of fear and dread. Only my face was hot. My cheeks still blazed from the thought that Tim could have seen what happened. What would he say? What would he do? Would he tell everyone? Then I thought about Tanner. *Oh shit. What have I done?* He kissed me, and I ran away like some scared little kid. I didn't want people to know, but that didn't mean I didn't want him. I always wanted him. Shame stung my face for a different reason. I'd probably hurt him. The one person who's ever accepted everything about me. The person I'm most myself with and happiest when I'm around. And I just ran out on him, leaving him to explain to our friends.

I'm a total asshole.

Should I go back? That would be even worse. Besides, he shouldn't have done that. He knows better. He's not out here either. Does he want to be? Is that how he planned on letting people know? Jesus.

By the time I got back to our room, I was soaked to the skin. Needing to concentrate on something normal, I turned on the shower, letting it run until it steamed, then stripped and climbed in. Cold had permeated straight through to my bones. I stood under the spray, not moving until I started to feel the heat seeping in. My muscles started to relax, and my mind let go of the endless loop of negative chatter. I'd just finished rinsing off the soap when I heard our door slam.

He's home.

I waited several minutes longer than I needed to be in the shower, wondering if maybe he'd come join me. He was probably cold too, unless it had stopped raining. Even then he might be. I knew he liked showering with me. Maybe that was what we needed. Some time to relax together and forget what just happened.

My skin was starting to prune, and there was still no sign that Tanner was coming into the bathroom, so I shut off the water and grabbed my towel. The closet door slammed, and I heard drawers being opened and closed with way more vigor than was required. *What the fuck?*

Wrapping the towel around my waist, I ventured into the room. Tanner had his suitcase on the bed, and it was already half full of clothes. Fear settled in my chest. "What are you doing?"

"I'm going home...." He paused for so long, I had the horrifying feeling he meant forever. "For the weekend."

"Oh. Okay." I don't know why I said that. It wasn't okay. The last thing in the world I wanted was for him to leave, especially if we were fighting. I ran my hand through my wet hair, hoping he'd say something.

He didn't look at me. He threw two pairs of socks into his bag and brushed past me into the bathroom, returning a second later with his toothbrush and toothpaste, which also disappeared into his bag.

"Tanner, I'm sorry I stormed out. I just... shit... you can't...."

"I can't what? Kiss the guy I like during a movie? Sorry, Collin. Didn't mean to be so offensive."

I flinched. "It wasn't offensive. Fuck. What if someone saw?"

"What if they did?" His eyes met mine, dark and passionate and so full of fire, I couldn't look away.

I swallowed hard, hoping my heart wouldn't beat its way out of my chest. "Are you saying you want people to know?"

"I'm saying I don't care. I don't care who knows. I don't care what they think. What I care about is you. And I'm trying to be patient. I know you've got reasons for keeping us secret. I get it. But Jesus, Collin, it was a dark room. And you pulled away like I'd burned you with acid."

"Tim was right on the other side of me."

"So?" His eyes blazed.

I felt like my brain was about to explode. "I don't know."

"Well, maybe that's the problem. Maybe you need to figure out the answer to that. Figure out what's more important to you. Because if we stay together, I've got news for you. I'm gonna wanna kiss you sometimes without giving a fuck about who might see."

If. He said if. Fuck.

Tanner tugged open the drawer beneath his bed and pulled out his gym bag. "Wendy said I could catch a ride down to the city with her. That'll give you the whole weekend to think."

The backs of my eyes stung. *He's leaving. He's still pissed. Are we breaking up?* My stomach lurched. "Tanner, I...."

He shoved a few T-shirts into the bag, swiped some things off his dresser, and zipped the bag shut. "She's leaving first thing in the morning, so I'm just going over now."

My brain couldn't keep up with what was happening. Tanner slung his backpack over his shoulder, grabbed the duffel and gym bag, and walked to the door. It creaked as he pulled it open. To me it sounded like the Earth had cracked in two. Like the world was ending.

"Wait."

"What?" He turned and looked at me, arm braced against the open door.

Say something. Anything. Laughter sounded in the hall, and Tim and Eric stopped outside our room.

"Hey," Tim said. "Where you going?"

"Wendy and I are headed home for the weekend."

"Nice. Have a good time." He elbowed Tanner and muttered something to Eric about Wendy's ass. Then he looked at me. "Where the fuck did you run off to in such a hurry?"

"I, uh, I forgot to turn in a paper. I had to e-mail it to my professor."

"Good thing you remembered." Tim walked past, heading toward his room.

Tanner looked at me again. Waiting. Prodding me with his eyes. And I couldn't speak, couldn't say one goddamned thing.

He nodded. "Yeah. That's what I thought."

Letting go of the door, he stepped into the hall and let it slam behind him. I listened as he clomped down the hall and into the stairwell, pretty sure everything I liked about my life had just ended.

Chapter Fifteen

Tanner hadn't even been gone twenty-four hours, but I was a wreck. I made it through my shift at work, wanting nothing more than to go home. Then I got back to the dorm and felt even worse. With him gone our room felt beyond empty. Devoid of energy. The kind of alone I didn't want to ever feel again.

I knew he was right—right to be angry, right to be hurt, right to say all the shit he did. I did need to get more comfortable, with everything, including myself. How crazy was that? I'd been me for twenty years, but the only time I was comfortable about it was when I was alone with him. All shades of wrong. Not because I felt good about myself with him, but because I needed to feel good about myself, period.

Late-afternoon sun shone through the window. I knew I should get work done or go to the library, but I didn't want to. Instead I stripped off my clothes. Stupid as it sounds I'd never done that before—been naked alone in my own room. Sure, once in a while, if I was changing, there might be a second or two when I didn't have anything on, but other than that? Nope. Even when I showered, I always waited until right before I stepped under the spray to remove everything.

When it was all off—shirt, pants, boxers, socks—I stood there. Nothing happened. The world didn't end. I didn't spontaneously combust. I'd seen Tanner walk around nude countless times. It seemed the same rules of nature applied to me. I could be naked.

I walked over to the fridge and grabbed a Snapple. I drank half of it, then screwed the lid on and put it back. My backpack sat next to the bed, so I rooted through it, found my laptop, and sat down on the bed. Turning it on and waiting for the browser to load was enough to make my heart beat faster. I typed in the website Tanner had told me about—the porn site he recommended. Before the page even loaded, I started getting hard.

You can do this. Up popped a half-dozen windows, each with a guy jerking off, two with a helping hand. My cock took special note of the two young guys who easily could have been me and Tanner. The dark-haired one worked the blond's cock with obvious familiarity. Instinctively I reached for my erection, but the moment I made contact, I scanned the room.

Jesus. There's no one here. The blinds are down. The door is locked. Tanner's not due home for two days. There's no reason in the world not to do this. There's not even any risk.

Still I hesitated. The old feeling of nervousness roiled inside me.

I clicked the arrow and went to the next set of images. The same couple, further along, with the dark-haired one murmuring encouragement as the blond struggled to contain his orgasm. He moaned, and again my gaze darted to the door. *Too loud? Could someone walking by hear? Would they know it's porn? Think it's me?* Not ready to take that chance, I lowered the volume but didn't let go of my cock. Moisture beaded at the tip, and I swiped it away, then rubbed it into the swollen skin. My balls puckered, and the tingling in the base of my cock increased.

The guy on the screen arched his back, pressing his head deep into the pillow. His hands traveled down the length of his body, then replaced his buddy's hands as he started to stroke his own cock. *Fuck.* I jerked a little faster. Watching made me hot and clearly had the same effect on his helper, who had immediately started jacking himself with his eyes glued to the blond. Who could blame him? I could watch Tanner get himself off day and night and never get tired of it. It was me that was the problem—my issues, my insecurities. My stuff to get over.

Blondie moaned and lifted his head off the pillow, cupping his balls and beating off so fast the camera couldn't keep up with the speed of the movements. His stomach tensed in knots as he jizzed all over his chest. It didn't take more than three seconds before his friend unloaded too. He groaned even louder than the blond, pumping until he was totally spent, and then he collapsed onto the bed alongside his partner, leaned in to kiss him, and they both started laughing. *Jesus. What a moment of bliss.* Thanks to Tanner, I knew what that felt like. And I didn't want to lose it. Didn't want to fuck it up because I had some stupid hang-ups.

I scrolled the other images—mostly guys going at it solo. All totally into it, all recording themselves to put the images online. Why? Because they could. Because they didn't care if someone saw them or knew what they were doing. Because they were comfortable with themselves and not paralyzed with fear. Plus they were fucking hot.

My cock throbbed in response to each come shot I watched, but I paused my stroking in between. I didn't want to come yet. And when I did, I thought I owed it to myself to be completely in the moment. I closed the laptop and settled myself on the bed, propped up enough to have a clear view down the length of my body.

I loved this view when it involved Tanner. Loved watching his head bob up and down on me or his arms flex as he stroked me. Loved having his golden skin sprawled alongside my paleness. I tried to remember if I'd ever just studied my own body. I hadn't. All those times in my car had been spent looking over my shoulder and into the side-view mirrors to make sure no one was coming. Every time I'd been in a bed, it had been under the covers. Even in the shower, I closed my eyes.

This time I looked. Watching made it feel different. Not only could I feel every vein, every ridge, I could see them. Tremors shook through me as I varied the stroke, thumb up, thumb down, two fingers, whole fist, head rubbing against my other palm. Every variation felt better than the one before. My abs clenched hard and tight. My feet slid against the blankets, looking for some place to brace. My thighs flexed, and I slipped a hand beneath my balls, rubbing my asshole. Wet from precome, I didn't bother with lube. I eased a finger inside... a little more. I breathed out, controlling my arousal and relaxing the right muscles. Relief rumbled in my throat when my fingertip made contact.

Holy fuck. Why had I not been doing this for years? The skin on my dick pulled so tight it glistened. Deep red gliding in and out of my fist. My lower back ached with tension, and my shoulder cramped from reaching between my legs. I didn't care. I felt so good, I didn't care about anything but keeping this feeling going as long as possible.

The pounding on my door nearly sent me careening off the bed. My heartbeat thudded behind my eyes.

"Collin. You in there? We're going to Starbucks."

I could hear shuffling and mumbling. Tim and whoever he was talking to were right outside the door. Not eight feet away from me with my hand up my ass and my cock seconds from spewing. Panic overwhelmed me, but I fought it. I wanted to grab the blanket and cover up or dive for my clothes and yank them on. Or sink into the bed and disappear altogether. Any other time I'd have chosen one of the above. This time what I wanted most was to come. To prove to myself that I could do this.

Letting my hand glide slowly up and down my length, I could tell my cock was thoroughly on board with this plan. The pounding came again. "Where the fuck is he?"

The doorknob rattled, and for a split second, I could imagine Tim walking in, seeing me like this, the stunned look on his face, the humiliation I'd feel. My face heated, but I kept going. I needed this. Needed it more than self-control or self-preservation or caution or sanity. I stroked faster, kneading the knot deep inside me, riding the crest of arousal until my legs started to shake.

More muttering in the hall, then a final loud thump on the door. They were still there. Right there. And so was I. Waiting was no longer an option. Come crept up my length, inch by inch until I tumbled over the edge into oblivion as it jetted out of me, right onto my face and my neck, coating my chest. Footsteps echoed down the hallway, but all I could concentrate on was the contractions inside my body as my ass milked my finger and my hand milked my cock.

My heart rate and breathing finally leveled off, and my hands fell to my sides. The room spun, but it started to slow down. I surveyed the damage. The mess was impressive. Instead of getting up right away, I lay there enjoying the moment. Every muscle in my body had relaxed and all that was left behind was this floating sensation. Smiling, I thought of Tanner. This was what he was talking about. Letting go. I did it. Even with Tim banging on the door, I did it. And I knew I could do it again, with Tanner right there, watching me. For the first time, I truly wanted that, and I couldn't wait to tell him.

I just hoped he still wanted to hear it.

Chapter Sixteen

I'D TEXTED Tanner twice and left a voice mail, but there'd been no reply.

Fuck. What if I blew it? I checked my cell again, jiggling the charger to make sure it was plugged in all the way. It was. And there were no missed calls or messages. He wasn't answering me.

I reread the same page of my English Lit homework for the tenth time. All the words blurred together. I couldn't concentrate on a damned thing.

My phone buzzed, and I nearly dropped it as I grabbed it off my desk. A text. From Wendy.

I don't mean to be rude or anything, but what the fuck is wrong with you?

I stared at the screen, stunned.

What are you talking about?

Her reply came in seconds.

You know what? I can't even type this. I'm calling you and you'd better pick up.

I'd gotten a grand total of maybe a half-dozen texts from Wendy in the year I'd known her. I certainly wasn't used to her bitching me out in them. My phone vibrated, and even though I knew it was her, my heart skipped for a second as I checked the number, thinking maybe, just maybe, it was Tanner. It wasn't. It was her. I almost didn't answer, but curiosity got the best of me.

"Hello?" I said.

"Seriously, what the fuck is wrong with you?"

"I… what?"

She sighed into the phone so loud it sounded like static. "I know what happened. At the movies. And before you go into a world-class panic, no, Tanner didn't say anything until we were alone."

My mind tried to play catch-up with her words. "What did he tell you?"

"First off, he didn't have to tell me much of anything. He was totally miserable the whole drive down. I knew something was up, and the only person who gets to him that way is you."

I am? Is that a good thing? It sounded like maybe it was a good thing. I didn't want him miserable, but I'd been a fucking basket case and a not-so-proud part of me was kind of happy to hear that he was in bad shape too. Maybe I hadn't wrecked everything. Yet.

"Hello-o-o?" Wendy's impatient voice rang through the phone.

"I'm here."

"Well, good, because I'm not done yet. You know, I was actually superhappy when you guys finally got together. I love Tanner. I want him to be happy, and I really thought he would be with you. I fucking hate seeing him like this."

"Like what?"

"Jesus, Collin. He's not even sure you want to be with him."

Oh. Shit.

"Well?" she demanded. "Do you? Or is this some kind of experiment for you? Because if it is, or was, you need to tell him, so he can move on."

Experiment? Is she kidding? "No. It's not. Of course it's not."

"There's no 'of course' involved here. He seriously thinks you're not into the relationship. And I don't want to be reassuring him if you're not. I mean, fuck, I backed off when you two got together because I knew how much he wanted this, but I'll be damned if I step aside to let you hurt him."

I hated the fact that she was yelling at me, but at the same time, I was kind of impressed. It's not like I didn't know she cared about Tanner. They'd been friends forever, and I'd heard firsthand how much she enjoyed his company when they'd been hooking up. But this was different. Her angry-mama-bear routine forced me to wake up. She was right.

"I don't want to hurt him."

"Well, then, you need to cut this shit out and be straight with him. Sorry. Poor choice of words."

"Very funny."

"I'm serious," she said. "If you want to be with him, you need to show him. And tell him. Because he's not sure of anything right now, and I hate it. Do you have any idea how hard it was for him to come out last summer?"

He'd told me some. And he'd certainly been patient and understanding about my situation. But I never really thought about what it had been like for him. "I guess not."

"Well, it was. Believe me, it was. I was there."

"You were?"

"I was one of his housemates on Fire Island."

"Oh." I didn't know that.

"When he first got together with James, he didn't tell anyone."

James. Even hearing the other guy's name made my stomach tie itself in knots. "Did he tell you? When it happened?"

"Sort of. I picked up on the vibe between them, and I started asking him questions. Eventually he told me and then the rest of our friends. Everyone was really cool with it. But he still didn't want to tell his parents."

"But he did." I knew he had. And they'd been okay with it too, which was not the response I'd get. That much I knew for sure.

"Yeah, he did. But it still wasn't easy. I mean his parents are really open-minded, but it's still not the kind of thing you really want to bring up with Mom and Dad, you know?"

I hadn't thought about that. He was braver than I was. I'd known that since I first met him. Confident, sure of himself. I loved that about him. And envied it. And hated that I'd made him feel less of any of those things.

"Fuck."

"What?" I could see Wendy scowling at her phone, eyebrows drawn together.

"I'm sorry."

"Well, I'm really happy to hear that, but I'm not the person you need to say it to."

"I know." God, I knew. "I've been trying to get in touch with him for hours. He didn't text me back, and he's not picking up."

"He's at a play. He's probably got his phone turned off."

Relief prickled through me so fast it tingled. *He's not avoiding me. Probably.* "Do you know what time it's over?"

"Should be anytime now."

"Do you think he'll call me back? I could call him again...." My phone made a *clickety* sound and lit up. Tanner was calling through. "Shit. That's him on the other line. I have to go."

"Good. Go. Be honest with him, would you? Please."

"I will. And Wendy... thanks."

"Go."

"Going." I tapped the touch screen and pressed the phone to my ear. "Hello?"

"Hey." He sounded tense, but it was so good to hear his voice I felt like crying.

"Hey. I'm glad you called."

"I got your messages."

"Good. I've been going kind of nuts waiting to talk to you."

"Yeah?" He sounded so far away.

My heart hammered so loud, I was pretty sure he could hear it. I gripped the phone hard, trying to hold it steady. "I'm sorry, Tanner."

"For what?"

A list swirled through my head. Not knowing what to start with I blurted out. "Everything. For the movies. For letting you walk out last night. For not speaking up. For being a goddamned coward. For...."

"You're not a coward." His voice sounded softer.

I closed my eyes, wishing he were with me so I could touch him. "No, I am. And I'm sorry. You deserve better than that. I want you to have better than that. I want you to have everything."

"I don't want everything," he said. My heart fluttered just from the sound of his voice, deep and rich and flowing around me like warm water. "I just want you."

Heat pricked the backs of my eyes as I struggled to take a deep breath and absorb what he'd said. *He wants me. He still wants me.* "When are you coming home?"

"Why? You miss me?" I could hear him smirking his lopsided grin, and I'd have given anything to tackle him onto the bed.

"Yes."

"Good." That was the Tanner I knew. Cocky. Sexy. Mine. "I'll text you tomorrow and let you know what train I can catch."

He was coming back. To me.

Chapter Seventeen

THE TRAIN wasn't due in until seven thirty, but I drove to the station right after dinner. Waiting in our room was making me crazy, so instead I sat in my car in the parking lot, staring down the tracks. By the time the train finally pulled into the station, I was ready to burst.

Just seeing him made my entire body react. My heart beat faster. My mouth went dry, then watered. My stomach tensed to the point the muscles in my thighs pulled. I ached to put my hands on him.

His hair blew in the night breeze as he walked over to the taxi stand, looking like some goddamned jeans commercial. I tapped the horn and he jumped, eyes squinting before he smiled and strode toward the car. The passenger window opened much slower than I wanted it to. Tanner leaned down and peered in.

"How much for a ride to campus?" The curve of his lips tugged at my heart and everything south of it.

"Just get in, would you?"

The crazy-hot grin widened as he opened the door, shoved his bags into the backseat, and swung into the car. I wanted to put the car in park and wrap my arms around him, and I almost did, until headlights from a car behind us filled my car. Nerves won out. Tossing a quick look over my shoulder, I pulled away from the curb, then out of the lot.

Every time I glanced Tanner's way, he was staring at me.

"What?" I asked.

"I didn't expect you to pick me up."

"I didn't want to wait to see you." The words were so true, I ached as they came out.

"Oh, yeah?"

Heat crept over my cheeks. I nodded.

Tanner reached over and rubbed my leg. Even that small gesture was enough to make me groan.

"I missed you too," he said.

He shifted his hand closer to my crotch and nudged my bulge. I swerved a little, and Tanner laughed. Strong fingers traced the outline of my erection through my jeans. "Shit, you're gonna make me crash the car."

"I'll take my chances." He shifted in his seat, leaning closer to me.

I shot a look at him, and the heat in his eyes was enough to set me on fire. *Fuck.* I'd missed him even more than I realized.

Tanner opened the button on my jeans and pulled down the zipper. My cock strained against my boxers, begging to be touched.

A car whizzed by in the other lane. "I don't think this is a good idea."

Craning his head to look out the windows, Tanner unhooked his seat belt. "There aren't any other cars around. Besides, you're getting off at the next exit. Ha. See what I did there?"

I almost laughed, but his fingers slid inside my fly, and the sound that came out of me was barely human. "Fuck."

"Maybe later," he said, stroking my cock as he extracted it from the folds of fabric. "Right now let's say we concentrate on turning the Batemobile into the Blowmobile."

"Tanner, I don't...."

Whatever I was going to say in protest disappeared in a puff of happy nothingness the second his tongue touched my cock.

"What was that?" he asked, licking his way from balls to crown, then back again.

"Nuh... I...."

"Yeah, that's what I thought. Just drive, okay? Try not to get us killed."

His mouth slid down my length in one smooth motion that felt so fucking good I almost came right then and there. I gripped the steering wheel like my life depended on it. It kind of did. My leg shook, and it took every ounce of concentration for me to keep my eyes open. My knuckles burned and cramped. Ten and two, ten and two. Eyes on the road.

I signaled and took the exit ramp onto the darkened side road that led to campus. There weren't any cars around, which was good, but unlike the main road, this was curved and winding. The scent of Tanner's shampoo wafted up to me as his head bobbed in my lap.

"God, you taste good," he said, stroking and running his tongue over me again.

Before I could answer, he took me deep into his mouth again. A growl left me as he sucked, moving up and down with short, quick thrusts. Surrounded by all that heat, I could barely breathe. I strained to keep my eyes on the road. Needing to touch him, I let one hand slip from the steering wheel. His silky hair felt surprisingly cool as I wove my fingers through it. His tongue twisted and turned until I knew I couldn't hold off any longer.

"Oh, God." I panted, and Tanner gripped my hip hard, steadying both of us as he increased his pace. "Fuck."

Come shot out of me so hard and fast my eyes rolled up into my head. Panic fought with pleasure, and I quickly refocused on the road as the orgasm pumped out of me. *Holy shit.* My heart pounded so fast, I could feel it in my fingertips.

Tanner continued to suck and lick until he emptied the last drop out of me, then sat up with that lopsided grin in place again. "No wonder you missed me."

I snorted. "Only one of the reasons."

"Oh yeah? What were some of the others?"

"Well, there's...." A deer jumped into the road, right in front of the car. I swerved, narrowly missing it, and Tanner slammed into the passenger door. "Jesus. Are you okay?"

Tanner shifted in his seat, shaking his right hand. "Jammed my shoulder."

"Shit, I'm sorry."

"Not your fault. Shoulda put my seat belt back on."

I turned to look at him, hoping his shoulder wasn't too bad. The second deer appeared out of nowhere. By the time I saw it, it was too late. I swerved again, slamming on the brakes, but we hit.

The moment of impact felt more like a brick wall than a living, breathing animal. I heard the *thud* before I felt it. The car fishtailed, and the rear wheels went off the road, spinning on gravel. Then I saw the other car. I jerked the steering wheel away from the headlights and felt my car go up and over the low rock wall. Braking didn't keep us from tumbling down the embankment, and tipping, flipping, rolling, until my foot was off the pedals and I didn't know which end was up.

Another *thud* brought the car to a halt on its side. Branches covered the windshield. It took me a second to catch my breath, and in that instant I tried to make sense of what had happened. I saw headlights in the distance—shimmery beams of light running through the dense night air above me.

I heard voices yelling. "You okay? I'm calling for help."

My chest ached, and I realized the seat belt was holding me in place. Then I saw Tanner.

He hadn't said a word. Hadn't moved. He was pressed against the passenger-side door, his body slumped in a weird position. *Oh God. No seat belt. Fuck.*

Scrambling to undo the buckle on my own seat belt, I realized my pants were still open. "Jesus. Tanner? Tanner, say something."

The latch on the belt was jammed, and it wouldn't let go. Growing more frantic by the second, I finally wrenched it open. The metal clanged as it hit the steering wheel, and I reached for Tanner. He was so still, it scared the shit out of me. *Be okay, please be okay.*

I grabbed his shoulder and tugged. "Tanner!"

Fuck. At the angle the car was at, I couldn't move him. Sirens blared in the distance.

"Tanner." I leaned as close as I could. I passed my hand over his face and felt warm air. *Thank God. He's breathing.*

Then I felt wetness—warm, thick. I pulled back and saw the dark smear on my fingers. *Oh fuck, he's bleeding.*

Fumbling in the glove compartment, I managed to find the flashlight. I pulled it open, illuminating the car with the soft yellow glow. Blood trailed from the curtain of hair that hung in front of Tanner's face. Lifting the hair as gently as I could, I saw the gash. Hairline to eyebrow. *Jesus.*

I tugged my sweatshirt off, balled it up, and pressed it against his head, desperate to remember my Boy Scout first aid training. *Don't move the victim.* Victim. *Oh, God, I did this. Apply pressure. Okay.* I shifted closer, aware again that my pants were still gaping. *Son of a bitch.* I yanked them up, shoving myself inside with one hand as I kept the shirt over Tanner's wound.

The voices sounded again, this time through a bullhorn. "Is anyone hurt down there?"

"Yes." I tried to yell, but my voice stuck in my throat. I reached for the driver's door enough to pull the handle and kick it open with my foot. "Yes. Please help me."

Light flooded the car as a spotlight shone through the darkness. It grew brighter as several people climbed down the embankment toward us. *Tanner, please wake up.*

"How many are in the car?"

"Just me and my friend. He's bleeding." Saying the words out loud turned my stomach.

One of the paramedics approached my side of the car while the other went around to Tanner's door.

I scrambled out of the car. "I'm fine. Please help him."

"We'll help both of you, son. Let's take a look at your friend. Has he been conscious since the crash?"

"No, sir, I don't think so."

"Was he wearing a seat belt?"

A shiver ran through me. "No, sir."

He whispered something to the other paramedic that I didn't hear. One of them climbed into the driver's seat while another pried open the passenger door.

Please, God.

They eased Tanner onto a backboard and strapped him to it. He had a thick foam cuff around his neck and was still out cold.

Please, God. Please let Tanner wake up. Please let him be all right.

Chapter Eighteen

I REMEMBER being ushered into the ambulance and having my hand wrapped in an Ace bandage. Someone kept shining lights into my eyes and asking me if I'd hit my head. I hadn't, though my nose felt bruised. Had I hit it on the steering wheel? I didn't remember. Everything was a blur. Paramedics buzzed around Tanner. I heard the word "concussion," but they wouldn't tell me anything else.

When we got to the hospital, they rushed him off in one direction and made me get on a gurney to wait for my wrist to be X-rayed. It seemed as if every nurse in the ER made her way over to me at one point or another. Fill out these forms. Answer these questions. None of them could tell me where Tanner was or what was happening with him. When I got back from X-ray, a nurse practitioner finally came in and sat down to talk to me.

"It's not broken," she said, "but you will need to keep it wrapped. And I can give you some painkillers if you think you'll need them. They may help you get some rest tonight."

I didn't give a shit about sleep or my wrist. I just wanted to know about Tanner. "Can you tell me how Tanner D'Amico is doing? We were brought in together."

Her gaze searched mine. "You were in the same car?"

"Yes, ma'am. I was driving. I need to know how he is."

Sympathy passed over her face. "Are you a relative of Mr. D'Amico's?"

Shit. No. Did that mean she wouldn't tell me? There was no way she'd buy I was his brother. Different last names, opposite coloring. *Family.* My mind raced. Boyfriend didn't count. Fiancé? Would that do? Worth a shot.

"I'm his fiancé."

A smile warmed her face. "Congratulations. I'll go check on his condition for you. Give me a minute."

That minute felt more like a decade. I said every prayer I could call to mind and made up some of my own. I didn't even care that I'd lied about the fiancé part, never mind that I'd just basically come out to a total stranger. I just wanted Tanner to be all right. *Please let him be all right. Please, God.*

She tugged the curtain aside, then yanked it closed again. "He's had some stitches for the gash on his head, and he has a concussion, but it doesn't sound too serious."

"Is he awake? Can I see him?"

"He's been admitted. It's after visiting hours, but I'll bring you up as soon as we get your wrist taken care of, okay?"

"Thank you."

Thank you, God.

Chapter Nineteen

Sitting in the hospital room waiting for Tanner to regain consciousness was killing me. I couldn't stop staring at him, looking for any sign he was ready to open his eyes. I didn't care if he yelled at me for being careless or told me off, I just wanted to see his eyes open and know he was okay.

The nurses had been reassuring and supersweet. One had even brought me a sandwich and a soda. I hadn't touched either. I didn't want to eat or drink or do anything other than hold Tanner's hand and wait.

"I'm sorry." I whispered the words over and over, hoping maybe he could hear me. *Please wake up.* I rested my forehead on our joined hands.

"Collin Dane Fitzpatrick."

My mother's voice was the last thing I expected to hear, yet there she was, standing in the doorway, glaring at me with the heat of a thousand suns. I'd seen fire in her eyes before, but nothing like this.

"Put that boy's hand down and come into the hallway this minute."

"Mom? What are you doing here?"

"The hospital called. I rushed right over, and they told me... never mind what they told me. It's absurd. Just come with me. Now."

The tremor in her voice told me she was keeping herself under control by only the tiniest of measures. The last thing I wanted was her screaming and causing a scene in the middle of the hospital. I squeezed Tanner's hand, waiting long enough to be certain I hadn't felt any movement in reply, and then I stood. If I'd been filled with lead, I couldn't have felt any heavier.

As soon as I reached the door, she grabbed my arm and tugged. "We're leaving."

She might have been determined, but I was a lot stronger. I planted my feet and shrugged away from her. "No. I'm not going anywhere."

"Oh, yes, you are. And after we've had a talk with Father Thomas, you're moving home. I'm not paying room and board to that school so my son can turn into a...."

A mix of fury and disgust crossed her face as she struggled for the right word. The word that would convey how perverted and blasphemous and overall wrong she undoubtedly thought it was for me to be holding Tanner's hand.

"A what, Mom?"

The heat in her eyes cooled to ice. Two wide blue pools of disappointment. "Never mind. Just come with me. Now."

"No."

That wasn't a word my mother was accustomed to hearing. Her eyes blazed brighter. Her voice lowered to a harsh whisper.

"You're not thinking clearly. You're upset. You need to speak with someone who can talk sense into you."

"I'm not leaving Tanner." I couldn't have said a more loaded sentence if I'd tried. It hit me like a wrecking ball how much truth was crammed into those four words.

"Yes. You. Are."

She reached for my arm again, but I jerked away and stepped toward the door, closer to Tanner. "I'm going back inside."

"No!" My mother's voice was shrill enough a nurse down the hall looked our way.

"Yes. Tanner needs me."

"I'm sure his girlfriend would feel otherwise."

She threw me a look so triumphant I felt sorry for her. For a second.

Taking as deep a breath as I could manage with my sore ribs, I looked into her eyes. "Tanner doesn't have a girlfriend. He has me. I'm his boyfriend. He's my boyfriend. We're together."

"You're talking nonsense. I won't have this."

My fingers tingled. "Then don't. That's your choice."

"Collin." Desperation leaked into her voice. "We can fix this. Come with me, and we'll get this all straightened out."

Straightened out. Good one, Mom. "There's nothing to fix. I'm gay, not broken. And I'm in love with Tanner."

The look on her face would have been comical had there been anything funny about that moment, but I'd never been more serious in my life. It knocked the air out of my lungs to have said it out loud like that. Not the gay part, either. The love part. Fuck. It was true. My heart skipped at least a few beats. *Holy shit. I'm in love.*

"Don't say things you can't take back," she said.

"I'm not."

She pulled herself to her full five foot four inches. "I'm leaving. And if you don't come with me, then I think it's best you don't ever come home."

The words stung, but not as much as I'd expected. "Don't say things you can't take back."

She swallowed hard, and for a second I saw a flicker in her eyes, a split second of doubt, instantly eclipsed by the cold, hard stare. "I'm not."

She held my gaze, then turned on her heel and walked away. Down the corridor. Into an elevator. And out of my life.

A tremor shook through me that was equal parts adrenaline and relief. I'd never stood up for myself like that. Not to her. I don't think anyone had. It felt... good. Weird, but good. I shoved my hands into my pockets, cringing as my wrist ached, and walked back into the hospital room.

Tanner's eyes were open. *Thank you, God.* "Are you all right? You want me to get a nurse?"

"No nurse."

"I'm getting a nurse." I bounded into the hallway, straight to the nurses' station. "My friend is awake. Can you check on him, please?"

The warm smile she gave me filled me with hope. "Sure, hon."

I watched as she took Tanner's blood pressure and pulse and scribbled into his chart. "Looking good, Mr. D'Amico. I'll have the doctor come in and check on you, see if we can arrange to send you home."

"Thanks." Tanner gave her his signature smile, and she flushed a warm pink. Even with a bandage on his head, he could charm the pants off anyone, male or female.

As soon as she left the room, his gaze focused on mine. "Happy now?"

"Very."

"Good." He gestured to the spot next to him on the bed.

I sat down, so thankful to be near him, to have him speaking again, I could barely breathe. "I'm sorry."

"For what? You didn't run me over. You hit a deer."

"I should have... I don't know, been paying more attention or reacted faster. Something."

"Dude, it's not your fault. If anything, it was my fault for distracting you. Not to mention I'm the one who thought it was a good idea not to have my seat belt on."

He was letting me off the hook too easily. "Will you just let me feel bad about this? You got hurt. I feel responsible."

That crooked smile flickered across his face. "Is this because I'm your boyfriend?"

My face flooded with heat. "You heard that?"

"Little bit." He reached for my hand and slid his palm over mine. I couldn't take my eyes off the sight of our fingers twined together. I couldn't tell which were his and which were mine, and I didn't care. I just didn't want him to let go. "So you're in love with me, huh?"

My gaze darted to Tanner's. I expected to see playfulness or teasing. All I saw were dark eyes staring straight into mine. Waiting. Tears prickled behind my nose. *Is that okay? Does he love me too?* It didn't matter. Even if the answer to both those questions was "no," it didn't change the facts.

"Yes."

His face stayed motionless. My chest tightened as I braced for his response—any response. His thumb stroked my wrist as his fingers squeezed mine. "Good. Because I love you."

The emotion in his voice hit me harder than the actual words. Their meaning sunk into my pores, wrapping around me like a blanket. He sat up, moving slowly, or maybe it just seemed slow in my mind because this all felt like part of some crazy dream. If it was one, I didn't want to wake up. I leaned in, meeting him halfway. His lips slanted over mine, and he let go of my hand to grab my neck and pull me closer. I could taste my tears on the back of my tongue, and I wondered if he could taste them too.

He broke the kiss but left his hand on my neck. I kept my eyes closed, concentrating on the warmth of his fingers.

"I hated being away from you this weekend," he said.

"Me too."

"I'm sorry about what happened with your mom."

My eyes flew open. "Don't be. I needed to tell her. She needed to know. I'm through with lying."

Tanner's pupils were wide and dark. Cartoonish. I knew that look, and it wasn't from the concussion. He wanted something. *What? Me?* He kneaded a knot in my neck and opened his mouth, then closed it, like he wasn't sure how to phrase what he wanted to say. He was so rarely at a loss for words. My stomach clenched in anticipation.

"How about if this summer you come to New York with me? We could stay at my mom's place in the city for a few weeks, and I'm sure I can get you a job with me at the restaurant on Fire Island."

I didn't know what to say. *He wants us to spend the summer together?* My heart soared.

Tanner must have taken my silence for hesitation. "I mean, you can make good money. And you wouldn't have to worry about a place to stay. I mean, you can't go home, and we could be, you know, us. Together. But if you don't—"

"Yes."

His fingers stilled. "Yes?"

"Yeah. Sounds… perfect."

The grin returned, tugging the side of his mouth into that irresistible curl. "You ready? To go public?"

"With you? I'm ready." My lips met his again, hard. I didn't care who saw us or what they thought. And in that moment, I was ready.

For anything.

Moment of Truth

To WM, who spent many happy summers on Fire Island. You are missed.

Acknowledgments

Many thanks to Karen Booth, KD Wood, Kira Decker, Amanda Usen, and Mandy Pennington for being beta readers extraordinaire. Couldn't have done it without you!

And a special thank-you to my agent, Saritza Hernandez, for making this book possible, and to Sue Adams and the rest of the Dreamspinner staff for making the editing of these books such an enjoyable experience. You're the best!

Chapter One

I DIDN'T expect the bed to be so big. And I didn't know there would only be one. Tanner had described the beach house to me in detail. Five bedrooms, right on the beach, old and weathered but still in good shape. It looked exactly as I'd pictured. Gray shingles. Sandy driveway. Creaky wooden staircase. He'd even told me that he'd made sure we got the one room on the top floor for extra privacy.

But I hadn't realized that room had only one bed. One big king-size bed. Compared to the twin-size ones we'd had in our dorm, it looked enormous. Decadent. I couldn't wait to sprawl out in it with Tanner and put it to full use. I also couldn't help but think about how everyone in the house would know we were sharing a bed.

My heart rate accelerated, and it had nothing to do with the two flights of stairs we'd just climbed. We'd been together for three months, but still almost no one knew we were a couple. My family, a disaster that still made me cringe when I thought about it. His family, who couldn't have been nicer—his mom had let us crash at her place for the week between moving out of the dorm and to the beach, and his dad had gotten us tickets to two shows and taken us out for an expensive dinner. And Wendy, who quietly referred to herself as our personal fag hag.

Tanner dropped his duffel on the floor by the big window and yanked the cord to raise the blinds. The view took my breath away. I knew we were only a short walk to the beach, but I hadn't realized there was nothing but sand and tall sea grass separating us from the ocean.

"Wow."

"Told you. Pretty awesome, huh?"

"I'll say."

Tanner undid the latch and shoved the window open. It squeaked as he lowered it a bit, then hooked his fingers underneath the wood and hoisted it higher. The muscles in his arms and back flexed, making my pulse race for a different reason. He turned and caught me staring. His sexy mouth curved into a wicked smile.

"You know," he said, eyeing me in a way that made me feel like I was melting from more than just the summer heat. "They say everything tastes better at the beach."

"Oh they do, do they?"

He tugged me into a kiss. Hot. Hungry. His tongue swept around mine, but it might as well have been circling the head of my cock. I pressed against him, sighing into his mouth and grinding my hips into his.

Tanner's mom couldn't have been more welcoming, but she was also home all the time, and I hadn't felt comfortable enough in her small apartment to do anything more than kiss him good night. The week of celibacy had me so horny, I could barely see straight.

Kissing him deeper, I sank my fingers into his hair. I'd missed the silky feel. The humid air filled with the coconut-lime scent of his shampoo, and I breathed it in, savoring him—his smell, his taste, his hardness. I pulled away enough to tug his shirt up and over his head.

Tanner grabbed a handful of my T-shirt and flopped backward onto the gigantic bed, pulling me along with him. For a solid week, I'd wanted nothing more than to feel his body against mine. Rubbing against him had stars dancing behind my eyes. I could have come just from that. Just from feeling him next to me. Just from knowing he was as hard as me, that he wanted this as much as I did.

Forcing myself to breathe, I rolled away, not sure what I wanted to take off first, my shirt or his shorts. Either way I wanted fewer clothes separating us, the sooner the better. Before my sex-scrambled brain could figure out what to do, a door slammed.

"Woot! We're here!"

Voices boomed from downstairs followed by the muffled sound of suitcases rolling into the house and footsteps thudding up the stairs.

My body stiffened, and not in a good way. I sat up so fast I nearly fell off the bed.

Tanner sat up alongside me and rubbed my back. His hand felt warm and comforting, but it wasn't enough to calm me.

"Collin, it's okay. Everyone living here is totally cool. With everything."

He'd said that before, but I'd been too freaked-out to ask what that meant. "You know them all?"

"Yep."

"And they know… about me?"

"They know you're my roommate from school. And yeah, they know you're my boyfriend. Trust me. No one gives a shit. Besides, they'll like you."

My eyes darted to his. He looked sympathetic but amused. His fingers kneaded my shoulder, and I wanted to shove him down on the bed and finish what we'd started, but I heard voices again.

"Tanner? You up there?" a guy called.

"Be down in a sec. We just got here too." He smoothed his hand over my hair and cupped the back of my neck, forcing me to look at him. "You'll feel better after you meet them. Unless you want to stay up here until we're done.... You might be calmer if...."

Tempting. So fucking tempting. I shook my head. "No. I can think of better first impressions than having them hear me moaning."

"You think there'd be moaning, huh?"

"I haven't come in four days."

Tanner laughed. "We were at my mom's place for seven."

"I jerked off in the shower one morning."

"I'd have come with you." His eyes twinkled at me. Fucking *twinkled* like goddamned gemstones. Like they thought his joke was the funniest thing they'd ever heard.

"I know you would have. That's why I got up early that morning."

"Just that one time, though? The whole time we were there?"

I looked down at the floor again and nodded.

"Well, we're gonna make up for that. And you're not going to have to feel like that here. This is our house, for the whole summer. And we are most definitely not the only people who will be having sex in it."

Even the thought of us having sex made me smile. "Tell me again who's living here."

Meeting my new housemates with a raging erection was not part of my plan, so I needed to focus on something other than Tanner.

"Suzanne and Bill own the house. They're in their late twenties, married about five years, I think. My dad knows them from the theater circuit. Bill's a set designer, and Suzanne's a writer. They can't afford this place and their apartment in the city unless they rent the other rooms."

"That's how you lived here last summer?"

"Yep. The last two summers. My dad heard they were looking for renters, so Wendy and I each took a room. That's how Wendy hooked up with Dex, who's also living here again."

"So they've been together two years?"

"Almost to the day. Last summer they shared this room, but this year they took one of the smaller rooms downstairs since Wendy can only be here on the weekends."

She'd told me she was bummed about that, but she'd scored an internship at some fashion magazine—her dream job—and she hadn't been able to turn it down. "Is Dex working at the restaurant with us?"

"Nah. He's a trust fund brat. Pretty sure all he'll be working on is a tan. I don't think I've ever seen him do anything other than read and play guitar, and I've lived with him two summers."

"Do you not like him?"

"He's nice enough. We just have nothing in common."

Except that you've both slept with Wendy. I kept that comment to myself. "Is that it? Housemate-wise?"

"Nope. There's Bryan. He's Suzanne's younger brother. Pretty sure he's our age. He goes to NYU. He's a photography student, but he's also a kickass musician. His band plays all over, but in the summer he books a bunch of gigs out here. So he'll be here when he's not touring around." Tanner paused, a smile playing at his lips. "Oh yeah. And he's gay."

My eyes bugged. "Really?"

"Yes. And very out. When I said no one here would think twice about us, I meant it."

That sounded too good to be true, but I really hoped it was. "That it?"

"No." There was an edge in Tanner's voice I hadn't heard before. "There's Maggie."

Something about his tone made me think "ex-girlfriend." Was that it? Were there two women in the house Tanner had slept with? "What's she like?"

"Maggie is...."

A giggle echoed through the stairwell. "Maggie is what?"

A pixie-ish girl with heavy black bangs and a ponytail high atop her head peered around the corner of our doorway.

Tanner rolled his eyes.

Pixie-chick fluttered her long fake lashes and gave him an exaggerated innocent-face. "Maggie is what, Tanner? And who's your friend? He's cute."

Tanner threw me a look I couldn't quite read—a cross between annoyance and concern. He drew in a breath. "Maggie is a dancer-singer-actress who works on a ton of my dad's productions."

Maggie grinned. "I prefer the term ingénue."

Nothing about her looked the least bit innocent or naïve to me.

A muscle in Tanner's jaw twitched, but he kept his voice even. "And she's his ex-girlfriend."

Wait. This was who he was talking about when he said his dad was dating someone our age? *Holy shit.*

"See?" she said, looking straight at me with her cartoonishly big black-rimmed eyes. "Ingénue. The femme fatale stole him away from me."

"No new director to seduce?" Tanner teased, but I could hear the hint of edginess behind his words.

"Not yet. I'm between... projects." Her gaze flitted between Tanner and me. "I think I'll go younger this time. Maybe a student in my class."

"You teach?" I asked. I couldn't imagine her teaching anything.

"Yoga and tai chi. On the beach. Three mornings a week. You should come." The breathy pause before she said the word "come" earned another eye roll from Tanner.

The screen door slammed again. "Anyone home?"

Maggie's eyebrows rose. "Who's that? He sounds hot."

Tanner took a step toward the door, ushering Maggie into the hall. "It's ninety degrees out, and the house isn't air-conditioned. Everyone's hot."

"Everyone in this room, at least." She winked at me and trotted down the stairs.

"That's your dad's ex?" I'd met Tanner's dad. He was like an older, graying version of Tanner. Easygoing. Smart. Movie-star attractive. And clearly able to get girls I'd have been too scared to talk to even if I'd been into them. Especially if I'd been into them.

"Yep. Ready to meet the rest of the house?"

"Let's do it." After Maggie, I was pretty sure nothing would be a surprise.

Chapter Two

The first floor of the house had become a sea of boxes and suitcases. It amazed me how much stuff there was. With Fire Island's no-cars-allowed policy, everything had to be carted to the houses from the dock by wagon or wheeled case. Not conducive to bringing a lot of stuff. Tanner had warned me, so all I'd brought was a backpack with my laptop and a suitcase full of clothes. Pretty much everything else I owned was in storage at the auto shop that was doing bodywork on my car after the accident. I'd worked for the owner a few times, and he'd said he didn't mind keeping my stuff for the summer.

Tanner and I stepped around the boxes as we made our way into the kitchen. "How'd they get all this shit here?" I asked.

"Those kids at the dock with the wagons are like island bellhops. They'll haul your stuff for a few bucks. Plus Suzanne owns one of those big wagons that were in that lot by the dock."

Crazy. I never imagined I'd live anywhere that didn't have cars. It was cool, but it was going to take some getting used to. I'd had a hard enough time being without a car since the crash. I really hoped I'd make enough money this summer to cover the cost of the repairs I couldn't do myself.

The kitchen was by far the largest room in the house, open and light with windows along one entire wall and a slider out to a big deck, which wrapped around two sides of the house. The cabinets were old and whitewashed, but the countertops looked new—black and shiny. Marble or granite. All the appliances were stainless steel and looked pretty new too. Rows of pots and pans and bowls covered the shelves that lined one of the shorter walls. Someone here must like to cook.

I tensed as we entered the room. We were spending an entire summer here, with all these people I didn't know. *What if they don't like me? What if Tanner's wrong about everyone being "okay" with us being here, as a couple?*

A woman in cut-off jeans and a black tank top stood on a step stool getting pitchers out of the cabinet over the double-door fridge. Her brown hair was twisted into a makeshift bun and held in place by what looked like a binder clip. She grimaced as she tried to reach farther into the cupboard.

"Need some help with that?" Tanner asked.

She turned toward him and broke into a huge grin. She had the bluest eyes I'd ever seen. They lit up as she hopped down from the stool and threw her arms around him. "Tan-Man!"

Tan-Man? If I hadn't been so nervous, I'd have laughed out loud.

"Hey Suzie-Q." He hugged her tight, lifting her off the ground.

She gave him a loud smooch on the cheek, then her blue laser beams focused on me, intent, studying. My heart tapped out Morse code against my ribs. Then her warm smile returned. "You must be Collin."

"Nice to meet you." I held out my hand, but she ignored it and went straight for a hug.

She popped up onto her toes and squeezed me tight as I nervously patted her back like I'd never given a hug before. "Welcome. We're so glad you can spend the summer at the Nut House."

The what? "Nut house?"

Tanner chuckled. "Their last name is Nutley, so this is officially the Nut House."

"The nuttier the better" came a deep, melodic voice behind me.

"Bryan." Tanner reached out a hand, and the guy took it and pulled him into a one-armed hug.

He had blue eyes that matched the woman's, except that his were rimmed with guy-liner and half-covered with spikes of dyed black bangs. I'd never met anyone I'd describe as stunning—until then. His sister had a natural beauty, high cheekbones, slender nose, no makeup or jewelry—just her. Bryan had all the same features, but amplified. More sculpted, thicker brows, redder lips, squarer jaw, ears lined in small rings, arms covered in tats.

His eyes narrowed as he looked at me, turning the bright blue smoky. "You must be the boyfriend."

My cheeks heated before I could answer. Tanner's hand lightly brushed over my back. Even that brief second of contact reassured me. He gestured between us. "Bryan, this is Collin. Collin, this is Suzie's wayward brother."

Bryan laughed and shook my hand. "Welcome."

"Thanks." I forced myself to breathe normally.

"Nice," he muttered, throwing Tanner a wink as he walked past us.

My face burned hotter.

Tanner stepped closer, his breath soft against my ear. "Relax," he whispered, "you're doing great."

I love you. I thought the words so hard, I was sure he was receiving them telepathically. And it was true. I loved him more than I could say. More than I'd ever loved anyone. Which still scared the crap out of me.

"A little help here?" The sliding glass door banged open as two guys struggled in, carrying an enormous ice chest with a milk crate balanced on top of it.

I was closest to the door, so I grabbed the crate off the top. It was full of groceries. Maple syrup, bags of flour and sugar, boxes of pasta. No wonder they were struggling—it weighed at least thirty pounds on its own. God knows how much the two-handled cooler weighed.

"Thanks, dude," the older guy said.

"No problem."

The guy who'd thanked me was Bill, Suzanne's husband. He seemed as down-to-earth and friendly as she was, casually dressed in board shorts and a worn T-shirt. He kissed her hello in a sweet, natural way that somehow announced to the entire room how totally in love they were. I smiled just watching them together.

The other one had to be Dex. I'd heard Wendy talk about him so many times I'd constructed a mental image without even realizing it, and the short-haired Tommy Hilfiger-wearing guy I was looking at didn't even remotely match what I'd expected. Wendy was so bubbly and free-spirited, wild hair flowing in every direction, gigantic purse always one item away from bursting at its seams. This guy looked like he wouldn't have a hair out of place even if he were in the middle of a monsoon. He could easily have been on the cover of anything from *GQ* to a J. Crew catalog. Everything from his haircut to his shoes screamed money.

Suzanne made the introductions this time, then everyone got busy unpacking the cooler and filling the pitchers to make lemonade and iced tea. Everyone except Dex. He gave a cool nod hello, then flopped onto the window seat scrolling through something on his phone.

"Hey, no lifting." Bill took the box Suzanne had hoisted off the floor.

She rolled her eyes, then smiled. I recognized the look that passed between them. I'd seen it on Sean's face every time his wife Laura had been pregnant—protective, concerned, proud. My stomach twinged. This would be the first summer of their lives that I wouldn't be seeing my nieces and nephew.

The last time Sean and I had spoken, we'd argued. He wanted me to talk to my mom. To "make things right." And he didn't want to talk about my relationship with Tanner. He wasn't all fire and brimstone like Quinn had been. Hadn't told me I was wrong or condemned me to hell or even disowned me. But he hadn't listened either. He just wanted to make peace where peace couldn't be made. Not unless I was willing to forget about Tanner, forget what I wanted, and change who I was. Three things I was in no way willing to do. I'd spent too long doing all of that. I was done. Even if that meant not having a family anymore.

"Okay, everyone, listen up," Bill said, wrapping his arms around Suzanne from behind. "We have a little announcement to make, and it affects all of you."

Tanner stopped stacking cereal boxes in the pantry, Maggie stopped stirring her pitcher, and Dex looked up from his phone for the first time since he'd entered the house.

Suzanne's face flushed a rosy pink as she rubbed Bill's hands and hugged her stomach. "We're pregnant."

The room buzzed with everyone offering congratulations. I knew it. As much as it made me miss home, it warmed me to be included in this announcement. They looked so insanely happy, beaming at each other.

Bryan grinned at his sister. "I'm so glad you're finally making me an aunt."

She grabbed the dishtowel off the counter and smacked him with it. "Freeloader. You owe me years of babysitting."

"Gladly. I'll get junior his first earring."

"What if it's a girl?"

"Then I'll get her her first tattoo."

Suzanne growled at him, but it was obvious how close they were. My stomach pangs returned.

"Anyway," Bill said. "This changes our plans for the summer a little. We won't be out here quite as much because we're going to be getting our place ready for the baby. And we're going to need you guys to pitch in a little more than usual with the cooking and cleaning."

"No, we don't," Suzanne said. "We'll do the schedule just like last summer. Everyone takes turns. We'll just be here a little less, so you'll have to factor that in."

Tanner had already gotten busy drawing lines down the huge chalkboard on the wall behind the long picnic bench-style kitchen table. He wrote breakfast, lunch, and dinner down the side and the days of the week across the top. Whatever meals you were signed up for meant you had to make sure the food for that meal was in the house—even if you wouldn't be there for that meal—meaning if you were responsible for breakfast on a day you were working in the morning, you had to make sure there were donuts or muffins or something for everyone else to eat. Seemed reasonable.

I hadn't said more than two words the whole time we'd been in the kitchen, so I asked something I'd been wondering since we'd gotten off the ferry and dragged our luggage the half mile or so to our house.

"How do you grocery shop here?"

"I'll show you," Tanner said, pointing to the schedule. "We're on dinner duty tonight, so we'll go get stuff now."

"Perfect," Suzanne said. "Just no chicken, okay? That's the only thing I can't deal with. Apparently this baby can't stand poultry, not even the smell of it cooking."

"Got it." Tanner nodded. "You ready?"

"Sure thing, Tan-Man."

He snorted and tried to look annoyed, but I saw the smile tugging at his lips. "Shut up."

I grinned and followed him out the door. I had no idea where we were heading, but I'd have followed Tanner anywhere.

Chapter Three

WALKING INTO Dylan's General Store was like stepping back in time. The wooden floors were old and bare. Half the customers were wearing flip-flops, while the other half remained barefoot. Sand had been tracked everywhere. For a tiny shop, they had an amazing stock of food. Baskets of fresh fruits and veggies, artisan bread, every herb I could name. Deli case full of cheeses and smoked meat plus a butcher case.

"What are you thinking for dinner?" I asked.

Tanner shrugged. "You know me, I'll eat anything."

I scanned the shelves. "Okay, how about pasta with meatballs? And maybe some of those pies over there for dessert. French toast for breakfast? Everyone should like french toast, right?"

"Who do you think is going to do all this cooking?"

"Me." The stunned look on Tanner's face amused the hell out of me.

"You can make all that?"

"And plenty more. Gino lets me cook a lot. I know my way around a kitchen."

"Awesome." Tanner reached for a jar of ready-made tomato sauce, but I shook my head.

"We can do way better than jarred." I tossed fresh garlic and a bunch of basil into my basket along with cans of crushed tomatoes and a package of ground beef. I'd seen plenty of pasta in the pantry at the house. We picked up several loaves of fresh crusty bread, milk and eggs, brown sugar, enough butter for the french toast, and some homemade garlic bread.

The produce looked amazing so I picked out some tomatoes and cucumbers for salad along with some mixed baby greens, and raspberries and blueberries to go with the french toast.

"What kind of pie did you get?"

Tanner had four pie boxes in his hands. "Mixed berry, apple, strawberry rhubarb, and peach. I think we need some vanilla ice cream too."

"Good thinking."

I couldn't wait for dinner. Tanner hadn't ever seen me cook before. I was looking forward to it. I hoped like hell I got stuff right and he liked the food.

After we paid we shoved all the perishable stuff into the big cooler and wheeled the wagon home, making it into the house just in time to miss an afternoon thunderstorm. Huge raindrops poured down, turning the deck from light to dark gray as we unpacked the food. I went to work cooking. Chopping garlic nice and small for the tomato sauce, cutting up the cucumbers so they could marinate in some vinegar. I wanted everything perfect.

I put half the garlic in the big stockpot with some olive oil, sautéed it until it was fragrant, then added in the tomato paste, stirring just until it started taking on a deeper color. The crushed tomatoes went in last with a canful of water, a half dozen fresh basil leaves ripped into pieces, and the lid so it could all simmer until the flavors merged and formed one new, better one.

I cut the tips off the other heads of garlic, put them in a small ceramic dish, covered them in olive oil, then wrapped them tightly in foil and set them to roast in a hot oven. While they were cooking, I made the meatballs.

Tanner came in and sat at the table, watching. "Jesus, you actually know what you're doing."

I grinned. "Imagine that."

"You know what I mean. I've lived with you a whole year, and I had no clue you could cook. How'd that happen?"

"If we'd had a kitchen, you'd know. Trust me. I'd have cooked for you all the time."

"Sex and cooking all in one place? I'd never leave the house."

I laughed, knowing he was serious. "Then my plan's working, because I don't want you leaving the house tonight."

"Good, because I'd kinda planned to spend the whole night in our room." That smile. Jesus, that smile of his was enough to make my knees weak and give the rest of my body ideas that involved pressing up against him or dragging him into the pantry. If there weren't so many other people home, I would have done one or both of those. I wanted to slam him down onto the kitchen table and blow him within an inch of his sanity.

"Can I at least help with some of this?"

"Sure." I was wrist-deep in ground beef, starting to shape meatballs. "You can slice the bread. Two loaves longways for garlic bread and the other two into one-inch slices for tomorrow morning's french toast."

"Cutting bread I can handle."

I loved watching his arms as he worked. The way they flexed caused a corresponding flex inside my jeans. Jesus, he had a strong effect on me. I'd never been this unstoppably drawn to someone before. Ever. And now I had him for the whole summer. It seemed too good to be true.

Worries popped into my head without warning. What would happen back at school? We'd managed to stay under the radar, but people were bound to find out eventually. Wendy was our only ally. My mother could arrive and make a scene at any moment. Gino could fire me. I shook those images out of my mind. *That's three months away. Focus on the here and now. This is paradise. Enjoy it.*

I planned to try.

Chapter Four

DINNER WAS a huge hit. Tanner declared my sauce better than Gino's, and Maggie proposed having me take over all the cooking shifts. We strolled down the beach, watching the moon rise over the water, then ate pie out on the deck under the stars. I couldn't remember a time I'd laughed more or felt more at home.

Since Tanner and I had shopped and cooked, it was everyone else's responsibility to clean up, so we finally got to head upstairs. Alone.

Tanner climbed the stairs to our room so slowly, I was tempted to try to fireman's carry him just to get us there faster.

He meandered at the second floor landing, stopping to look at me with that damned smirk on his face. "Need to brush your teeth or anything?"

He pointed at the bathroom, all innocent, like he was the maître d' at a restaurant asking if I wanted to check my coat before being shown to my table.

"I'm good, thanks."

His smile twitched as he started up the next staircase. The last one. The one that led to our room and nowhere else. My heart hammered hard and fast, and not from stair climbing. I needed to touch Tanner, soon, or every part of my body from my brain to my balls was going to simultaneously combust.

Tanner pushed our door open with exaggerated care and stepped inside. *Jesus, is he trying to make me crazy? All I want is to....*

My back slammed against the wall, and before I could complete my thought, Tanner's mouth was on mine. The kiss was savage, tongue hot and heavy against mine. Even through our shorts, I could feel how ready he was. My head swam.

Desperate for more, I grabbed on to him, rolling us toward the door and kicking it shut. Tanner let out a grunt as I pressed him against the hard wood. Could anyone hear us? I didn't care. I just needed this. Tanner. Now.

As soon as I shoved his T-shirt up his ribs, he yanked it off and tossed it aside. Warm smooth skin greeted my fingertips, filling my nose with his scent. God, I missed this. My mouth returned to his, tongues dueling as my hands fumbled with his fly. I couldn't stop rubbing against him enough to get the zipper down. Tanner grabbed my ass, crushing his cock alongside mine, humping against me with enough intensity I had to force myself not to come.

I didn't want that. Not yet. Not standing against the door when that crazy big bed was only feet away. As if he read my mind, Tanner shoved me backward, taking advantage of the moment our bodies parted to strip off his shorts. I tugged off my shirt, and before I could launch it across the room, Tanner had my shorts undone and down. Kicking them away put me off-balance, and Tanner steadied me with one hand clutching the back of my neck and the other wrapped around my cock.

Whimpers echoed through the room. My whimpers. His thumb slicked over my swollen head, round and round in circles that left me dizzy and panting.

"Let's try out the bed." Tanner's voice was low and thick. I'd have said yes to anything he asked with that voice.

I couldn't actually say a word, so I nodded and pulled us down onto the mattress. Holy Jesus. Soft cool sheets, warm hard body, wet velvety tongue. Heaven. Fire Island was heaven.

Tanner straddled me, rocking his hips back and forth, skin gliding against skin as his tongue circled mine. His arms shook. He was as close as I was. The thought alone was enough to turn me on even more. Wedging a hand between us, I wrapped my fingers around both of us. Our very first time together he'd done this—stroked us together. I wanted our first time in our new place to be like that. A first of many.

The room filled with the sweet sound of our cocks, slick and ready, pumping together in my fist. As I teetered on the edge of insanity, my hips arched beneath Tanner, my balls pressed tight against his. My mouth slid to his neck, needing his taste, but no longer able to keep kissing. I nipped at his collarbone, licked at the salty hollow at the base of his throat.

His groan sounded low and deep alongside my ear. Drawing that sound from him was my undoing. My dick spasmed, unleashing jet after jet of come. My hand kept the rhythm as Tanner swelled, then joined me, exploding in thick wet bursts.

Panting hard, he slowed his hips, still rubbing our bodies together. Good. So insanely fucking good. My stomach muscles contracted again and again as the last shudders of the orgasm rippled through my cock.

Tanner kissed me, slow and deep. I wanted to drown in that kiss. To sink inside it and let it carry me away.

Tanner's eyes drifted shut. His voice was sleepy, like a purr. "I'm glad you're here."

"Me too."

It didn't matter that I'd had nowhere else to go this summer. Wherever Tanner was, that's where I wanted to be.

Chapter Five

I'D FALLEN into a deep sleep, but something had woken me. A door slam? A dream? I wasn't sure.

My phone? I reached for it before I remembered. *No one has this number. No one but Tanner.* My mom had cut off my family plan when she stopped speaking to me. I checked anyway. No missed calls. No messages. My stomach tensed, but I forced myself to breathe. *No sense in worrying about things you can't change or a future that's an unknown. For now all I can do is focus on tomorrow. And tomorrow it's our turn to make breakfast. Might as well go down now and get that started.*

Tanner's slow, deep breaths told me he was fast asleep. I pulled on a pair of shorts and a T-shirt and crept downstairs. The kitchen was empty so I only turned on the small overhead light at the sink. That's all I needed. I grabbed a bowl and got the eggs, butter, and milk out of the fridge and the brown sugar and vanilla out of the cupboard. Whisking together the eggs and milk with the sugar and vanilla made the kitchen smell sweet and enticing even though nothing was cooked yet.

I got out two rectangular pans, buttered them, then found the bag of french bread Tanner had sliced earlier and placed them in the pans. The egg mixture covered all the slices, and I poked them with a sharp knife, making little slits to make sure it was getting absorbed. The aluminum foil crinkled, then screeched when I tore it off the roll. I placed the covered pan in the fridge. Overnight to soak and then forty-five minutes to bake in the morning and we'd have awesome french toast for breakfast. It was the breakfast my brothers and I had asked for every year on our birthdays since I could remember. My stomach knotted again.

Slinking up the stairs, I tried to be as quiet as possible, but I paused on the second landing. There were voices, a guy and a girl, coming from Dex's room. Wendy wasn't visiting until the weekend.

The door opened just as I walked by, and Maggie flounced out, giggling. "Hey, Collin, you're up late."

"Just fixed breakfast for the morning."

"Mmm." She walked around me like a predator assessing her prey. "There's something irresistible about a man who can cook. Tanner's father makes the most amazing breakfast potatoes. I don't even like potatoes that much, but his? Oh my God. That was my first thought when we broke up. No more potatoes? Cruel and unusual punishment, if you ask me."

"Why don't you just learn to make them?"

"Because I despise cooking. I like eating food, just not making it."

"Thanks for the warning. I'll remember to eat at work on the days you're in charge of house meals."

She smirked. "You're pretty smart for someone so adorable."

My cheeks burned, and I cursed them for giving her the satisfaction.

She walked toward me, licking her lips, a devilish gleam in her oversized eyes. "So tell me, Collin, how gay are you? I know Tanner swings both ways. You too?"

"Nope. Sorry, on a scale of one to gay, I'm afraid I'm very gay."

She gave an exaggerated pout. "What about threesomes? Another guy for you to play with while I play with both of you?"

"Not the man for the job. Tanner's it for me."

"Wow. Such loyalty. What about him? Are you it for him, or does he still have girls on the side? Like Wendy. Is she still his snack cake when she and the boyfriend are apart?"

Her teasing tone grated on my nerves, plus I thought that was a secret. My eyes narrowed. "You knew about that?"

"Everyone had a hunch. Now I know." She gave me an even more wicked smile. God, I'm an idiot. I fell right into her trap and confirmed what she wanted to know. Shit. Should I tell Tanner? Warn him? Or Wendy? If Dex found out, it seemed like that could cause a good bit of tension in the house. I didn't want any tension. I had enough of that with my family. I didn't want it here.

Maggie sauntered closer, running her finger along my arm. "Have you had pussy?"

"Yes."

"Didn't like it?"

"Not my favorite, no."

She stroked her fingers over my chest. "I bet I could do some things you'd like."

"I'm sure you could, but I'm sorry. I'm taken." I was sure she wouldn't have any trouble finding someone else to take her up on an offer like that.

The pout returned in full force, but I could tell it was mostly for show. She peeled off her shirt, revealing a lacy black bra, and gave a tall stretch. Then she bent to touch her toes, ass in the air, right in front of me. Any straight guy would have carried her off to bed or started humping her right there in the hallway. I felt nothing. Except that I wanted to get up to my room and finally go to sleep alongside Tanner. I'd been away from him for less than an hour, and somehow I missed him.

"Good night, Maggie."

I heard her sigh and close her bedroom door as I made my way up the final flight of stairs.

Climbing into our big comfy bed felt heavenly. I let myself sink into the cushiony mattress and breathed in deeply. Cool salty ocean air mixed with Tanner's warm sleepy scent. I already knew I wasn't ever going to want this summer to end.

Chapter Six

French toast. The sweet aroma drifted around me. I recognized it even before I was fully awake. For a second I thought I was home, at my mom's house, then I opened my eyes and saw the dim light filtering through the window. Breathing deeper, I smelled the ocean under the toasty, sugary scent, and I remembered. Not Mom's.

"Morning."

Tanner's voice startled me. The bed was so fucking big, I hadn't even felt that he was still in it.

I turned to look at him, and my mouth dropped. Dark hair, damp and slicked back. Dressed. Well, sort of. A pair of khaki shorts on. No shirt. Smelling clean and fresh from the shower.

I rubbed my eyes with my fists. "When did you get up?"

"About an hour ago. You were out cold. It's the ocean air. Awesome, isn't it?"

"I think there was more to it than the ocean air." My cock twitched as if it were trying to remind me what had made me sleep so well.

Tanner chuckled. "You're gonna sleep really well this summer."

"Sounds good to me." I didn't ever want to get out of that bed.

"I stuck the french toast in the oven like you said. The timer should go off in about a half hour. Iced tea?" He held out a tall glass. Moisture beaded on the side, and a drop ran down, landing in a cold splash on my chest. I jumped, my cock continuing to plump.

The tea was strong and sweet, but I gulped it, not realizing how thirsty I was until I swallowed the first mouthful. "Thanks."

Tanner grinned as he took the empty glass. "You gonna grab a shower before breakfast?"

His gaze darted from my erection to my eyes. Huge pupils filled his dark brown irises.

My throat tightened. "A shower would be good."

"You have something else in mind?"

One dark brow arched as he leaned over and kissed me, sending me to full mast with two sweeps of his tongue.

I groaned, and Tanner chuckled again, glancing down my body. Precome trickled onto my stomach. Tanner nodded toward my erection. "You might want to take care of that before you venture down to the bathroom. Unless you're looking for a hands-free way to carry your towel."

My cheeks heated, and my heart picked up speed.

He held my gaze, eyes dark with desire. He'd said I might want to take care of it. I shot a quick look at the door.

"It's locked," he said, reading my mind.

My face burned hotter as my hand went to my cock. I'd jerked off in front of him more times than I could count, but there was still a rush of self-consciousness every time I started. The first stroke alone felt so good, it lessened some of the embarrassment. The second elicited a low moan from Tanner, which made my dick jump, and took the heat in my face lower, to my throat. By the third stroke, Tanner was rubbing his own bulge as he watched, and all I wanted was for us both to get off.

I cupped my balls with my free hand, lightly touching the puckered skin. Jesus. This wasn't going to take long. Tanner ran his fingers up and down my thigh, then slid them up my torso and flicked my nipple.

"Fuck." The word came out as a whisper as my head pressed back into the pillow. My eyes fluttered open. The look on Tanner's face—intense, full of lust—urged me to pump faster. My hips rose off the bed. The tip of my cock was so red, I doubted any blood was left to color my face.

"So fucking hot," Tanner said, his eyes locked on my dick. He knelt alongside me, unzipped, and pulled out his erection. I went to reach for it, but Tanner caught my wrist and moved my hand back to my balls. "No. You."

I loved that he wanted to watch. His fingers traced the underside of his cock. I loved to watch him too. Loved it too much. I teetered on the brink for a few more precious seconds. *Make it last. Make it last. Just one more stroke. One more. One. One. One.* Tanner's hand braced against my chest as he thrust into his fist and I tumbled over the edge. The world went black as hot streaks painted my body. *Mine. His. Oh God.*

My heart pounded in my ears as bright lights flicked on and off behind my eyelids. Our panting breaths filled the room. Laughter bubbled up from deep in my chest.

"What's so funny?" Tanner asked, wiping my chest with a small towel.

"I'm ready for a nap."

Tanner snorted and gave me a shove toward the edge of the bed. "Hit the shower, then we eat. You need sustenance if you're gonna survive this summer."

Chapter Seven

WALKING INTO Dorothy's for the first time was like walking into a new school on the first day. Only weirder. Most of the servers and busboys seemed to already know each other. At least three girls made beelines for Tanner, giggling and hugging him hello like he was their long-lost best friend. Manicured hands flitted over his arms as they giggled and asked how his year had been. I hung back and watched.

I'd seen the restaurant online, and Tanner had described it, but in person it was overwhelming. The entire place was done in black and white. Not just the two colors but all the shades of gray as well. And not just the floor, walls, and ceilings—everything. Black tablecloths, white napkins, black-and-white chairs. Enormous framed black-and-white photographs lined the walls. It was like stepping into the opening of *The Wizard of Oz*. If Tanner's shirt hadn't still been bright blue, I'd have wondered if it was all an optical illusion.

"Okay, kiddies, listen up...." A woman with a booming voice swept into the room, clipboard in her hand. "Come on, I don't have all day."

Tanner rolled his eyes as she snapped her fingers. He leaned close and whispered, "That would be Dorothy."

I'd spoken with Dorothy on the phone after Tanner had asked her if there would be an opening for me at the restaurant. Cell service didn't do her justice. She was loud, imposing, and a sea of colors. Shocking red hair with blonde streaks that made it look like a sunset. Blue-and-purple swirly summer dress. Nails painted every color of the rainbow.

"Where are my newbies? Collin? Jason? Sarah?"

I hadn't expected for my name to be one of the first orders of business. "Here."

She motioned me forward with an impatient wave of her hand. I headed to the front of the group along with a guy and a girl who both looked as hesitant as I felt. "Okay, gang, Collin and Jason are our new servers. Make them feel welcome, get them acclimated. Sarah will be in the kitchen. She'll be plating the apps and desserts and prepping all your setup. Be nice to her. You'll need her to like you when you're in the weeds and forgot to order someone's smoked salmon."

I scanned the group as Dorothy kept talking, detailing how specials would be announced, how black was the only option for pants, how lateness wouldn't be tolerated. It was a lot to take in but didn't sound too terribly different from working at Gino's. I was used to big crowds. I knew how to deal with customers. Besides, Tanner had said he'd show me the ropes.

"One more thing," Dorothy said. "A few changes in the lineup. The downside of hiring Manhattan's beautiful people to work for you is that sometimes they get better offers. Scotty and Marie will not be joining us this summer, so I've done some juggling. Jane, you're going to be playing hostess three nights a week. And Tanner, you're going to Oz."

Shit.

Oz was the club next door to Dorothy's. The two establishments were separated by a winding yellow brick path and a sea of flowers I was guessing were supposed to look like poppies. Tanner said Oz was one of the island's premier hot spots and was one of the wildest clubs on the island, apart from the bars in The Pines and Cherry Grove, Fire Island's two gay towns. He'd said we'd hang out at Oz after my birthday. He'd only been twenty-one for a month and a half, and I wouldn't turn for another three weeks.

He shot me a glance and shrugged. I wondered what he'd be doing there. I didn't even know if they served food.

"Collin, Jason, let's get you settled with the menu. You've got a lot to learn. Questions, ask the kitchen staff. There's a quiz in an hour—not kidding. Then one of the servers will take you around and show you how we set tables, where we bus dishes, all that good stuff."

She snapped her fingers again and ushered me and the other new guy to a table on the side of the room. She handed us each a menu, then rattled off a list of house favorites, tapping each section with a bright orange fingertip before leaving with a swish of her dress. She headed straight for Tanner, who threw me a small wave before she sent him packing out the side exit.

"How'd you land this job?" the guy asked.

I wasn't sure how to answer. What did I call Tanner? My roommate? My boyfriend? While my brain raced for an answer, the guy kept talking.

"My friend Ashley got me in. She's the short blonde." He pointed to a girl with a pixie cut who was folding napkins on the side of the room. "She's worked here two years. I bussed tables at the Seaside Inn last summer, but my ex still works there and I didn't really feel like dealing with seeing him every day, if you know what I mean."

Him? His ex was a guy? I sucked in a deep breath. "My roommate, uh, boyfriend, worked here last summer. We go to school up in Connecticut. He talked to Dorothy for me. She hired me over the phone."

"Cool." He seemed unfazed by everything I'd babbled out. "I'm Jason, by the way."

"Collin." He shook my hand. I tried not to stare at the tattoos that twisted from his wrist all the way up his arm.

"So which one's your boyfriend?" His pale gray eyes flitted around the room, then landed on mine. His gaze was open, friendly.

"The one that just left to go work at Oz."

"Oh wow. He'll be raking in the bucks. I hear the bartenders there clean up."

"Bartender?"

"Yep. Before you got here, I heard Dorothy talking about how one of their bartenders quit this morning. Modeling gig at some magazine. Oz is known for their hot staff. That's why they make so much in tips."

Jesus. Not that that should have surprised me. If Tanner was my bartender, I'd probably hand over my paycheck to get his attention. My stomach wiggled in a way that made me wish I'd eaten less breakfast.

Chapter Eight

JASON WAS definitely the highlight of working at Dorothy's. The other servers were nice, but it was clear they'd worked together before and had already formed cliques. With Jason and me as the new guys, we were left to do a lot of the grunt work. Making salad dressings, restocking the walk-in with seafood and salads, precutting the cakes, gathering up the laundry. We were earning our spot on the floor, working our way toward tables in the better sections of the restaurant. Having him to talk to made it all bearable.

Our first major task was learning the menu, which included passing the short quiz on the first day and a more elaborate one at the end of the week. Not only did Dorothy expect us to have the menu and all possible specials memorized, we needed to know what allergens they contained, how they were prepared, and what wine we should recommend with them.

I wasn't the only one with homework either. Tanner came home from his first night at Oz with the master list of Great and Powerful Concoctions—their signature drinks, which he needed to know how to prepare for an on-site exam before his first shift behind the bar.

Luckily the house had a pretty well stocked liquor cabinet, so all we had to do was buy some juices, milk, cherries, and spices. Tanner's goal was to have us all order off the menu, and then he'd have to see if he could remember and prepare the proper drinks. Needless to say no one balked at this except Suzanne, who whined that she couldn't drink but perked up as soon as he offered to make her a special nonalcoholic drink instead.

Playing Tanner's assistant was my job. I liked watching him toss the cocktail shaker around as he practiced his routine. In no time he was serving up drinks with a flourish. I had no trouble at all imagining him charming customers.

All the cocktails had goofy names that related to Oz. Ruby Slippers, Glinda's Wand, Flying Monkey, Oil Can. I'd quizzed him every night for a week. I knew he had it all memorized—he just needed to see if he could perform under pressure.

I invited Jason over. Another warm body to try out the drinks. Plus I had the feeling he was lonely. He jumped at the chance to come to our house, which made me glad I'd asked him. No one should spend their summer feeling lonely. I was grateful I wasn't. Besides, I thought it was possible he'd hook up with Bryan.

Bryan had a lull between gigs and had been lolling around the house for days. I'd only noticed one morning when a guy slunk out of his room and left the house. Other than that he'd either been alone or he'd taken to dating ninjas. With Bryan the latter wasn't out of the question, but I still thought he might give Jason a shot. They were both tattooed musicians. That should have been enough for them to at least get a conversation going. God knows they were both attractive enough. Bryan with his pouty Jared Leto look and Jason a dead ringer for Adam Levine. Maggie was going to be beside herself with two gorgeous guys so close but yet so gay.

Jason walked home from work with me the night Tanner was going to do his practice run. He seemed nervous, asking if he should go home and change first, then wanting to know who was going to be there.

"So did you live with your boyfriend at school too?" he asked.

"Yeah, we were roommates for seven months before we got involved."

"Oh wow. I assumed you were a couple first, then decided to live together."

"Nope. I didn't even know he was bi. He thought I was straight too. Then everything just... clicked."

Jason nodded. "That's cool. It's good he was able to get you the job too. They're not easy to come by."

"Yeah. And I was desperate to earn as much money as possible."

Jason's eyebrow rose. "For school?"

I felt embarrassed admitting the reason. "When I came out to my mom, she disowned me. No contact. No more tuition dollars. So the more I earn this summer the better. Thank God it's my last year, but let's face it, a bachelor's degree in social work isn't exactly going to land me a job that pays big bucks. I'm gonna have loans coming out of my ass for the next few decades."

Jason nodded. "I hear you. Same thing happened to me, only it was my freshman year. I've been on my own for the past two years."

I'd never met anyone else who'd been kicked out. "Do you still talk to them?"

"Me? The family disgrace? No. They can't have that. My father is a Conservative rabbi. I'm the shameful outcast. There's nothing to talk about. As he sees it, he has no son anymore."

"I'm sorry. That sucks."

He shrugged. "Your mom sounds a lot like him. Let me guess, Catholic?"

I nodded. We walked in silence. He knew what it was like. The humiliation and judgment. The rejection. "Do you have brothers or sisters?"

"Only sisters, and they're all the do-as-you're-told type. Not one of them stood by me. It was more 'Why are you doing this to us? Can't you just be normal?'" Jason scrubbed his hand through his hair. "I don't do normal. What you see is what you get."

"Normal's overrated in my book. You're much better off. Hey, this is our place." I headed up the sand-and-gravel driveway, but Jason paused. "You sure it's okay you're bringing me? I don't want to be a fifth wheel or anything."

I laughed and grabbed his arm, pulling him up onto the deck. "You'll be fine. Trust me." I held open the door, motioning him in. "Welcome to the Nut House."

Chapter Nine

I INTRODUCED Jason to Maggie, Dex, and Bryan who were hanging out in the front room. I wondered where Wendy was. Last I'd heard she was planning to catch the ferry after work. Suzanne and Bill had sent word that they were spending the weekend in Manhattan. I headed to the kitchen in search of Tanner. He was studying the recipe book more intently than I'd ever seen him study anything for school. I loved the serious look on his face.

"Time's up," I said. "You either know it or you don't. Ready for me to bring everyone in?"

"Ready as I'll ever be." There was no one else in the kitchen, so I gave him a hug and then a kiss, and he seemed more relaxed.

"You've got this."

"Thanks, Collin."

And he did. No matter what we ordered, he mixed it up right. Within a half hour, everyone was on their second cocktail and having a great time. Bryan and Jason seemed to hit it off. They took charge of the music and had a steady stream of tunes blaring. I decided with all the drinking going on, people should probably eat something too, so I mixed up some dips and chips and made some quick wraps—turkey with coleslaw and cranberry mayo, and roast beef with horseradish sauce and spicy pickles.

"Let's go eat on the beach." Maggie suggested, packing the food into a big picnic basket. "Tanner, make a few pitchers, and we'll take the plastic glasses out with us. Please."

She'd given him her best puppy-dog eyes, so he'd mixed up another batch each of Ruby Slippers and Glinda's Wands. Those were the biggest hits. I loaded ice and the plastic glasses into one of the big coolers along with the pitchers. Tanner grabbed a few blankets off the bench by the door, and we made our way out to the beach.

Bryan brought a keg speaker with him and kept the music going. It was a perfect summer night. The moon was high and bright enough, we could easily see well enough to eat and keep pouring drinks. I'd been out on the beach nearly every night since we'd arrived, but that night there seemed to be more stars out than usual.

Tanner still looked tense, so I offered to go for a walk down the beach with him. We kicked off our shoes, and he cuffed up his jeans. Then we strolled along the damp sand right at the point where the water licked at our feet every wave or two. The surf was gentle and warm from the calm weather we'd had all week.

"You nervous about your exam?" I asked.

"A little. The other bartenders are so much more experienced. I feel like a dork half the time."

I hadn't seen this side of him very often. I was usually the worried one. "You need to chill. People go to bars to wind down and stare at hot bartenders. You've got half that taken care of just by showing up and being you."

"Thanks." He turned and started walking backward, facing me.

"You'll have girls all over you. And guys." My stomach clenched at the thought.

"You're kinda hot when you're jealous."

I kicked water at him, and he jumped out of the way, laughing.

"If we didn't know each other and you came into the bar, would you stare at me?"

"Absolutely not," I said.

He gave an indignant grunt.

I chuckled. "I'd do everything I could not to notice you at all. Then I'd go home and spend the whole night masturbating, thinking about you."

He stopped short and I banged into him. "God, I love you."

Hearing those words from him sent a boulder-sized lump straight to my throat. My eyes prickled, and I knew if I tried to say anything, I'd botch it completely. Instead I grabbed a handful of his shirt and yanked him close so hard, he almost tripped on the uneven sand. I kissed him long and deep, gripping my other hand against the base of his neck, possessively, fiercely. A kiss I'd have kept going all night if I hadn't heard shrieks from in the water. Maggie and Dex had decided it would be a good idea to have a splash fight and were now wrestling around in the surf together like drunken otters.

"Do you think we should go get them? They could drown."

Tanner shook his head, his brow tensed in a straight line. I knew what he was thinking—Wendy. She'd missed the last ferry and wasn't coming out until the next morning. Dex and Maggie appeared to be making no effort to get out of the water. Was she on top of him? Were her legs wrapped around his waist? Wait—was that a kiss? Oh fuck.

"Dammit, Dex," Tanner whispered, running both hands through his hair.

"Shit. Are you going to say something to Wendy?"

"I don't know." He sighed. "I don't think so. The last time something like this happened and I told her, she pulled a shoot-the-messenger routine and didn't talk to me for six months."

"Did she not want to know?"

"No, I think in the long run she did, but at the time it was easier to be mad at me than at the guy. I don't know. Women are weird that way."

"So you're not going to say anything?"

"I'll keep an eye on it. But for now, no."

"I suppose that means you don't want me to say anything either?"

"I can't tell you what to do, but I can warn you that she'll get really pissed off at you and may not even believe you."

"But would it stop her from getting hurt? That's all I want."

"Agreed. Maybe Dex and Maggie are just friends who are a little too touchy-feely. That could be all that's going on."

Peals of Maggie's laughter sounded as Dex tossed her into a wave and dove in after her. They came up kissing again. It looked more than "touchy-feely" to me when they wound up on the sand together, still attached at the mouth.

"You don't think Wendy will feel really stupid if we don't say anything and she finds out?" Maybe I was projecting. I'd feel like an asshole if Tanner were hooking up with some guy and I was the last to know of all my friends. I didn't even want to imagine how bad that would make me feel. I didn't want that for Wendy.

"I know you want to play knight in shining armor here, but I'm asking you not to. I don't know exactly what their friends-with-benefits rules are for the summer. Let's not make trouble where there may not be any, okay?"

"Okay." Benefit of the doubt. I could do that. Although my doubts got stronger with each rolling wave.

They were still kissing. You might roughhouse with your friend or wrestle around, but kissing was a step beyond that. I hoped it was just the power of Tanner's drinks making their judgment a little shaky. By morning, when they were both sober, they'd have to see that even an FWB thing wouldn't work while they were housemates. Not with Wendy visiting every weekend and everyone under the same roof.

Warm arms wound around me, behind my back, up to my neck. Tanner's lips hovered in front of mine. "Let's say we forget about them. We can go the long way back, through the tall grass, behind the dunes."

He kissed me, soft at first, then deeper. I forgot there was anyone else in the world, let alone on the same beach.

When Tanner pulled back, the grin on his face had my full attention, except for the part of me that was focused a bit lower. "It's very quiet back there. Super private. We could look at the stars."

I knew stargazing wasn't his top priority. And I was hard from the mere suggestion that we sneak off together. Hell, yeah. Dunes, tall grass, sand in all the wrong places? Sounded perfect to me.

Chapter Ten

I'D NEVER thought about the fact that I hadn't lived with any woman other than my mother, until I moved into a house inhabited by three of them. At first I'd thought it was mostly a difference of more attention to decor and way more products in the bathroom, but the longer I lived in the house, the more I realized it was everything. The TV shows recorded on the DVR, the types of snacks in the kitchen, and the magazines. I'd never seen so many magazines. Fashion. Beauty. Gossip. I didn't realize people even still read magazines.

Part of the suck factor of Tanner working at Oz while I worked at Dorothy's was that our shifts didn't match up. Even when I worked dinner, I was home several hours before him. I couldn't hang out at Oz until my birthday, which was still a few weeks away, so that left me with time on my hands on more nights than I would have liked. Spending time alone was risky. It was too tempting to check e-mails. Or worse, answer them. Both my brothers were still sending regular messages, and there was nothing I wanted to say to either of them. Not yet, at least.

Most nights I'd take walks on the beach. It was peaceful by the water. I loved the sound of the waves rolling in and out. Before I'd moved to Fire Island, I'd never been to the beach at night. We'd taken day trips when I was a kid but always headed home before it got dark. I loved the soft, cool feel of the sand under my feet.

Other nights I'd just hang in the living room watching TV with whoever was home. One night a magazine headline caught my attention. "Manscaping: Boner Bonsai." I laughed but had to admit I was curious. Between sharing a bathroom in a coed house and living on the beach, I'd seen more half-dressed bodies in the past few weeks than I had in my life. It was clear that lots of guys had had work done, so to speak. Smooth waxed chests were everywhere, and the low-riding board shorts usually showed enough to indicate that they weren't growing any dense shrubbery down below either.

No one else was in the room, so I picked up the magazine. Makeup ads. Perfume ads. Then there was the article. A guy with a shocked look on his face as a girl ripped a wax strip off his hairy stomach. That looked scary as hell.

"Care for the hair down there...." Okay. I read four pages of quips and suggestions for grooming.

I knew Tanner trimmed. I loved the way his body looked. Loved the line of silky dark hair pointing from his waist to my favorite part of his body.

The neat patch of short dark hair atop his cock. His balls were smooth and hairless, although I didn't know if they were that way naturally or not.

I was so blond, I didn't have a ton of hair to worry about. But still. Would he like it better if—

"Whatcha readin'?" Wendy leaned over the back of the couch, right over my shoulder, scaring the shit out of me.

I closed the magazine as fast as I could, but she'd already seen. She climbed over the couch and settled in next to me, then offered me the cup of M&M's she was munching from. I took a handful, sure I was the same shade as the red ones.

"Thinking of doing some maintenance?"

"Can we not discuss this?"

She snorted. "Do you have any idea how much grooming women do? We're hair removal experts. What are your plans?"

My jaw twitched, and I popped M&M's in my mouth to keep the tendons in my neck from snapping. "I don't have plans."

"Well, you should. No one wants a mouthful of hair. Especially if a long one gets stuck in your teeth or the back of your throat."

She made a gagging sound, and I looked around to make sure we didn't have an audience. Thankfully no one else was around.

"There's not that much."

"I didn't think so. You're so fair and all. So what are you doing? Just some pruning? Maybe an arrow?"

"He knows the way just fine without directions."

She giggled. "Don't use scissors, too pointy and too hard to get it even. Do you have clippers? You know, like for cutting hair?"

I sighed. She wouldn't leave until we'd talked this out, so I figured I might as well get the advice. "My electric razor has those plastic attachments for different length beards."

"Perfect. Use one of the shorter ones. You'll love it. And those keep you from cutting yourself. Just take it off if there's anywhere you want, you know, a closer shave. And try to hold the skin taut, it makes it less likely to pinch or pull." I flinched at the thought, and Wendy laughed again. "You'll do great. Oh, and use a mirror for the parts that are hard to see. It'll make your life way easier."

"Thanks."

She grinned, then hopped up from the couch. "I'm gonna go wake Dex. He's in a sex coma from this afternoon, but he's gonna have to get over that."

"Go get him."

"You bet I will. I'm only here two days, he's gotta be a sexual camel the rest of the week. I need to make sure his hump is full."

She winked at me and practically skipped up the stairs. I didn't really know what she saw in Dex. I mean, he was nice enough, but he didn't really do anything. Ever. I'd never seen him go out. He seemed content to read on the hammock, go for a swim, and sit on the deck or in his room strumming random chords on his guitar. The only thing I'd seen him show any real interest in was Maggie. The only time I ever heard him talk was when she was around.

Whatever he had going for him, Maggie seemed to like it too. I'd seen them spending more and more time together since the night they'd made out on the beach. Maybe they had a lot in common. Who knows? Obviously he and Wendy had something going for them or they wouldn't have lasted two years. I repeated Tanner's advice in my head. *Stay out of it.*

I glanced at the magazine cover again, then at my phone. Tanner wasn't due home for about an hour. That seemed like enough time. Before I could chicken out, I stood and headed upstairs.

Chapter Eleven

Manscaping sounded simple enough when I read about it. It seemed a lot more complicated once I was standing naked in our bedroom.

Just trim, don't shave yourself bare. How hard could that be? I snapped the clipper attachment onto my electric razor and leaned back staring down at my pubes. Combing my fingers through them, I sucked in a breath, flipped the switch, and took a pass at the blond curls. They drifted to the floor around my feet like feathers. Nice and steady. Right side. Left side. My cock got hard from the combination of being held and moved from side to side along with the vibrations of the actual trimmer. I took off the plastic guard and went to work at the hair that climbed the base of the shaft. Zip, Zip. Zip. And it was all gone.

With a Kleenex I swept up the scattered bits of hair on the floor, then ventured toward the full-length mirror inside the closet door. I looked up slowly, not sure what to expect.

I sucked in a deep breath. I'd never really looked at myself naked before. Not more than a passing glance in the mirror after a shower. Standing there, fully erect, dick looking at least two inches longer than usual without the cloud of pubes around it, I couldn't stop staring.

I propped one foot against the doorframe and got the first-ever view of my asshole. My dick twitched. I ran a finger past it, feeling the fringe of hair. *I can do this.* Bracing against the frame, I turned the razor back on. Holding my breath, I ran the razor gently over the skin.

I tested the area with a light pass of my fingertips. Smooth. Then I gave my cock a stroke. Just one stroke. I wanted to see what I looked like touching myself.

Only I didn't stop at one stroke. One became two, which became three, and before I knew it, I was watching myself jerk off. When the door to our room opened, I nearly fell into the closet before I realized it was only Tanner. I still hid behind the partially closed closet door.

The grin on his face told me he had already guessed what I'd been doing. He tugged off his shirt and tossed it onto the bed, then came up behind me. His nose ruffled through the hair at the back of my head, and he kissed my neck.

"I missed you." He ran his fingers down my back, hard enough I'm sure they left red trails.

My cock stiffened more. "Yeah?"

"Uh-huh. So, how's your night been?" Tanner asked.

I could hear the smile in his voice. "Boring?"

"Definitely not boring. Hot." His hands slid around my waist as he pressed himself against my back. He was still wearing his shorts, but I could clearly feel how hard he was. Warm fingers stroked my shaft, and he leaned to the side to watch in the mirror. "Do you have any idea how fucking hot you look jerking off in a mirror. First off, you're watching yourself, which is sexy as fuck. Second, there are two of you. Which is probably the hottest fucking thing I've ever seen."

I swallowed hard. I loved when he told me he thought I was sexy. It wasn't how I thought of myself. My cheeks flushed, and this time instead of just feeling it, I could see it too.

"Jesus." My hand went to my face.

"So warm." Tanner's lips grazed my cheek. "I love it when you blush."

His hands trailed down my neck, and he followed the path with his lips. "First your cheeks turn red, then it spreads down to your neck. Then when you're really excited, like when you're getting ready to come, your neck gets redder and your whole chest turns pink."

"Really? Every time?" I had no clue.

"Yep. That's part of how I know you're about to come."

The fact that he knew that, that he paid close enough attention to know that, made me blush harder. It also warmed me in a way I couldn't quite explain. He cared enough to notice those things. *He loves me.*

Tanner brushed his fingertips over my newly trimmed bush. I held my breath, waiting for a reaction. "Nice. Less between us now."

I swallowed hard, trying not to pant.

His hand swept under my balls. "Didn't trim these yet, I see."

"Ran out of time."

"You want some help?" He kissed his way down my chest.

With Tanner down on his knees in front of my erection, he could help with anything he wanted. "Sure. If you want."

"Give me the clippers." He blew into the blade and turned it on, then tested it against his hand. "Yeah, let's not use this. Give me a sec."

He got up and walked over to his dresser, rooted around, and came back with a different razor. At least I thought that was what it was. It was silver and cylindrical and looked like a saltshaker. "This works better. Stay really still, okay? You trust me?"

I nodded. Nervousness coursed through my body, but I did trust him. He'd never hurt me on purpose.

The sound made me more anxious than anything else, so I concentrated on Tanner. The intent expression on his face. The shadows the dark wings of his eyelashes cast on his beautifully sculpted cheeks. The way his tongue kept flicking out and wetting his lips. He wanted my cock in his mouth, I could tell. I needed it to be there as much as he did.

The razor wasn't off for more than two seconds before he had one of my balls in his mouth, then the other, then licked up my shaft like it was a goddamned Popsicle. I stared down at him, then met his gaze.

"Don't watch here," he said. "Watch in the mirror. Stroke yourself while I suck your balls."

That was an offer that was impossible to turn down. My fingers glided back and forth as I watched in the mirror. Watched myself. Watched Tanner. When I got closer, he stood and stripped, then came up alongside me, pulling me into a kiss—a kiss we could see in the mirror with our eyes open. He rubbed his cock against my hip, then moved behind me, rubbing himself against my ass.

I spread my legs wider, and he slipped a hand between them, stroking my balls and my ass. Then he switched his fingers out with his cock. Wetness made me jump. Not lube, just precome from his erection. He didn't press in, just massaged the head of his dick back and forth over my taint and hole until I was so hot and bothered I could barely breathe.

"You like that?" he asked, voice hoarse from his own need.

"Yeah. A lot."

"Good. So do I."

He turned us sideways so we could both watch in the mirror. Watch his cock rubbing my ass and disappearing between my legs. Watch my hand moving ever faster over my erection. I leaned back to kiss him, needing to taste him. That was too much for Tanner. He groaned into my mouth, pumped himself harder along the crack of my ass, and shot his hot wet load onto my back. Feeling his come running down my back undid me. In three strokes I felt my climax peaking. I turned toward the mirror just in time. The first spurt splattered on the smooth glass, running down in thick white streaks as I painted more lines on either side. *Jesus.* Tanner was still pumping himself. Still watching, eyes dark as night.

His breath was warm against my neck. "That was fucking amazing. Forget porn. You're way better."

I laughed, long and hard and so loud, I wondered if we'd wake the rest of the house.

Tanner handed me a towel, and I went to work wiping off the mirror while he cleaned my back. Even after all these months, it felt weird to be cleaned off by another person. But I liked it. I liked the care he took. I liked that he always remembered. Most of all I liked how afterward things would go back to normal between us.

"You hungry?" he asked.

"Kind of."

"I'm starving. How do I always wind up working at places that don't serve food?"

He tossed me a pair of shorts, then tugged on his own, and we headed downstairs. Snacking with Tanner in the middle of the night had become one of my favorite things. Without the other housemates around, it seemed like we had the whole house to ourselves. Even when they were awake, it was like family. Maybe a slightly dysfunctional family, but what family wasn't?

Suzanne was over her chicken aversion, and there was cold fried chicken left over from dinner. I handed Tanner a leg and took one for myself. I don't know why food always tasted better after sex, but it did. Flavors, textures, smells, everything was heightened. That chicken leg was the best I'd ever eaten. Tanner followed it up with a chocolate cupcake. I only had three bites of one before I was full. He polished off the rest of mine and a big glass of milk.

"Did you like watching?" he asked.

"Yeah. You?"

"Hell yeah." He paused. "What about when I was rubbing on you? Was that okay?"

"It was great. It made me think... well, it felt like if you'd gone further we could have maybe... I mean if you wanted to, I don't know if you're into...."

"Anal sex?" Tanner was so much more straightforward than I could ever be.

"Yes. Are you?"

"Dunno. I've never done it."

"You mean you and Paul...."

Tanner's face darkened, but he stayed calm. "No. Tried once, and I couldn't relax enough, so it hurt. Never tried again after that."

"He tried to top?"

"Yeah."

"You were okay with that?" I couldn't imagine Tanner as a bottom. Actually, I could, in my mind, but not in reality.

"I was willing to try. I didn't know what I liked. I'm still not sure. But I'd like to try with you. Both ways."

"Really?"

"If you want."

"You mean you on top sometimes and me on top others?" I didn't even know that was an option.

"Hey, if you're not comfortable—"

"No," I said, waving a hand to stop him. "I'll try anything you want. Seriously. Anything." I moved toward him and kissed him hard, locking my hands in his hair. "Anything."

He stared straight into my eyes, serious and intense, but the wheels were clearly turning behind the darkness. His lips curled into his crooked grin. "I like the sound of that."

He kissed me back, slow and lingering. I almost didn't hear the footsteps padding toward the kitchen.

"Shhh, we'll wake everyone."

Maggie came around the corner with Dex right behind her, and they both jumped and yelled when they saw us.

"Jesus, fuck," Dex said. "Way to give your roommates a coronary."

"Bad boys," Maggie scolded. "You'd better not have eaten all the chicken."

"No," Tanner said, giving Dex the coldest look I'd ever seen him give anyone. "There's still plenty of chicken."

"We were just heading up to bed." I gave Tanner a nudge toward the door. His jaw clenched, but he followed.

"You still think we shouldn't tell Wendy?" I whispered as we climbed the stairs.

"Yeah."

I hoped he was right.

Chapter Twelve

DOROTHY'S WAS closed on Mondays and Oz was usually quiet that night, so Mondays were most often our common day off. We'd taken to spending them at the beach, then heading home to grill, usually with a group of friends. More and more I'd noticed that Amy, a summer resident from the next town over, had been making a point to be on our beach on Mondays.

Tanner had introduced us and was up front about the fact that we were a couple, but I could tell Amy didn't care. Not about me, at least. All she cared about was Tanner. She'd scan the crowd if she didn't know where he was, and once she found him, she'd be by his side every second he'd let her.

I'd never seen him do anything to lead her on. Not really. He was chatty and funny with everyone. But the way Amy looked at him? The grin that crossed her face whenever he paid her the least bit of attention? The way she leaned her body toward his when they talked and used any excuse to touch him? She was interested in way more than his witty repartee. She wanted *him*. And from everything I'd seen, she wasn't afraid to go after him.

Tanner was busy chatting with Bryan while they stacked coals in the Weber on our deck. Amy had followed us home for dinner for the second week in a row. She stood next to them holding the box of matches, like this was a job that required a special assistant. I couldn't hear what Tanner was saying, but pretty much anytime he opened his mouth, Amy giggled and her free hand went to his arm or shoulder. My nostrils flared, and I looked away.

Wendy sat down next to me, bumping her hip against mine to scoot me over on the picnic bench. "Don't let little Gigi over there mess with your head."

"Gigi?" I had no idea what she was talking about.

"GG—Gabby and Grabby. I always forget her real name. Allie? Annie?"

"Amy?"

"Yeah, that's it. I prefer GG. It's easier to remember. And way more accurate."

I had to agree. "She's pretty forward."

"Pretty forward? Every time she's here, I expect her to suggest spin the bottle, then tape the bottle to Tanner's leg."

I laughed. "She's not that bad."

"Trust me, I know women. She's worse."

My stomach churned. Wendy knew Tanner better than pretty much anyone else. Her opinion mattered to me. I took a deep breath. "Do you think he... I mean is she his... type?"

Wendy's lips pulled into a frown as she studied Tanner and Amy. My heart sank with each passing second. I'd hoped for an instant response of "no way" or "you're his type"—instead she sighed.

"If he wasn't with you, maybe."

She might as well have punched me in the stomach. It must have shown on my face because she quickly shook her head. "That didn't come out right. I just meant she's pretty. It doesn't matter. She doesn't matter. He is with you. She's a non-issue. She's just annoying to watch."

I nodded, trying to believe what she just said. The sound of Amy's giggling seemed to crawl under my skin. I didn't want to hear it anymore so I grabbed a soda and headed down the path to the beach. Dinner wasn't something I was in the mood for anymore.

I walked for a short way, then sat down, watching the surf. The sun was setting, and the sky was pink and purple, making the water glow like it was fake.

"Hey, Collin. Food's almost ready." Tanner was only feet behind me.

"Oh, thanks. Not that hungry."

He sat down next to me. "You all right? Wendy told me you went for a walk. I got the feeling it wasn't for exercise."

That just made me feel stupid. I liked Wendy, but sometimes I wished she'd mind her own business. Which was, I guess, part of the reason I went along with Tanner's insistence that we not tell her about Dex's extracurricular activities with Maggie.

"I'm fine."

"Okay." Tanner stood up and took a few steps back toward the house. Then he turned around. "I'll save you some food."

I nodded and looked back at the water, then took a sip of soda and noticed he was still standing there. "What?" I asked.

"How come you didn't tell me Maggie hit on you?"

The mouthful of soda surged high enough in my mouth to tickle the back of my nose. "How did you find out about that?"

"That's not an answer."

Shit. "I don't know. I didn't think it was important."

"But it's important when someone flirts with me?"

My shoulders knotted, and I shifted to try to loosen them. "It's... I don't know. It's different. I'm not into girls."

"So because I'm bi, I'm not trustworthy?" His jaw muscles twitched. I could tell he was trying not to be angry, but his face betrayed him.

"That's not what I meant."

"Well, that's what it seems like. What if it was the other way around?"

"What do you mean?" I fiddled with the metal tab on my Coke.

"What if some guy made a move on you? Would you tell me that? You're into guys. Would that be something I should be concerned about?"

I snorted. *Like that's ever going to happen.* "No."

"No, you wouldn't tell me? Or no, I shouldn't be concerned?"

His eyes were getting a buggy look to them I hadn't seen before. "No. I mean, yes. I might tell you, but no, it's not something you should worry about."

"Why's that?"

My stomach rolled. Talking about feelings still didn't come easily. "Because I'm not interested in anyone else."

"Well, neither am I."

"Good."

Tanner's expression softened, and the tension started to ebb from my shoulders. I hated arguing with him. "Speaking of people being interested in other people, is it just me, or was Maggie all over Dex this morning?"

"I don't know if I'd say 'all over.'"

"I would. She was practically in his lap all through breakfast."

I had seen her wrestling with him for the half-and-half and then smashing a strawberry into his mouth. "Maybe she's that flirty with everyone. He is the only straight guy in the house."

"Maybe." Tanner's eyebrows drew together, and I could tell he was worried.

"Did you ever ask Wendy if they have their special arrangement over the summer?"

Tanner shook his head. "They don't. She said since she's out here every weekend, they didn't need it."

"Oh."

"Yeah." He paused, and I could see the wheels turning in his head.

"Have you changed your mind about giving her a heads-up?" I kind of hoped he had.

"I worry about her—you know?"

"I know." The idea of someone hurting Wendy didn't sit well with me either. I wasn't as close with her as Tanner, but she'd been really nice to me. Not to mention that she was the only person who seemed to really support me and Tanner being together. Plus no one deserved to be cheated on. Having a deal about seeing other people was one thing, doing it when there was no such deal was another thing entirely. Dex was so laid-back, I had a hard time imagining him summoning the energy to chase after someone, but Maggie was aggressive. That I'd seen firsthand. And Dex didn't seem to have the ability to say no. Which sucked.

"I could tell her," I said. "That way if she gets mad, it's just at me."

Tanner smiled. "You're only saying that because you've never seen her mad."

"I'm serious."

"So am I." He laughed and ran his hands through his hair. "And I know you're serious. Thanks for offering. I still don't think we should say anything. We don't even know for a fact they're fucking. Right?"

"True." They could be watching movies in his room. All we'd really seen them do was kiss.

"Let's go grab some dinner. I'm starving." He held out his hand, and I took it. He pulled me up, then linked his fingers with mine as we walked back to the house.

Amy's eyes lit up the second she saw us approaching the house, and then they drifted down to our hands. Her face darkened, and she busied herself stirring potato salad. I squeezed Tanner's hand tighter, and he gave me a quick kiss before letting go.

Chapter Thirteen

Jason's face was so pinched and furrowed, I knew something was wrong the second I laid eyes on him. He was behind the prep counter plating dishes for the crab cakes, fried calamari, and whatever tonight's special seafood app was going to be. Smoked salmon, if I were to guess, based on the piles of capers he was balancing on each of the square plates.

I tied my apron, folded it over, and stuck my check holder into the waist. "Have you seen my corkscrew?"

Jason nodded. "Sharon took it. She snapped hers last night. Here, I brought you my extra." He fished around in his pocket and came out with a shiny silver corkscrew, nicer than the one I used to use.

"Thanks. I'll pick one up tomorrow so I can give it back."

Jason wiped the back of his hand over his forehead. "Just keep it, okay? It's a corkscrew, not a fucking engagement ring."

Whoa. I'd seen Jason in a bunch of different moods, but I'd never seen him quite so on edge. I helped him move the salad plates to the service fridge. When we finished, I followed him to the napkin-folding station. He usually talked nonstop, but he stayed silent.

I waited until he focused on getting the silverware lined up just right to ask, "What's going on with you today?"

A cross between sadness and defeat flashed behind his eyes. "Family bullshit. I keep telling myself that after three years it shouldn't get to me anymore, but it still does."

Good to know. It had only been three months for me, and it definitely still got to me. Looked like I had years of the same thing in my future. Fan-fucking-tastic. "You want to tell me what happened?"

"I ran into this woman who knows my family. She recognized me, so she started talking. Said she'd see me next week at my sister's wedding."

Jason looked at the ground, then closed his eyes. His fingers clenched and unclenched, and I could tell he was doing one of his breathing exercises to calm down.

Swallowing hard, he looked up at me. "Rachel's getting married next week, and no one even told me."

The exercise might have calmed him down, but it did nothing to mask the hurt in his eyes. I wondered if I shouldn't suggest he go for a walk or even take the night off. I could cover his tables if I had to. We could say he'd puked or something.

"Do me a favor?" he said.

"Sure." Plans for covering for his absence were already swirling in my mind.

"Come with me after our shift is over. I need to do something, and I don't like going by myself."

"Okay. Sure. What do you have to do?"

Jason held out his arms, nodding at the collage of tattoos that decorated them. "Tats are kinda frowned upon in Jewish tradition, so when my family cut me off, I went out and got my first one. I was all melodramatic about it at the time, but it wasn't just a rebellion thing. It was like a way of me making my own decisions about my life. Ever since then, if I get left out of a family event or family decision, I get a new tattoo. Kind of stupid, I guess. But it makes me feel like I'm owning what's happening rather than just letting it happen to me, you know?"

"That makes sense." It did. I liked it. Liked the symbolism and the permanence of the statement. "I'll definitely go with. Hell, I may even get one."

Jason's eyes bugged. "Get one? I thought you hated needles."

"I do, and I'm a bad Catholic, but I'm still a Catholic. The pain will be like penance. I can take it."

"Cool. We'll head out as soon as the dinner shift ends." Jason bit his lip. "You don't, uh, I mean Tanner won't be pissed, will he?"

"About me getting a tattoo? Nah. He's pretty open to anything. I wish you had a chance to get to know him better. You'd like him."

"All I know is he's one lucky bastard to have hooked up with you."

I couldn't keep from grinning. Taking compliments still made my face burn hotter than a stove coil, but for the first time in my life, I'd started to let kind words be felt on the inside too. I liked people thinking Tanner's lucky to have me, even if the truth was that I'm ten times luckier to have him.

Dinner was slow that night leaving me with plenty of time to debate what kind of tattoo I wanted. And where. Where was definitely the harder thing to decide. I didn't want it anywhere superobvious, but I didn't want it somewhere it would never be seen either. Tanner would probably be shocked. Would he like it? Think it was stupid? Sexy?

Anticipation built in my stomach, and by the time our shift was over, I was wound like a top.

"You sure you want to do this?" Jason asked. "You can just tag along, not get one. Lots of people bring a friend just for company."

"I'm doing it."

Jason gave me a smile I'd never seen from him before. Was he proud of me for making a bold move like this? Appreciative of the show of solidarity, so he wouldn't have to get it alone? He stayed quiet for most of the boat ride across the bay to Long Island.

The tattoo parlor was a tiny storefront in an old wooden house. Inside, everything was neat and tidy. The walls were covered with artwork, and rows of design books filled three long shelves and a big coffee table.

"What can I do for you boys?" A woman who couldn't have been much over thirty looked us up and down. "Y'all gettin' your girlfriend's names tattooed on your arms? Or your mama's birthdates?"

Jason and I both laughed. "Not even close," he said. "Does Billy still work here? He's done my others."

Jason rolled up his sleeve, and the woman whistled with appreciation. "Oh yeah, Billy's still here. I bet he'd love to add on to what you've got goin' on there. Hey, Billy, you got a repeat out front."

I don't know why, but I expected Billy to be some biker-looking huge dude with a bushy beard. He was actually a wiry, nerdy-looking guy, who I'd have guessed was a physics teacher, not a tattoo artist.

"Dude." He greeted Jason with a hug. "What are we doing?"

As Jason described what he wanted, I caught the spiky-haired blonde eyeing me again. "What about you, sugar britches? You here to watch, or you gettin' some ink too?"

"Ink. Black. I want a phoenix and a date underneath."

"Okay." She nodded in approval. "I like a man who knows what he wants."

She ran her fingers across a row of thick green binders and pulled one off the shelf. "Flip through these and see if you find what you're lookin' for. I can size the designs up and down, but I need to know what you want."

"Sure." I flipped through the pages, getting a little discouraged when I reached the halfway mark and nothing had caught my eye. Then there it was. Black scrollwork on the bottom. Sharper lines to the phoenix head up top. And the perfect size to fit from my hipbone to my ribs. I held the book up. "Page twenty-seven, design C."

"Nice. That'll look real good on your pale skin." She ran her finger over the design and took the book. "Where'd you say you're gonna be wantin' this?"

I gestured around my right hipbone.

She cringed. "You ever had ink before?"

"No."

She picked up my wrist and ran her finger over the knobby bone. "Places like this, where the skin is thin over bone, they hurt like a son of a bitch. You sure you want that? There are other places...."

"I'm sure. I can take it." In fact that seemed the most fitting way to get it. Suffer a little. You can't take the Catholic out of the boy. I chuckled, and the blonde woman just shook her head.

"I'll get you your consent forms while I go make up your template. That'll give you enough time in case you change your mind."

"Don't worry. I won't." I took the clipboard and started filling out the forms.

Chapter Fourteen

"Son of a bitch" was a bit of an understatement, but a few hours later, Jason and I were heading back to the island with brand-new tattoos.

Jason had gotten a group of small black doves scattering from his shoulder to his neck. A symbol of both weddings and freedom....

"How long does it take to heal?" I asked.

"It'll be sore for a few days, then probably a bit itchy. Then you'll forget you even have it."

I couldn't imagine forgetting I had it. And I didn't want to forget. It was part of me now. A permanent reminder.

"It'll peel too," he added. "It's kinda gross, but it's supposed to happen."

"Good to know." I smoothed my hand over the bandage, surprised I'd had the nerve to go through with it. "Thanks for asking me to go with you."

"Anytime." Jason smiled and held my gaze. Whenever there was eye contact, it had that same weird quality I couldn't quite place. Whatever it was, it seemed things between us had changed. Like we were brothers now, or something. Maybe I was just delirious from spending the last hour in pain.

"You working tomorrow?" I asked.

"Nope. Not until the weekend."

"What do you do on your days off?" I knew he lived in a studio apartment. Without Tanner and the other housemates, I didn't know what I'd keep busy with on the island.

"Read. Watch movies. Sleep."

"Nice." I hadn't done much of any of those things recently.

"Sometimes I head over to a club in Cherry Grove."

I knew that was one of the gay towns. Bryan's band played there sometimes, and he'd been saying he wanted to take me and Tanner with him sometime this summer. The idea intrigued and scared me in equal parts. I'd looked it up online, and it seemed like a 24-7 all-gay version of Mardi Gras. I wasn't sure I was ready for that. I wasn't sure I wanted to be either.

"You been to any of them yet?" Jason asked.

I shook my head.

"You should. Take a walk on the wild side."

The boat docked, and I twisted to stand up, hissing as the tattoo stung. "I think I've had my share of wild for the week."

Jason laughed. It was good to see him in a better mood than he'd been at the start of the night.

"See you in a few days." I turned up the street toward my house, running my hand lightly over the bandage.

As I headed up the driveway, I saw someone sitting on the front porch.

"Hey," Tanner said.

"Hey." I trotted up the stairs. "What are you doing out here?"

He raked a hand through his damp hair. He must have showered after work. "Just don't feel like being in the house right now. And our room is like a sauna. I put the fan in the window so it'll cool off a little."

"Good idea." I took a seat next to him on the wicker couch and sucked in a breath when the rawness of the tattoo pinched.

"You okay?"

"Yeah." I shifted carefully, trying not to pull the sensitive skin. "I just… I got a tattoo."

Tanner's eyes bugged, and he shook his head. "No way. Really?"

I liked that he was surprised. Predictability isn't exactly exciting. "It was a last-minute sort of thing."

"Well, can I see it?"

His eyes raked over me, and I could tell he was trying to figure out where it was. My cock attempted to point him in the right direction.

"Not for another hour or so. I'm supposed to keep it covered a bit, then wash it and put some stuff on it."

One side of his mouth had lifted into his sexy grin. "I never really thought of you as the tattoo type."

I shrugged. "Me neither. It just seemed… right."

"I didn't even know there was a place on the island."

"There might not be. Jason took me to see the guy who's done his. It's over in Bay Shore somewhere, I think. I had no clue where we were."

Tanner's smile flickered, but just for a second. "So you went with him?"

"Yeah, he wanted another one. It's kind of a ritual for him."

Tanner nodded, then moved closer, tilting his head. His eyes surveyed my body again, sending a fresh wave of heat rolling over me. My abs clenched, and I sniffed in a short breath. With his hair still wet, the scent of his shampoo was even stronger than usual, sweet and heavy in the thick night air.

"You gonna tell me where it is? Or do I have to find it on my own?"

My cheeks heated. We were on the front porch. Not that that was particularly public, but still. Tanner's hand grazed my arm, then raised the sleeve of my T-shirt. Goosebumps tickled their way over my skin.

"Not even close."

Tanner chuckled and moved his hand to my neck. He leaned way closer than was necessary to look. His hair felt slick and cool against my overheated cheek as his lips moved over my ear.

"Warmer?"

"No." The word came out more like a groan. I could hear people talking inside the house, probably not fifteen feet away from us, right on the other side of the open screen door. Instinct told me to move away from Tanner before someone saw us, but everything else in me pulled me closer.

His hand slid down to my chest, moving so slowly it felt like torture. The edge of his thumb brushed against one nipple, then slid across to the other. "No?"

I shivered and shook my head, wishing we were playing "find the tattoo" up in our room rather than on the creaky porch couch. Instead of running his hand down my abs, he placed it on my hip. Down the length of one leg, up the other. *Jesus*. My cock strained against my pants, begging to give Tanner a personal set of directions to the tattoo or anything else he wanted.

"Not the arms, neck, pecs, or legs." Tanner's voice rumbled low in his throat, meaning he was just as turned on as I was. He palmed my bulge, giving a light squeeze that sent air rushing from my lungs.

"I think it's been two hours. How about if we go upstairs so I can show it to you?"

"I thought you'd never ask." He kissed me hard and fast, letting go of my dick and cupping the back of my neck as he drew me up off the couch with him.

Tanner pulled away, eyes heavy lidded and lusty, mouth back in that fucking irresistible grin. "You're gonna have to keep your check holder in the other side of your apron for a while."

Fuck. "You knew where it was?"

He laughed as he pulled the screen door open. "Yep. You flinched when you sat down. Figured it had to either be there or on your ass."

"You're such a dick." I shoved him through the door, grabbing the spot just under his ribs where I knew he was most ticklish.

He laughed harder as he headed for the staircase. The rich sexy sound tugged me right behind him.

Chapter Fifteen

I KNEW how anxious Tanner was to get a look at the tattoo. So was I, to be honest. It all went so fast at the tattoo parlor, and then it had been covered up. I knew it would be red and probably a bit puffy, but I hoped it was still easy to see. I wanted Tanner to see it.

Taking my time in the bathroom, I changed the gauze pad. It didn't look too bad, and it only stung if I pressed on it or twisted at my waist. Tightening those muscles pulled the skin and made it feel like flexing when you're badly sunburned. That pinchy, tearing feeling like your skin can't stretch as far as you need it to go. The writing looked great, though. That was my biggest worry, that it would be too small or illegible. It was perfect. Hidden alongside the bottom of the phoenix in scrolling black ink, the month, day, and year. Only one person in the world knew the significance of that date, and I hoped he remembered what it was.

I walked up the stairs to our room, moving slowly. I was a bit sore, but it had also occurred to me that Tanner might not like it. Might think it was stupid. Entering our room, I took a deep breath, then turned to close and lock our door.

Tanner was on the bed. Not just sitting there—lying back against the pillows, shirt off, pants undone, stroking a very firm erection.

"Am I interrupting?" I asked, moving closer.

"Yes. My boyfriend's about to show me his new sexy tattoo, and I'm so turned on I can't fucking stand it."

My boyfriend. God, I loved it when he said that, even when there was no one else to hear. *Boyfriend.*

"So...."

He turned on his side, exposing every beautiful line of his body. He could be the life model for an art studio. Any artist would be able to sketch and paint him forever and never tire of it. I never tired of looking. Tanner didn't know, but some mornings I'd wake before him and just watch him sleep. I loved to see his chest rising and falling, see his eyelids twitch as he dreamed. My favorite part was spooning behind him. Even half-awake he'd grind his ass against me, letting out soft, sleepy moans. When I'd reach around, I was always greeted by a large erection, happy to see me. Stroking him like that, warm from sleep, my cock sandwiched against his back, was my favorite way to start any day. Touching him while I humped his ass somehow felt like I was jerking off both of us at the same time. It was hot and sexy and made me feel immersed in our love.

"Do I get to see this tattoo or not?"

I'd left my pants unzipped. I removed my shirt and draped it on the desk chair. Tanner's eyes locked on mine, and I could see how excited he was. His pupils were huge and black like they always were when he wanted something. Moving closer, I let my pants fall open wider. I could tell by his expression when he'd gotten his first glimpse.

He inched toward the edge of the bed, examining the design. "A phoenix?"

"It's a symbol of rebirth and new beginnings."

Tanner's finger ran in a gentle path just outside the area that stung. It tickled, but at the same time, I wanted his hands on me any and everywhere. His head turned to the side, sending that silky curtain of dark hair sweeping across his face. He tucked it behind his ear and sucked in a breath.

"The date."

My cheeks heated. "Yeah. It's just a reminder."

He smoothed his finger up the midline of my chest, then over my collarbone, tracing the hollow, then trailing higher and cupping my face. "That was the best day of my life."

"Why?" I needed to know why he thought it was so important.

He pushed my hair back, away from my face, and held it there with both hands. "Because that's the day that you and I became us."

I'm sure my heart was actually still in my chest, but it felt like it was in my stomach, in my throat, ready to burst out of me altogether.

Tanner kissed me, soft at first but with strength and passion. I could tell he was afraid to touch anywhere near the tattoo, so instead he focused on my mouth, my neck, stroking my back. It all felt so good, I grew dizzy from the attention.

I reached for Tanner, but he said, "No. Tonight let's just be about you."

He climbed out of bed and stood before me, eyes still glued to the tattoo. "What hurts more, standing or lying down?"

"Probably lying down."

"Good to know. " He inched me up against the wall, stroking my chest, being careful not to go too near the raw skin. His fingers made quick work of what was left of my zipper, and he went onto his knees to remove my pants. I tried to help but hissed when I bent. "Don't," he said. "Let me take care of everything."

So I did. I backed up against the wall, resting my head against the cool smooth paint, and waited. Tanner took his time. Caressing my legs, slipping his fingers between my thighs to tease my ass and taint. Then he went to work on my foreskin. Generally we just used it to stroke, then slicked it down and out of the way when we meant business. Tonight he decided my foreskin was the business. He rolled it up past the crown of my cock, then ran the pads of his fingers around the sensitive fold of skin. My cock swelled, begging to be the main attraction. With a gentle grip, he lightly pinched the skin between his thumb and index finger, giving a little tug that sent electric zips straight to my balls. Jesus, Tanner. Where'd he learn that? Holding my cock with one hand, he used the other to dip his finger inside my foreskin and trace the wetness that had accumulated. The tip of my cock strained against his fingers as I struggled to keep breathing.

By the time he finally, blissfully decided to show me some mercy, I was so revved up I could barely see straight. With one painstakingly slow stroke, he unrolled the skin, stretching it over my swollen length, pulling it taut enough that I sucked in a sharp breath when the bit just under the head got a solid tug. His thumb went straight there. He knew that was my favorite spot to be rubbed. I could come from touching just that one tiny area, massaging those nerve endings, feeling the come bubble up the length of my shaft.

He moved so slowly and intently it killed me to wait. I wanted to buck, but he slammed a hand onto my chest, holding me steady against the wall. "Don't move," he whispered. "Your tattoo will hurt. All I want you to feel is pleasure."

"I do."

"Not yet...."

The gleam in his eye made me groan. He dropped to his knees once more and took a long, slow lick. The wetness combined with the breeze of the fan felt electric. He licked the sides, the top, the base, then huffed to mix his warm breath with the cool air. My cock twitched like mad, begging to be stroked or sucked or fucked—anything—desperate for release.

Tanner traced a finger over my hip bone, just under the ink. "So fucking sexy. Not to mention that you're the first tattooed guy I've ever been with."

I grinned. I loved being his first anything. I always thought of Tanner as so much more experienced than me. Doing firsts together seemed like the coolest thing I could possibly offer him.

Holding my hip steady with a firm hand, Tanner sank his mouth down onto my cock. He swallowed it whole, till the head bumped the back of his throat. No gagging, just a sensual moan that almost had me shooting the second I heard it.

Up and down he licked and swiveled, using his hands along the shaft while his tongue twirled and lapped at the precome flowing out of me. I couldn't last much longer. "Tanner, I can't... I need... I have to."

"So come," he said, leisurely sliding my dick back into his superwet mouth. He sucked harder, drawing me all the way in, still licking circles against the underside. *Jesus. Can't last. Too good.* I clawed at the wall, finding nothing, then sank my hands into Tanner's silky mane. Tangling my fingers in his hair released its coconut-lime scent, and I was surrounded by him. His fingers, his mouth, his aroma. It overwhelmed me. My cock was thick and full, ready to burst. With three final pumps into that beautiful mouth, I exploded, straight down his throat. I felt him swallow, knew he was sucking every last drop from me, but it was too much to keep up with and some ran down his chin. I wiped it with my finger, then pulled him up to my mouth, sliding the finger between his lips before I ravished him with my mouth.

His dick was rock hard, jutting from his shorts. I started stroking without even bothering to take his pants the rest of the way off. I loved the way he looked with a huge erection sticking out of his clothes. Like he was so desperate and so consumed by the need for sex, he'd forgotten the most basic skills like how to disrobe.

I stroked him fast, knowing how close he was to coming, then stopped, releasing his dick the moment before I knew he'd come. He groaned in disappointment, but he'd taught me the stop-and-go game. Taught me too well. I could do it for hours, sensing each time he was about to orgasm and stopping all stimulation until he settled down enough to wait. Cruel while you're doing it, but so worth the reward.

That moment when you don't have to wait another second and you finally let go—it's unreal. Like every orgasm you managed to tamp down is now bursting to get out along with all its other orgasm buddies. The amount of come is doubled, tripled, or more, like you could keep shooting forever and not run out. Pass Go. Collect $200. Winner, winner, chicken dinner.

I edged him four times. Each time his moans of protest grew louder. I distracted him by sucking his nipples. Nipping his neck. Kissing him hard and fast until he'd whimper. I never thought of myself as controlling, but when it came to orgasms, I loved giving them but loved it even more if they were superintense and entirely on my terms.

"Collin, please. Now."

He was about to burst. I could feel it. Every inch of his body seemed taut, tensed, stretched to its limit. I pumped him faster, the way he liked to stroke himself when he was ready. In half-a-dozen strokes I heard the groan that tipped the balance. The ridges of his cock swelled and pulsed. I got my mouth on him just in time to swallow his load, sucking him deep into my throat so he could finish in the warmth and safety of my mouth.

"Holy Christ, Collin. Where do you learn this shit?"

"I seem to remember someone encouraging me to watch porn."

"Damn, I give good advice."

We both laughed. "You're a fucking genius."

"I am. We didn't even fuck up a single sheet, which means no laundry tomorrow."

"You're without question the best boyfriend I've ever had."

"Dork. I'm the only boyfriend you've ever had."

"Still the best."

I cringed as I sat down on the bed.

"Hurt that much?"

"Feels pinchy. Like a bad sunburn. I think I better lie on my back, not my side. Too much pulling."

"Good idea," Tanner scooted to his side of the bed, propping pillows against the wall, then propping another near him. "Try this."

I lay down on the pillow with my head resting near his stomach. I could hear his heart beating in the background, steady and even. I closed my eyes, knowing I could fall asleep like this. Any position that involved our bodies touching was fine with me for sleeping. I liked the constant reminder that he was there with me.

Tanner snuggled deeper into the pillows, then started to run his fingers through my hair, lightly scraping my scalp with his short nails. The orgasm had felt amazing, but somehow this felt better. I sighed and closed my eyes, focusing on the sensation. Tanner warm beneath my head, his taste coating my mouth, his fingers caressing my scalp. Nothing had ever felt that soothing, that relaxing, that incredibly blissful.

I didn't want it to ever end.

Chapter Sixteen

"Woof."

I was sure that's what I heard the guy in the black T-shirt say after he stamped my hand. One of the bouncers whispered something in response, and they all nodded and chuckled.

I leaned closer to Tanner as we made our way through the crowd. "Did that guy just bark at me?"

Tanner grinned. "Yep. That's gay for he thinks you're hot."

"Oh." My cheeks prickled.

Tanner slid his hand across my back and tugged me toward him as we kept moving. Leaning in close, his mouth grazed my ear. "He's right."

His warm breath made me tingle from head to toe. The urge to pull away from him stiffened my shoulders, but as I glanced around the crowd, I realized no one here would care. Two guys leaning against the bar had their hands in each other's back pockets. Two others were dancing on one of the raised platforms, in full view of everyone, moving together like their dicks were magnets that couldn't be pulled apart. No one stared. No one pointed. I didn't even see any sideways glances.

Tanner's lips moved near my ear again. "You okay?"

It was too loud to talk, so I nodded.

"You want a drink, or you want to dance?"

The sound of his voice vibrated through me, making the hairs on my arms stand at attention. *Dance?* Before I could answer, I heard a familiar shriek.

"Birthday boy!" Seconds later Wendy had catapulted herself into my arms and planted a mushy kiss on my cheek. "Twenty-one! Wooo!"

"Hey, when did you get here?"

"I caught the early ferry. Dex texted me and told me everyone was meeting up here to celebrate, but I haven't seen anyone else yet."

Even though she was yelling, it was hard to hear, but I could tell Tanner had made out what she'd said. He shot me a look and a subtle headshake. "I think they're on their way. We just got here too. This place is a madhouse."

"I know. But I managed to get the bartender's attention." She shimmied her boobs and they jiggled in her low-cut tank. I was pretty sure she'd had at least a few drinks while she was waiting. "What are you drinking, Collin? Birthday booze is on me."

Tanner nodded, and I knew he wanted me to keep Wendy busy so he could scan the crowd and see if Dex or Maggie had made an appearance yet. Why would Dex tell Wendy to meet them here, then not show up? He couldn't be that stupid. Or that mean. Could he? *Shit.*

Wendy gave a little jump and propped herself up on the bar like a gymnast on the uneven parallels. The bartender saw her and threw her a devilish grin. "You ready for another already?"

"Sure am. And I need drinks for my two fuck-hot friends. Card the one in the blue shirt. It's his birthday." She winked at me.

"Happy birthday, man. What can I get you?"

I had no idea. Tanner was still looking around. He shrugged at me, so I guessed there was no sign of Dex. "I'll have what she's having."

"Me too," Tanner said, stepping behind me. His hand rubbed against my back and the tingles returned. I glanced around, still nervous that someone would see. All I saw was a tall blond guy leaning in to kiss the heavily tattooed, very beefy other bartender on the lips. My jaw dropped. I didn't mean to stare, but I couldn't help it. Right there, in front of a packed club of people, a guy who could have been a model for anything from designer underwear to imported vodka was making out with a guy who looked more like a bouncer than a bartender. And no one seemed to notice.

When I finally managed to look away, what I noticed was Tanner. The lopsided smile on his face told me he knew exactly what I'd been looking at. His hand was still on my back, and his fingers pressed into my side. I moved closer.

"Sex on the Beach with beer chasers. Courtesy of the lovely lady." The bartender lined up three rocks glasses of some dark red concoction and three tall-neck Rolling Rocks.

"Sex on the Beach?" Tanner said to Wendy, eyebrows scrunched together. "You're a walking cliché."

"And that's why you love me." Wendy stuck out her tongue, then handed glasses to me and Tanner. She raised hers. "To Collin. Cheers."

We clinked them together and all drank. Sweet, icy coldness filled my mouth. Liquid Popsicle.

"God, I love Sex on the Beach." Wendy giggled as she slammed her empty glass down on the bar.

The bartender winked at her. "My kinda customer."

I finished off what was left of my drink and grabbed the beer bottle just in time to see Dex come up behind Wendy and nibble her neck. She shrieked and turned in his arms. They were making out in under ten seconds.

The look on Tanner's face told me he was less than 100 percent pleased to see Dex. He took a few gulps of his beer, then looked at me. His expression changed as soon as we made eye contact. Mischief sparkled behind the darkness.

"Finish that beer. I want to dance."

"Yes." Wendy chugged her beer, then nearly knocked it over setting it back on the bar. She grabbed my hand and Dex's and dragged us both out onto the dance floor.

Tanner followed close behind. Closer to the speakers, the music was so loud it shook the floor. Between the thumping bass, the flashing lights, and the mass of gyrating bodies, it was impossible not to move. One song seamlessly blended into the next as the videos on the huge screens shifted to match the songs.

Song lyrics echoed through my brain along with the beat as I watched Wendy swiveling her hips. Dex had a beer in one hand and swayed more than danced. Tanner moved in a way that electrified me more than all the other sights and sounds combined. I'd never seen him dance before. The smile on his face made my stomach spin faster than the turntable.

Ricky Martin blared through the speakers, and Tanner and Wendy danced closer, shimmying together in a routine they'd clearly done before. Laughter bubbled out of them, and I couldn't help but join in. I had no idea dancing could be so much fun.

The beat changed again, and the crowd started jumping. Tanner mouthed the words at me.

My cheeks hurt from grinning—yes, he was sexy and I knew it, very well. Tanner's hand rested on my hip as he rocked in toward me. I don't know if it was the booze or the song or a mix of everything, but I moved with him, our bodies finding the rhythm and totally in sync.

Our eyes met, locking for a second, and then Tanner kissed me. The panic I felt was fleeting as his lips pressed against mine, making me forget what I was nervous about and focus on what was right in front of me. The guy I loved was kissing me in a room full of people, and it was okay.

It was better than okay. It was amazing. It was my birthday. This was my life. And at that moment, I had everything I wanted.

Chapter Seventeen

WE MADE it less than halfway up the first staircase at the house before we started kissing. By the second landing, Tanner's shirt was off. By the time we made into our room, our pants were undone and en route to the floor.

Tanner shoved the door shut and flipped the lock while I kicked off my shorts. We fell into the bed, naked, attached at the mouth, hands roaming everywhere. His cock rubbed against mine, and I reached my hand between us, needing to feel him. I stroked up and down, feeling his wetness against my fingers.

"Stop." He grabbed my wrist. "I don't want to come yet."

I let go reluctantly and shifted to my side as he climbed over me and fumbled in the drawer. The snap of a lid popping open made my dick twitch with anticipation. We'd left the lights off, but there was enough moonlight in the room to see pretty well. The clear stream of liquid glistened as he poured it onto his hand.

My heart raced, then skipped a beat as his slippery fingers slid over my balls and then over my asshole. I rocked against his hand, wanting more. He drizzled the lube over my cock and stroked as silky liquid ran down the crease of my leg. His finger slid inside me.

I arched my neck against the pillow. So good. "Fuck."

"Do you want to?"

It took a second for my brain to register what he was saying. *Do I want to fuck? Hell yes.* We'd talked about it a few times. We'd both been tested—him twice, me once, for insurance exams. We were clean. We were monogamous. And we both wanted to try it. I nodded and took the lube from his hand, then squeezed some over his erection. He groaned as I stroked. Yes, I wanted to fuck. *Now.*

I rolled to my side, and Tanner stretched out behind me, his fingers still inside me. He withdrew them, and I groaned in protest, but he reached around and stroked my cock instead. *Jesus.*

He pressed against me, rubbing back and forth against my ass, between my legs, sliding against my balls. The head of his cock pressed against my hole, and I tried to relax. He slid inside the tiniest bit, and I tensed.

Tanner stopped and stroked my cock until I relaxed more, then tried again. I gasped, and he stopped immediately, pulling away.

"Get on your back." Tanner's voice was thick and low.

I rolled over, feeling the cool sheets under my overheated skin. Had he changed his mind? Were we not going to try anymore? I didn't care. Well, that's not true. It just didn't matter to me what we did. Being with him was all that mattered.

"Sorry," he said. "If we're going to do this, I need to see your face."

His eyes were dark and serious as he stared down at me. Looking at him was one of my favorite pastimes. Looking at him now, with that expression on his face, was beyond hot.

I reached for his cock, but he locked his fingers with mine, leaned forward, and pressed my hand into the mattress alongside my head. He shifted so he was between my legs. The heat and weight of his body felt amazing as he moved on top of me. His cock rubbed back and forth against mine, drawing moans from deep inside my chest. Tanner nipped at my lips, then kissed me full-on, his tongue exploring my mouth. God, he tasted good. My body responded from head to toe until I was sure I must be glowing. When I opened my eyes, the room looked shimmery, like I could actually see the heat rising off our bodies.

Tanner raised his hips and slipped a hand between us. My cock twitched, expecting him to start stroking, but his fingers moved lower. Lube coated them again. When did he do that? The silky, slippery liquid coated my ass, and Tanner slid in one finger, then two. I groaned into his mouth and felt him smile against my lips. He scissored his fingers, opening me more. Need took control, and I bucked against his hand, wanting more, wanting him.

Tanner's other hand was still locked with mine, clutching my fingers. I squeezed back, trying to let him know everything was okay. We could do this. I knew it. I wanted it. I needed it.

Moving slowly, Tanner slid back and forth against me, painting wetness on my skin. His cock caressed my balls, then stroked against my taint. The slow passes of his fingers deep inside me became like torture. The best possible type of torture. When his fingers withdrew, I cried out, but before I had a chance to speak, the head of his cock replaced them.

"Breathe, Collin."

My eyes fluttered open and locked with Tanner's. His expression was serious, forehead furrowed, lips parted. If every fantasy and wet dream I'd ever had were spliced into a single image, that would have been it—Tanner's face as the tip of his cock pressed into my ass.

He was always hot, but he'd never looked sexier. I could have come just from looking at him, but that wasn't what I wanted. I took a deep breath and blew it out slowly, feeling my muscles start to relax. Like magic he inched inside me. Not much, but enough to make me moan again, with pleasure this time. No pain.

A smile twitched at his lips. "Good. Again."

Breathing deeper this time, I tightened the muscles deep inside me, then released them. As I felt them relax, my body drew him deeper. This time it was Tanner who groaned. I loved the sound. Loved knowing I made him make it. Loved the feel of him sliding inside me. Filling me.

"Pull your knees up, to your chest."

I did as he asked, flinching for a second as he pushed deeper. I clenched and released the muscles again, and Tanner sighed. His warm breath passed over my sweaty skin like fire. He moved so slowly it was barely noticeable on the outside, but inside my body, every nerve ending ignited each time he did so much as breathe.

The intensity made me shudder.

"You okay?" His voice shook.

"Better than okay." I hissed as he rocked in deeper. "You?"

"Fucking awesome."

My heart soared at his words. My vocabulary failed me, so I let the sensations wrap around me instead.

Tanner let go of my hand and shifted so he was kneeling between my legs. Swallowing hard, I hooked my hands under my knees, drawing them up as close to my chest as possible. Tanner's cock throbbed, stretching me more as he sank deeper, nudging the spot inside me that seemed to have swollen to five times its normal size.

Spikes of pleasure rushed through me so fast my eyes rolled back in my head. White lights flickered in my peripheral vision like flashing Christmas lights. I forced my eyes open, needing to look at Tanner, needing to see him as much as he needed to see me. It took a minute for my brain to process the image, and when it did, it took my breath away.

Tanner's gaze was locked on me, filled with heat and lust and something that looked almost like wonder. His lips were puffy from kissing and hung open as breaths rasped out in short gasps. Strong hands gripped my hips, dragging me closer, so my ass rested against his firm thighs. There was control in his movements. Slow. Steady. In and out and in and out, but the tremble in his arms made me think he was about to lose it.

"Good?" he asked, his voice a whisper.

My mind scrambled, looking for any words, but there were none. I nodded.

"You okay?" He sank into me again, and we both groaned, but I managed another nod.

Tanner's hips pressed against my ass, and his cock twitched deep inside me. Spasms shook through me as precome pooled on my abs.

Warm fingers closed around me, and my eyes drifted closed as I lost myself in all of it. The whole world slid back and forth. The bedsheets, bunching under my shoulders. Tanner's cock as he rocked in and out of me. My dick as his hand pumped up and down.

Pressure built inside me. Not just in my cock and balls. Everywhere. My chest felt tight. My brain felt like it was about to burst. Tanner's thumb rolled around my swollen head as he pumped faster.

"Fuck," he whispered.

I couldn't agree more.

His hips moved faster. He was close. So close I could feel him swelling, feel his balls pebbling as they rubbed against my ass.

"In you or on you?" Tanner asked.

"What?"

"You want me to come in you or on you?"

The thought of either pushed me to the brink. "In me."

He changed his angle, bumping the spot inside me that tipped me over the edge. I groaned long and low as thick ribbons of come shot out of me.

"Jesus," Tanner moaned.

I came so hard everything went black. My ass clamped around him so tight I could feel every fucking ridge of his erection, every swell, every curve. Then he moved again, grunting out a sound I'd never heard him make before—the sexiest noise in the history of sounds. He pulsed inside me, followed by a burst of liquid heat. My body clenched along with his as the last of my orgasm drained out of me and the first burst of his shot through me.

His hips slammed against me so hard my hands lost their sweaty grasp on my thighs. My legs fell to the sides and Tanner leaned forward, his chest hot against my slick stomach, his breath hot against my face, until our mouths found each other.

We kissed hard and fast, inhaling the air out of one another's lungs like each breath might be our last. My ass shuddered as his cock slowly withdrew.

I couldn't kiss anymore. Giving his lower lip one last suck, I pulled back, wondering if the tingling sensation in my extremities was permanent. Not that I cared. The rest of my life could stay exactly like this moment and I'd be happy. The weight of Tanner on top of me was the only thing keeping me from drifting away on a goddamned cloud.

His fingers raked through my hair, pushing it off my forehead. I understood why dogs liked to have their heads rubbed. It felt good. Somehow I'd managed to live twenty-one years without anyone ever running their fingers through my hair. Now I couldn't get enough of it. My head rolled from side to side, prolonging the feel of his fingertips massaging my scalp.

He cupped the back of my head and kissed me one more time before easing off me. Without his heat the air in the room felt thick and cool.

Tanner's breaths were still coming fast.

"You okay?" I asked.

He nodded.

Role reversal. He was always the one checking to make sure I was all right. I was the one who could never find words. It unnerved me a little that he didn't have a verbal answer.

Propping myself on my elbow, I reached over the edge of the bed for something to wipe up what was quickly turning sticky on my chest. I grabbed a T-shirt, but it was pointless. Between the humidity and the sweat, all I was doing was pushing the mess around.

"You think I'd wake anyone if I took a shower?"

A lazy grin curled Tanner's sexy lips. "Not if we use the one outside."

We. My new favorite word.

Chapter Eighteen

It wasn't until I woke up the next morning that I realized my birthday had come and gone without a word from my mother. I wanted to say it didn't matter. That I'd expected as much and it didn't hurt. But it did. A lot.

As I scanned my e-mails, my heart sank further with each message. At least the letter from the university said my loans had been approved. That was something. It meant a shitload more debt, but it also meant I could attend my senior year. And we could keep our room in the dorm.

Tanner had said that if my loans didn't go through, he'd have paid, but I couldn't have let him do that. Enough things seemed to be working against us without letting something weird like money come into play in our relationship.

I replied to my student advisor and hit Send. As I was about to close my laptop, my e-mail dinged. One new message. From Sean.

Not opening it seemed like a valid option. I wasn't in the mood for another please-talk-to-Mom guilt-inducing e-mail. Trying to prolong the high of yesterday already wasn't working, and the subject line seemed innocent enough—Day Late—so I clicked.

> Didn't realize the date yesterday. Sorry I missed your birthday. Happy 21, Collie. Maybe we can grab a beer when you get home.

Sent from his mobile.

That was odd. He never sent e-mails from his phone. They were always from his computer. Then again, if he had my phone number, he probably would have texted instead of e-mailing in the first place. I considered answering from my phone. Would it hurt for him to have my number? It might. I hit Reply instead. My fingers paused over the keys. I'd never had trouble talking to Sean before, but now even "thank you" seemed hard to type. Everything I could think of sounded stupid.

"That would be nice"—how lame was that?

"A drink would be great, maybe even a burger, but hold the moralizing." No. Not a good idea. And not the right person to send that message to anyway. In all fairness, he hadn't really moralized. He'd seemed more desperate and sad than judgmental, which left me somehow more unsettled than my mom's harsh words and Quinn's lecturing. Truth was I'd always been closest to Sean, and I missed him. Just not enough to change who I was to get him back.

Thanks. Sounds good.

I hit Send before I could write anything else or change my mind, then turned off my laptop.

My stomach rumbled, so I headed downstairs. Tanner was sitting at the kitchen table, eating one of the dozens of birthday cupcakes Suzanne had baked.

"Is that your breakfast?" I asked.

"What, like it's worse than a Pop-Tart or a donut? It's got strawberry filling. It's practically a serving of fruit."

I rolled my eyes, but leaned in and kissed him. He tasted sweet and tangy from the lemon frosting. I swiped my finger through the frosting and stuck it in my mouth.

"Get your own," he said, laughing and shoving the Tupperware full of cupcakes toward me.

I grabbed a chocolate one with fluffy white icing and a sprinkle of coconut. "Coconut's a fruit too, right?"

"Sure." Tanner shoved the remainder of his cupcake into his mouth. "Come outside."

"I'm trying to enjoy a healthy breakfast here."

He gave me a shove off the bench. "Enjoy it on the go. I never gave you your present last night."

Present? Tanner's birthday had been right before the end of school, when I was pretty much broke. I'd taken him out for dinner, and we'd gone home and watched movies in bed all night. And had sex. I hadn't gotten him a *gift* gift.

"You didn't have to get me anything."

"Get your ass outside, would you?"

He held the door open, and I stepped onto the deck. Before I could say another word, I saw it. It was hard to miss the huge red bow, but all I could see was the shiny black bicycle it was attached to.

"The bow was Wendy's addition," he said as I moved toward it.

"You got me a bike?" *Duh, Captain Obvious.* I couldn't think of anything else to say, I just stared.

"I know it may be a while before the Batmobile is up and running, so I wanted you to have a way around campus. That's why I got black. It can be the Bikemobile. Or the Batbike."

"I don't know what to say."

"Say you know how to ride a bike."

Laughter snorted out of me, but I quickly choked up. No one had ever bought me a gift like this. "Thank you."

"Do you like it?"

"I love it." My voice cracked.

Tanner grinned at me. "Good. Let's go for a ride."

Chapter Nineteen

After two straight months of weekend shifts, Tanner and I both had a Friday night off, so Bryan insisted we go see his band play. I wanted to see them perform, but the venue concerned me. It was known to be the rowdiest gay bar on the island.

"Rowdiest on any island," Bryan had said. "You'll love it."

I wasn't so sure. I'd just barely gotten used to the idea that Tanner and I could kiss or hold hands in front of our housemates without anyone reacting. I'd been able to make out with him at the bar we'd gone to for my birthday, but even that was after a few drinks. I just didn't know what to expect from this place. Other than my birthday celebration, I'd never even been to a straight club, let alone a gay one. Pictures on the Internet led me to believe that this would be a whole new level of wild. One I wasn't sure I'd be comfortable with.

Tanner knew I was tense. "We'll go hear the band play, and if we don't like it, we'll leave. No big deal."

He always knew my limits. When to push them and when to accept them. I don't know how he read me so well, but he did. Sometimes I felt like I couldn't tell what the fuck he was thinking. Especially with girls. I knew he was still attracted to them, and I knew of at least three in addition to Amy who were regulars at Oz and had massive crushes on him. I'd hear them talking about him. Amy was by far the most forward of the bunch. She hung out at Oz every night Tanner worked and lit up like a sparkler every time he talked to her.

I'd asked him about her, and he'd said she was "nice." Her boyfriend was supposed to share her house with her, but they'd broken up right before summer, so she was there with her sister instead. He said she was still getting over the breakup and was lonely. She didn't look lonely or sad when I saw her. She looked *hungry*. And Tanner seemed to be what she felt like having.

Plenty of guys flirted with him too. Somehow that didn't bother me as much. I knew he was happy with me. Or I thought he was. But women had things to offer that I simply didn't possess. Things I knew he still liked. That made me nervous as fuck, especially when I could tell there were so many women willing to give him those things at a moment's notice if he showed any interest.

I got dressed for the club. Khaki shorts, black T-shirt. It was as close as my wardrobe came to being trendy. Tanner came into our room, fresh from the shower, smelling so good I wanted to spend our night in bed, not at some loud club. I knew he wanted to go, though. And when I saw how insanely hot he looked, I wanted to go just so I could keep looking at him. Slim-fit red shorts, black V-neck tee. There was no way I could pull off that look, but on him? *Jesus.*

Staying home and wondering about other people ogling him would have made me crazy. Plus I was actually curious to see Bryan's band perform. Wasabi Incident had gotten good reviews for their NYC shows. Bryan had shown us the write-up from *The Village Voice.* They'd been compared to Green Day, which was pretty fucking cool since they'd only been together for three months.

We arrived at the club with Bryan, so we got to go in through the back entrance, but after we met the band, the manager sent us into the main bar. Oz was flashy. Or at least what I considered flashy. This place was surreal. Everyone wore something glowing. Necklaces, headbands, bracelets, body paint, even people's tongues were neon electric blue or pink. Attire ranged from casual shorts and shirts to beachwear, including a good number of guys wearing just a mankini or a thong. I couldn't imagine going out in public dressed like that, let alone grinding in a crowded room dressed like that.

What I did like was that no one seemed to give anyone a second look. I felt like I was probably the most judgmental person in the room. Not that I was trying to judge anyone. It was just all new to me. Not bad. Just… different. What I loved was that when Tanner wanted to dance, I didn't feel the least bit weird about joining him on the dance floor, not even when we got close and the crowds packed tighter, not even when I could feel him hard against my ass or when he leaned over and kissed me.

Being able to be with him like that, out in the open, was freeing. Like there wasn't anything I needed to hide or pretend. I watched the men around us. Guys in tank tops rubbing against men in button-downs. Couples holding hands. Some just meeting. Some with matching wedding bands. All of them out, letting the world know they were gay. It gave me hope and scared me in equal measure. This was paradise, not reality. While it was nice to know paradise existed, I also knew it wasn't where I lived. The land Tanner and I were going back to at the end of the summer wouldn't look kindly on us. Hiding had been hard before. After being out like this, for months, I couldn't imagine going back in the closet. But I couldn't imagine not being there either. Not at school.

Bryan's band performed two sets. He had the most beautiful voice. I'd heard him sing around the house, but onstage, with microphones and a band backing him up, he was mesmerizing. It was no wonder there was a revolving door of men in and out of his bedroom. He oozed confidence and sex appeal onstage. And he was gorgeous no matter where he was.

"Well," Bryan asked when he came offstage. "What'd ya think?"

The bartender handed him a beer and gestured to see if I wanted another. I waved a hand to say no.

"You were great. I only recognized a few covers. Are all the rest originals?"

He flashed his movie star smile at me. "All mine. Except that last song. The drummer wrote that."

"Well, you sounded amazing. I can't believe a label hasn't picked you guys up yet."

He leaned closer. "Can you keep a secret?"

"Sure."

"A producer came to hear us last night. They're going to offer to sign us, and I think we're gonna say yes."

"Wow. Shit. That's insane. You must be stoked."

"I won't believe it till we've signed the paper, but yeah, I was pretty blown away when I heard about the offer. That's been my dream for, like, six years."

"All good things to those who wait, man...."

"You said it." He clinked his beer against mine.

Tanner came up behind me. "What are we toasting?"

"Can I tell him?" I asked.

"Sure. You two are practically married. I just assume what one of you knows, the other knows."

Married.

Do we give off a married vibe? Is that a good thing? A happily married couple? The thought didn't scare me as much as I thought it should. I couldn't imagine not having Tanner in my life. Agreeing to spend the rest of my life with him didn't seem like it would be a bad thing in any way. In fact it sounded awesome. Maybe not now... but some day.

Tanner put his hand on my back, and I leaned into his touch. The smile on his face made my heart switch places with my stomach. Did he know what I was thinking? Did he feel the same way? And when the fuck had I started thinking about spending my life with another person? Electricity hummed through me as he stroked his thumb against my back. I knew the answer. I'd started thinking about it the first moment he'd touched me.

Chapter Twenty

We'd talked about going to brunch at the famous Bay Side Inn all summer, and finally we had a Sunday morning free.

The view was amazing. Sparkling water with sunlight dancing off it. Boats sailing by. Fresh salt-air breeze. We sat at a table on the deck overlooking it all from the peaceful shade of a huge umbrella.

The food was every bit as amazing as I'd heard. Eggs Benedict with house-cured bacon instead of Canadian bacon. Eggs perfectly poached, hollandaise as rich and creamy as ice cream. We'd each polished off an order along with crispy hash browns, a basket of their signature cinnamon mini muffins, and a huge fruit platter with local honey and assorted cheeses. I couldn't remember ever having a better meal. Or a better time. We talked and laughed and held hands right at the table. I could have stayed there for the rest of the day and been happy.

"Tanner, Collin." I recognized the voice immediately, even out of context. It was Eric from our dorm.

Tanner and I turned just in time to see him approaching the table. Our hands slipped apart, but the look on Eric's face made it clear—he'd seen. Breakfast suddenly felt like a cement mixer in my gut.

"Hey, Eric."

Tanner stood and offered his hand. The same hand that had been holding mine. *Jesus.*

"Hey." He shook it, then leaned across the table and shook mine. "I saw you while we were waiting for our table. My folks have a dock a few blocks up. I came up for the weekend."

A woman who looked insanely similar to Eric came up behind him and put her hand on his shoulder. "Our table's ready, honey."

"Mom, this is Tanner D'Amico and Collin Fitzpatrick. We've lived in the same dorm the past three years."

A warm smile brightened her face. "It's nice to meet you. Are you here with your families?"

"No, ma'am," Tanner answered. "We're renting a house with a bunch of friends. We've been working at Dorothy's and Oz."

"I love Dorothy's." Her eyes settled on me. "I think you waited on us a few weeks ago."

"I think you're right. Mahimahi with pineapple salsa?"

"Yes." She beamed. "Impressive memory. I hope I tipped you well."

I smiled politely. She had. "Yes, thank you."

"Well, it was lovely to meet both of you, but our table's ready and Eric's dad will be wondering where we are. Enjoy the rest of your meal."

"You too," Tanner said, but his eyes were on Eric's.

Eric nodded. "See you back at school."

I watched as he waved and followed his mom.

"Fuck." My voice came out as a whisper, but inside my head there was nothing but yelling. *Fuck. Fuck. Fuck.*

Tanner blew out a slow breath. "You all right?"

"I don't know." I had a headache behind my left eye, and my heart was beating in my throat. If that was all right, then yeah, I was fine.

Tanner's leg bobbed up and down, but other than that, he looked calm. "All things considered, he didn't seem too shaken up."

"No, he didn't. But it's not like he's gonna start screaming 'look at the gay guys' while he's trying to eat brunch with his parents."

"I know. But he didn't look that freaked-out. I think it'll be okay. Eric's a good guy. I'll shoot him a text later, make sure he's cool. Okay?"

I nodded.

"Collin, look at me."

I raised my eyes to his, knowing I must have looked like I was about to lose it. My insides were still shaking.

He held my gaze. "It's going to be okay."

"It's not like I don't want to believe that, I just... I don't know. I thought we'd at least get to tell people when we decided to, and how we wanted to. I didn't expect to just get... caught."

It felt wrong to use that word. "Caught" made it seem like we were doing something wrong, and we weren't. That didn't make it feel any less like he'd caught us.

"I'll talk to him. As much as I don't care if people know, I agree. It's better if we tell them. I'll take care of it."

If we tell them. As happy as I was being out with Tanner this summer, I couldn't imagine us being out at school. My mother's reaction played over in my head. What if everyone was like that? What if Gino fired me? What if Tanner couldn't talk Eric into staying quiet and everyone knew by the time we got back to campus? Would they be okay with it? I didn't know a single out person at our school.

"Collin."

Tanner's voice shook me back to the present. "What?"

"Don't worry about Eric, okay? He's a good guy."

I nodded, not at all sure that being a good guy meant he could keep a secret, let alone that it meant he was okay with the idea of me and Tanner as a couple.

The waitress brought our check, and Tanner stuck cash in the folder. "Ready?"

I was more than ready to be anywhere but there.

Chapter Twenty-One

ALL THOSE old sayings about bad luck coming in threes and how when it rains it pours seemed to be coming true. I woke up to e-mails from the school about how one of my loan forms had gotten lost and if they didn't have a signed copy on their desk by the end of the day, I could be un-enrolled from my classes.

After three hours of phone calls and e-mails proving they already had the damned forms, they finally figured out that they'd put them in someone else's file. By then I was late for work, so Dorothy stuck me in the worst station at the restaurant. My shift seemed endless, but I knew I'd be in better favor with Dorothy if I stayed to help close, so I did. So did Jason. I think he took pity on me because I was having such a shit day.

When the last chair was up on the tables and the floor had been swept, I took off my apron and sighed. Jason clapped a hand on my shoulder. "It's after midnight. It's a new day."

"Thank God. Let's hope it's a better one."

"You headed home?"

I thought I was, but then I realized that since I was twenty-one, I could go to Oz. We could grab a drink, and then I could walk home with Tanner when he got off. "You want to get a beer or something?"

"Sure."

Oz was pretty quiet. Only a handful of people were outside the door instead of the usual mob. I wove through them and headed inside. Scanning the bar, I saw it was slow there too. Two bartenders stacked glasses, and only a handful of customers were in the row of seats. I wondered if maybe Tanner had headed home early because it was slow.

I recognized one of the bartenders Tanner had introduced me to a few times. "Hey, Tommy, is Tanner still around?"

"Yeah, I think so." He leaned to the side to look around. "He went out on the floor for a while. He was with that Amy chick."

Amy. It figured. I wasn't in the mood for her tonight, but I did want to let Tanner know I was there. I turned to Jason. "I'll be right back."

He nodded, and I heard him ordering a beer as I headed off across the dance floor. I couldn't find Tanner anywhere. He wasn't in any of the booths, wasn't by the restrooms or the DJ table. I'd even peered into the storage area behind the bar. Jason caught my eye, and I shrugged to let him know I was still looking.

The only place I hadn't checked was outside on the deck. I poked my head out the door and took a quick look around. Most of the tables were empty, and neither Tanner nor Amy were anywhere in sight. I was about to go back inside when I noticed a couple on the far side of the deck. They leaned against the wooden banister, heads close. My stomach recognized them before my brain. It was Tanner and Amy. I couldn't see them clearly, but it was definitely them. His dark hair against her blonde mane, her pink nails against his black Oz shirt. They were hugging, at the very least. If Amy had her say, they'd be doing more than that soon—if they hadn't already. I didn't want to see that.

I turned so fast, I bumped into someone who was coming out onto the deck. She sloshed her drink down her arm and cursed at me. I think I apologized. I couldn't hear anything. Not even my own voice. Just my heart beating in my ears.

I headed straight for the exit and made it into the parking lot before I took a full breath. With my hands on my knees, I bent forward, trying desperately to clear my head.

They're just friends, right? It was probably just a hug. Unless maybe he's thinking it would be a hell of a lot easier to have his talk with Eric about how things are if he has a pretty girl along with him.

My mind raced, bouncing between images of Amy with her arms around Tanner and things I couldn't even put into words.

Jason came up behind me, and I nearly jumped out of my skin. I'd forgotten he was there.

"Dude, what's going on?"

"Nothing."

"You look like you've seen a ghost."

"Can we get out of here?" *I need to go. Now. Please.*

"Sure," he said. "Let's go to my place."

Anywhere I didn't have to watch Amy and Tanner sounded like exactly where I wanted to be.

Chapter Twenty-Two

Jason pushed open his apartment door, and I followed him into the small front room. He tossed his keys onto the coffee table and gathered a few books off the worn leather sofa.

"Have a seat," he said. "You want a drink?"

I was still too upset to speak. Shrugging, I flopped onto the couch. Visions of Tanner with Amy refused to stop popping into my brain. His arm around her tiny waist. The way her hand clutched at him, possessive, desirous. My stomach churned.

"Drink this."

Jason handed me a glass with way more than one shot worth of tequila in it. My nose crinkled.

Jason laughed. "Sorry, I forgot. Hold on a sec."

He disappeared into the small kitchen and rummaged. The fridge opened and closed with a sigh. Jason returned, saltshaker in hand.

"Come on. Hand out. Lick."

I closed my eyes and forced a deep breath, then licked the inside of my wrist. Jason sprinkled a good amount of salt onto me.

"Go on," he said, setting a plate of sliced limes down in front of me.

Why not? Licking my salty wrist, I raised the tumbler with my other hand. The pungent aroma singed my nostrils, but I ignored it, slugged back a huge mouthful, swallowed, drained the rest of the glass, and swallowed again. My eyes watered as I shoved the lime into my mouth, biting down as hard as I could.

"Dude, that was supposed to be, like, three shots." Jason stared at me, eyes wide with surprise.

"Oh," I muttered, trying to suck as much lime juice into my mouth as possible.

"Cheers." He licked, salted, drank and shoved a piece of lime into his own mouth.

I didn't feel particularly cheerful, but the tequila had already taken a little of the edge off. Warmth spread through my body, and I relaxed into the couch enough to take a full breath.

"Here, this'll help get rid of the taste." Jason handed me a beer. The cold bottle was covered in beads of water.

The icy liquid frothed in my mouth, the bubbles tingling as they worked down my throat. I was starting to feel less. Less sad. Less angry. Less everything.

Jason sat on the couch, one leg folded under him, facing me. Studying me.

"What?" I asked.

He shrugged and took a long drink. "Just thinking Tanner's a fool."

"He's not." My instinct to defend Tanner kicked in before I could even think about it. Besides, if anyone was the fool in this scenario, it was definitely me.

"Whatever." Jason stared at his beer, tracing a pattern into the bottle sweat. "Have you noticed that I've only hooked up with blond guys this summer?"

A small laugh huffed out of my lungs. "Yeah, actually I had."

"I don't like blonds."

Ouch. "Jesus, Jason. Way to kick a guy while he's down."

Jason shifted and stretched his arm out along the back of the couch. "They're just not usually my type. Every one of them was a substitute because the guy I really wanted was unavailable."

I took another swallow of beer, waiting for him to finish his thought. Hearing about his love life was way better than dwelling on the disaster of my own. He stayed quiet, and when I looked up, he was studying me again.

"You don't get it, do you?" he asked, dark eyes narrowed, head tilted to the side.

"Get what?"

"All those guys were a substitute for you."

Wait, what? I set my beer down on the coffee table before I dropped it.

Jason continued to stare, then looked down at his own beer.

My mind tried to race to come up with something to say, but it just inched around in circles. *A substitute for me? Seriously?* I'd been so caught up, thinking about all the people I knew who were into Tanner, it hadn't actually occurred to me that someone might be into me.

"Jason, I…." Words wedged in my throat.

"Don't…," he whispered, shifting closer. "Just… let's just…."

My gaze met his. I don't know what I expected to see, but it wasn't hunger. It wasn't lust. It wasn't desire. But that's what I saw. Two shiny pools of need.

And then his mouth was on mine.

The kiss knocked me back from a mix of sheer force and shock. Jason's hand cupped my neck as his tongue parted my lips. My brain struggled to make sense of what was happening, but my tongue went along with what Jason had in mind, wrestling his.

This can't be happening. Sure, I was pissed at Tanner. Yeah, maybe we were breaking up. Yes, at that very moment, he could have been in the middle of fucking Amy. But that didn't change the facts. I loved Tanner. I didn't want anyone else. Not even Jason. My cock didn't seem to entirely agree. When Jason palmed my crotch, it strained against my pants trying to convince me that maybe this was a good idea after all.

Giving Jason's shoulder a solid shove, I pushed away from him. "I can't."

Jason stopped kissing but barely budged. "Sure you can. Does Tanner ever let you top? I would. I'd let you do whatever you want."

Again my cock begged to differ with my brain. Jason took the moment of silence as acquiescence and went in for another kiss. His lips were warm and soft, vaguely salty from the tequila shots, and with my eyes closed and the help of my one-track Tanner-centric mind, I could imagine it was Tanner starting to climb on top of me.

Then I heard the voice of the guy I was wishing I was tangled with on the couch. It didn't come from the mouth that was working mine, it came from the porch, accompanied by the sound of footsteps and knocks on the shaky wood frame around the screen door.

"Jason, you here? Have you seen Collin? I'm worried. He left his bike at...."

I wrenched out from under Jason just in time to see the stunned look on Tanner's face as he saw us through the screen. "Stunned" didn't quite cover it. He looked like he'd been punched in the gut. And he didn't look like he was having sex with Amy. Shame and horror washed over me. *Oh shit. I fucked up.*

Scrambling off the couch was harder than it should have been. Jason wasn't being very helpful, and my legs were rubbery and uncooperative. Tanner's image got blurrier as he backed away from the door without turning around. Even through the haze of the screen door, I could see the hurt in his eyes. He looked like I'd felt when I'd seen him hugging Amy. Except he'd seen me with Jason practically sprawled on top of me.

"Wait." The word came out quieter than I wanted and didn't stop Tanner from moving away.

"Sorry." The cold tone in his voice didn't mask the underlying pain. "Didn't mean to interrupt."

Managing to get past the suddenly monstrous coffee table, I choked out, "You're not interrupting anything. We weren't... I didn't...."

By the time I made it to the door, Tanner was on his bike. I tried to chase after him, but his legs pumped fast and strong. There was no way I'd catch him. The crunch of gravel as he sped off crackled in my ears like static as I processed what had just happened. *He saw us. Us. There is no us. Oh God. What have I done?*

Tequila, lime, and beer churned into a giant swirling puke-a-rita. My stomach turned traitor and lurched up into my throat. I made it to the side of the road and hurled into the bushes. Acid stung the back of my nose and made my eyes water.

"You okay?" Jason's voice was soft and full of concern, making me feel worse. Was it possible for anyone to be friends with me without me stomping on their feelings? *What the fuck is wrong with me?*

"I'm fine. Sorry."

"I'm sorry. I shouldn't have given you so much tequila."

"You didn't make me drink it. You didn't make me do anything." This was all me. Every stupid fucked-up minute of it.

"I meant what I said. I wouldn't have told you if I didn't mean it."

What am I supposed to say to that? And how the hell did I manage to hurt the two people I cared about most without trying to hurt either of them? Jesus. "I'm sorry, Jason. If I made you think… I mean, I never meant…."

"Just wishful thinking on my part. Not your fault."

Forgiveness didn't feel like something I deserved.

"I have to go after him."

"You love him, don't you?"

My throat felt like I'd swallowed a handful of sand. I nodded.

Jason dug his hands into his pockets and stared at his shoes, then his eyes met mine. "You want me to talk to him? I'll tell him it was all me. It's true."

"It's not. I'll take care of it." *I hope.* "And I really am sorry."

"Don't be. At least now I don't have to feel like I never even tried."

The sadness in his voice wrenched my guts even further than they were already twisted.

"I have to go."

Jason rocked back on his heels. "You okay? You want me to walk with you?"

"No, thanks. I'm fine." That was sort of true as long as "fine" meant "okay to make it home without wandering into the ocean." Not even a hint of a buzz remained.

Jason gave a halfhearted wave, and I turned, unable to look at him anymore and desperate to get home. I needed to talk to Tanner. The sooner the better.

I knew I should go by Dorothy's and get my bike, but that wasn't my priority. As much as I loved it, I didn't care what the fuck happened to it. I didn't even feel like I deserved the damned thing.

Walking as fast as I could toward home, my mind wandered. When I was a kid and I fucked up, I'd wish I had superpowers so I could turn back time, like Superman or Hermione, and go back to fix whatever I'd done wrong. I'd never wanted that more than I did right then.

Tanner's bike wasn't on the rack and wasn't up on the porch either. My stomach threatened to stage another revolt, but I breathed in through my nose and willed my body to settle.

Maggie was curled into the recliner, reading. Her brow furrowed when she saw me. Great. Someone else disappointed by me. *Just what I need.*

"Have you seen Tanner?" I asked.

"Came and went. About ten minutes ago." The puzzled look remained on her face.

"Did he say where he was going?"

"Nope. Didn't ask. I assumed he was meeting you somewhere."

"Why?"

She chewed her lip, and my stomach twisted more with each second. "He, um... well."

"Maggie...." I pleaded with my eyes. I'd have gotten down on my knees and begged if it would have made her tell me where he was or what he said.

"He borrowed some condoms."

Chapter Twenty-Three

My heart felt broken. Like it wouldn't beat right. Like it might never be able to find its rhythm again.

Then my stomach won the battle we'd been waging. I made it to the downstairs bathroom just in time to puke what was left of my stomach contents into the toilet. Maggie's feet thudded up the stairs. Thankful not to have her bear further witness to my humiliation, I rested my forehead on my arm, wanting to make sure I didn't have to throw up anymore before I attempted to stand.

The sound of her trotting back down the staircase made me cringe. I flushed the toilet and turned on the water in the sink, trying to keep from trembling. Maggie knocked and opened the door at the same time.

"Mouthwash," she said, handing me a bright blue bottle and a bathroom Dixie cup.

"Thanks." I dried my hands and took the bottle from her, not sure if I was more grateful for the mouthwash or the fact that she had the decency to leave as soon as I took it from her.

The minty liquid succeeding in taking away the puke taste along with what felt like half the skin on my tongue. The burn gave me something to focus on other than thoughts of what Tanner was doing, pissed off, out, with condoms he'd needed badly enough to borrow them from his dad's ex-girlfriend.

I couldn't even look in the mirror. Feeling it was more than enough—a visual wasn't necessary.

"You wanna talk about it?" Maggie said the minute I set foot in the living room. She'd curled back up in the chair but didn't have the book this time, just an intent look on her face. She raised an eyebrow at my silence.

"Not really. Thanks for the mouthwash."

"Anytime."

I headed for the stairs but stopped with one hand on the banister. "Did he say anything else?"

Maggie shook her head. "Just grabbed a hoodie, asked for the condoms, and left. I take it you two had a fight?"

I wish. "Not exactly."

"You're not gonna tell me, are you?"

Telling someone would only make it worse. The only person I needed to talk to was Tanner. Wherever he was.

It felt as if our room had moved to the thirtieth floor. My legs grew heavier with every step. The idea of sitting down in the stairwell was tempting. I didn't really want to be in our room without Tanner. Not when he was the only thing I could think about. Not when he was probably in someone else's room at that very minute, doing things that made me think twice about being more than a foot away from the toilet.

Breathing in and out through my nose helped some. I opened the window wide, letting the night air rush into the room. Realizing I was still in my work clothes, I stripped and put on a fresh T-shirt and shorts. Sleep didn't seem remotely possible, but I got into bed anyway.

I'd thought the bed felt huge when Tanner and I were both in it. Alone it felt immense. Bottomless. Endless. Like I could drown in it and never be found again. At that moment, that didn't sound like a bad idea.

I stared at my phone, desperate to text Tanner. I wanted to know where he was, who he was with… things I felt like I'd lost the right to ask, given that he'd caught me with Jason. My stomach churned. I had to at least know he was all right. My hands shook as I typed *Are you okay?* and hit Send. Seconds later a phone buzzed. Not mine. His. It was on top of the dresser. *Shit.*

I closed my eyes tight and willed myself to listen to the ocean. The breeze washed in and out of the room as the steady rustle of the waves came and went. None of it could block out my thoughts. Jason's face moving closer to mine. His hands on me. How could I not have seen that coming? Tanner had. He'd been dropping hints all summer, and I'd been too damn busy worrying about him to see what was really going on. *I'm an idiot.*

The front door opened and closed a half-dozen times, and I strained to listen each time—Maggie, Bryan, Dex—no Tanner. Fuck. It was nearly three in the morning. Wherever he was, I had the feeling he was spending the night.

My heart sank into my disgruntled stomach. They both seemed to be conveying their overall disgust with me for their treatment.

I pinched the bridge of my nose, willing away the headache that threatened to erupt behind my eyeballs. *Water.* A hangover might have been what I deserved, but it was the last thing I needed.

Moving with care to avoid the extra-creaky steps so I wouldn't wake the whole house, I made my way to the first floor. The chimes on the front porch jingled, and I held my breath, hoping they'd moved because Tanner had walked by. No such luck. They sounded again, louder, and I felt the accompanying breeze through the open kitchen window.

Where is he? My insides twisted around one another. I drained a glass of water, then rummaged in the cupboard until I found the Tylenol. My mind wandered through all the events of the evening as I downed the pills with a Snapple. Amy. Jason. Tanner. Everything swirled together, making me dizzy.

Fresh air seemed like a good idea. I tugged on a sweatshirt, gingerly opened the front door so it wouldn't squeak too much, and headed for the beach.

It had been cloudy earlier, but the winds had blown enough to clear out the sky. Stars twinkled everywhere in the darkness, and the moon shone bright white, high and full in the night sky. Shadows from the tall beach grass danced along the sandy path as I made my way toward the water.

As I neared the first row of fences, my heart skipped a beat. There was a bike on the sand. The royal blue and silver frame glinted in the darkness. Tanner's bike.

He's here.

Chapter Twenty-Four

The sand shifted under my feet as I made my way toward him. My legs felt rubbery. It seemed possible I might actually shake apart before I reached him.

His shoulders tensed, but he didn't turn around. I knew he'd heard me coming. Forcing myself to inhale, I took a deep breath in, then blew it out slowly and sank down onto the sand next to him.

"I'm so sorry, Tanner."

He snorted out a breath, still not looking at me.

My chest ached. "I don't even know what happened. Seriously. I saw you hugging Amy and I got upset, so Jason invited me over to his place to calm down. It didn't even occur to me that anything would happen."

"How is that even possible? The guy's had a boner for you since day one."

"I didn't know. I mean it."

"Well, then, you're pretty fucking stupid."

That stung. Largely because it was true. Tanner still hadn't looked at me. He studied the sand, raking it with his fingers. I got on my knees in front of him, willing him to look up. I needed him to see it in my eyes. To see how sorry I was. To see that it was killing me to think I'd hurt him.

When his eyes met mine, I wished I hadn't been looking. His brow was furrowed, eyes narrowed and rimmed in red. Shit. He'd been crying. I made him cry. Tears prickled behind my own eyes, making everything blurry, then superclear when I blinked them away. The knot in my throat felt like a giant ball of yarn, dry and scratchy and impossible to swallow.

I rasped out the only thing I kept thinking. "I love you."

Tanner's expression turned darker. "Do you?"

"Of course I do." How could he question that? After all the stuff we'd done together. After all we'd been through.

"Well, you sure as hell didn't act like it tonight."

"That was just one minute of bad judgment. A mistake. It doesn't mean—"

"It doesn't mean what?" He was angry now, his voice low and rumbly. "Doesn't mean I saw you with another guy's tongue down your throat and his hand on your dick? Do you have any idea what that felt like for me? It felt like my fucking guts were being ripped out. It was humiliating. And painful. It sure as fuck didn't feel like *love*."

"Oh God. I'm sorry."

"I would never do that to you. Do you hear me? Never. If I wanted someone else, I'd have the decency to tell you and end things between us first."

"Tanner, you have to believe me. If I wanted someone else, I would say so. I never want to do anything to hurt you. I didn't know Jason thought of me that way. When he kissed me, I was more shocked than anything else, and I swear that's all it was, just a kiss."

He turned and looked out toward the ocean. His hair fluttered in the breeze, and he looked so unbearably sexy. I wanted nothing more than to reach out and hold him, to run my fingers through his hair and kiss him and tell him how much I loved him. But it seemed like I might have lost my right to those privileges. Like he didn't want those things from me anymore.

My heart hurt so bad I thought it might cramp up and stop beating altogether. I'd ruined everything. I couldn't even look at him for fear of what I'd see. I closed my eyes tight. "I can't lose you." I wasn't even sure I'd said the words out loud, but Tanner sighed, so I assumed he'd heard them.

"What do you want, Collin? Seriously, do you even know?"

That took no thought whatsoever. I opened my eyes. "You."

Tanner shook his head, eyebrows knitted together again.

"I'm serious," I said. "*You.* You're all that matters to me. You're all I think about. I'm so fucking worried about losing you, I do stupid shit like get jealous of all the other people who want you, and I'm so damned stupid I don't even see it when someone's interested in me. But you. You're the one thing in my life I never question. I never doubt how I feel about you."

"So does that mean you still want us to be together?"

I couldn't believe he asked me that. "Of course I want to be with you. I love you."

Tanner's gaze lifted to meet mine. The dark brown was glassy as he searched my eyes.

"Do you realize that tonight's the first time you've said that to me since the night of the accident?"

"Said what?"

"I love you."

Wait. No. That's not possible. Is it? I struggled to remember another time. Tanner had said it to me a bunch. *Have I really not said it back? Ever?* My heart sank into my stomach. I hadn't. I'd thought it eight million times a day, but I hadn't said it out loud.

"I'm sorry." My voice cracked. "I've loved you every fucking second since then. I didn't know I wasn't saying it. I didn't realize."

"How can you not realize something like that?"

I shrugged. I didn't have a good answer. "My family never said it. I mean, like, *never*. Only in general statements like 'We're a family, we love each other.' You were just supposed to take it on faith."

"Well, that kinda fucking sucks."

"Yeah, I guess it does."

"I'm not like your family, Collin. I don't want to take things on faith or assume anything. You need to tell me what you're feeling. Not just now—all the time. I don't want to guess and find out later I was totally off base."

The back of my nose tingled, and my eyes prickled as I willed myself not to cry. I rested my elbows on my knees and rubbed my forehead, kneading the balls of my hands against my eyes. My legs had cramped from kneeling on the cool sand. Tanner shifted, and my stomach rolled over. *He's getting up. He's leaving. He's done with me. I'm closed off and fucked-up and fucking cruel. And he's had enough.* The cool breeze caught the wetness on my fists, making them feel ice cold. Then Tanner's hands gripped my shoulders.

He hadn't left. He'd shifted to his knees in front of me. His hands slid to my neck, fingers sinking into my hair as he pulled me upright. Even on our knees, we were the same height. My arms hung limp at my sides. I wanted to touch him but wasn't sure if he wanted that anymore. My hands ached, still balled into tight fists.

Tanner's eyes were crystal clear now, glinting in the light as the sun rose behind us. I stared into them for what seemed like an eternity. I didn't mind. I wanted to look into them forever. He opened his mouth, but nothing came out. I'd never seen him at a loss for words before, and it scared the shit out of me, thinking of all the things he might be about to say.

He gnawed his bottom lip, something he only did when he was really struggling. *Oh Jesus. Are we over? Is this it?* I tried to contain myself, but a tear leaked out and rolled down my cheek. Tanner's gaze followed its path. It reached my jaw and clung for a moment before starting down my neck.

Leaning forward, Tanner kissed it away. My heart shuddered like an engine on a cold day. His lips slid to my cheek, and he placed another kiss, then pulled back so his face was inches from mine.

"We're gonna have to learn to trust each other more."

I nodded, breathless.

"And you're gonna have to get better at telling me how you feel. About everything."

"I will. I promise."

"And please, for the love of God, will you realize that other people find you attractive?"

"I'll try."

"Okay, then." His thumbs stroked my cheek as he gripped the back of my head harder.

"Tanner, I—"

Words wouldn't come, they were all stuck behind the massive lump in my throat. It didn't matter. I didn't need words for what I needed to let him know. Lunging forward, I smashed my mouth against his. My arms remembered how to move and wrapped around him, clawing at his shirt, gripping his neck, anything to get his body as flush with mine as possible.

Now that I'd touched him again, I never wanted to let him go.

Chapter Twenty-Five

TANNER AND I walked back to the house hand in hand. For the first time in hours, I felt like I could breathe again.

I opened the front door, and we snuck in as quietly as possible so we wouldn't wake anyone. All I wanted was to go up to our room, get into bed, and finish making up. Before we even got across the living room, a door slammed upstairs, followed by the sound of tears. Wendy barreled down the staircase, sobbing.

Shit. What the fuck?

"What's wrong?" Tanner asked her.

"Nothing." She grabbed her purse, rushing for the door. "I have to go."

Tanner dropped my hand and stepped in front of her, throwing me a wide-eyed look. "Hey. Talk to me. What happened?"

"I got a ride over on my boss's boat. I wanted to surprise Dex by getting here early." She let out a cross between a hiccup and a squeak, then dissolved into another storm of tears.

Tanner wrapped his arms around her as she cried.

Dex appeared in the stairwell, wearing sweatpants and tugging on a T-shirt. The look in Tanner's eyes sent a chill through me. I'd never seen him so angry.

Dex walked straight to Wendy and put his hand on her back. She pulled away, clinging tighter to Tanner.

"Come on, baby," Dex said. "Let me explain."

"Get away from me." Wendy's voice was muffled against Tanner's chest.

Tanner's jaw was clenched so tight, I could see the veins in his neck. "Why don't you give her some space?"

Dex scowled. "This doesn't concern you, man. This is between me and her."

A high-pitched giggle sounded, and Maggie appeared, wearing a T-shirt and a grin. "Not exactly."

"Stay out of this," Tanner said, glaring at her.

Maggie perched on the edge of the couch and crossed her long bare legs, wagging a foot in the air. "You're one to talk. She's back in your arms in under five minutes. I'd have thought it would take at least a few days."

Fuck. Dex stared at her, face screwed up in obvious confusion. "What are you talking about?"

"Your weekend princess and her schooltime fuck buddy," Maggie said, answering Dex but looking straight at Tanner, eyes gleaming.

Dex flinched. "What?"

Maggie gave me a mischievous smirk, then turned her wide eyes to Dex. "Oh, did you not know? About Wendy and Tanner's extracurricular activities?"

Wendy had pulled away from Tanner, tears still streaming but now with fear in her eyes.

Dex's face darkened, nostrils flared. "Seriously?" He glared at Wendy. "This guy?"

Wendy held her hand up. "Dex, it was a long time ago...."

Maggie snorted and rolled her eyes. "A long time in dog years, maybe."

"Jesus." Dex's voice was full of disgust. "You couldn't even find a straight guy?"

My blood went from simmer to boil. "Back off, Dex."

The sound of my voice startled me. It came out more like a growl. My hand ached and I realized my fists had clenched.

Dex raised an eyebrow. "So the wife's gonna defend the mistress? This is fucked-up."

I lunged at him without thinking, catching him totally off guard and landing a punch right on his smug face. The impact shot through my knuckles and up my arm like a bolt of lightning. Before I knew what was happening, Tanner had grabbed me from behind, pulling me away from Dex. Bryan appeared out of nowhere and stopped Dex from swinging at me.

Wendy shoved her way between all of us, yelling, "Stop it! Just stop!"

Dex struggled out of Bryan's grasp and backed away, rubbing the bruise already forming on his cheek. "So not worth it." He spat. "You know what, Wen, you can have your bunch of faggots. Do whatever you want with them. I'm outta here."

He stormed out of the house, slamming the screen door behind him. Wendy went to follow him, but Tanner grabbed her arm. "Let him go."

Tears were rolling down her cheeks again. "I don't want to let him go."

I could see the exasperation in Tanner's face. *Don't say it. Not now.*

"He's been hooking up with Maggie all summer. Let him go. You don't need this bullshit. You can do so much better."

Wendy looked as if Tanner had slapped her across the face.

Oh Jesus.

"What did you say?" Her eyes darted from Tanner's to Maggie's, then back. "All summer?"

Bryan puffed out a breath and took a step back like he was afraid she might literally explode.

Wendy's eyes grew bigger as she glanced from Bryan to me. "And you knew? You all knew?"

I wanted to say something. Something comforting. Something to defend the fact that we hadn't told her. Words failed me.

"Wendy...." Tanner reached for her, but she recoiled.

"Don't even talk to me." She backed away, looking at all of us like we were dangerous predators, then turned and raced up the stairs.

Chapter Twenty-Six

Bryan was the first to speak. "I just came down for a glass of water."

Maggie giggled. I'd forgotten she was still there. I couldn't deal with her or her self-satisfied grin.

Tanner looked more stressed than I'd ever seen him. "You were right, I should have told her. Shit," he said and took off after Wendy.

I watched him go, flexing my fingers. My whole hand still tingled.

Bryan raked his hands through his hair. "I think I'll get that water now."

"I'm sorry you got dragged into this," I said. "Thanks for stopping Dex."

"No worries." He gave a wave of his hand and disappeared into the kitchen.

Maggie hummed and flopped onto the couch, letting her T-shirt ride up high enough that I could see she wasn't wearing anything under it. She grabbed a magazine and started to thumb through it.

"This is all your fault, you know."

"Excuse me?"

Her shoulders rose to her ears as her round eyes stared up at me, dark and treacherous. "If you'd have taken me up on my offer at the beginning of the summer, none of this would have happened."

My blood ran cold. "Fuck you, Maggie."

"That was the plan." She smiled in a way that made the hair stand up on my arms. "But you weren't up for the challenge. So to speak."

I'd had enough.

Without another word, I turned and climbed the stairs, wanting to be as far away from her as possible before I said or did something I'd regret.

Tanner was on the second floor landing. "Come on, Wendy, open up."

"No." Her voice sounded muffled through the door.

Tanner shook his head at me. "She's just being stubborn now. She'll let me in. Go on up. I'll be there as soon as I can."

"Take your time." I knew that was the right thing to say. Truth was I wanted him to get up to our room as soon as possible.

I hadn't even reached the top floor when I heard the squeak of Wendy opening her door and the gentle *click* of it closing behind them. Our room glowed pink from the sunrise. It felt like it had been days since I'd slept, but the last thing I wanted to do was get into bed. Not without Tanner.

I busied myself folding laundry for as long as possible, trying to pretend I wasn't straining to see if I could hear anything from downstairs. There were no voices. No doors opening or closing. I put on headphones and turned on my laptop. Music wasn't as much of a distraction as I hoped, but my in-box caught my attention. For the first time in weeks, there was an e-mail from Sean.

Don't open it. You don't need any more shit right now. The voice of reason was drowned out by the subject line: "I need to talk to you."

I pulled my hand away from the mouse pad three times before I gave in and clicked to open the message.

> *Collin,*
>
> *I know you don't owe me any favors, especially not the way things have been between us lately, but I need you, bro. Laura and I split up a few weeks back. We're getting a divorce. I don't want to discuss the sordid details in an e-mail, but suffice to say I caught her fucking some other guy. Mom's not speaking to me. Quinn's lecturing me about marital counseling. All I want is for everyone to shut the fuck up. I guess I know how you must feel with everyone telling you what you should and shouldn't do and how you should and shouldn't feel. I'm sorry. Seriously. I can't tell you how sorry I am.*
>
> *Through all this shit, you're the one person I wanted advice from. You always give me such good advice. I'm sorry I couldn't return the favor when everyone was coming down on you, but I promise, I'll do better. I don't know when you're heading back up here, but could you give me a call? The kids miss their uncle. I miss my brother.*
>
> *Hope things are better with you than they are here.*
> *Really hope we can talk soon.*
> *S*

Holy fucking shit. My mother must be having a cow. Divorce? Adultery? I bet homosexuality was looking a lot better to her. Well, maybe not. But at least I was no longer the only person she was furious at. Poor Sean. I'd felt like shit even thinking about Tanner cheating on me. I couldn't imagine what it would be like to have someone you were married to betray you like that.

I looked at my phone. It was still way too early to call him. I typed a message instead.

> *Sean*

Remember when we were kids and we'd try to see who could make Mom madder? Which of us do you think is winning?

Tanner and I are moving back to school on the 26th. Call me anytime. I can't pick up while I'm at work, but other than that, I'm here for you. Whatever you need.

Miss you too. And the kids.

Talk to you soon.

C

I hit Send, took off the headphones, and rubbed my forehead. The floorboards creaked and Tanner entered our room, looking like he'd been through a war.

"How'd it go?" I asked.

He closed and locked the door. "Not well."

Sighing, he looked around the room, eyes zooming in on me. "You okay?"

Telling him about Sean could wait. "What happened with Wendy?"

He raked his hand through his hair and shook his head. "Captain Douchebag came back right after she let me into her room. He said he loves her and he'll never see Maggie again on one condition."

Uh-oh. "What's that?"

"That she severs all ties with me."

"Fuck."

"Yeah."

"What'd she tell him?"

"They're heading back to the city. Together. She wants to give it another try. Somehow she's got it in her head they're 'even,' since he didn't know she'd been with me and she didn't know about Maggie."

"But...."

He waved a hand to stop me.

"I know. Don't even. Her mind's made up. She said she didn't want to hear another word from me. Or you. Sorry. Again, you were right. We should have said something."

"You don't know that. She could have gotten just as pissed if we had. Like she did the other time."

Dark circles ringed his eyes. I wanted to hug him, so I stood up. He took a step back, looking nervous. "She'll come around eventually. Look, I don't want to talk about Dex and Wendy anymore. She's a big girl. She's gotta make her own decision. But I need to ask you something. About us."

My breath caught in my chest. "Shoot."

"We're going back to school in two weeks. I need to know. Is this what you want?" He moved his hand in the air between us. "You and me?"

I couldn't believe he was asking me that. "Yes!"

His eyes searched mine, and I thought my heart might burst. "Because if you don't... I don't want us to wind up like the two of them. If you're not sure...."

"Tanner, I'm positive."

He swallowed hard and ran his hands through his hair again. I hated seeing him so shaken. Hated that I was part of why he felt that way. He reached into his pocket and pulled out two condoms, placing them on the dresser.

"After I found you and Jason, I grabbed these and went out. I planned on using them."

My throat ached so bad, I couldn't swallow, couldn't speak, could barely breathe. *With who? Did you?* I couldn't get the words out.

His gaze met mine. "I couldn't do it. I made it halfway to town, then turned around and went to the beach. I don't want anyone but you."

Relief swept over me so fast, my skin tingled. I stepped forward and put my hand over his heart, feeling it pounding hard beneath my fingers. "I'm sorry for being such a jerk. It was never because I doubted how I feel about you. You're who I want. You're what I want. You're all I want. No question. I love you."

I'd have said more, but Tanner stopped me with his mouth. Firm, warm lips moved over mine, parting them, tongue seeking tongue. I don't know if he shoved me or I pulled him, but we banged into the wall. Tanner pressed against me, grinding his hips into mine. My cock thrummed with a mix of desire and need.

A door slammed below us, and I held still. Tanner ran his hand down the side of my face, forcing me to look into his eyes. "We're not them," he said.

"Thank God."

"There's no trust in their relationship. Do you trust me?" His eyes were as dark as I'd ever seen them.

"Yes." I meant it. My heart stuttered. "Do you trust me?"

He stared for what seemed like an eternity, and I thought my heart might stop beating. If he said no, I knew it would. His fingers massaged the base of my skull, and he nodded. "I trust you. I need you."

His mouth slammed into mine, hard and hungry. I kissed him until I ran right out of air, then gulped a breath and kissed him more. Our bodies moved together, stroking, rubbing, straining to be closer. Clothes were tugged, up, down, off, flung in every direction until we were naked and back in each other's arms.

Tanner's hand circled as we thrust together in and out of his fist. I'd never needed to come so badly in my life.

I couldn't focus on kissing anymore. Sliding my mouth off his, I licked a path to his neck, tasting salt. Tears. Sweat. Ocean. It didn't matter. It all tasted like him. Tanner moaned, and I nipped at the pulse beating fast beneath my tongue.

He groaned and swelled against me, pumping faster.

"*Come.*" The word rasped out of me.

"Yes." He groaned, bucking against me, slamming his fist up and down around our cocks.

I don't know who shot first, him or me. I didn't care. I sank into the feeling of us, together. No Maggie. No Dex. No Wendy. No Jason. No Sean. No Eric.

Just us. Me and Tanner.

I wanted this. Only this.

Now. Always.

Moment of Clarity

Acknowledgments

Many thanks to Karen Booth, KD Wood, Kira Decker, Amanda Usen, Saritza Hernandez, and Mandy Pennington for their continued support throughout this series—without you, none of this would have happened (and I mean that in a good way).

Special thanks to Sue Adams and the amazing staff at Dreamspinner Press—it's a pleasure to work with all of you.

Chapter One

I HADN'T particularly been looking forward to the dinky twin beds in the dorms, but I'd at least expected them to be indoors.

"What the fuck?" Tanner stared out one side of the cab while I gaped out of the other. Mattresses and dressers covered the quad as far as I could see. Then I saw the fire truck.

We paid the driver, unloaded our bags from his trunk, and made our way toward the crowd by the main entrance of Downing Hall.

Eric was sitting under a tree with a pile of suitcases alongside him. I knew Tanner had talked to him after Eric saw us holding hands on Fire Island. Eric had said he was cool about us being a couple—he'd agreed to keep it quiet—but my instinct was to avoid him. No such luck.

He stood and yelled over to us. "Can you believe this shit?"

I set my bags next to Eric's. "Dude, what's going on?"

Eric rolled his eyes. "Some dipshit on the second floor put a Pop-Tart in the illegal toaster oven in his room, then went to take a shower. It started smoking and set off all the water systems on the second and third floors."

Fuck. We're third floor. "How bad is the damage?"

"All I'm hearing is rumors, but it sounds like it'll be a few weeks before we can really move in."

"Shit." I scrubbed my hand through my hair.

Tanner came over and dropped his duffel alongside mine. "I just talked to the RA. He said we're going to be temporarily housed in the gym, on cots."

Eric grumbled. "Perfect. A $45K-a-year shelter."

"At least there are showers. Did they say how long?"

Tanner took a seat on the grass and started plucking out random leaves and shredding them. "Nope. Could be a week, could be two or more. There's a long line of parents busting a gut over there yelling at people."

I didn't want to cause problems. I just wanted to be with Tanner. We'd spent our last week of summer break at his mom's, and it had been great—sleeping late, going out to shows, eating takeout on the roof—but it had once again been a chaste week. I still wasn't comfortable with us doing anything with his mom right down the hall. She'd been so kind to us, I didn't want to do anything to offend her. But I was horny as fuck and looking forward to getting Tanner all to myself behind the closed door of our dorm room, not sleeping on a cot next to him in a room with fifty other displaced students.

"We're supposed to check in over there." Tanner pointed to two makeshift tables that were propped by the far side of our building. "They're giving out the passes for the gym and some sort of credit from food services for our inconvenience."

"Guess we better go check that out."

"I'm gonna wait for Tim to get here," Eric said. "He was stuck in traffic, and his phone died, so he doesn't even know. You think you two could save us cots?"

I looked Eric in the eye, searching for any sign of disapproval or fear, but I saw neither. It either didn't matter to him, or he was going to pretend it hadn't happened. Either way, maybe this wouldn't be as bad as I thought.

"Sure. We'll try to get a good spot."

"Thanks. See you there in a bit."

I joined Tanner in line at the tables. He shifted his duffel from arm to arm, and I stared at the muscles of his back as they flexed and rippled under the thin fabric of his T-shirt. *Goddamn he's gorgeous.* I already missed seeing him walking around barefoot and shirtless in his board shorts. Thinking about that made me want to get him anywhere we could take off our clothes and spend some quality alone time getting reacquainted. As we were handed our gym pass and a set of industrial blankets, I realized naked time was going to be a long way off.

"Want to go check this out?" Tanner asked.

"Might as well."

The gym was as loud and dreary as I expected. With the extra-high ceilings, any sound echoed all around. Everyone was complaining. Parents who'd stuck around were bitching loudly to staff, who were apologizing and looking more stressed by the minute. What a mess. And what an ass to have burned food and caused such havoc. Lots of people had illegal appliances, but usually that made them more careful not to get caught with them.

We picked out four beds in the far corner of the room, thinking maybe that would be quieter with fewer people walking by. Once our stuff was set, we headed to the cafeteria. By the time we got there, Tim had arrived and Eric was filling him in.

"This is bullshit," Tim said. "My parents pay good money so I can have a room, not a spot in a homeless shelter."

"Hopefully it'll only be for a week," I said.

Tim shoved a huge bite of macaroni and cheese into his mouth. "What are you two doing in the gym anyway? I assumed you'd crash at Wendy's. I've seen her apartment. There's plenty of room, even if she and Tanner are getting busy."

Tanner poked through the fries on his plate, plucked out a thin crunchy one, and popped it into his mouth. "Yeah, that's not an option."

"You and the Wendster have a fight?" Tim's eyebrow popped high.

"Something like that. She's trying to work on things with her boyfriend right now, and that involves not talking to me."

"Summer lovers cramping your style, eh?"

"Just giving them space." He looked sad, which made me want to reach over to him. Knowing I shouldn't touch him was making me crazy.

"You know the guy, right? Is he a douche or what?"

Tanner shook his head, and I could tell he was done with the conversation. "My opinion's not relevant here. She's the one who wants to be with him. It's her call."

Tim nodded, looking satisfied with the answer. "Sucks she wouldn't even give you a piece of her floor. Even that would be better than those fucking cots." Tim waved his fork at me. "You've got family nearby. Can't you just live at home until this is settled?"

"Not exactly." My stomach twisted as I tried to think of how to explain this without really telling him anything. "My mom and I don't exactly get along, and my brother's got some marital problems, so I don't want to get in the way."

"Maybe you could go stay at the convent with your other brother."

I laughed. "They don't keep priests in a convent. You're thinking of nuns. And I'm not about to move to a rectory. No thanks."

"Rectory. Sounds dirty." Tim laughed and shoved another huge mouthful of food into his face. "Guess you're doomed, then. I'm gonna ask some of my buddies if I can crash at the frat house. I bet they'll let me. I helped a bunch of them pass statistics last quarter."

"Good idea," Eric said. He'd remained quiet the whole time we were chatting, and I got the distinct feeling he wanted Tim to stop talking to me as soon as possible.

Tanner stayed quiet, and I wondered what was going on inside that beautiful head of his. I bussed my tray, then got another soda and sat down next to him.

Leaning close enough that only he could hear, I murmured, "You all right?"

He smiled and nodded. "Just disappointed I have to go another night without you in my bed."

His voice was low, but I still glanced around to make sure no one had heard. No one had. Except my dick, who wholeheartedly agreed about us needing a night together. In fact, fuck the night. Right now. In a roomful of people. My dick didn't have the best judgment or sense of decorum. It was just hyperfocused on Tanner. Rubbing against Tanner. Being stroked by Tanner. Being sucked by Tanner.

I have to stop listening to my cock before I come right here in my jeans. That was the last thing I needed.

I managed to get my laptop connected to the cafeteria's shitty Wi-Fi. Sean had sent an e-mail asking that we meet for breakfast after he dropped the kids at preschool tomorrow. I didn't have to do anything but finish registering, so I said that was fine. I hoped at least something would get resolved from our talk. I was looking forward to having my brother in my life again.

Tanner clapped me on the back the way any two friends might, but we weren't any two friends, and the warmth of his hand sank through my T-shirt and warmed me all the way to my bones.

"Everything all right?" he asked.

"Yep. Meeting Sean at the coffee shop for breakfast tomorrow."

"Good. I hope you guys set things right between you."

"Me too."

Chapter Two

Showering in the gym was never one of my favorite things. Doing it with so many people, all cranky from a bad night's sleep on wobbly cots, made it all the more unpleasant. Tanner had taken off early for his shift at the bookstore, and I wasn't ready to deal with more cafeteria food, so I headed to the diner a few minutes ahead of schedule.

A waitress came straight to my table and asked if I wanted a coffee. I ordered two, and she turned over both cups and poured them nearly full. "I'm sorry," she said, flustered, "did you need room for cream? I'll dump them out."

"Don't worry. They're fine. My brother should be here any minute. I'm not sure what he'll order, but can you bring us a grilled cinnamon roll and a toasted pumpkin muffin for now?"

"You got it, handsome."

She winked at me. She couldn't have been more than a few years older than me. A part of me wished I'd respond when a girl flirted like that, but I didn't. Nothing. I mean sure, it was always fun to flirt. Who didn't like some banter with a side of flattery? But it didn't turn me on. She seemed extra nice, though. Maybe Sean's type....

"Sorry I'm late." Sean slid into the opposite side of the booth. "This mine?"

"Yep. Coffee's yours. Grilled cinnamon bun and muffin are on their way."

"Aw, Collie. Just like old times." He ripped open sugar packets, two at a time, and shook them into his cup, then poured in two of the mini cups of cream.

I couldn't help but smile. I'd missed this, missed him.

Sean took a few swallows of coffee and sighed, then dumped in some more sugar and another cream. He stared at me as he stirred. "You look good. Did you have fun this summer?"

"Yeah, Fire Island was great. Beautiful place."

"You make good tips at that restaurant?"

"Excellent."

"Good." He bent his head to take a sip from the brimming cup. "And Tanner? You two still together?"

I bristled but tried not to show it. My leg bobbed under the table. "We're together. We're doing great. You okay with that?"

Sean looked up from his coffee, eyes serious. "I am. I really am. If you're happy and this is what you want, that's good enough for me."

My throat tightened. "It's not just what I want. It's who I am. You're all right with that? With having a gay brother?"

"You're my brother. Period. And I missed the shit out of you this summer. I'm just glad you're back." He fiddled with the silverware, straightening it on the napkin, and then looked at me. "And I'm hoping you can forgive me."

I took a deep breath, knowing I wouldn't be able to squeak out a word if I didn't settle some of the emotions that were stirring inside me. "I'm glad I'm back too. I missed you. Now tell me, what's going on with Laura? Are the kids okay?"

His expression darkened, and he stirred his coffee again. "They're stressed, but I'm doing my best to keep their schedules as normal as possible. Fucking Laura, though. Christ. I don't know how she walked out on them. I mean, it's bad enough she cheated on me, but who the fuck walks out on three little kids?"

The pain in his voice made my heart hurt. "She just left? She doesn't even see them?"

"Nope. She said she was done being a mother and was going to live a little—whatever the fuck that means. She's got this apartment in a high-rise on the far side of town, and I bet you anything she's shacking up with that accountant I caught her fucking."

"Caught her? Literally?"

"They were in our bathroom. Can you fucking believe that? I tiled that damn thing myself. I love that bathroom. Now when I see it, all I think about is his dark head bobbing between her legs with her all splayed out on the countertop."

"Sorry."

Sean shrugged and scratched his head. "It's over. She made her choices. And you know what? I'm glad the kids are with me. She's nuts right now. So what's going on with you? When do classes start? You all moved in?"

"Well, actually, no. Our dorm situation is fucked-up."

Sean's pale brown eyebrows furrowed. "What's up? Did they screw up your room assignment?"

"No. Some dickwad almost burned down the building with a Pop-Tart or something, so they need to do repairs for a week or two, and we've all been herded over to the gym for temporary shelter."

"Oh man, that sucks." Sean leaned back so the waitress could set down a cinnamon bun the size of my head and a muffin bigger than my fist. Sean pulled off a piece of the cinnamon bun and moaned as he popped it into his mouth. "You should come stay with us."

I was sure I'd heard him wrong. "What do you mean?"

"I mean live with me and the kids until your room's ready. We've got space, and frankly I could use the help. It's killing me doing all the Mommy-and-Daddy stuff by myself."

My chest felt heavy as I tried to figure out how to ask my questions. "I can't leave Tanner alone in the gym."

"Bring him." Sean pulled off another strip of cinnamon bun.

"You want us both? You'd be okay with that?"

Sean took a deep breath and raked a hand through his sandy hair, making it look even more disheveled. When his eyes settled on mine, they were serious, tinged with sadness. "I owe you a major apology. When Mom kicked you out of the family, that didn't come from me. That wasn't how I felt at all. I need you to know that."

"Okay." I fidgeted with the doily under the muffin.

"And I'm sorry I tried to make peace between you and her and Quinn. They were both so upset. All I could think about was trying to calm the situation down. I should have known better. And more than that, I should have stuck by you, listened to what you wanted."

"I understand. You were in a rough spot. You see them a lot more than I do. Hell, I might have done the same thing if the situation was reversed."

"You're letting me off the hook way too easy."

I smiled. "You're my brother."

"I really am sorry, Collie."

"I know. Thanks." My heart tapped out a Latin rhythm against my ribs, pulsing and throbbing in what couldn't be a healthy beat. "You're sure you're okay with it now?"

"I'll be honest. When I first heard you were gay, I was upset. And I think it was mainly selfish. I wanted you to meet a girl and have kids and have your kids play with my kids or some shit like that."

"I can still have kids, you know. Adopted or biologically mine."

Sean nodded. "I know. I was being old-fashioned and judgmental. Then, when Laura pulled all her crap this summer, I started thinking about how fucked-up everything was with my marriage, with the way Mom and Quinn were handling it—pushing me to get back with her when she's the one who cheated—and I felt so cut off. Then I realized that's what we did to you, and I felt like such a fuckup."

Sympathy washed over me. Sean looked so sad, so full of contrition.

"Are you and Tanner happy together?"

"Very."

Sean nodded. "That's good enough for me. That's all I want, Collie, for the people I care about to be happy. And Tanner's a good guy. I've only talked to him a few times, but I can see why you like him. I'm glad you found each other."

"Thanks. That means a lot." It really did. I didn't realize how starved for approval I was until I had some. It settled something deep inside me that had been in a state of unrest for months, like a knot of tension melting away.

"So you'll come stay at the house?"

"You *positive* it's okay?"

"It's my house. And the kids will be ecstatic. They've missed you so much. Plus the girls adore Tanner. Fucking charmer."

I laughed. "He's got a way with women of all ages. Even Mom, before she found out we were a couple."

Sean laughed too. "Yeah, I remember her singing his praises once upon a time."

"You know, having us move in with you isn't gonna make her come around to your side. Or Quinn. I don't want to cause you more trouble."

"Don't care. You two can move your stuff in whenever you want. It'll be good to have other grown-ups to talk to. There's only so many Barbie conversations I can have before I start doubting my sanity."

"That's too bad. I was just about to bring up Barbie."

"Dick."

"Ass."

"Collin?"

"Yeah?" I broke off a piece of muffin, realizing just how hungry I was.

"Have I mentioned how happy I am that you're home?"

"Me too. Let's get that waitress over here so we can order the rest of our food. I'm starving."

Chapter Three

Eric dropped his backpack on the chair next to me and set his tray next to Tanner's. "You guys are lucky as shit. I can't believe you only had to spend one night at the fucking gym."

Tanner smiled. "You won't hear me complaining."

Tim grumbled. "You two definitely lucked out. I'm sleeping with four other guys on the floor at Alpha Phi."

Tanner shot me a look, and I could tell he was thinking of cracking a joke. I bit my tongue to keep from laughing.

Wendy walked past us carrying her tray of food, and sat at a table alone.

"Jesus," Tim said. "That was cold. What the fuck happened at that house this summer?"

"Nothing reality TV-worthy," I said, hoping to change the topic.

Tim chuckled, eyeing Tanner. "I bet you did something. What'd you do? Hook up with one too many hotties at that club you worked at? Looks like a jealous kind of pissed off to me."

"Not exactly." Tanner glanced over at Wendy, who was still ignoring us even though I know she saw us when she walked by. His gaze shifted to Eric, then to me.

Oh God. Is he going to tell Tim? Here? Now? I shoved a forkful of food in my mouth but missed and banged a tine into my teeth. "Fuck."

Tim raised his eyebrow at me. "Easy there, Tiger, eat the food, not the silverware. Come on, Tanner, spill it. What's got Wendy's panties in a bunch?"

"Like I told you, she's working shit out with her boyfriend. Not spending time with me is just part of that... process."

"Chicks." Tim shook his head.

Eric remained silent. I knew Tanner had said he wouldn't say anything, but if things like this kept coming up, he was bound to slip. He met my eyes, and I silently pleaded with him. Having Wendy give us the cold shoulder was enough to deal with, I didn't want to add Tim to the list of people I felt weird around. Not when he was going to be living right across the hall from us all year—assuming they actually got our building fixed—and certainly not when he had one of the biggest mouths of anyone on campus.

Eric chugged his milk, then stood up. "I'm late. I've gotta stop at the bookstore before class."

Tanner got up too, grabbing the apple off his tray and shoving it into his backpack. "I'll walk with you. My shift starts soon."

I knew he wasn't on for over an hour. And I knew he'd have gone up for another tray of food under normal circumstances. He must have wanted to talk to Eric some more, which probably meant he was still worried about him spilling. *Fuck.*

When Tim left, I took my time bussing my tray. Wendy was still sitting alone, flipping through a book. Not a textbook, a paperback. A romance novel judging by the cover—shirtless guy, ripped, hairless chest, jeans unbuttoned. I slipped into the seat next to her, and she threw me a dirty look, then shoved her nose back into her book.

I took a deep breath. "I never had a chance to apologize to you."

"Save it. I'm not interested."

"Well, you should be. If you want the truth, I thought we should have told you about Maggie right away, but Tanner didn't think it was a good idea."

"I'm thrilled. Thanks so much for supporting him in his plan to deceive me and have me made a fool of in my own house."

"You're not listening to me. He had good reasons for not wanting to tell you. For one thing, we weren't sure what was up between Dex and Maggie. We didn't want to tell you they were fucking if all they did was kiss a few times, and that's all we saw them do."

Wendy's mouth pinched, and she turned her attention to her salad, staring at it like she needed to study each piece before she took a bite. I kept talking.

"Tanner was also really afraid you'd get mad at him. He said that happened once before and he hated it when you stopped talking to him. This time he did the opposite and didn't tell you, and guess what—you stopped talking to him again, so he had a lose-lose situation. Either way he knew you'd be mad at him."

"I don't care. You all knew, and no one had the decency to give me a heads-up. I'd have done that, for any one of you. You hurt me."

"I'm sorry. I'm sorry for anything I did that hurt you. But please, know that we just wanted to look out for you. And please, Wendy, you really have to know how much Tanner misses you. We both do. We're worried about you."

"Worried?" Her brow crinkled, but she finally turned toward me. "Worried about what?"

"We don't want to see Dex break your heart."

"Then you'd better look away. It's just a matter of time."

I sighed and started tearing a napkin into strips. "If you believe that, then why do you stay with him?"

"Stubbornness? Bad judgment. If I was smart, I never would have let Tanner go."

Wait, what? My hands went cold. "You think you and Tanner would have gotten serious?" I didn't think that had been what either of them wanted.

"I don't know. Maybe. I know he'd never treat me like Dex does, that's for sure. And I love him. I've loved him since I first met him."

My heart felt like it was beating in mud. *Glub-glub-glub.* "You mean as a friend, right?"

She shook her head, her light eyes glazed with sadness. "No, I mean I've been in love with him since we were kids."

Shit. "Does he know that?"

She shrugged. "Not sure. I never told him. I figured keeping things casual was the best way to keep our friendship, but I always thought... I don't know, maybe someday he'd have this big awakening and realize I was the perfect woman for him."

I tried to remember how to breathe. *Does Tanner know any of this? Would it make a difference if he did?*

She sighed and stared at the book balanced across her leg. "That's why I read these novels. Everything always works out in the end in the books. It's comforting. Gives me hope."

"You'll meet someone better than Dex. Better for you. Better to you. And Dex'll spend the rest of his life regretting what an ass he was to you."

"You make it really hard to stay mad at you when you say nice shit like that."

I smiled. "Oh yeah?"

She scowled. "Yeah. But I'm still mad."

"Fair enough."

Wendy shoved her book into her backpack, then stood. "I'm late for a meeting with my advisor."

"See you around."

She took two steps, then turned around, gnawing at her lip before she spoke. "I heard about your dorm. I hope they let you move in soon."

I knew that was her way of saying she hoped we were okay. It wasn't much, but it was a start. "Thanks."

She wove through the crowd, and I watched until I couldn't see her anymore. *She was in love with Tanner? Was? Or is?* I wasn't sure I wanted an answer. What I was sure of was that it didn't matter, at least not at the moment. For now, she was still pissed off. I hated myself for thinking maybe that was for the best.

Chapter Four

Breakfast with Sean and the kids had become part of the routine. I made breakfast, Tanner set the table, and Sean got the girls ready for school. It reminded me of mornings on Fire Island—only with a lot more hair ribbons and shoe tying and significantly fewer hungover people.

Sean paced around, phone at his ear. He looked tired and stressed. "I'll see what I can do. I'll call you back later."

"What's wrong?" I flipped the last pieces of french toast on the griddle.

Sean shoved his phone into his pocket and started dropping granola bars into the girls' lunch bags. "My lawyer wants me to come by this afternoon to sign some papers, but he can't meet until after three, and the kids will be out of school by then."

"Sorry. I work until the dinner shift today. Otherwise I'd help you out."

Tanner shook a carton of orange juice. "I don't have classes today, and my shift at the bookstore got moved to tomorrow. I can watch them."

I almost dropped the piece of french toast I was shoveling onto a plate.

Sean raised an eyebrow. "You do realize there are three of them, right?"

"Three of them?" Tanner pointed to each of the kids, mouthing the numbers as he counted. "Oh my God, you're right. There are three of them."

The girls giggled like that was the funniest thing they'd ever heard, which made the baby giggle too.

Even Sean cracked a smile. "I just mean they can be a handful."

"We're not a handful, Daddy," Megan said.

Emma nodded. "We'll be good for Tanner, Daddy. We promise."

I snickered. I must have heard Sean use that line on our parents a hundred times when we were little. "How can you argue with that?"

Sean looked from me to Tanner. "You sure you want to?"

"Positive. I like kids. Especially yours." Tanner winked at the girls, and they beamed back at him.

I could have kissed him. My nieces and nephew were good kids, but Sean was right, they were a handful sometimes. I couldn't believe Tanner was volunteering to babysit—like our lives weren't a big enough mess commuting to school and working. I wouldn't have blamed him if he'd gone to live at one of the frat houses or sucked up to Wendy until she let him crash at her place. Instead he was crammed into my brother's small house, changing Pull-Ups and agreeing to be at the beck and call of three little kids, by himself, just to help my brother.

God, I fucking love him. The urge to grab him and at least hug him nearly overwhelmed me, but I knew I was already late for class. "I'll be home by five, so I can help you out then."

"No worries." Tanner took a seat next to Emma and filled her glass with milk. "We'll be fine."

Sean zipped up all three backpacks. "Call my cell if you have any questions."

"Will do."

"Thanks, man, you're a godsend."

"Something like that."

Tanner grinned at me, sending warmth washing over me from head to toe. *Eat your breakfast before you do something stupid like tackle him.*

"I'll drop them off here around two," Sean said.

Tanner nodded. He'd already started folding Megan's napkin into a flower for her. Giggling resumed before Sean and I even made it to the table.

When breakfast was over, I followed Sean outside with the girls. I put Melissa in her car seat while he strapped in the baby.

"Hands out of the way." Sean slammed the minivan door shut, then turned to me. "He sure has a way with kids."

"Tanner? Yeah. They love him."

Sean paused, rubbing the car door handle, then looking up at me. "You love him too. I can see it."

"Sean, we don't have to talk about me and Tanner as a couple. I know you're not completely comfortable with it."

"That's the thing. I am. Jesus. I mean, I thought it would be awkward, and I planned to just push through it, but it's not. You guys, I don't know. It's like you belong together. You... fit."

"Thanks." I couldn't imagine a nicer thing for him to have said.

"I'm thankful you both decided to come stay here. And I'm glad I'm getting to know him."

Except that. "I'm glad too. So is Tanner."

"Good. See? Maybe Quinn's right about one thing."

I raised an eyebrow. "What's that?"

"He always says things happen for a reason, but sometimes we're just not ready to see the reason right away."

"So you think that dude set his Pop-Tart on fire so you and I could reconnect?"

"Okay, so maybe not that. Still. Something brought us back together."

I nodded. "Good luck with the lawyer. We'll take care of the kids and get dinner ready."

"You guys are better as wives than Laura."

"I won't tell her you said that."

"Tell her whatever you want. It's too late for anything to make an impact on her."

Chapter Five

BETWEEN CLASSES, my work at Gino's, Tanner's shifts at the bookstore, and commuting back and forth to Sean's house, Tanner and I were busier than we'd ever been. I always knew it was more convenient to live on campus, but I had no idea what a hassle it was to make the added drive daily. By the time we got to Sean's, had dinner, spent time with the kids, and did some studying, we were exhausted.

I hadn't touched Tanner for yet another week, and I didn't think I'd last the day without changing that. Tanner must have felt the same. I'd seen the looks he'd been throwing me, particularly the night before while we were watching a movie together, but I wasn't about to do anything with Sean and the kids in the house. I didn't care that the doors locked. It didn't feel right. And I didn't trust either of us to be quiet enough. Especially since it had been so long.

Sean handed me the last dirty dish to load into the dishwasher while Tanner put the juice and milk in the fridge.

"I'm gonna run to the grocery store while the kids are at preschool. Any requests?" Sean asked, grabbing his wallet off the counter and shoving it in his pocket.

"If you get a can of crushed tomatoes and some spaghetti, I'll cook."

"Thanks. The kids loved that the other night. Anything else?"

I tried to think but couldn't. All that registered in my brain was that Sean was going out. Tanner and I would be alone in the house. My cock was totally onboard with this thought and already looking for an escape plan from my pants.

"I think that'll do it. Tanner, you need anything?"

Tanner looked up from wiping off the kitchen tables. His pupils were huge. I knew that look. I *loved* that look. He was thinking the same thing I was. My cock twitched in anticipation.

"I'm good," Tanner said, tossing the rag on the counter.

"Okay, then." Sean headed for the door. "It's my turn to drive carpool home, so I'll probably take the kids to Mickey D's for happy meals. Lock up if you both leave, okay?"

"Sure." My heart raced as I watched Sean trot down the back porch steps. I held my breath, listening as the car door slammed, the engine revved, and the tires crunched down the gravel driveway.

I turned to look at Tanner, but before I could even focus my eyes, he was on me. Hands on either side of my face, body pressed up against mine, lips prying mine open, tongue—oh, God, I'd missed that tongue—swirling in circles with mine.

Groaning, I grabbed his ass and tugged him closer. I needed to feel as much of him as possible. All of him. Immediately, if not sooner.

We banged into the kitchen wall, rattling the pots that hung on the metal rack by the stove. Tanner humped against me with firm, deliberate thrusts, his cock stroking mine through the thick layers of our jeans. A pan bounced loose from its hook and clattered to the floor, making us both jump, then laugh.

Tanner pulled back, hands still planted in my hair. "Maybe this isn't the best room."

"Probably not."

I tugged him through the doorway, intending to head upstairs, but the couch was right there, so big and inviting and so close. My leg bumped into it, and that momentary pause was enough for Tanner to take the opportunity and plant his mouth on mine again.

His tongue wrapped around mine as his hand slipped under my shirt, up my back, his fingers kneading and caressing. I wanted more. I opened my eyes, sneaking a glance at the stairs. They seemed so far away, and Tanner was right there, warm and ready. I couldn't wait. I tugged him down onto the couch and sprawled atop him.

So good.

Having him under me, his cock hard alongside mine, his hands hot and strong, stroking my back, was heaven. I whimpered, bucking my hips against his, wishing like hell our jeans would disappear like magic. Like stripper pants. I'd rip them away and fling them over the couch, and then we could be naked together and—

The woman's scream scared the shit out of me.

Tanner and I fell apart, me onto the floor, him scrambling upright on the sofa. Laura stood in the doorway to the house, not ten feet away from us, house key still clutched in her hand, mouth and eyes wide and round like dark Os.

"What the hell is going on here?" she said, inching along the wall, still staring.

I straightened my clothes, silently thanking God that I was still wearing them. "Nothing. We were just—"

Her head shook as if she was about to have a seizure. "Get out of my house."

Tanner held up his hand. "Laura, we're sorry we startled you. We were alone in the house. We didn't know you were coming by."

Her eyes somehow widened. "You didn't know I was coming by? I live here. My children live here. And you two... what is wrong with you?"

My stomach turned. She sounded like my mother. "Nothing is wrong with us. Tanner and I have been together as a couple for months."

She gasped. Actually fucking *gasped* like I'd just said I was a murderer. "Oh my God. That's why your mother's not talking to you anymore."

I nodded. "That's her choice."

"Choice?" Her voice raised an octave. "Choice? How else did you expect her to react? I mean, Jesus, Collin. Are you telling me Sean knows about this?"

Tanner stood, moving slowly as if he didn't want to spook her more. "There was a fire in our dorm. Sean's been letting us stay here the past few weeks. He's been—"

"Stay here? You're staying in this house? With my kids? Oh, no. Fucking hell, no. Over my dead body."

The anger in her voice chilled me to the bone. "Laura, we've been helping him around the house. We're not doing anything wrong."

"Are you kidding me? It's... you're... the whole thing is...." Her mouth worked as she struggled for a word.

Tanner shot me a pained look, then glanced at Laura. "I think if we sit down and calm down, maybe—"

Laura glared at him. "You can calm down all you want, but not in my house. I want both of you out. Now. The thought that you two have been around my children makes me sick."

My hands went cold and started to shake. "Laura, we'd never do anything in front of your kids."

"I don't trust perverts."

Tanner flinched. "We're not perverts."

"I just saw you two on top of each other. You're disgusting. It's immoral. For Christ's sake, Collin. You know better. You weren't raised to act like this."

I snorted. "You're going to lecture me on Catholicism? I seem to remember you needing to marry my brother when you were sixteen because you were pregnant. What part of being a good Catholic were you practicing when that happened?"

Her gaze turned steely. "I made a mistake, but we did the right thing. We got married. We had the baby. Don't you dare compare what we did to what I just walked in on."

"Why not? We're in love, just like you and Sean used to be. Or can you not remember that long ago?"

She shook her head. "I'm gonna throw up. You literally make me sick. Take your things and your freak of a friend and get out."

Tanner looked like he'd been slapped.

My body felt numb, but my mind raced. "What are you even doing here? Sean said you haven't been home in over a month."

Her shoulders squared. "That's none of your business."

"No, it's probably not, but Sean is my brother. And your kids are my nieces. And they all seemed to think you were gone."

"I'm here to get my things from my house. And I don't need to explain myself any more to someone like you." She pushed past me and stormed up the stairs.

Tanner's gaze met mine. "I'm so sorry."

"Sorry for what?"

He raked his hands through his hair, but that didn't hide the fact they were shaking. "I shouldn't have. Not here."

I'd never seen him so shaken, and it scared me. I stepped closer and cupped the back of his neck with my hand. "We. Not you. We."

He nodded, then footsteps sounded at the top of staircase, and he pulled away from me, hands shoved deep into his pants pockets. Laura continued with whatever the hell she was doing upstairs—banging drawers and slamming closet doors—for what felt like an eternity. Tanner must have cracked his knuckles two dozen times before she finally stomped down the stairs.

Laura had a suitcase in one hand and a shopping bag in the other. "Since you're still here, you can deliver a message to your brother. Tell him he'll be hearing from my lawyer."

She headed straight for the door and walked out without another word.

Shit.

Chapter Six

I TEXTED Sean immediately, but I got no reply. He'd probably already picked up the kids, and he rarely checked his phone when he was busy with them.

Tanner paced around the family room, looking more rattled than I'd ever seen him. "What are we going to do?"

I didn't have an answer. "What do you think she meant by Sean will be hearing from her lawyer?"

"I don't know, but I doubt it's good." He traced his fingers over one of the ceramic bowls the girls had made at school. "Is this what it felt like? For you? When your mom disowned you?"

I shrugged. "Not exactly."

"No one's ever talked to me like that." His voice was different. A cross between sadness and disbelief.

"I'm sorry. She's… that's the way a lot of people here think. It's why I was so scared to come out to anyone."

"I get it now. Fuck. I mean, I thought it was hard when I came out to my parents, but that was nothing. That was like a goddamned Hallmark moment compared to this shit."

I smiled. "You think they make a card for this?"

Tanner flopped onto the couch. "Maybe. 'Sorry your son's gay, but at least now you don't have to worry about him knocking someone up!'"

I sat next to him, needing to be as close to him as possible even though I knew touching wouldn't be a good idea. Sean and the kids could be home any time now, and the last thing I wanted was to make things worse. "God, this sucks."

Tanner reached for my hand, but before he made contact, a car pulled in to the driveway. He peered around the curtain. "It's Sean."

"Let's go help with the groceries."

My heart pounded as we walked toward the car. The kids were skipping around on the grass, and Sean was leaning into the back of the minivan, loading supermarket bags onto his arm. The second we made eye contact, I knew he knew.

"We'll talk about it later," he said in a tone that turned my stomach to stone. "Come on, girls, take your brother and go in the house."

Tanner came up beside him. "I'll take the food inside and keep an eye on the kids. You two can talk now."

Sean handed over the bags, and I watched as Tanner held the door and ushered everyone inside.

"I take it you heard from Laura?"

"What the hell happened?" He sounded angry and confused.

My cheeks heated. "Tanner and I haven't laid a finger on each other the whole time we've been here, but there was no one else home. We were just kissing. I'm sorry."

Sean slammed the minivan door, then rested against it, massaging the back of his neck. "She was hysterical when she called. To hear her describe it, she walked in on a goddamned porn shoot or something."

"It wasn't like that." I shook my head, not believing this was even happening. "Sean, I'm sorry."

He closed his eyes. "Don't apologize. It's not your fault. I understand. But she's not letting it go."

"What do you mean?"

He stared at the gravel, then slowly looked up at me. "She's having her lawyer file papers. She's suing me for full custody on the grounds that I endangered the kids by letting you and Tanner live here."

The words stung as they sank in. "I never, we never—"

"Collin, don't. I know. You and Tanner are great with the kids. Having you here has been a blessing, not a problem. But I can't lose them."

I hadn't seen tears in Sean's eyes in years, but they were there now. I'd put them there. "We'll move out. Right away."

"I wish I could argue with you. I don't want you to go."

I held up a hand. "I know. But the kids come first. It's not your fault. You've been great letting us stay here. It never even occurred to me we'd cause a problem for you."

"Me neither." He rubbed his forehead. "Where will you go? You haven't heard from the housing department yet, have you?"

"There was an e-mail update that said maybe by Monday it would be ready."

"Shit. Do you have some place to stay for the weekend? I don't want to toss you guys out on the street."

"Don't worry about it. Seriously, man, we'll be fine."

He nodded. "I better go check on the kids."

"Tell Tanner I'll be there in a minute. I'll make some calls."

Chapter Seven

TANNER WAS going to be pissed at me. That much I knew for sure. But it didn't stop me from calling Wendy.

"What do you want?" she said.

I was too relieved that she'd answered her phone to let the snotty tone in her voice bother me. "I need to ask a favor."

"Are you fucking kidding me? You've got a lot of nerve, Collin Fitzpatrick."

"We've got nowhere to live."

"What?"

"Our dorm's still not ready. We were staying at my brother's place, but his wife doesn't want her kids exposed to 'people like us,' so we have to leave. Tonight."

"She actually said that? People like you?" Wendy's voice had softened.

"She had a much more colorful way of phrasing it, but that's the gist of it."

"Oh. That sucks." She paused, and I could imagine her arguing with herself over how nice to be about it. "What does this have to do with me?"

"I don't know if we can even go back to the gym. I think we forfeited our spot when we left. Can we crash at your place? Just for a few nights. They're supposed to have our building ready by Monday."

She sighed so loud, her breath whistled through the phone.

Please, Wendy, come on.

"I shouldn't say yes. I'm still mad at both of you."

"Shouldn't? Does that mean you're saying yes anyway?"

Please-please-please.

This time she blew directly into the phone. "Fine. But only because I won't be here. I'm heading to Dex's in a few hours—keep your comments to yourself, thank you very much. I can leave a key for you at the front desk."

"Thank you. Seriously, you have no idea how much I appreciate this."

"Yeah, well, be glad I was already going out of town, or I might have said no. And be nice to my roommate. I'll tell her you guys are desperate. She's got friends staying over all the time, so she shouldn't mind."

"Thanks."

"How come you're calling instead of Tanner?" I could tell she was trying to sound nonchalant, but disappointment leaked into her voice.

"It's my family that's kicking us out, so I wanted to be the one to find us a new place." Mostly true. Tanner wouldn't have called her, though. He'd have slept in a cardboard box in an alley first.

"Oh. Okay. Look, I have to go. Tell the guard I left an envelope for you. And don't let Tanner eat all my microwave popcorn."

"I won't. I owe you one."

"You owe me more than one."

I chuckled. "Have a safe trip."

Now all I had to do was convince Tanner it was a good idea to stay at her place.

Chapter Eight

SAYING GOOD-BYE to Sean and the kids was one of the hardest things I've ever done. Not just because they were sad and I didn't want to leave, but because I wasn't sure when I was going to see them again. None of us had any clue how serious Laura was about the lawsuit or what the ramifications would be if we had continued contact with Sean and the kids.

"Don't worry, we'll see you soon," I told them as we hugged them good-bye, knowing very well that could be less than true.

As I was getting in the car, Sean stopped me. "It's not your fault," he said.

I didn't know what to say. It might not have been my fault, but there was no questioning that what was happening was due to me. My actions. My decision to be with Tanner. Didn't that make it at least somewhat my fault? It felt like it did. And that didn't feel good.

"Stay in touch." I gripped the car door to keep my hand from shaking.

Sean pulled me into a hug. "I'll keep you posted. Take care of yourself."

Tanner and I drove away in silence. As we neared campus, he finally spoke. "Where exactly are we going, anyway?"

All I'd told him was that I had a place for us to stay. "Wendy's apartment."

"What?" Tanner's eyes bugged.

"Before you say anything, yes, she's okay with it, no, she won't be there, and I'm sorry, but we didn't have a whole lot of options."

Tanner cracked his knuckles, a new habit I'd noticed since we got back from Fire Island. "Let me guess, she's visiting Dex for the weekend."

"Yep."

He shook his head.

I pulled in to the parking lot behind her building. "We'll make the best of it. Hopefully our room will be ready by Monday like they said."

"I almost wish Wendy was around this weekend. This whole not talking to each other thing is getting old."

I knew he missed her. "She agreed to let us stay here. That's gotta be a step in the right direction."

"Maybe. I still wish she'd wise up and get Dex out of her life before he hurts her again."

I didn't feel particularly qualified to talk about people who hurt other people, considering I'd just gotten my brother into a custody battle. We took a minimal amount of stuff out of the car and headed into the building.

The guy working the front desk had been in my Social Welfare Policy class the semester before. He found the envelope with Wendy's key in it and signed us into the building. "I'll register you as guests for the weekend so you can come and go no matter who's working the desk. Just tell them you're on the list."

"Thanks, man."

I'd been in the Towers before, but hadn't seen Wendy's room. The elevator quickly brought us to the eighth floor. Most of the campus-owned buildings were ancient, but this one was only two years old, built by a grant from some wealthy alumnus. The hallway still smelled like new carpeting, and it looked more like a hotel than university housing.

"Here goes nothing." Tanner knocked on the door.

Giggles sounded on the other side along with some fumbling. When it finally swung open, we were greeted by a tall thin girl with super-curly long black hair, wearing pajama pants and a white tank top with no bra. "You must be Wendy's friends Tyler and Conner?"

Tanner's lip twitched, and I could tell he was trying not to laugh. He gave her one of his killer smiles instead. "Close. I'm Tanner, he's Collin."

"Oh, well, nice to meet you. Come on in. This is my friend Laney."

A petite red-haired girl waved from atop a pink bedspread.

"Oh, and I'm Sarah, by the way. Ignore the mess—we were trying clothes on for tonight. We're having some friends over for Jell-O shots and Truth or Dare. You should come."

"Thanks." I took a quick look around the room. I'd thought the Fire Island house got girly with Wendy, Maggie, and Susan. That was nothing. Sarah's side of the room looked like cotton candy had exploded all over it. Everything was pink, from the trash can to the pictures on the wall to the furry pillows all over her bed.

Laney stopped painting her nails long enough to look Tanner up and down. "You guys can bring your girlfriends."

My cheeks flushed, but Tanner pulled off another killer grin. "We don't have girlfriends."

Laney beamed at him. "Then you both should definitely come."

"We'll try," he said.

For the life of me, I couldn't tell if he meant it or not. After almost two weeks of Sesame Street and then the blowout with my toxic sister-in-law, maybe he wanted a night of Jell-O shots and giggling girls.

We put our duffel bags on Wendy's bed. Wendy's *very narrow* bed. Sarah must have read my mind. "Wendy's got a sleeping bag in the closet.

I'm sure one of you could use that. Unless you make a friend tonight at the party."

More giggles filled the room.

My head ached, and a deep breath filled with nail polish fumes wasn't helping.

I nudged Tanner. "You want to grab some food and head to the library? I've got a paper due Monday."

"Me too. We'll catch you ladies later."

Laney looked disappointed as she watched Tanner walk toward the door.

"We'll be here," Sarah called as she closed the door behind us.

"That's what I'm afraid of." Tanner whispered the words into my ear as we walked down the hall.

I laughed, partly because I felt the same way and partly because I was relieved. He seemed as ready to get out of that room as I was. Thank God.

Chapter Nine

It took me four hours to finish writing my paper, probably in part because I kept stopping to check my phone. I'd been hoping for an update from Sean even though I knew that wasn't likely. It was the weekend, and any more info from his lawyer probably wouldn't arrive until Monday. I also kept thinking maybe we'd hear something from Housing, but so far, silence.

After I'd saved my document, I went in search of Tanner. He'd finished his work an hour earlier and said he'd be reading in one of the lounges. I found him in one of the alcoves, sprawled on a big couch under one of the heavily leaded windows. An open book lay tented on his chest—Dostoevsky's short stories. His eyes were closed, those thick black lashes casting shadows on his cheekbones.

I approached slowly, wanting the time to keep looking. Tanner hadn't had a haircut in weeks. Silky dark bangs fell across his forehead, begging for my fingers to sweep them off his face. Perfect lips, ever so slightly parted, looking desperately in need of a kiss. My gaze passed lower, taking in his long strong fingers as they rested on the book, his narrow waist, slim hips. I struggled to swallow. My cock enjoyed the show with me, not so silently encouraging me to climb on top of Tanner, toss that book aside, grind against him....

Tanner's eyelids fluttered open, and he shook his head, craning his neck to look around. He yawned and stretched as he sat up. "What time is it?"

"Little after ten." I sat next to him, needing to be close to him. He smelled warm and sweet. I breathed in, taking in as much of his scent as possible. God, I missed that. Sleeping apart for two weeks had me waking in the middle of the night craving him—his touch, his smell, his taste—all of him.

My thigh knocked into his, and he pressed back against me. "You wanna get out of here?"

I nodded, wanting to be anywhere as long as he was there too.

A light rain had started to fall, so we half jogged to the Towers.

"What do you suppose is going on in Wendy's room?" I asked as we rode the elevator.

Tanner brushed rain droplets off his backpack. The elevator dinged and opened. "Guess we're about to find out."

Wendy's door was open. Music and voices filled the hallway, and as we approached the room, a purple bra came flying out, followed by the sound of drunken laughter and cheering.

Tanner caught the elevator door just before it closed. "What do you say we go for a drive instead?"

"I say that's the best offer I've had in weeks."

Chapter Ten

Rain was coming down in sheets so fast, I could barely see two feet in front of the car.

Tanner fidgeted in the passenger seat. "I don't mean to be a pain in the ass, and I learned my lesson about taking off my seat belt in a moving car, but I swear to God, if you don't pull over soon, I'm gonna die."

"From what?"

"ACD. Acute Collin Deficiency."

I laughed, trying to keep my eyes on the road even though I wanted nothing more than to look at him. My fingers ached to touch him, but I forced myself to grip the steering wheel instead.

"It's not funny. I'm serious." His voice was deep and lusty.

Pull over, my cock weighed in urgently. *Here. Over there. Anywhere. Pull the fuck over!*

"Hang on, I know a place."

"Thank God."

Tanner shifted in his seat, and it took every ounce of self-control I could muster not to reach over and see if he was as hard as I was.

I slowed to make sure I didn't miss the turnoff in the rainy darkness.

"Where are we going?"

In the distance I saw what I was looking for. An unpaved road cut through a small patch of woods and led to an abandoned barn on acres of land that had been for sale for as long as I could remember.

"There."

The car bumped on the uneven pavement. As soon as we neared the barn, I cut the lights and pulled behind the old wooden building.

Tanner leaned closer to the window. "Call me a city kid, but that's one spooky-looking barn."

Laughter snorted out of me. "Very spooky. And very private. No one drives down this road even when there's no monsoon."

I put the car in park and turned it off.

"No one, huh?" Tanner's voice was even lower, thick and seductive.

My cock pulsed in reply.

Tanner's seat belt clicked as he released it. Before I could reach for mine, his hand was on it. The belt slithered up across my chest, followed by

Tanner's fingers. I groaned, shivering with need and wanting to savor every second of his touch.

He cupped my neck, leaning closer. "You're sure?"

He didn't say it, but I knew he was thinking about Laura barging in on us. I hated that we had to be so hesitant, so cautious. Nodding, I pointed out the front window. "Even if someone was coming, we'd see the headlights way before they got—"

Tanner interrupted with a kiss that stopped my sentence and my brain. His lips pressed against mine, irresistibly warm in the cold, damp night air. I shifted closer, feeling his fingers tighten on my neck as our tongues touched. So sweet. He tasted so fucking sweet. I nipped at his lower lip, breathing him in as he moaned.

"Jesus, I miss this."

My hand couldn't move fast enough as I reached for him, grabbing his shirt and tugging him closer, then sliding my fingers down the ridges of his abs, inching lower, passing from thin T-shirt to thick denim. Heat radiated through the fabric as I stroked his erection, pressing against him with the heel of my hand and feeling him throb in response. I fumbled to undo his fly.

Smooth metal button. Jagged zipper. Cottony boxer briefs. Each texture left me aching more for what I really wanted. *Finally.* The hot silky feel of him sliding into my waiting hand had me squirming in my seat.

"Fuck," Tanner groaned as I freed him from his clothes, shoving his pants lower, stroking him as slowly as I could make myself go.

I slicked my thumb across his swollen tip, vaguely aware that the windows in the car were already steaming up around us.

Tanner's head fell back against the seat as his hips lifted to thrust harder into my hand. "Christ, that feels fucking amazing."

"Good." I leaned forward, kissing his neck, his chest. "Because I believe I owe you a cargasm."

Tanner's laughter vibrated through me. His fingers wove into my hair, and he tilted my head so I had no choice but to stare into his eyes. Not that I minded. I was happy to gaze at him all night, especially when he looked like this, hair disheveled, face flushed from need, pupils so huge and dark I could get lost in them. His desire was palpable, and what he wanted was me.

I kissed him hard and fast, maintaining my grip on his cock but not stroking at all. He twitched in my hand, impatient and demanding. I wasn't about to keep him waiting any longer. Pulling away from the warmth of his mouth, I lowered my head, swept the bead of precome off his swollen crown, and eased him between my lips.

Tanner hissed, tightening his grip on my hair, then massaging my neck as I slowly teased him. Short licks swirling around his head, first one way, then the other, then up and down over the sensitive seam. He whimpered, raising his hips off the seat, but I pushed him down, anchoring him with a firm hand to his chest. His heart pounded beneath my fingertips, the booming audible even with the rain drumming onto the car.

Knowing he was that excited pushed me to the brink of control. My cock had worked its way up to my waistband, leaving damp streaks on my belly each time my head bobbed in Tanner's lap. I sucked him deeper, reveling in his taste, clean, slightly salty, all Tanner. I missed this so much.

His breathing grew more ragged with each pull of my mouth. I was lost in thoughts of making him come, feeling him fill me, but insistent hands tugged me upward, bringing my mouth to his.

I considered protesting, but with his tongue wrapped around mine and his hand freeing my erection, I couldn't say anything more complex than a muffled "Good."

Tanner's lips pulled into a smile against mine as his fingers shoved my pants open and wrapped around my length. He stroked with reverence, up to the tip, flipping his hand over, then sliding down to the base, flipping over, then back again, like sliding into an endless tunnel of his warmth. I panted, not wanting him to stop but longing to have him back in my mouth. Kisses distracted me, and I was caught up in wave after wave of pleasure as his tongue spiraled mine. My heart raced, my head swam. I didn't want it to stop—ever.

Tanner pulled away, breathless, and I let out an exasperated grunt as the cool air rushed between us. Then I saw his lopsided grin. "Show me the Batemobile in action."

Heat filled my cheeks. *Seriously? That's what he wants?*

My cock weighed in quickly—*Give the man what he wants! Show him. Now!*

Out of habit, I threw a nervous glance over my shoulder, then checked the sideview mirror. Nothing but rain and darkness, and Tanner's hungry stare. His seat creaked as he turned to face me, his head resting on the seat back, his fingers lightly stroking the underside of his cock. *Jesus.*

I wrapped my hand around my erection and sighed, from the feel, from the sight of Tanner, from the memory of how many times I'd done this alone, from all the times I'd wished for him, from—everything. Lifting my hips, I shoved my jeans farther down my legs. The waistband of my boxers hugged my balls, caressing them as I stroked. Tanner matched my pace, up and down, up and down, swivel over the head, up and down. Fuck, I loved watching him.

The wet, rhythmic sound filled the car, mingling with the drumbeat of rain. My breath puffed out hard and fast, turning the windows opaque with steam. As insanely good as it all felt, I needed more. Switching to my left hand, I reached for Tanner with my right. Stroking us both at the same time was nearly enough to push me over the edge. Then he leaned forward and kissed me. I moaned into his mouth, and his hand covered mine. Two hands were more than my cock could manage. My balls drew up so full and tight, they ached. Tingling ran down my thighs and up my torso, concentrating at the base of my cock as my body started to shake. My knee vibrated against the keys that still hung from the steering column, and the jingling added to the chorus of sounds. Tanner's fingers sank into my hair, holding me steady as he worked my mouth with his, my cock thrusting in and out of our hands. With a low growl, my orgasm ripped through me, racing up my length and coating us both. Pleasure seeped over me like warm honey.

Tanner slowed his tongue, allowing me to breathe. My eyes struggled for focus. He slid his hand off me and hit the automatic window. Rain bounced off the doorframe into the car as Tanner stuck his arm out the window letting the downpour rinse him clean. I was about to do the same, but he caught my hand in his, brought it to his lips, and gave my fingers a long, slow lick.

Everything he did was sexy, but something about him licking away the come he'd just stroked out of me drove me wild. I traced my finger around his tongue as he sucked, quite sure I'd never seen anything hotter in my life. I withdrew slowly, reluctantly. Without thinking, I lowered my head. Having him back in my mouth went beyond need or desire. I had to have him. All of him.

Cries of pleasure echoed through the car as I sucked, stroked, cupped, squeezed—no matter what I had to offer, I wanted to give more. I tilted my head to catch a glimpse of his face and found him staring down at me, mouth open, brow furrowed, eyes locked on mine, though it was clear he was struggling to keep them open. I sucked slower, more deliberately, rubbing my tongue in just the right spot, making his eyes slam shut as he growled and came inside me.

I swallowed, hard, continuing to lick and suck until his breathing slowed. I'd have been happy to fall asleep right there, head in his lap, surrounded by the darkness. Tanner massaged my back, running his fingers through my hair, along the side of my face. I sat up enough to kiss his hand, and he pulled me into his arms. Our tongues lazily rolled around each other, sweet and salty. Satisfied.

Tanner rested his forehead against mine. "You think they're having this much fun at that Truth or Dare party?"

I laughed. "Doubtful."

"You think they're done and maybe we can get some sleep? I'm exhausted."

I turned the key in the ignition. According to the clock, it was past midnight. "They started early. They might have passed out by now."

"I'd almost rather sleep here."

"I think we'd regret that in the morning when we can't move our necks."

"True."

I stretched and shifted back to the driver's side, straightening my pants and zipping them up. Tanner did the same. I waited until he had his seat belt on, then flipped on the headlights and let the car roll along the bumpy pavement. Our lives were still a mess—no place to live, Wendy still pissed, my family in a shambles—but I'd never been more thankful, because I had Tanner. As we reached the main road, I stopped.

"What's wrong?" he asked.

"Nothing." I pulled my shoulder strap aside and leaned across to give him one more kiss. "I just love you."

At that moment, nothing else mattered.

Chapter Eleven

THE FIRST thing I saw was pink. Everywhere. Sunlight filled Wendy's apartment and seemed to be reflecting off every pink surface in the room. And there were a fucking million of them.

I squinted and pulled the balled-up sweatshirt I'd used as a pillow over my head.

A high-pitched female groan sounded across the room. "Coffee...." the voice whined. "If either of you guys are willing to walk to the deli and get me a coffee, I'll do anything you want. *Anything.*"

I chuckled, thinking she was definitely using the wrong bargaining chip.

"I'll go."

Tanner sounded way more awake than I expected. I opened my eyes and noticed he was sitting at Wendy's desk, already showered, hair still damp. I was grateful a sleeping bag had my lower half covered, because the morning wood I'd been sporting turned into a damned sequoia at the sight of him.

"Morning, sunshine." He winked at me.

Sarah groaned again, the distinct sound of a hangover. "I think I love you," she murmured. "Light and sweet, please. And a donut if they still have any."

"Sure thing." Tanner tucked his wallet into his pocket. God, I loved that pocket, pulled tight against the curve of his ass. "Want anything?"

The smile he threw me was enough to set my face on fire. "You know what I like."

"I do indeed." His grin widened. "Be back in a few."

The door closed behind him, and the pink covers rustled again. "Where were you guys last night?"

My flush deepened, and I was glad Sarah was still buried under her blankets instead of looking at me. "Library, mostly. Seems like you all had fun back here."

"Too much fun. Well, too much rum is more accurate."

"Sorry."

"I'll live. Maybe. If your friend brings back that coffee fast enough. Tanner, right?"

"Yes."

"He's cute."

I laughed. "So I've been told."

Sarah yawned. "You can use the bathroom, by the way. I'm not leaving this bed until after caffeine."

"Thanks." I stretched and crawled out of the sleeping bag, tugging my clothes into place. My phone was plugged into the charging station on Wendy's desk. I grabbed it, hoping to maybe see a message from Sean. Instead I found a text from the Housing Department.

Your room is now available. You may move in any time after noon on Saturday. Your key will be available with the RA for your floor.

Saturday? Today's Saturday. I couldn't help myself. "Woo-hoo!"

Sarah moaned and sat half upright. "Oh my God, please stop making such loud noises."

"Sorry." I kept my voice as soft as possible, even though I felt like shouting from the rooftop. "Good news. Looks like you'll get to enjoy your coffee in peace. We've been given clearance to move into our dorm this afternoon."

"Mazel tov." She settled back under the covers.

Not only was I thrilled that we'd finally get our room, but this gave me a reason to text Sean. I typed a quick message:

Just wanted to let you know we're moving into our dorm later today. Hope all's well with you. Hug the kids for me.

I hit Send, then immediately checked to see if there was a reply. *Stop it. Give him time.* My mind bounced around. I couldn't wait for Tanner to get back. I couldn't wait for us to finally be in our own space again. My shift at Gino's didn't start until three o'clock, which gave us enough time to unload our stuff and go get the rest of the things I was storing at the auto shop. Then, when I got off work tonight, we'd be alone. Together. I couldn't wait.

Chapter Twelve

THEY'D TAKEN their sweet time getting the building ready for move-in, but they'd done a good job. The halls smelled fresh and clean, like new paint, and every piece of woodwork shone like new, which was impressive for a building nearly a hundred years old.

It had taken most of the day, but Tanner and I had managed to get all our shit moved before I headed to work. Saturdays at Gino's were busy as hell, so the time flew by. When the crowd thinned around eleven o'clock, Gino stuck three pizzas in the service window. "Go home," he said.

"I'm on till close."

"Not tonight, you're not. We've got it covered. Take these with you—I'm sure someone at the dorm will eat them. Go celebrate move-in day."

Marissa came up alongside me. "You better watch it, Gino, your reputation as a hardass is gonna go south real fast if word gets out you're this nice to people."

"You complaining about picking up extra tips for the night?" he asked.

She grinned. "No, sir."

"I can stay," I said.

"Get the hell out of here. And put a stack of menus out while people are eating. I'm not that nice, I'm just a marketing genius."

I took the pizzas and a handful of our take-out flyers. "Thanks. I owe you."

My heart fluttered as I drove back to the dorm. I couldn't wait to spend the night in our room. My cock was in full agreement. *Not yet.* I focused on how and where to dispense the pizza to try to distract myself.

The first floor of the building was empty, but in the stairwell of the second floor, I ran into the RA, who gladly took one of the pizzas off my hands with an enthusiastic thank-you. I saw him stick some menus into the side of the bulletin board before he started knocking on doors.

Tim and Eric had their door open. They were still carrying in boxes of shit.

Eric saw me first. "Oh, man, tell me you're bringing food."

"Best pizza in town."

Tim appeared on the spot. "Hell yeah. I fucking love you."

The expression on Eric's face defied description. "We missed dinner because that was the only time we could borrow his brother's car to go pick up our fridge."

"Take a whole pie," I said.

"Seriously? Thanks. What do we owe you?"

"Nothing. On the house, courtesy of my boss." I handed him a flyer. "Just stop by some time to give him business."

Tim already had the box open and was inhaling a slice. "Like you've gotta tell me to do that? Their food's the best."

The door behind me opened. Our door. Tanner leaned against the doorframe wearing a dark T-shirt and jeans. Barefoot. Looking so goddamned sexy, my entire body was ready to say hello.

"Hungry?" I asked, holding out the remaining box, knowing he was always ready to eat.

"Nah, just exhausted."

He stretched, cracking his back. His ready-for-bed sounds sent tingles straight through me. I wanted nothing more than to get out of that hallway and into our room, behind that closed door, ASAP.

"Me too. Looks like we'll have pizza for breakfast."

"Fine by me." Tanner gestured to the few crates still left in the hall. "You guys need help with anything?"

Eric shook his head. "This is the last of it. Soon as we finish this pizza, we're heading to Duncan's for drinks. You want to come?"

Tanner yawned. "Not tonight."

"I'm pretty beat too. I slept on Wendy's floor last night."

Eric's gaze shot between us, and my cheeks heated. I still wasn't used to people knowing about us—not here at least—and I had the feeling he sensed that Tanner and I wanted time alone.

He just gave a smile and a wave. "Catch you guys tomorrow. Thanks again for the food."

"Anytime."

Tanner stepped aside, and I walked into our room. The sound of the door clicking shut behind me was like music to my ears.

The look in Tanner's eyes had me mesmerized. Dark heat, drawing me into his imagination, making me wonder which dirty thought he'd act on first. He took the pizza box from my hands and slid it onto the desk as he nudged me so that my back was against the wall.

Leaning so close that I could feel his warm breath, he whispered, "If we're both so tired, I guess we'd better get to bed."

His hips pressed against mine as I arched away from the wall. Jesus, he was hard. Our cocks rubbed against each other through the thick fabric. I stifled a groan, staring down between us as our bodies moved together.

"Fuck." I breathed the word, unable to think of anything else.

"If you insist." His mouth was on mine before I could answer, laugh, or take my next breath.

Good. All I felt was good. His warm tongue circled mine, thick and sweet, as we continued to grind. *God, I missed this.*

I slid my fingers under his T-shirt, gasping deep in my throat as they passed over his smooth hot skin. He pulled back enough to yank the shirt over his head and jettison it across the room before reaching for mine.

Skin against skin, the heat between us rose exponentially as our mouths found each other again. As much as I wanted the rest of our clothes gone, I was grateful to have our jeans separating us. The friction felt amazing, but layers of denim were the only thing keeping me from coming right then and there, and I wanted this to last as long as possible.

Tanner's hand slid to my nipple, plucking on it as he sucked my tongue, and I began to think, jeans or no jeans, I was going to come. Then my phone rang, buzzing harshly against my ass, startling us both.

"Ignore it."

My brain was barely functioning, but I recognized the ringtone. "I can't. It's Sean."

Tanner let out a slow breath and eased away. I fished the phone from my pocket. "Hey, what's up?"

"I, um, just wanted to check and see how you're doing. I got your message."

"We're all moved in. Everything okay there?" He sounded funny. Tense and strained.

"Not exactly. I just got off the phone with my lawyer."

Shit. "And?"

"He said the guy Laura's hired is a real shark. Loves anything down and dirty. He didn't come out and say it, but I can tell. He thinks I'm gonna lose the kids."

"Jesus."

Tanner gestured for me to tell him what was going on. I shook my head and held up a hand for him to wait a second. "She abandoned her children. The judge will just hand them over to her because she says so?"

Tanner's eyes widened.

Sean sighed. "I never officially filed for custody. When she walked out, I just focused on keeping things normal for the kids. I didn't want to go public with her affair either."

The desperation in his voice made my mind race. "That doesn't change the fact that she left."

"What matters is that she's back now, with a way better lawyer than mine. And judges almost always side with the mom in a custody fight." Sean took a deep breath, and my stomach knotted. "If she can prove that I wasn't using sound judgment while they were with me, I'll lose."

"But you take great care of the kids."

"Not according to Laura."

He paused, and my heart filled with dread. "What do you mean?"

"She's saying I endangered them… by leaving them with you."

Thank God the desk chair was right next to me, because I needed to sit down. "Sean, I'm sorry."

"Stop. I already told you, it's not you. You didn't do anything. I know that. But I'm not supposed to see you. Or talk to you. That's my lawyer talking, not me. This isn't what I want." He sounded as choked up as I felt.

I nodded before I realized he couldn't see me. "Whatever you need to do. I understand."

"Thanks."

"Please don't thank me. Shit. I feel like this is all my fault."

"It's not. And don't listen to Mom if she tries to tell you otherwise."

"She knows?" *How the fuck does she know?*

"Yeah, get this. Laura called her. How's that for a kick in the head?"

"What can I do to help? You want me to talk to Mom? Talk to Laura? Your lawyer? I'll sign an affidavit—anything you need."

"I'll let you know. For now, just… lay low. I'll be in touch when I can, okay?"

"Yeah."

I hung up. My fingers felt numb.

Tanner sat down on the bed, facing me. "What was that all about?"

My stomach churned as I relayed to him the things Sean had said.

Tanner listened in stunned silence. He fiddled with the edge of the blanket, then cracked his knuckles. "I can't believe this is happening. It's so fucked-up."

The anger in his voice mirrored what I felt. *How can people act like this? How can they even think for one second that because we're gay we'd endanger kids?*

"I'm sorry." I didn't know what else to say. There was nothing for anyone to say. This was a complete nightmare. The last thing I wanted was for him to feel bad or responsible. This was my fucked-up family, not his.

I rubbed my forehead as if maybe I could massage a thought into my mind. Nothing. Tanner crossed to my side of the room. I looked up at him. The anger I'd seen and heard moments ago was gone. All I saw was need.

His head lowered to mine, his lips soft and gentle. I cupped the back of his neck, pulling him closer, tasting him. Kissing him was enough to make me forget. At least a little. Tanner's hands settled on my hips, and he tugged me to the edge of the chair. Impatient fingers went to work on my fly. I struggled out of my jeans while Tanner stripped in silence, then knelt in front of me.

Again he moved closer, eyes closed. I swallowed hard, leaving my eyes open so I could look at him as long as possible. Not that I didn't have every inch of him memorized. I did. I had for ages. But I still couldn't get enough.

He smoothed his hands up my thighs, up my chest, down my arms. Every molecule in my body stood at attention, electrified from his touch. His lips brushed mine, distracting me more with each pass as he kissed his way from my mouth, to my neck, to my abs, to my cock. Every worry turned to heat.

Goddamn, his mouth feels good. Warm and wet, pulling me in as he swallowed me whole. His tongue flicked out, grazing my balls, then slithering up my length, around my head, taking every last thought right out of my brain and swirling it into nothingness.

My fingers sank into his hair. Cool silky strands slipped between them as his head bobbed up and down, up and down, making me dizzy. I gripped tighter, drawing his lips down harder, but he clasped my wrists and pinned them to the arms of the chair. *Fuck.* My neck arched back as pleasure shot through me. *Close. So close.* He slowed his mouth, then sped up again, keeping me on the brink.

I whimpered when he pulled away.

"Not yet," he said, pulling me up from the chair and kissing me again before he gave me a shove onto his bed. He fumbled in the nightstand drawer.

Lube. I tensed. As aroused as I was, I wasn't sure I could relax enough for anything we usually did with lube. I closed my eyes and breathed through my nose as I lay back on the bed, waiting to feel his fingers.

I felt them, but not on my ass. Slick wetness stroked down the length of my cock as he drizzled more lube over me. One hand pumped me while the other reached behind him. My heart pounded unevenly. *He's lubing his ass. Jesus.*

"Tanner."

"Please."

I didn't need to think anymore. I'd do anything he wanted. He started to climb on top of me, but I stopped him. "Wait."

He opened his mouth, but before he could protest, I shoved his hip so he'd lie down. Spooning behind him, I ran my hands over his ass, kneading, reaching beneath him to tickle his balls. He hissed, parting his legs to give me better access.

My heart raced with anticipation. I wanted this to be as good for him as possible. I grabbed the lube and squeezed some into my hand, then slid my fingers up his crack. He clenched, then relaxed as I worked in one finger, then two, just as he'd done with me.

Tanner's moans encouraged me. I kissed his back, his neck, his arm, letting my teeth graze his skin as I tasted him with my tongue.

My dick pressed against my stomach, hard and ready, waiting its turn as I probed inside Tanner, stroking my fingers over the knot that made him suck in his breath. He reached behind him, sliding a hand down my chest, then wrapping it around my erection. He gave two slow, heavenly strokes, then let go.

"Can you sit up?" His voice was deep and rumbly.

"Sure." I could do anything he wanted.

"Scoot back."

I eased my fingers out of him and scooted to the head of the bed, resting my back against the pillows.

Tanner raised himself off the mattress, braced one foot on the floor, then lowered himself like he was about to sit on my lap. Gripping my cock again, he rubbed the head against his ass.

Fuck. Warm, slippery skin. *So good.* He pushed down, and the tip of my dick pressed against his asshole. I felt it shudder, closing tight, then giving way, little by little. I stayed still, as still as I could, given that my arms were shaking as I steeled myself on the bed.

"You okay?" I whispered.

"God, yes."

The need in his voice made my erection swell, and he groaned, settling himself farther down my length.

Jesus.

Nothing had ever felt like this. Nothing. Smooth… tight… hot. His body was always warm, but inside him felt like an inferno. He drew in a deep breath and blew it out, sinking the rest of the way onto me.

My eyes clamped shut, blocking out everything but pleasure. I moaned as he raised and lowered himself on me, trying to resist the urge to slam my hips against him.

Needing more, I pressed my mouth to his shoulder, biting and licking my way down his arm.

"Can you turn?" I panted. "I want to kiss you."

He stilled atop me, then twisted at the waist, swiveling ever so slightly on my lap. *Holy Christ.*

Our lips could barely reach each other, but we managed a kiss, tongues lashing together, hungry for more. Tanner braced one arm against the mattress, turning a little more so he was straddling my leg and anchoring his other arm around my shoulder. I kissed him harder, drawing his tongue into my mouth and sucking as my hand slid over his thigh and clamped around his cock.

Tanner sighed into my mouth, plumping in my fingers as I stroked. My hips rocked as he raised and lowered himself, sliding in and out of my fist with the same rhythm I was sliding in and out of him. *Jesus.* It was like fucking, jerking off, and jerking him off all at once. My head swam.

Leaning back for better leverage, Tanner wrapped his arm tighter around my back, clutching at my shoulder as he increased his pace. His thigh muscles flexed hard against my legs. Dizzy from the mix of sensations, I stared at his cock. With him on my lap, turned to the side, I had a clear view. Deep red, thick, so close I could see every one of the veins and ridges of his shaft, the high gloss of the swollen head. But I wanted more. I wanted to see him come.

I kept my grip loose enough that he could thrust freely, but tightened on each upstroke. His breaths came faster, more irregular, as we moved together. I nipped at his shoulder, craving his taste. Smooth, firm flesh grazed against my tongue.

Tanner cried out. "Fuck!"

The desperation in his voice fueled my desire, and I bucked harder. *I'm inside him.* The thought overwhelmed me as much as the sensation. Tanner tensed and jerked, swelling in my fist as come pulsed out of him.

Watching him erupt put me right over the edge. I tried to breathe, but he clenched so hard around my cock, I forgot how. Nothing existed besides my cock in his body. All I wanted was to come. I gripped the back of his neck, needing to hold on to him. *Oh God, oh, yes.*

The breath I was holding huffed out of me as if I'd been underwater for too long and finally made it up for air. I'd meant to ask him the same question he'd asked me, "In you or on you?" but it was too late. I came hard and fast, pulsing deep inside him.

We collapsed on the bed in a tangled heap, and I eased out of Tanner, feeling him wince as I pulled the last bit out. The sound of panting filled the air as my heart continued to hammer, finally slowing down to a seminormal rate.

Tanner rolled toward me and our mouths met for a lazy kiss that grew deeper as we wrapped our arms around each other.

"Was that okay?" I asked.

He answered with a laugh that shook us both. "Okay? Uh, yeah, that was better than okay."

He anchored his hand on the back of my neck and pulled me in for another kiss.

Pulling back, I waited until he looked me in the eyes. "I love you."

"Good," he said. The smile I hadn't seen enough of lately tugged up one corner of his sexy mouth. "Because I fucking love you too."

Chapter Thirteen

For the next twelve hours, we fucked, sucked, slept, showered, rinsed, and repeated until we were both sore in the most awesomely good way. I could have stayed in our new room forever and been a happy man.

We debated running out to grab breakfast but opted for cold pizza and Coke, the only things in our fridge. The perfect way to start our Sunday, especially since eating them didn't involve putting on clothes or keeping our hands off each other. I was already thinking about going for—what would it be? Round five? I'd lost count—when a knock on the door interrupted us.

"Ignore it," Tanner said, before kissing me in a way that could have made me ignore it if our room had burst into flames.

"Collin, Tanner, I know you're in there. Open up. Please."

Shit. It's Wendy.

Tanner closed his eyes and took a deep breath. I could see him struggling.

"We've gotta let her in. Come on. She let us crash at her place this weekend. Besides, she sounds upset."

He nodded and grabbed a pair of shorts off the floor. "Just a sec, Wen," he yelled.

I tugged on jeans and tossed Tanner his T-shirt while I rooted around for mine.

His comforter was in a pile at the foot of the bed, and I pulled it up, covering any splatters that might be on the sheets. I knocked the bottle of lube into the drawer and pushed it shut, then nodded to Tanner.

He opened the door and gasped. "What the hell? What happened to you?"

I looked past him to see what had him so shocked. I'd seen Wendy in various states of dress and undress, with and without makeup, but I'd never seen her like this. Her normally bouncy blonde curls were straggled and wet, as were her clothes, including her leggings, which had a rip on one knee and what looked like blood on her leg. Black eye makeup ran in streaks down her face, smudged under both eyes like grease.

"Jesus," I said. "Are you okay?"

She sniffled, shoulders rising in a shrug as tears rolled down her cheeks. "I'm kinda having a shitty weekend."

Tanner reached toward her, and she flung herself into his arms, sobbing. He pulled her into the room, stroking her hair.

I closed the door. The last thing she needed was an audience, and someone was bound to walk by.

Tanner walked backward toward his bed. "Come on, sit down. Tell us what's going on."

His voice was calm and soothing, but I could see in his eyes that he was freaking out. So was I. Not knowing what else to do, I got her a glass of water while he settled her next to him on the bed. Her face was still buried in his chest, and she continued to cry.

I rubbed her shoulder. "Here, have some water."

Sniffling she turned to peer up at me.

I handed her the water, and she took it, wiping her face with her other hand and smearing more eye makeup around.

"Drink," Tanner said.

She nodded and took a sip.

I crouched on the floor next to her while Tanner rubbed her back.

"I'm sorry." Her voice was shaky, but the tears had let up. "I know you guys don't have to be nice to me. Not after the way I've been treating you."

Tanner took her hand. "Hey, we've been here before. I know the drill. You and I get pissed at each other for something, we don't speak for a while, then something happens, and we know we're still there for each other."

Wendy nodded and sniffled loudly.

I still wasn't sure what was going on. "You gonna tell us what's got you so upset? And what happened to your clothes?"

Wendy took a deep breath. "I got home at 3:00 a.m., and my roommate was 'occupied.' The last thing I wanted was to spend the night listening to some happy couple getting it on. I'd been hoping to find the two of you there, but then I figured you must have moved in, so I came here."

Tanner looked at the clock. "You stood outside in the rain for seven hours?"

"No, I went for a walk and got a coffee part of the time. And tripped on the curb, hence the ripped pants."

I ran my fingers lightly over the torn fabric. Her scrape was scabbing over but still needed to be cleaned. I was pretty sure I knew where the first aid kit was.

Tanner studied Wendy, then glanced at me. His look said, "Get ready." "Wendy, why'd you come home early from the weekend?"

Tears welled in her eyes, and her entire face screwed up in an attempt to keep them from falling. She blinked rapidly, head tipped back, not looking at either of us. "Dex and I are over."

Oh, jeez.

Tanner closed his eyes and took a breath. "What'd he do?"

"He told me to meet him for dinner, but I was running early, so I went to the film school. They said he was editing, so I went to the booth he'd signed out, and I opened the door." A gulping sob made the tears start rolling. "I'd seen her before. He'd sworn to me that they were just friends, but he's been with her for a whole year. The only reason he went to the beach house this summer was because she was in Europe, otherwise he said he'd have just dumped me before Fire Island."

What a class-A fucktard. Jesus. Who treats people like this? "I'm so sorry, Wendy. We didn't know any of that."

"I know you didn't. He's a master liar. And I'm really sorry I got so mad at you about the summer. He's the one I should be mad at, not you guys. I love you guys. Do you still love me?"

She was rumpled and crying and bleeding and pleading. "Of course we do."

"Always." Tanner pulled her closer and kissed the side of her head.

Wendy burrowed her face in his neck. She looked so comfortable all cuddled up with him. It gave me major flashbacks to when we first lived together and she used to be Tanner's Monday night regular. They fit together so well. Wendy looked up with more streaks of mascara leaving haphazard stripes all over.

"You too, Collin. I need a group hug from the two best guys I know."

She kissed me on the cheek, then wiped off whatever makeup she'd left behind, and pulled me into a hug with her and Tanner.

I don't know how long we stayed there, but it felt... nice. Wendy was still upset but seemed to be calming down, Tanner was in full protection mode, and I was planning what we'd need to eat since Wendy said she didn't want to leave the room.

She was napping closer to dinnertime, so I pulled Tanner aside. "You think she'll be okay?"

"She'll be fine. She's got us to get her through. Then she'll meet someone or get involved in some new project. I'm not worried."

That last bit was a lie. He was cracking his knuckles, and his brow hadn't unfurrowed since she'd arrived. He was definitely worried.

Chapter Fourteen

WHEN I returned with dinner, Wendy was awake and wearing a pair of Tanner's sweatpants and one of his T-shirts. For some reason it made me bristle to see her in his clothes. It was silly, I know, but it seemed... I don't know... intimate. And I didn't particularly like it.

She and Tanner seemed more relaxed. We sat on the floor in a circle. I'd picked up Indian takeout. Tandoori chicken, tikka masala, pakoras, potato-stuffed paratha, and some dipping sauces. I knew Wendy loved Indian food, and the sight of it seemed to cheer her up.

"Oh my God, Collin, it smells so good. And you remembered that I like pakoras. Tanner, you're so lucky—you have the best boyfriend ever."

Tanner came up behind me and put his arms around me. "She's right. I do." He leaned over my shoulder, and I craned my neck to kiss him. He'd already managed to sneak a bite of chicken, and he tasted warm and spicy along with his own delicious flavor. I didn't want to be mean, but I really hoped Wendy would be heading home to sleep and not crashing at our place.

When dinner was over, we packed up the leftovers and shoved them in the fridge. Wendy suggested we watch a movie, which meant she wasn't leaving anytime soon. The minute she hit the Netflix list, some sappy chick flick popped up and she started crying all over again.

"No sad movies," Tanner said.

Wendy nodded and wiped her eyes. "Comedy. Or action. Do you guys have any Kleenex?"

"I can get you a roll of toilet paper." I headed for the bathroom.

"No, I think I've got some in here." She dragged her ginormous purse up onto the bed. Out came two miniskirts, three pairs of patterned socks, a pair of shoes, and a flowered bag bursting with makeup. Then finally a tiny tissue packet. "Found them. Oh, by the way, Tanner, did you get one of these?"

She held up a fancy envelope with calligraphy writing.

Tanner shook his head. "Mail's been all screwed up from the whole dorm thing. Why? What is it?"

"It's an invitation to Sam and Tina's wedding. We should go. We should all go. It'll be so much fun, and we can get away from here for five days. Come on, guys, say you'll go with me, please? I can't go to this by myself. But I can definitely show up with two gorgeous men on my arms."

Tanner picked up the card and examined it. "Jesus. I can't believe they're getting married. I mean, I guess I can. They've been a couple since, like, third grade."

Wendy plucked the card back from Tanner's hand. "There was a note here somewhere about how they're getting married at a family ski resort way up north in Maine. It's off-season, so they're getting it free. Apparently the aunt and uncle who own the resort are the only family members who approve of the marriage."

"I can relate to that."

Tanner threw me a look complete with an apology and a reassuring smile.

Wendy pointed to the map. "Looks like it'll be about a four-hour drive from here, maybe five. And it's the whole Columbus Day weekend. Doesn't that sound awesome? Away from here with nothing to worry about other than eating and drinking and seeing old friends?"

"And moose," Tanner added. "Lots of moose up there. And no cell signal."

"Seriously?" I mean, our local reception was crappy, but I didn't realize there were still places with no reception.

"I went to this ski lodge with them once a few years ago. No one could get their phones to work. We got snowed in three days when the big nor'easter hit, and none of us could call our parents to say we were all right."

"See?" Wendy said. "That's what we all need. A secluded getaway in the woods. Come on, say you'll go."

"We'll need to rent a car," Tanner said.

"No, we won't," I said. "We've got the Batmobile."

"Awesome. You can drive, and we'll navigate."

"Whoa, I didn't say I could go. I meant I could loan you the Batmobile. I'd need to check with Gino first. I can't ditch him if he can't find someone to cover my shifts."

Wendy gave a real smile for the first time since she'd arrived. "Well, then we'll have to find Gino a replacement for a few days. 'Cuz the three of us are goin' to Maine!"

Chapter Fifteen

WENDY STAYED in our room that night and the entire next day, refusing to even go out to grab food. We brought her a sandwich and a box of Froot Loops from the cafeteria. She ate a few pieces of cereal but mostly just sniffled and hugged Tanner's pillow. Her sadness seemed to come in waves, and when one hit, she was down for the count for at least an hour.

As I suspected she might, she slept in Tanner's bed, wearing Tanner's clothes. I was having flashbacks of the way things used to be with them until Tanner kissed me and pushed me down onto my bed. We didn't do anything in case Wendy woke up, but having him spooned behind me was enough.

I loved feeling him behind me: strong, solid, warm. He wrapped an arm around me, and I could feel his breath on my neck. *Is he smelling me the way I sniff him?* Coconut lime filled my nostrils. I wondered what I smelled like to him. *Good, I hope.*

"I can't be this near you and not at least kiss you," Tanner whispered.

Who could say no to that? I shifted as quietly as possible. In our one night in the dorm, I'd already gotten used to sleeping naked again. Now I was in shorts and a T-shirt. With Tanner so close and his mouth on mine, our chilly room became an inferno. We kissed, soft and gentle, until we ran out of breath, and then we kissed some more. Tanner's hand explored my back beneath my shirt while I wove my fingers through his irresistible hair. *God, I love kissing him.* Round and round and round our tongues spiraled until all the thoughts in my head were a big swirl of nothingness and all that was left was Tanner. I belonged with him. Hell, I belonged *to* him. There was no one else I wanted. For a second I was envious of the couple getting married. Jealous of strangers. *When did that happen? Me thinking about wedding bells? Jesus. I swear the coconut lime shit lowers my IQ every time I inhale it. Or maybe I'm just that crazy in love. Either way, fuck.*

At some point we must have dozed off, because before I knew what was going on, Wendy was whispering and shaking me awake. "Collin, I'm heading back to my dorm, okay? I've got a ton of studying to do for quarter finals this week. Thanks for letting me crash here."

"You sure you're okay to go?" My brain felt muddy.

"I'm sure. Tell Tanner I'll call later."

"I will."

She rooted around the room, putting on her shoes and jacket. She'd already changed back into her own clothes. Seeing the torn pants made me feel bad for her again. She'd had a suckfest of a weekend. As the door clicked shut, I realized she was gone and Tanner and I were alone.

Inching the sheets down, I eyed his sleeping body. *So fucking hot.* His shirt had ridden up exposing nearly a foot of beautifully sculpted abs. Abs I loved to stroke, to lick, to frot against, to come on, to watch him come on. My cock was in full agreement, standing tall and nodding inside the shorts I quickly decided were no longer necessary.

Tanner shifted onto his back, which made the outline of his cock clear beneath his sweats. *Fucking perfection.* Kneeling alongside him, I leaned down as close as possible without resting my head on him and huffed hot breath on his bulge. Even through the layers of fabric, it responded, twitching, then thickening. The head was most prominent, standing away from his body. I breathed again, feeling the warm moist air, knowing he was feeling it too.

He moaned but didn't open his eyes. I placed a kiss on the tip of his cock, pressing my lips firmly and moving them back and forth. The fabric grew slick, and my lips grew salty. My cock was yelling for more action, but I had Tanner on my mind first. Grabbing the waistband to his pants, I stretched them far and high, then gently pulled them down. His erection sprung free, and I couldn't wait anymore. Starting at his balls, I licked and sucked and nibbled my way up his length, tugging his foreskin gently between my lips, tickling beneath it with my tongue.

Tanner's hips bucked, and I wondered if he was still asleep. I got my answer when his hand clamped around his cock tugging his foreskin way down, exposing the full meaty glory of his dick. A stream of precome flowed from my cock, and I could no longer ignore it. I lowered my mouth onto Tanner's swollen head and took matters into my own hands.

"Fuck."

I didn't know which of us muttered it. I could guarantee we both thought it. *Jesus, it all feels too good.* Having Tanner in my mouth made me feel everything all at once—powerful, vulnerable, loved, in love, and fucking sexier than I ever imagined I could feel. His hand replaced mine on my cock, and he stroked while I sucked.

Soft moans filled the room. I hoped they were soft. I couldn't hear much over the pounding of my heart. *Ba-boom. Ba-boom. Ba-boom. How long can it keep that up before my entire body bursts?* I didn't care. I was so close to coming, all I could think of was making sure Tanner was ready along with me.

I fumbled in the drawer for lube, squeezed some out, and slicked it back and forth against his hole before sliding in a finger. "Please, yes," he said. "Oh, God, yes."

I loved hearing him ask. Circling my finger wide to loosen him, I inserted a second, stroking across the knot inside him until I felt him tense and jolt.

"Oh, fuck." He sounded desperate to come, but the hand on my cock told me he wasn't going to until I did.

I pumped my hips, reveling in the feel of his hand on me while my lips pulled him into my throat as far as possible. Sucking and stroking and groaning with my own pleasure, I felt him stiffen the last little bit. His balls pruned beneath my thumb. Knowing he was about to bust was enough to put me over. Come sprayed out of me, landing right on his chest in big white globs. Tanner stared down at them, and then his gaze met mine. Deep, intense, smoking hot. His eyes narrowed, and I could see he was losing focus. Then the first burst hit the back of my throat. I held still and swallowed, then continued to lick and suck as he pumped inside me, his gaze never leaving my face.

Panting I sat up, then collapsed alongside him.

"Fuck, it's hot when you look at me while you're blowing me."

I laughed. "Glad you approve of my technique."

I pulled a towel from the bedside drawer and wiped off, then handed it to Tanner.

He seemed to be in a postsex haze. Even after I got out of the bathroom with brushed teeth and jeans and a T-shirt on, he was still sprawled on the bed, naked with a bedsheet covering none of the important bits.

"You have no idea how bad I want to take a picture of you like that."

Tanner chuckled. "Yeah? What would you do with it?"

"Beat off to it when you're not home."

Tanner flung his arms wide in a very provocative pose.

"Remind me to buy a better camera, would you? The one on my phone sucks. Actually, I do pass that camera store on the way to work...."

He tossed a pillow at me, and I batted it onto his bed. With him looking that sexy, I wanted nothing more than to stay in bed with him the whole day, but I'd already missed Statistics a bunch of times when we were living at Sean's, and I couldn't afford to fail a class. Especially one I needed to graduate.

I leaned down and gave Tanner the hottest kiss I could manage that I knew I'd still be able to pull away from. "I'll be home by lunchtime. You want to meet me at the cafeteria?"

"Sure. If I ever find the motivation to get out of bed. Maybe I'll just lay here and take some sexy selfies and torment you with them all day."

I laughed. "You do what you've gotta do."

Laughter still filled the room when I pulled open our door. Tim was inches away from me, leaning against the wall.

"You dog," he said, his voice barely above a whisper. "I got up early to go for a run and I've been out here listening to you and your sex noises instead. Who've you got in there? Is it Wendy?"

He pushed past me, barging into the room before my brain could even focus. I turned to stop him, but it was too late. The look on Tanner's face was something I wish I'd never seen. Fear, shock, terror, mortification. He was nude, alongside a tangled sheet and a very used come rag with a bottle of lube at the side of the bed. And there was clearly no girl in our room.

Fucking hell.

My heart raced so fast I worried I might pass out. Tanner appeared frozen. I'd never seen his face so red. He made an initial grab for the sheet, but it was so twisted it barely covered anything.

Tim looked around the room. "The fuck. Where is she? I mean were you two both with one chick?"

And then it hit him. Tim's face screwed up as he looked from Tanner to me to that damned lube bottle. "Oh, fuck no. You two? No fucking way."

Tanner remained immobile. I stepped between him and Tim. "Take it easy. I know it's a shock."

"A shock? A shock is finding out your dad's been fucking around and you have three half sisters. A shock is when you buy one lottery ticket and you win. This… this is… you guys make me want to puke."

The words hit me like a punch to the gut. It was like Laura all over only ten times worse—at school, with one of our friends. One of our friends with a very big mouth.

"Tim, please. It's not that big a deal."

"Not that big? Are you fucking insane? I'm hanging out with goddamned faggots for two-and-a-half years. I can't even…." He backed out of the room, shaking his head, and tripped over the trashcan, which he proceeded to kick into the open closet. "You make me sick."

"Tim—"

"Don't even talk to me, fag."

He scrambled over to his room and slammed the door behind him.

I closed our door and counted to five to try to steady myself before turning to face Tanner.

He was still in bed, although he'd pulled on a T-shirt and the pair of sweats he'd loaned Wendy instead of the ones he'd been wearing. "What are we gonna do?"

My head shook, partly because I didn't know and partly because I couldn't hold it steady. *Jesus. What now?*

"Do you think he's going to tell everyone?"

For the first time, I heard fear in Tanner's voice. I knew he wanted us to come out to people, but at the right time, in the right way, so we had support before the whole world knew. And Tim didn't make it look like we were off to a good start supportwise.

"I don't know. He seemed so freaked, he may not want to talk about it. At least not right away. Hopefully he'll talk to Eric first, and he'll talk some sense into him."

"Yeah. That would be good." Tanner raked his hand through his hair. "I'm sorry, Collin. I should've at least pulled the blankets up before you opened the door. I was stupid."

I sat down next to him. "I'm the idiot who opened the door and then didn't stop him from barging in. I'm the one who's sorry."

"Now we're both screwed."

"Probably. But at least we've got each other."

"And Wendy."

"Yes, and Wendy. We'll be fine."

I kissed him hard and solid, trying desperately not to let him see how scared I was.

I don't think it worked.

Chapter Sixteen

I HEARD raised voices before I even got to the top of the staircase. I took the remaining steps two at a time and threw open the door to our floor. Tim and Tanner were standing in front of our room.

"You're being a douche about three different ways right now. You going for some sort of asshat-trick?" Tanner's voice vibrated with anger.

"Ass trick? That's more your speed, D'Amico."

"Jealous?"

Tim let out an ugly cackle. "Yeah, right. You're nothing to be jealous of. Fucking degenerate."

Tanner's fist clenched and unclenched.

"Hey, guys." I approached slowly, heart pounding, not wanting to set either of them off.

Tim's lip curled. "Oh, look, your wife's home. Or are you the girl?"

Tanner lunged before I could reach him and hit Tim hard enough to slam him into the wall. He'd taken Tim by surprise with that punch, but the shock didn't last long and Tim swung back, catching Tanner under the ribs before he tackled him to the ground.

The sounds—grunts and thumps—coupled with the image of Tanner getting hit, and something inside me snapped. Tim had at least twenty pounds on me, but I pulled him off Tanner like I was ripping open a cardboard box. I don't even remember aiming, I just remember my fist smashing into his jaw.

Tim regained his footing almost instantly and shoved me into his door. Before I could react, he landed a punch so hard, I thought my eye was going to explode. Tanner was on him, tugging him away from me, and then I heard Eric's voice.

"Jesus. What the fuck?" Eric stepped between all of us.

For a second I thought Tim was going to take a swing at him too, but Eric had his hands up. Tim bounced with energy. "Fucking faggots!"

Tanner lurched toward him, but I grabbed him and held him back while Eric blocked Tim's way.

"Stop it," Eric said. "You're gonna get us all kicked out of the dorm."

Tim's eyes bugged. "I don't understand you, man. Did you not hear me?"

"I heard you."

"Why are you sticking up for them? Are you one too?"

"No." There was enough disgust in Eric's voice for Tim to believe him and for my stomach to turn.

Tanner broke away from me. "What the fuck is it to you anyway, asshole? Trust me, neither of us has any interest in you. Unless, is that it? You feel left out?"

Jesus. Don't antagonize him.

"I'm gonna fucking kill you, D'Amico."

"Go for it."

Fuck.

Eric threw me a look. "No one's killing anyone. We're all just gonna go back to our rooms before… *shit.*"

Footsteps echoed in the stairwell, and the RA from the floor below us came through the door, followed by two other guys I didn't know. "Is there a problem up here?" the RA asked.

"No," Eric said.

The RA looked back and forth among us, and then his gaze landed on our door. I hadn't seen it before, but now it was as if it was the only thing in the hall. Bright red letters shone against the black door. "FAGS LIVE HERE."

My entire body went cold.

The guys with the RA muttered something I couldn't hear. The RA took a deep breath. "What's going on here?"

"I'll tell you what's going on," Tim said. "These two queers are out of their goddamned minds. This one attacked me."

Tanner was angrier than I'd ever seen him—his face was deep red, his fists balled so tight his knuckles were white. "This dickwad wrote on our door."

Tim let out an ugly laugh. "Prove it. You think I'm the only one on campus who's disgusted by the two of you? Think again."

The RA held up his hands. "Do I need to call campus security, or can you two settle down? You can't be beating the shit out of each other on university property."

Eric nodded. "We're okay. It was just a misunderstanding."

Tim scoffed.

The RA looked at Tanner. "Is that true?"

Tanner's jaw clenched so hard, I could see his pulse beating in his neck. "Just tell him to stay the fuck away from us, and yeah, we'll be fine."

"You agree with that?" The RA turned his gaze to Tim.

"Whatever."

"I'm gonna have to report the graffiti on the door."

"Fine," Tim said. "The more people who know, the better."

"Asshole," Tanner muttered.

The RA's eyes shot to him. "Do we still have a problem here?"

"No."

"Good. Maintenance probably won't get to the door for a while, but it'll be repainted. You can, I don't know, hang a sheet over it or something in the meantime."

Seriously? A sheet?

Tanner's eyes darkened, and I could tell it was killing him not to say anything else.

"Are we done?" Tim asked.

"I hope so." The RA shook his head as he looked at our door again. His gaze drifted back and forth between me and Tanner, and I saw it—he was trying to mask it, but I saw it—disapproval. Repulsion.

Heat prickled through me followed by a rush of icy cold. There was no hiding anything anymore. Like it or not, we were out.

Chapter Seventeen

The last thing I wanted to do was go to work. Tanner was still shaking with rage, and I didn't want to leave him alone, but I'd promised Gino I'd work the kitchen, and I knew he had a huge catering job booked. He'd be screwed if I didn't show up, and I couldn't afford to get fired.

Tanner reassured me he'd be fine, and I finally agreed to leave. I missed every traffic light and wound up being over half an hour late. Hoping like hell Gino had been too busy to notice, I snuck in through the back door.

I hadn't even had a chance to tie my apron before Gino called my name. "In my office. Now."

Marissa shrugged at me and mouthed. "Good luck."

I finished tying the knot on my apron, but it felt more like I'd tied up my stomach. Walking as fast as I could convince my legs to go, I entered the tiny office.

"Shut the door," he said, sitting down behind his desk and leaning back in his chair. "You wanna tell me what the hell happened to your face?"

My fingers went to my eye, and I cringed as I made contact with the bruised flesh. "Just a misunderstanding at the dorm. Nothing to worry about. It won't happen again."

Gino nodded, tenting his fingers. "How's the other guy look?"

"Worse. Tanner tackled him. He's got a black eye, and I don't imagine his ribs are feeling too good."

"Tanner all right?"

"Yeah, just a cut on his cheek from the guy's class ring."

"Well, good for Tanner jumping in to help you. That's a true friend."

"I was actually trying to help him."

Gino leaned forward, head down, then looked up at my face. "He's, uh… more than just a friend to you, isn't he?"

No. Not here too. I can't lose this job. I was seconds away from begging. Gino kept talking. "Did I ever tell you about my friend Mickey Denuzio?"

What? "No."

"Mickey and I grew up together. Went to Immaculata together, same schools you went to all the way through high school. Only Mickey wasn't allowed to graduate because senior year one of the nuns caught him making out with one of the other football players and they were both kicked out of school."

"I remember that in the news. I must have been in fourth grade or so."

Gino shook his head. "It was hell for those kids after that. No one wanted to hang out with them. Their cars got spray-painted with dicks and words I won't bother repeating. The other kid went to live with relatives in Boston, but Mickey stayed in town and was homeschooled to finish out senior year. His mother put him in some freaky Bible class that was supposed to deprogram him and make him not gay."

"Did it work?" This whole conversation scared the shit out of me.

"No, it didn't work. Bunch of assholes moralizing and giving electric shocks to a bunch of scared kids. The second he turned eighteen, he took off for Florida. I gave him all the cash I'd earned bussing tables that year so he could get down there safe and start a new life."

"Did he?"

"He sure did. That was twelve years ago. He owns a club in Miami now. Has a nice place to live and just got engaged to a guy he's dated for three years. No one's fucking up his car or trying to give him shock treatments. He took charge of his life."

"Why are you telling me this?"

"I like you, kid. You know that. And I like your friend Tanner too. I don't want trouble for you guys, and it seems like the dorms are giving you nothing but."

"We can't afford anything else." It was obvious he knew at least some of my situation. Might as well tell him the rest. "My mom cut me off when I came out. I need every penny to pay tuition, and we already paid housing for the semester."

"That's where I can help you out, if you want. You know the place upstairs, where old lady Maria used to live?"

"Yeah."

"Well, she's moved in with her granddaughter down in Jersey. I need someone to update the apartment a little, strip some wallpaper, fresh coat of paint, put in some new appliances. Bring it into the twenty-first century. It's a one bedroom, but it's got a nice living room and a small eat-in kitchen. Two people could live there, easy, while they do the work."

I stared at him.

"I'm offering it to you and Tanner if you guys want out of the residence hall. You can stay free for the rest of the semester. Just do some of the renovations while you're there. Then, when the semester's done, if you can swing it, you pay me instead of the housing board—whatever you can afford."

I didn't know what to say. "You're sure you're okay with this?"

"I just made the offer. Of course I'm okay with it."

"I meant okay with us being... you know, a couple." I sighed. This never seemed to get easier. "A gay couple."

"Yeah, I'm okay with that. When Mickey went through his problems, I made a promise that if I ever saw anyone struggling like that, I'd do what I could to help them. You and Tanner are good guys. You've helped me out. Let me do this for you."

"What about business? My whole town is furious with me. My mother, my priest, my sister-in-law. I don't want you to lose customers because of me."

"Let me worry about the customers. You just do the jobs I pay you to do and work on graduating. I'll pay you and give you a safe place to land at the end of the day. Deal?"

"I'll have to run it by Tanner, but I know he's dying to get out of that dorm, so I'm guessing he'll say yes."

"Good."

"Gino, I... man, I don't even know what to say. Thank you."

"You're welcome, kid. I wish you'd told me sooner, before your face got in the way. You should put some ice on that. It's still swollen."

"I will, after my shift. Thanks."

"And do me a favor, will you?"

"Sure. Anything."

"Someone gives you a hard time, you or Tanner, tell them they need to speak with me. No bullshit on my watch, got it?"

"Got it. I mean it, Gino, thank you. Means a lot to hear you say that."

"Good. Now that that's straightened out, get your ass out of my office. You've got work to do."

"Yes, sir." I headed out the door.

"Hey, Collin."

"Yeah?"

"That bruise on your face? I'm glad you clocked the guy."

"Me too."

I headed back to the kitchen, feeling lighter than I had in days.

Marissa was stirring the giant pot of sauce. She lowered her voice and leaned closer. "He didn't fire you, did he?"

I laughed. "No. He offered me the apartment over the pizzeria."

"Are you fucking kidding me? I'd love to live there."

"Well, we need to fix it up as part of our rental agreement, but yeah, sounds pretty cool."

"So he's okay with it?"

"With what?"

She rolled her eyes. "The gay thing."

My cheeks heated. "You know?"

"Honestly, I guessed a while ago, but now it's kind of everywhere. It made the school's Facebook page."

My eyes bugged. "It made what?"

"Hang on." She rooted around in her apron pocket and came out with her phone.

My stomach churned as I waited for her to pull up the page. She handed me the phone. *Disagreement Erupted in Downing Hall. Should residents be asked to leave because they're gay? Should charges be pressed for the altercation?*

"Fuck."

Marissa put her hand on my shoulder. "Sorry, I thought you'd heard about the post."

"I hadn't. Thanks for showing me."

"For what it's worth, I always hoped you and Tanner were a couple. You seem so happy together. Don't let this stuff wreck it for you."

I'd worked with Marissa for two-and-a-half years, but it felt like I was seeing her for the first time. I leaned over and kissed her cheek.

She grinned. "What was that for?"

"You have no idea how nice it was to hear someone say that. I really appreciate it."

"Well, you better start appreciating some chicken parm, because we don't have any made and that catering gig's in a few hours."

"Deal. I'll make the sauce. You make the cutlets?"

"You got it."

I breathed a sigh of relief. We had a new place to live—as long as Tanner agreed. And my job was safe. Not to mention that Gino knew and didn't care. I hadn't had that much weight lifted off my shoulders in months. I couldn't wait to get home and tell Tanner.

Chapter Eighteen

To say that Tanner was in favor of us moving to the apartment was an understatement. For the next four days, we spent every spare moment over there, trying to get it livable. Gino had stuck all the furniture in one room, so the carpet could be ripped out of the main living area. The previous tenant had owned a cat more elderly and senile than her, and the rug was beyond disgusting. Tearing it up and removing the baseboards was a pain in the ass, but so worth it. Once the new carpet was in, we had a new place to stay.

After work I'd done a final check upstairs to make sure everything was ready for the installer, and then I headed back to the dorm. Things had been tense in the building, but there hadn't been any more incidents. I knew Eric had told Tim to back off, and at least for the time being, Tim seemed to be taking his advice. I still didn't trust him, but it helped knowing I'd only be living across the hall from him for a few more days.

I heard the shower running as soon I opened the door to our room. The thought of Tanner wet and naked instantly brightened my day. Plans of stripping and joining him popped into my head before I could even kick off my shoes.

"Hey." His voice startled me. He stood in the bathroom doorway wearing a pair of low-slung jeans and a smile that brought my cock the rest of the way to attention.

"I thought you were in the shower."

Tanner shrugged, and my gaze raked his body, watching all the muscles in his chest and abs bunch. *Jesus, you're beautiful.* He still had a bruise on his side, where Tim had landed a punch, but it had faded to a pale yellow-gray.

"Does it hurt?"

Tanner glanced down and frowned. "Nah. For such a big dickhead, he can't punch for shit."

I knew from personal experience that wasn't entirely true, but I was glad Tanner was able to joke about it. "A hot shower will help."

"Yeah. I was gonna get in, but then I realized you'd be home any minute, so I decided to wait."

"Oh yeah?" My heart beat so fast, I could see my chest jumping under my T-shirt as he stalked toward me.

He reached for the hem of my shirt and tugged it up, letting his thumbs graze my ribs in a way that made me groan. The sound made him tense, and his eyes darted in the direction of the door. *Shit.* I could see it all over his face. He was still scared someone was going to barge in on us. Or overhear us. Or listen in.

He tried to seem casual as he reached for the doorknob.

I put my hand on top of his. "I locked it. It's okay."

Lie. It wasn't okay. It fucking sucked that we had to be this careful even in the privacy of our own room. I knew I'd been like this when we first got together—it had been new, and everything scared me back then—but Tanner had always been confident. Bold. I hated that I'd played any part in him wearing the look that was still on his face.

Closing my fingers around his hand, I pulled him closer and kissed him hard, coaxing his mouth open with my tongue until I felt him relax and kiss me back. Hunger could outweigh fear. That much I knew for sure. I wove my fingers into his silky hair, massaging his neck.

Pulling back just enough to talk, I whispered, "The shower's still going. That drowns out a lot of other sounds."

"Yes." He groaned the word as he turned and walked us toward the bathroom.

The air was thick with steam. Tanner pulled me back into a kiss as his hands went to work on my pants. He stroked my cock through my jeans, emitting a low growl as it flexed against his palm. I was so fucking hard, my brain felt fuzzy. All I wanted was Tanner naked and against me.

As soon as he unzipped my pants, I shoved them down and stepped out of them. He took the opportunity to take off his own, and finally there was nothing between us but clouds of steam spiraling from the breeze of the bathroom fan.

Strong fingers ran up my chest, making me shiver in spite of the warmth of the room. My cock bobbed, seeking contact with his.

Tanner leaned in for another kiss, backing me up against the door. I heard it click shut, then felt his hand leave my chest. He fumbled for a second, then pushed in the door lock. Now two doors and two sets of locks separated us from the outside world.

Is that enough? Enough for him to feel safe? My heart beat irregularly as my thoughts raced. Then his hand wrapped around my dick and all thought stopped.

So good. His fingers stroking my erection felt so damn good, I thought I might come before we even got started. My legs shook. I gripped his neck and gave him a bruising kiss, sweeping my tongue around his mouth. Sliding my back down the door, I inched him down with me. I positioned myself on the bath mat and motioned for him to stop kneeling.

"Sit. Hook your legs over mine."

Tanner rested one leg on each of my thighs, and I reached for his ass, tugging him so close our cocks slid against each other. "Fuck."

Moaning, Tanner reached between us and wrapped his hand around both of us, stroking slowly. I'd been leaking precome since I'd gotten home, and his touch inspired a whole new deluge. The slick sound of us rubbing together drove me completely wild. I nipped his neck, his collarbone, licked at the hollow at the base of his throat, kissed my way over to his shoulder. Tension still had his posture rigid. I massaged both shoulders, kneading the tight skin, then slid one hand down his chest, letting my thumb graze back and forth across his nipple. His cock pulsed against mine in response, but he still seemed... distracted.

I pushed the hair off his face, leaving my fingers anchored in it so I could see his eyes clearly. "What's wrong?"

"Nothing."

He went in for a kiss, but I put my forehead to his instead, waiting.

A deep sigh escaped him. "I can't completely relax. I keep trying, but it's like this cloud looming behind me."

I continued to rub his shoulder, trying not to focus on the sensation of his hand as he idly stroked our cocks. "What would distract you?"

He shook his head. "I don't know."

I took a deep breath. "Would it help if you knew I was thinking about your cock all damn day?"

Tanner laughed, then looked at me, his sly smile curving his tempting lips. "For real?"

"I was in my policy class, in the auditorium. I always sit in the back of the room because I can see better from back there. Someone walked by with something coconut, and the smell made me think of you."

He snorted. "Coconut?"

"Your shampoo. You've got no idea what that fucking scent does to me. I breathed it in as deeply as I could and regretted it almost immediately, because I wound up with a huge boner."

Tanner grinned and squeezed our cocks tighter together. The precome coating us was no longer just mine. "What'd you do?"

My face heated.

Tanner must have noticed. He ran his free hand across my cheek. "Seriously, dude, what did you do?"

"I put my hand in my pocket, you know, like I was lounging all casual."

"Jesus. Did you jerk off in class?" His eyes were wide and dark, and I wanted to stare straight into them until everything else disappeared.

"No."

"But you were stroking? Right there in a roomful of people?"

"There was no one for at least three rows around me. And it was more like barely moving. Maybe rubbing just a little bit. Crazy, I know."

"Crazy hot."

My eyes bugged. "Really? I felt like a pervert."

"I like your pervy side."

He let go of his cock and focused just on mine, slowing as he stroked base to tip, then down to my balls, pulling my foreskin taut. His other hand trailed down my chest until he reached my dick. Fingertips danced all around the crown as his thumb slicked back and forth across the slit. "When was the last time you jerked off?"

My cheeks burned hotter. "Yesterday."

"Tell me."

With both his hands on me, I had to reach over his arm to get to his erection, but I needed to feel him in my hands. Smooth hot skin rubbed against my palm, and I sighed with pleasure.

"Tell me, please." His voice rumbled with need.

"You weren't due home for hours, and I knew you'd be exhausted. Plus I couldn't wait. I'd wanted you since I left you sleeping in the morning." His dick swelled in my hand as I talked and rubbed. "I smelled like the pizzeria, so I got in the shower."

"Mmm... go on." He nuzzled my neck, nipping, then sucking my earlobe so hard my abs clenched.

I focused on not coming, counting my heartbeats until I was under control. "I wanted this. Us." I shifted so my hand encompassed both of us. "I missed this. So I soaped up the shower wall... then humped it."

I could feel his lips pulling into a smile against my neck before he inched back and looked at me. "You fucked the shower wall?"

"Yes. It was warm and hard and slick, and I pretended I was frotting against you instead of ceramic tiles."

Tanner's breathing had accelerated, and he was thrusting more vigorously inside my palm, making our cocks rub together harder. "Did you come?"

"Like a fucking volcano. All over the wall and me."

He groaned. "You think about this a lot?"

"Our cocks all hard and hot and sliding together? Uh, yeah."

"Christ, Collin. I didn't know you had this kind of dirty talk in you."

I laughed as much as I could, considering I was having a hard time with normal breathing. "Good?"

"Fucking fantastic."

His mouth closed over mine. *No more talking.* Soft moans filled the room as our breaths synced and our bodies moved in tandem. The head of his cock pressed against mine, creating friction at just the right spot to keep me going completely out of my mind.

His tongue spiraled mine, his balls, warm and firm, slid against mine, slick from precome too. *Jesus.*

Tanner broke the kiss. "I need to watch."

Our foreheads pulled together like magnets as we both stared down. I don't know whose cock was redder. Both were thick and swollen, glossy with need. "You've got the most perfect cock."

"Yeah?" His voice was breathy, and I knew he was about to come.

"Fucking beautiful."

I couldn't believe it had taken me this long to figure out that talking about sex during sex stoked his fire. He pumped like mad against my dick, then grunted. He swelled, then pulsed, the first shot hitting my chest, the next pumping out of him like lava and running down his fist. The combination of the visual and the extra-loud slapping sound as he stroked his come up and down my length pushed me over the edge. My balls clenched tight, and I sucked in a quick breath as I felt myself let go. Thick white come shot onto his abs, then added to the collection that coated us.

Tanner's mouth met mine, and he kissed me slow and deep. I wrapped my arms around him, drawing him as close as possible, legs still entwined. "I really needed that," he whispered.

"Me too." I stroked his hair. My mind was still numb and tingly from the orgasm, but I wanted to say something. "It'll be better, you know."

"What will?"

"Everything. When we move into the apartment, we won't need to feel like we have to lock every door in sight."

He nodded. "I'm sorry. I don't mean to make a big deal—"

"It is a big deal. And you've got nothing to apologize for." *You wouldn't have this problem if you were with Wendy instead of me. If anything, it's my fault.* I cringed as the words rattled in my brain.

Tanner stuck his hand behind the shower curtain. "Still warm. Care to join me?"

I forced a smile as I eased myself off the bathroom floor, untangling myself from his legs.

"There's nothing in the world I'd rather do."

Chapter Nineteen

CLASSES SEEMED extra boring because all I could think about was how there were only a few days left until we'd get to move into our new place. I never understood why some people would say they hated change so much. *Now I get it.* I just wanted things to settle down. Everything.

I took the stairs at the dorm two at a time, attempting to avoid contact with anyone in the building. There was only one person I wanted to see, and I knew he'd be in our room.

The second I opened our door, I knew something was wrong. Tanner was pacing around the room looking really wound up. Worry filled me from head to toe.

"I need to tell you something."

My skin crawled with nerves. I tried to keep my voice steady. "Okay."

Tanner ran his hand through his hair, then looked at me. "I kissed Wendy."

Whatever air had been in my lungs seemed to disappear. My head hurt. "Oh."

"I'm sorry. It wasn't… I mean, we didn't plan it. It just sort of happened." He paced and raked his hair again. "She was crying, so I hugged her, and we were sitting on the bed together. I don't know. She looked up at me with her big sad eyes.…"

"And you kissed her. I get it." I more than got it. It played out in my mind like a fucking movie.

"Actually she kissed me. But I kissed her back." He shook his head and started pacing again. "It was like, I don't know—a reflex?"

She kissed him? I knew it. Wendy wants Tanner back. My stomach clenched, sending a dull ache through my body. "Is that all that happened? You just kissed?"

"No." He sat with his head in his hands.

Fuck. "Did you, I mean, did the two of you…?" My eyes stung as I awaited the answer.

"We didn't have sex. But we could have." He closed his eyes, tight. "I don't know what happened. One minute it was a reassuring kiss, then the next we were rolling around on the bed, then clothes started coming off. She wanted to. I knew she did. She was rubbing me through my jeans, and she pulled me on top of her."

He sounded like he was trying to make sense of what had happened. I tried to focus on breathing. "Why'd you stop?"

"Why do you think?"

"I don't know. I mean, you two have history, and you're obviously attracted to each other."

"That's the scary part. It felt so... easy. I mean, we've done it before, so it wouldn't have been a big deal that way, and God help me, the first thought in my mind didn't even have anything to do with that. All I kept thinking was that Tim had seen us come into the room and that if he heard us having sex—and we all know Wendy's not exactly quiet in bed—then maybe, I don't know, maybe he'd get off our backs with all the gay shit. Stupid. I told you. Totally stupid."

I sat down on the edge of my bed. "It's not stupid at all. Tanner, you're not even gay. Not that gay people deserve to be harassed, but you're not. You like girls. It would be so easy for you to avoid all of this. Get a girlfriend. Take her out. People have short attention spans. They'd move on to the next scandal, and you'd be in the clear."

Tanner stared at me like I'd grown a second head. "And what about you?"

"I'm gay."

"I've noticed. I meant what about you and me? Collin, I'm in love with you. I may as well be gay."

"You have choices. Choices that won't get you beaten up. I just want you to consider your options." My chest hurt.

"I have. You're the only option I want. This was supposed to be an apology, and it's the suckiest apology of all time." He got down on his knees in front of me so we were eye to eye. "I'm sorry, Collin. I'm so sorry. It won't happen again. I promise. I don't want her. I want you."

"Don't you miss girls? At all?"

Tanner flinched. "Miss them? What do you mean?"

"I mean you're bi. Don't you miss being with women?"

"I don't look at it that way, like I'm missing something. I'm happy with you. I love you."

The words made my heart clench tighter than my stomach. "I know. But still... do you ever question it? Us?"

He paused, and I couldn't breathe.

"No. Not us. Sometimes I wonder what's going to happen. What other people are going to do. But I never question how I feel about you." Tanner's eyes locked with mine, and he reached up to cup the back of my neck. "You're all I want."

I wanted to believe him. A part of me did believe him. But another part knew this was an opportunity. Tanner had options, viable options. He could be happy with someone else. Someone female. I was sure of it. For the first time in a long time, I saw things clearly. Tanner didn't have to go through what we were going through. That was all because of me.

I forced myself to speak. "I love you too."

I meant it more than I'd ever meant anything.

"Good." He massaged the back of my neck and moved closer. "Are we okay?"

I nodded.

His soft breath brushed my lips for one delicious second before his mouth touched mine.

I kissed him back. Hard. Sweet. With as much passion as I could muster. I wanted to savor every second with him. Because there wouldn't be many more.

I finally knew what I had to do. I just had to figure out how.

Chapter Twenty

Focusing on writing my paper was next to impossible. Between all the shit going on in my head and all the boxes in our dorm room, I couldn't concentrate worth a damn. Plus the noises in the hallway were driving me insane. At first I thought maybe maintenance was cleaning the hallway, but the sound was concentrated near our room—it sounded like an animal was scratching at the door. Hoping it wasn't more artwork being scrawled, I opened the door, and Wendy nearly fell into the room.

"What are you doing?"

"Ta-da!" She held her hands in the spokesmodel pose, gesturing grandly.

"Holy shit. It's gone." The awful words were completely gone. "How'd you do that?"

"First I used nail polish remover. Then I buffed it with an exfoliating facial sponge. Then I painted it black."

"Well, it looks great. Thank you."

"You're welcome. I'm hoping it saves you guys the maintenance fee. Besides, I kinda wanted to apologize to you anyway."

I held the door for her to come inside.

She followed me and sat nervously on the edge of the desk, kicking her legs. "I know Tanner told you what happened. It was my fault. And I really didn't mean it as anything against you. I know that sounds stupid, but I didn't want to hurt you. I just…."

"You were sad and lonely, and you wanted Tanner. I get it. Believe me, you don't have to explain."

Wendy fiddled with the edge of her sleeve. "It just seemed so easy, you know? I love him, and we're so comfortable together. After everything with Dex, I just wanted simple. No drama. And someone who actually cares about me. Is that too much to ask?"

"Not at all. Everyone deserves that. And Tanner does care about you. He loves you."

She gave me a wistful smile. "Yeah. As a friend."

"You two have history as more than friends."

"I know. To be honest, sometimes I wish you weren't so fucking awesome, so I could have a shot with him. But I know that's just me being selfish."

My brain went into overdrive. "Is that what you want?"

"A nice stable relationship with someone I trust? It'd be like a dream come true."

"And a lot easier with me out of the picture."

"What do you mean?"

"I just mean you and Tanner are going to spend a whole long weekend together."

"With you."

I shook my head. "I can't go. It'll just be the two of you. Maybe you should see what happens. Think of it as fate giving you guys another chance."

I was so full of shit I couldn't see straight.

"What are you saying? That you want Tanner to hook up with me?"

I took a deep breath and blew it out slowly, then I nodded.

Wendy's eyes popped. "For real?"

"Jesus, Wendy, it fucking kills me to see Tanner hurt or upset by something some asshole says to him in passing. None of that started until people found out about me. It's all my fault. If he were with you, he wouldn't have to deal with that anymore. You could both be happy."

"Well, yeah, except for the teeny little issue that he's totally in love with you."

"You're gonna be alone together for days while you're at the wedding. Maybe he can remember what it's like to be with someone you don't have to hide."

Wendy eyed me warily. "Are you asking me to go for it with Tanner while we're in Maine?"

"You want to, right?"

"Yeah, but—"

"Well, I just want him to feel good about himself again. I mean, shit. Look at what I've done to my life. My mother won't speak to me, my sister-in-law is suing my brother for custody because of me, Tanner's getting harassed and getting into fights—and it's all because of me. I just want to fix it. I want everyone's life to go back to normal. Can you help me do that? Can you take care of Tanner for me on the trip? Please?"

My voice cracked on the last few words, and she threw her arms around me, holding me tight. She wouldn't do anything to hurt Tanner. I knew that for sure. She loved him. And I loved him enough to let him go.

"I'll take care of him, I promise," she said, making my heart ache and spasm. I felt like I was dying inside. *It's for the best. It has to be. Anything that hurts this much has to be for something good.*

"You're sure it's what's you want?" Wendy searched my face with her bright blue eyes.

"Yes. Work your magic, okay? Make him happy. All I want is him happy. I trust you."

"Thanks."

"Thanks for fixing our fucked-up door."

"Shit, I'm late for class." Wendy grabbed her oversized purse and perched her sunglasses atop her head. "You gonna be okay here alone?"

"I'll be fine. You just make sure he has fun at the wedding. Get his mind off everything. Remind him what normal feels like."

She stared at me, eyes so serious, it felt like they were trying to drill a hole in my soul. "I promise. I'll do my best." She popped up onto her toes and kissed my cheek, then quietly closed the door behind her.

The wedding was in two days. Tanner wasn't due back from class for hours, so I made arrangements. I called Bryan. Over the summer he'd told me I could crash at his place if I was ever in the city.

"Hey, Bry, it's Collin."

"What's up? You back at school?"

"Yeah, that's kind of the thing, though. I need to be in New York for a bit."

"What for? Did you get an internship?"

"Something like that. I need somewhere to crash. Can I stay at your place?"

"I just signed it away for a two-week sublet because I'm off on a short tour. But as soon as I get back, you're welcome to come stay as long as you want. You got a place to hole up until then?"

"Yeah, I can find one." *I hope.*

Bryan didn't ask any questions, which was great because I didn't want to be explaining myself all over the place. I just needed to get out of town. I needed to be someplace where there was no one left for me to hurt.

Chapter Twenty-One

Tanner zipped his suitcase closed and hoisted it off the bed. We'd just moved our stuff into the apartment earlier in the day. It was a miracle he could even find his suitcase in the mess. "Collin, this is ridiculous. Come with us. I really think Gino would understand your needing to get away for a few days if you'd just ask him. Or let me talk to him."

I shook my head, not entirely trusting my voice. We'd been having the same conversation since I'd told him I couldn't go to the wedding. I'd been adamant that I couldn't ask Gino for time off—especially not after he'd given us a place to live. The only problem was that now that it was time for Tanner to leave, I didn't want him to go. I just had to pretend I did.

Tanner's eyes scanned our new place. There were boxes everywhere. "This is crazy. We literally just moved in, and I'm leaving already. You know, I don't have to go. Wendy will be fine on her own—she'll know half the people there."

Don't go. Don't ever leave this apartment. I bit my tongue, willing myself to focus. "Stop. Go to the wedding. Have a good time. With all the work I've got, I won't even notice you're gone."

"Gee, thanks." He laughed and stepped closer, putting his arms around me. The warmth of his body, the coconut lime—I wanted to freeze time, right then, with him pressed against me and us safe and happy and together. "You sure you're all right?"

He studied my eyes, and I forced myself to nod and smile. "I'm fine."

"I was serious with what I said about the shitty cell reception. I probably won't be able to use my phone up there. I don't like that—not being able to reach you. What if there's a problem here?"

"Tanner, I'll be fine. I'll be working. Drive safe, okay?"

"Don't worry. I'll return the Batmobile in one piece. I promise."

"Good." I swallowed hard.

Tanner hesitated for a moment, and I knew he wasn't completely buying that I was okay. He leaned closer, mouth hovering a breath from mine, our noses brushing against each other, my eyes closed in anticipation and dread. Then we kissed. Sweet and tender. A kiss that said "take care, see you soon, I love you." A kiss that damn near broke my fucking heart right then and there.

I pulled back and forced myself to step away. "You better get going. Wendy's gonna give you all kinds of shit for being late."

He laughed, and the sound rattled around inside my heart.

"See you Tuesday. I'll try to call if I can get a signal."

"Don't worry about it."

He opened the door and gave a quick wave.

I waved back and closed it behind him, trying to keep breathing as I listened to his footsteps echo down the stairs. The front door of the building slammed shut, and I counted in my head as I listened. Car trunk. *Slam.* Car door. *Bang.* The engine purred to life, then grew fainter as he drove away.

My eyes were closed so tight, my head ached. *Breathe. And do what you have to do.*

I had people to cover my shifts for the week, and I'd told Gino I was pretty sure Tanner would jump at the chance to work for him. I knew he was sick of the bookstore, especially since a few people there had been giving him grief. I'd managed not to explain to Gino what I was doing. I didn't want him or anyone else to talk me out of my plan.

Packing went fast since I hadn't even unpacked everything yet. I'd written a letter to Tanner the night before, while he was sleeping. I read it one last time, then hit Print. Waiting for it to chug out of the printer, my mind raced. *Where should I leave it? The coffee table? The dresser? The bed?* I folded it neatly into thirds and eased it into an envelope. My hand shook, and I had to steady it to write his name. *Tanner.*

The black ink stared up at me. He'd read it when he got home, and hopefully he'd understand. If not right away, some day. I set it down on the kitchen table, trying not to picture him finding it.

The only thing left to do was call Sean. He picked up on the second ring.

"Hey, Collie, what's up?"

I hadn't heard his voice since we'd moved out. My throat tightened. "Nothing. I just wanted to let you know I'm going out of town for a bit."

"Everything okay? You sound weird."

Dammit. I inhaled deeply through my nose and blew it out in a steady stream. "I'm good. This thing came up. For school." *When had I become this good a liar?*

"Oh, okay. How long are you away?"

"I don't know. I'll be finishing up my classes online." *At least that much is true.*

The girls were arguing in the background, and Sean's voice sounded muffled as he told them to settle down. "Sorry."

"It's okay. Hey, I'll let you go. I just wanted you to be able to tell your lawyer that I won't even be in the area anymore. Tell him I won't be stopping by or having any contact with you or the kids. Maybe that'll settle Laura down."

Crying erupted from one of the girls.

"Shit," Sean muttered. "Megan, leave her alone."

"Sounds like you've got your hands full. Go. Take care of them. Tell them I love them, okay?"

"All right. Thanks for letting me know. And good luck. I want to hear more about this."

"I'll be in touch."

"Is Tanner going with you?"

My eyes stung, and I squeezed them shut. "No. Just me."

"… Daddy, she took my Play-Doh…."

"I'm coming, Emma. Look, Collin, I've gotta go. I guess text me when you get settled."

"I will."

And that was it. Everything was set. All I had to do was take my bags and head to the bus station.

So that's what I did.

I walked out the door and down the stairs, not looking back. Climbing onto the bus, I took one last glance around, swallowing hard. Then I did the only thing I could.

I left.

Chapter Twenty-Two

MY HAND shook as I reached for the buzzer. *What if there's no answer? What if I'm interrupting? What if I'm not welcome?* I had nowhere else to go.

I pushed the pale gray button and held my breath.

"Hello?"

"It's Collin."

The buzzer sounded before I could even get another word out. I shoved the door open and held it for the two women who were heading out of the building. The elevator they'd gotten out of was still open, so I got in and headed for the fifteenth floor.

My heart raced. *Is this the right thing to do? Should I even be here?*

I stepped out of the elevator and saw the door to the apartment was open. Mrs. D'Amico stood in the doorway. She smiled warmly, but her brow was furrowed. I'd never been so relieved to see anyone.

"Collin, honey, it's so good to see you. Are you all right? Is Tanner okay? Is he with you?"

"Tanner's fine. And it's just me."

The lines in her forehead deepened, but she put her arms out and pulled me into a hug. My chest tightened, and I wondered if she'd still be hugging me once she found out why I was there.

"Come inside. Put your stuff down. Are you in town for school? Do you need a place to stay?"

"I didn't know where else to go." My voice sounded small. I felt small. Like the world could swallow me in one tiny bite, and I'd just be gone... which didn't sound half-bad.

"Sit down." She ushered me over to the couch and took a seat, cross-legged and facing me, studying me with her dark eyes. Tanner's eyes. "Sadness is rolling off you in waves." She plucked at the air around me, shaking handfuls of nothing off to the side.

"Sorry."

"Let me get you some tea. That'll help." She rested her hand on the top of my head for a moment. It felt warm and comforting and made tears sting my eyes. "Here, hold this, I'll be right back."

I looked down at the smooth pink stone she'd placed in my hand. I didn't believe in crystal healing, though I wished something as simple as a rock could take away some of what I was feeling. Turning it over and over in my hand, I concentrated on the way it felt. Cool and smooth. By the time Tanner's mom returned, I had calmed a little.

"Ginger tea. It'll relax your muscles. Your body is so tense right now, it's a wonder you can walk. It'll help you think clearer too. Breathe in the aroma, then sip it."

I brought the cup to my mouth and inhaled. Sweet warmth filled my nostrils. Ginger, honey, and a hint of cinnamon and lemon. I closed my eyes and took a sip. My mouth tingled, and it burned a little as it slid down my throat, but the sensation quickly changed to a soothing warmth that seemed to radiate up the back of my head and down into my stomach.

She waited while I took a few more sips. "Do you want to tell me?"

Not really. But I knew she had a right to know. Especially as I'd shown up on her doorstep.

"I left Tanner."

I don't know what I expected her to do. Yell at me? Kick me out? Slap me? Instead she sat down next to me, took the teacup out of my hand, and took my hands in hers. "What happened?"

The eyes did it. Those dark Tanner eyes stared into mine, and before I knew what I was doing, I was spilling the whole story. Eric, Tim, the fight, Wendy, her breakup, Sean, the custody battle.

She listened, not commenting, just nodding. When I finished, I took a deep breath, and it caught in my throat. "I didn't know what else to do. I don't want to hurt the people I care about. Being there just causes problems for everyone."

I tried to keep my voice steady, but it cracked like an egg on a granite counter.

"Oh, sweetie."

I looked up at Mrs. D, expecting disapproval and anger. All I saw were the tears rolling down her face. I'd hurt someone else. That did it. I started to cry. Big fat fucking tears rolled down my cheeks, down my throat, inside my nose. My entire head seemed to have sprung a massive set of leaks, and I couldn't stop them, no matter how hard I bit my tongue or dug my nails into my palm.

Warm hands rubbed my shoulders, and she pulled me closer. Burying my face in her neck, I cried harder than I could remember crying in years. Maybe ever.

It felt like forever before I finally pulled myself together and got my breathing back to normal. I tried to focus. Mrs. D's hair smelled good. Sweet and spicy, like the tea—soothing and comforting. I concentrated on that and took deep breaths of it.

She rubbed the back of my neck.

"You're going to be okay, Collin. This will all work out."

I shook my head. "I don't think so."

"It will. My son loves you, and it's obvious you love him. This is just a bump in the road."

"Big fucking bump. Sorry, I didn't mean...."

"You're right, it is a big fucking bump. But that's okay."

It didn't feel okay. It didn't feel like anything would ever be okay again.

"Drink some more." She handed me the teacup.

I took another sip. "Thanks. I'm sorry."

She gave my knee a quick pat, then leaned back against the couch. "Don't ever be sorry for coming here. I told you, you're always welcome. And you can stay as long as you'd like. But I don't think this is where you need to be."

"Tanner's got Wendy. Maybe they can make things work. He loves her too, you know."

"Oh, I know he does. Wendy's been his friend for a long time. I know just how much he cares about her. But I've never seen him with anyone who makes him as happy as you do."

My eyes prickled again. "Being with me causes problems. Problems he wouldn't have with her. With any girl."

"Sweetie, if relationships were easy, they'd all last forever. They're not. You have to decide which ones are worth fighting for, then give it all you've got and then some. Do you love Tanner?"

"Yes."

"Do you want to be with him?"

"In an ideal world, yes, but...."

She shook her head. "There is no ideal world, only this one. Do you want to be with him?"

"Yes, but—"

"No buts. I'm not saying it's easy. I'm just saying it's worth it to fight for what you want. You're hurting. And I imagine he is too. He's not going to just substitute Wendy for you. It doesn't work that way."

"She loves him."

Mrs. D nodded and toyed with the fringe on the edge of the couch throw. "I know she does. But that doesn't mean she's meant to be with him. Those two are better off friends. Tanner knows that. If you and Wendy would accept it, I think you'd all be a lot happier."

"I just thought, maybe...."

"If another guy came along tomorrow and you really liked him, would you forget how you feel about Tanner?"

"No, but...."

She stared at me.

"Fuck. Sorry, I mean—"

"Collin, you're in New York City, everyone says 'fuck' here. Stop apologizing. And stop worrying about everyone else. It's an endearing quality, but you're hurting yourself. What do you want?"

I had no answer for her. My chest hurt. My head ached.

Her hand returned to mine, and she gave it a squeeze. "Close your eyes, take a deep breath, and tell me what you want."

I inhaled, ginger, lemon, the spicy scent of Mrs. D's hair, then blew out a long slow breath. "Tanner."

I hadn't been sure what I was going to say, but that was the only word in my head, on my lips, in my heart. *Fuck.*

"You need to tell him that. You need to go back and figure out a way to work this out."

"I can't. Not yet. The trial."

"How about if I give my lawyer a call and get his opinion on that? You can stay here. I meant what I said, you're always welcome. If you need to be here to think, then take the time you need."

"Thank you."

She leaned over and kissed me on the cheek. I nearly started crying again.

"Drink. I'll go get your room ready and place that call."

I watched as she crossed the room and disappeared down the narrow hallway. It didn't seem likely her lawyer would be able to do anything, but it couldn't hurt. It occurred to me that she'd probably try to call Tanner too, but that wouldn't be a problem. I'd tried his cell. He was right. There was no service. By the time she could get in touch with him, he'd have spent time with Wendy. Everything would be different.

Everything already is.

Chapter Twenty-Three

All I wanted was to stay in bed. Not sleep in. Stay there. Live there. Become one with the mattress. The idea of getting up and walking around hurt. I'd heard people talk about things like this. I'd seen it in enough movies. Heartbreak. Depression. I hadn't realized quite how much it sucked.

The only thing forcing me to crawl out from under the covers was the fact that I didn't want to upset Tanner's mom. She'd been so good to me—great, really—letting me stay there, not bombarding me with questions, even though I was the guy who was in the process of hurting her son. I couldn't wrap my head around it. My mom couldn't stand the thought of me, but Tanner's mom seemed to sincerely like me. I didn't get it, but I didn't need to. What I needed was to do something nice for her. I didn't have a whole lot to offer, so I cooked.

I realized it sounded crazy, but in some weird way it made me feel like if I did nice things for her, somehow Tanner would know. And maybe one day, when he looked back on this, he wouldn't think I was a complete asshole.

Maybe.

Tossing the blankets aside, I forced myself to get out of bed. My neck ached with tension, and no matter how much I tried, I couldn't get it to relax. I couldn't even remember the last time I'd jerked off, but that was okay. My cock and I weren't on speaking terms.

I'd been at Tanner's mom's for nearly a week. She gave me plenty of space but checked on me several times a day. She kept offering me healing sessions or angel readings. I knew she meant well, but I also knew nothing like that would cure what ailed me. My heart was broken. No amount of stones or balance cards was going to fix that. I just had to get over it.

The worst day by far had been Monday. I'd known all day that Tanner and Wendy were due back from Maine on Tuesday, and my stomach had been filled with so much dread, it had been all I could do not to spend the entire day puking. I kept my phone turned off until that night, equally dreading and hoping that when I turned it on, there might be a message from Tanner. He'd have read my note. Seen that my stuff was gone. I didn't even know what I expected or wanted from him. All I knew was that I craved something—anything—even if it was just him telling me to fuck off.

When I finally pushed the on button, I saw I had one missed message. My hands shook as I clicked.

It wasn't from Tanner.

It was from Wendy. One single word stared up at me from the small screen: *Thanks*.

My heart had spiraled into my stomach, and my stomach felt like a bottomless pit. Hopelessly empty. Like a freefall into absolute nothingness. My entire body ached.

The one bright spot had been Bryan. He said the guy who was subletting his place was moving out a few days early, so I was welcome to crash there as of next week. I told Tanner's mom I just needed another week, and then I'd move out. I hated being a burden to her. She owed me nothing. Her son and I weren't even together anymore. Tanner's silence confirmed that so loudly, it was deafening.

In keeping with her record as being the nicest mom in the history of the world, she said not to worry. But I did worry. About everything. As far as I knew, Tanner hadn't called her when he got back either. Every time I saw her on the phone, I prepared myself to pack my bags, certain she'd kick me right out the door if he was upset.

Maybe he wasn't upset. Maybe he was relieved.

I showered, then headed into the kitchen and started making chicken marsala. By the time Mrs. D got home, it was almost done. The kitchen air was rich with garlic and red wine.

"Smells heavenly, Collin."

"Thanks. It's really easy."

"You don't have to do this, you know." She said that every night when she got home from work to whatever I'd prepared for her dinner.

"Yeah, I do." I'd made her all of Tanner's favorite dishes, which I hadn't been able to eat a bite of. It hurt too much to think about preparing his favorite foods without him there to eat them—and killed what little appetite I had. Instead I'd wait until later in the evening and order Chinese takeout from the place Tanner and I had gone when we'd stayed at her apartment that summer. The nightly walk to pick it up helped me clear my head. I never ate more than a few bites. The food was cheap and greasy, but the sounds and smells of the place were comforting. They reminded me of Tanner—of better times, of us happy together—in a way that wasn't as painful, and for that I was grateful. Even if it only lasted a little while.

By the end of the first week, I was going crazy. I'd been working online, tutoring, and had picked up a ton of hours because midterm exams were coming up. I needed the money. Not only was New York expensive, but if I wasn't able to keep my grades above a 3.5, I might lose my scholarships, and then I'd have to drop out. Not being enrolled would mean I'd have to start repaying my loans. I tried not to think about that and focus on writing my papers and listening to the online seminars.

Work kept my mind off Tanner for part of the day, but no one wanted tutoring at 3:00 a.m., so I'd lie awake at night and let my mind wander. It always went to the same place. Straight to Tanner. Wondering how he was. Hoping he and Wendy were making things work. Praying I'd come to peace with things one day. Wishing with everything I had that I could go back in time to when we were together.

Tanner's mom had a convention to go to, in California.

"Are you sure you'll be all right?" she asked as she got ready for her flight. "I can cancel. Or you can come along as my assistant. I hate the thought of you here all alone."

It was touching. Her concern. Her willingness to help. She reminded me of Tanner and made me miss him a little less. "I'm fine. I can move into Bryan's in a few days, so I'll be out of here before you even get back. I can't thank you enough for all you've done for me."

She touched my face, her eyes filled with kindness. "We'll talk when I get back."

I nodded, even though I was pretty sure that wasn't true.

Chapter Twenty-Four

WITHOUT MRS. D in the apartment, I realized I was completely alone. The feeling nearly swallowed me whole. I didn't even have anyone to cook for. When nighttime fell, I made my daily call to Mrs. Chang's. Five-spice chicken, an egg roll, and cold sesame noodles.

The cold air made me shiver as I walked the three blocks to pick up the order. I'd never been in New York City in the late fall. I missed the scent of the changing leaves, but somehow the cooler weather made the city smell cleaner. I breathed in deeply, trying to let the air cleanse me.

The old woman behind the counter smiled when she saw me. "Every night, same thing. You try new order."

I tried for a smile. "No, thanks. I like this one."

She shook her head and handed me my change, then disappeared into the back to get my food. When she returned, she handed me two bags. "You try new tonight. You don't like, you don't eat."

"I really don't—"

"On the house," she said. "You go."

She shooed me aside and started taking the order of the guy behind me.

I felt ridiculous carrying two bags of food when I knew I wouldn't even finish the contents of one. The street was empty, but as I walked the first block, I heard footsteps behind me. They followed when I turned the corner. I didn't think anything of it until they stopped when I slowed to fish the keys out of my pocket. *What now? A mugger? Fuck.* I bristled, ready to beat the shit out of someone if I had to. Hell, I kind of wanted the opportunity to feel something other than sad. Adrenaline pumped into my veins as I turned.

Tanner was three feet away from me. Hair blowing in the night breeze. Hands tucked into the pockets of his jeans. "You gonna eat all that yourself?"

Chapter Twenty-Five

THE BAGS of Chinese food landed on the ground with a solid *thud*.

Tanner nodded at it. "Good thing they tie those tight, otherwise that would have been an awful waste."

He's here. He's here, and he's talking about Chinese food.

I stared at him, like an idiot. "What are you... how did you...?"

"My mom ratted you out."

"Oh." Of all the words in the English language, that was the only one I could come up with.

"Don't be mad at her. I was pretty much freaking right the fuck out when I called her."

"Sorry." *Just how many lame one-word comments can I make before he turns and walks away?*

He shifted his stance, hands still in his pockets. "So, are you all right?"

No. "Yeah."

"Because you didn't really sound all right in that letter you left me."

Oh God, the letter. Just the thought of it made my stomach cramp into knots. "I did what I thought was best."

The breeze sent his hair fluttering off his face, then settling back across his eyes. "Best for who, exactly?"

Jesus. This was why I'd written the damned letter in the first place. To avoid having to say it all out loud. But I guessed I owed him at least that much. "Everyone. You. Sean. Wendy."

"What about you?"

"I'll be fine."

Tanner raked his hands through his hair and left them linked around the back of his neck. "You will? Really? You left your family, you left school. You left me." His voice cracked a little on the "me," and I thought my heart might shatter. "Do you even have a place to live?"

"I'm moving to Bryan's next week."

Tanner's gaze shot to mine. "That's not... is that what this is about? Did you move to New York to be with him?"

"What? No. *Jesus.*"

"Collin, work with me here. I'm trying to understand. I know we've been through a lot the past few weeks, but everything was finally settling down. I mean if you changed your mind about us or you want to be with

Bryan now, fuck, I guess I'll have to figure out how to deal with that, but the other bullshit—this 'best for everyone' crap—I can't live with that."

I sucked in the biggest breath of air my lungs would allow. "It's not bullshit. And it's got less than nothing to do with Bryan. I'm tired of hurting everyone I love just by being with them. Don't you get it? I'm letting you go so you can be happy."

Tanner laughed. "Happy? You think I'm happy? I got back from the wedding thinking you and I were finally going to be able to be together again, and instead I found a Dear John letter waiting for me. Not to mention how you totally lied to me before I left."

I flinched at the accusation. He was right. "I'm sorry."

"So am I. It's not like I don't get why you're good at lying. I know you've had to do it a lot. But not with me." He scrubbed his hands over his face. He looked like he hadn't slept in days. "I don't get it. I really don't. What the fuck?"

Seeing him there, right in front of me, upset, pleading for answers, it occurred to me I didn't have any. Not good ones. All I wanted was to throw my arms around him and tell him how much I'd missed him.

I forced myself to remember why I'd left. "Wendy loves you."

Tanner's hands fell loosely at his sides as he stared at me. "What?"

"She loves you."

"That's why you left?"

I don't know what hurt more, my brain or my heart. "No. Well, yes. Sort of. It just seemed like that would make everyone's life so much easier. For you to be with her."

Tanner let out a loud groan and paced several steps away, then walked back, stopping right in front of me. "I probably should have mentioned this at some point, but whenever Wendy hits a rough spot with a guy, she convinces herself that she's in love with me."

"Maybe because she is."

Tanner shook his head. "She loves me. I know that. And I love her too. But neither one of us has ever been in love with the other."

"But—"

"No buts. I've just been nicer to her than the other guys she's been with. She dates assholes. All. The. Time. One day she'll find the right guy. I'm not that guy. Not for her and not for me."

"How do you know? I mean, maybe if you—"

He rocked back on his heels, then stared at the ground. With his hair falling in his face, I couldn't read his expression. My stomach felt like it was eating itself alive.

"I know because I know what it feels like to be in love."

He looked at me then. Eyes serious and dark, streetlights making them shine like two perfect reflecting pools. I couldn't have looked away if the city had exploded around us and Godzilla was heading our way. I couldn't even swallow.

"Do you?" His voice was so soft I almost didn't hear him over the sound of my heartbeat.

"Do I what?" *Can he tell that I'm shaking, or is it just inside my body that everything's about to vibrate apart?*

"Do you know what it feels like to be in love?"

"Yes." *God, do I.*

"Still?"

The lump in my throat had reached meteoric proportions. My eyes stung, but I was afraid to blink, afraid I'd start crying and not be able to stop or worse—afraid I'd open them, and he wouldn't really be standing there.

I nodded and forced myself to squeak out, "Very much."

"Then what the fuck are we doing?"

My head felt as if it was about to explode. Too many thoughts. Too many feelings. Tanner stepped closer. I braced myself as I watched his hand rise, knowing if he touched me, it would all be over. His fingers cupped the back of my neck, and I trembled.

He inched closer still. "What are we doing?"

I pulled him against me so hard, we both staggered as our mouths collided. His lips, warm and firm, sprung open beneath mine, our tongues lashed against each other, hot and sweet. For the first time in over a week, I felt like I could breathe.

Chapter Twenty-Six

I DIDN'T remember picking up the bags of Chinese food or riding the elevator to the fifteenth floor. All I knew was that we were in Tanner's mom's apartment, that the door had closed and locked. That we were alone. And that I couldn't have stopped kissing or touching Tanner if my life depended on it.

He ground his hips into mine, and the entire week's worth of need coursed through my veins. I moaned when he pulled back. His crooked smile melted what was left of my brain cells.

"I've missed that sound." He pressed himself closer. "You want to know a secret?"

"Sure."

"I've never had sex in this apartment."

"Never?"

"Nope. Want to change that?"

"Immediately."

We made it to his room before clothes started flying. My shirt joined his on the floor. His jeans got kicked across the room. He fumbled with the button on my pants and growled, "Jesus, this never happens in porn."

I laughed and reached down to help him. "People in porn don't wear pants."

"They're geniuses." He dropped to his knees and gave my cock a slow stroke that felt so good, my eyes rolled back into my head. "But this is way better than porn."

Silky hair grazed my stomach as his lips glossed over my tattoo. A groan rumbled deep in my throat. "Fuck."

"Maybe later." His warm breath tickled my skin. "I've been waiting all week to do this."

Tanner's tongue flicked the base of my cock, then circled each of my balls. *Please don't let this be a dream.* I grabbed on to the dresser to steady myself. He kissed his way up my length so slowly, it made it seem like my cock was a mile long. His warm breath caressed me, but I ached for more. Weaving my fingers in his hair, I tugged him closer. He grinned up at me, eyes sly and mischievous as he placed a gentle kiss on the tip and flicked the bead of moisture away with his tongue.

"You're trying to torture me, right? As punishment for leaving you?"

Tanner chuckled. "Maybe just a little. But I believe more in reward for good behavior than punishment for bad."

He finally slid his lips around the head of my cock. *Holy God.* The week without sex had me revved and ready. Tanner seemed hell-bent on making this the best blowjob of all eternity. He licked, sucked, twirled, tugged, cupped, and swooped, all the while kneading my ass and sliding the occasional hand north to tweak a nipple. He had me tingling from head to toe, not knowing what sensation to respond to next.

"Tanner, please." I didn't know how much longer I could do this without passing out.

"Please what?"

"Let me come."

"As you wish." He grinned up at me, locked our eyes, and sucked my cock so far into his mouth, I couldn't do anything other than grunt. His tongue swirled along my underside, tickling and licking all the right places. My hips bucked on their own, aching for release.

Tanner palmed my balls, sending streaks of pleasure racing up my torso. My entire body was ready to give in to every last sensation and explode. My legs shook, and Tanner braced his hands on my thighs. I loved the grip of his strong fingers, wrapped tight around the base as he worked my dick with his sexy mouth. Up and down, spiral the tip, tongue the slit, then begin again.

"Have to, Tanner. Have to come. Now."

Sucking rhythmically, he inched me in farther and farther until I was totally engulfed in his mouth. His perfect, steamy, "I could dream about this every night and never get bored" mouth. Once his tongue started the swooping thing, where it felt like somehow he was managing to lick the tip, underside and balls all at once—I was a goner. I let it wash over me in a white rush of light. My eyes slammed shut and colors appeared—a fucking rainbow—pinks and purples, blues and red, bright orange and yellow, all danced behind my lids as I teetered on the brink, shaking, then finally gave in.

I tumbled into the sensation, mind clear, arms held wide, ready and willing to drown in a pool of ecstasy. No regrets. Only desire. Only Tanner. He was all I wanted. All I needed. He was everything, and he was there with me. I groaned as the pleasure crashed over me, wave after wave, racking my body. I gripped the dresser, feeling my knees give out. But Tanner stood and caught me in his arms. His kiss was salty sweet, him mixed with me.

"I missed you," he said.

"I missed you too." The words panted out of me. It took me a second, but I caught my breath and shoved him down on the bed. "My turn."

With Tanner sprawled naked on the bed, my mind went too many places at once. Suck? Fuck? Stroke? Frot? I wanted to do all of it, then take a break and do it all again.

Straddling him, I kissed my way from his cock to each nipple, then up to his collarbone, where I nipped until he groaned, to that spot on his neck that makes him emit a vibratey sigh, to his beautiful, perfect lips.

Kissing. Jesus, I'd missed kissing him. I swirled my tongue around his until we both ran out of breath, then started again. Tanner was hard beneath me, his cock wildly bucking against my ass.

"Did you bring lube?" he asked.

"No. I didn't think I'd need any. You don't have any here?"

"I never used it here. Wait. This is my suitcase from Fire Island. Let me check the pockets." He reached over the edge of the bed, rooted around, growling in frustration, and then turned toward me with a grin, holding up a tiny travel-sized tube. "And where would you like this lube to go?"

"Everywhere. I want to fuck you and be fucked by you and do everything else we can possibly come up with."

Tanner grinned. "You know I hated being away from you, but if this is the welcome home, maybe I should go away more often."

"Don't even think about it."

"Why not?"

My heart swelled. "I love you. And I don't even want to think about us being apart."

"Does that mean you're coming back to school with me?"

"Is that what you want?" *Please say yes.* My heartbeat drummed in my ears.

Tanner shook his head. "I asked what *you* want. Tell me. Please."

"Are you sure you want me back up there? You know it's spread everywhere now. We can't hide anymore, anywhere."

"I know. And I don't give a rat's ass what anyone has to say. I mean it. I know I let it get to me, but that's just because it was the first time I'd ever dealt with it. I'm sorry. I won't do that anymore. Fuck them. Let them say whatever they want. All I know is, you make me happy. You're all I need."

That did it. I crawled on top of him, needing my mouth on his. The saltiness had faded. All I tasted was him, and I couldn't get enough. We rubbed together, our cocks caressing each other as our bodies slid back and forth across the sheets, across each other. It was a good thing he'd blown me, or I'd have already busted a nut.

I sat up and grabbed the tube of lube, coating first my cock, then his. Getting to stroke both our cocks until they were slick and shiny was just a perk. The real reward was so close, I could taste it.

"Who goes first?"

"You."

Tanner lay back, displaying his body in all its naked glory. Dark nipples in tight, aroused peaks, firm chest, silky happy trail, and the most beautiful cock on the planet. I hooked my hands under his thighs and bent his knees to raise them up. Shoving a pillow under his ass put it at the perfect height and angle. I lubed my fingers and circled his hole. Feeling it quiver beneath my fingertips was enough to make a stream of precome run straight down my cock and pool on my balls. One finger, then two, stretching, exploring, stroking until he gasped. He was ready and so was I. Holding his thighs up, I had the most perfect view. Ass ready and waiting for me, cock at attention, balls drawn up and full. *Jesus. So fucking hot.* I lowered myself toward him, teasing him with the head of my dick.

Every time his hips bucked, I knew he wanted more, and I wanted to give him everything. I slid inside, slow and deep. His groans were the most beautiful music I'd ever heard. I'd forgotten how warm and tight he was. How insanely good it felt to be inside him.

I leaned closer and kissed him. Not an ordinary kiss, a "my life depends on this kiss" kind of kiss. Tanner whimpered as I slowly fucked him, stroking his cock in the same rhythm while my tongue kept time in his mouth. I kept my eyes open. I needed to see that he was really there with me and not some figment of an elaborate fantasy I'd cooked up. He wasn't a fantasy, though. He was real. And by the grace of God or the stars aligning or pure luck, he was mine.

"Oh God, faster."

I sped up, thrusting into him as I pumped away at his cock. Angling myself with my knees based on the bed, I could stroke his prostate. Every time I did, I could tell from the noises he'd make. Sexy, erotic noises that made it harder and harder for me not to come. "Fuck."

"Yes, harder."

I held him closer, keeping one hand between us to work his cock while my mouth worked his. I'd thought about this all week, but it was like I'd dreamed it in black-and-white, and we were in Technicolor.

The pressure inside me became unbearable, bordering on pain. "I have to come."

"Come."

"Come with me."

"Deal."

Rasping breaths filled the room as we fucked, kissed, and stroked. Tanner cried out first, deep animal sounds, followed by a high-pitched keen as he erupted everywhere. That's all it took. Seeing his dick in action put mine straight past the point of no return. Hot come bubbled up my length, then burst forth, filling Tanner. He must have felt it because he flinched and clenched, which felt even more amazing than it already had.

I slowly withdrew, then collapsed in a heap alongside him. He rolled so we were face-to-face.

His dark eyes shone in the dim light of the room. "Glad we decided to try out the room. Good sex room."

"It is."

He laughed and kissed me, then stroked my hair off my face with a serious look. "Will you go back with me? I don't want to do this alone. If you don't go back, I won't either. We'll finish up school online and find a place to live and take it from there."

"You can't do that. You'd miss the award ceremony for your ad campaign."

Tanner put his hands on either side of my face. "You still don't get it, do you? You're more important."

You're more important. I repeated the words trying desperately to let them sink in. "So you want to go back?"

"I do. It's our college too, you know? I don't intend to let some dumbass old-fashioned pricks ruin everything. I say we go back, heads held high, fix up the new place, make Gino proud. Then after graduation we can move wherever the hell we want."

"Together?" The idea that he was making plans for us to be together all those months away just floored me. Not that I was complaining, I just didn't know he thought like that.

"Is that okay?"

The shakiness was back in his voice. A sound I wanted banned from existence.

"Tanner, I've done some jerky things, but I thought they were for the right reasons. I promise I'll never do them again. And yes, together. God, I'll say yes to anything you suggest if we're together and you're okay with it."

"I'm more than okay with it. I need it. I need *you*."

My phone buzzed with the Sean text sound. I leaned over the bed and rummaged through my pants until I found it. Two messages:

Tell Mrs. D'Amico her friend is fucking amazing and let her know how grateful I am. I didn't even understand half of what he said in that legal document, but it shook Laura's needle-dick attorney up so much, he advised her to settle out of court. I get to keep the kids, Collie, thanks to you.

I swallowed hard, noticing a huge lump had formed in my throat, then clicked to the next message.

Hope you can come home soon. The kids and I miss you. Let me know how you're doing, okay? Love you, bro.

Again with the tears. My face kept springing leaks like a faulty garden hose. I swiped at my eyes, hoping Tanner hadn't noticed, but he had. He swept a thumb under each eye. "Good tears or bad?"

"Good. Really good. Only how the hell did your mother set my brother up with a lawyer?"

Tanner shrugged. "She knows a lot of rich and famous people. You don't work Broadway for twenty-five years and not meet the stars. She asked around, got a name, and hired him."

"Sean can't afford that."

"She knows. She can."

"Why? Why is she doing this?"

"Because his wife is wrong, for one thing, but mostly because it was making you miserable and keeping you from me. She's annoying at times, but she's a good mom."

"She's the best mom ever. I can't let her pay for all this, though."

"Yeah, you can. Collin, she wants to do this for you, for your family. You're going to have to learn to accept that there are some people in your life who sincerely want you to be happy."

"You know what would make me happy?"

"What?"

"If we could go sit on the couch and eat some of that Chinese food. I'm starving."

"Sounds perfect to me. Just remember, when we read our fortunes, we're gonna make them all come true—*in bed.*"

"God, I love you."

Tanner's lopsided grin made my heart do a giddy jig. "I love you too. And no one, anywhere, will ever convince me that's wrong. You're the best thing that's ever happened to me. We can do this, together. I know we can."

In that moment everything became clear—Tanner was my past, my present, my future. "We *can*. We *will*. Leaving you was the hardest thing I've ever done. I don't think I could survive it a second time."

"Then don't do it."

"Never again."

That was one promise I knew I could keep.

Epilogue

Six months later

THE COOLEST thing about living over the pizza place—other than me and Tanner having an apartment all to ourselves, which was fucking amazing—was that anytime we wanted takeout, all we had to do was trot downstairs. That was particularly helpful when we were having company, which had been happening on a regular basis. I'd never been big on socializing, but I realized that was because I'd always had something to hide. Now that I didn't, and the people closest to me all knew the truth, I wanted to see them as often as possible.

I checked the clock over the stove. Five minutes and the brownies would be done. That was perfect, because it meant they'd be cool by the time Sean and the kids arrived and started poking their fingers into them. Wendy was due any minute too. Supposedly we were finally going to get to meet her new boyfriend. I didn't know if they were serious enough that she wanted to start introducing him to her friends or if she'd just gotten sick of Tanner referring to the guy as a figment of her imagination. Either way she looked happy, and that's great to see.

The bedroom door squeaked as it opened, and Tanner stepped into the living room, tugging on a T-shirt. I watched until every last inch of his fucktastic stomach disappeared beneath the black fabric, then my gaze drifted up to his lopsided grin. We'd been together a whole year, and that smile still made my heart do backflips.

Tanner breathed in deep, letting his eyes drift shut, then sighing. "It smells amazing in here."

I closed the distance between us, needing to touch him. He tugged me up against him, and I willingly gave up the view of him to close my eyes and focus on the sensation of his lips on mine. Warm and solid. Sexy as hell. I pressed closer, feeling every inch of him align with me. We'd had sex twice already today, and I still wanted more. His hair was damp from his shower, and I breathed in the coconut lime, wondering if we had time to sneak off for a few minutes.

The oven timer answered with its shrill beep. Tanner groaned.

I chuckled. "Brownie interruptus."

"It's a good thing I love those damned brownies so much."

Before I could even turn off the timer, I heard footsteps coming up the stairs, followed by Sean holding the baby, telling the girls to knock and not just barge in. It didn't matter. Tanner opened the door before they had a chance and scooped Megan and Emma into a big hug.

"We made you a cake," Megan said, beaming at Tanner.

"For yours and Uncle Collin's abi-nursery!" Emma said.

Megan rolled her eyes. "Anniversary."

I set the hot pan of brownies on the stove, then shoved some bags of chips out of the way so Sean could set down the bakery box he was carrying.

He leaned closer to me, keeping his voice low. "Don't worry, the cake is from Carmine's. I just let the kids decorate."

I nodded, then turned toward the girls, who were bouncing on their toes with excitement. "You guys made this for us? Can we look at it now?"

They yelled "Yes!" and Tanner came over to take a peek as I lifted the lid: "Collin + Tanner" written in squiggly purple icing with tons of blue icing hearts surrounding it and even more blue heart-shaped sprinkles.

"We made blue hearts because you're boys," Megan said, looking so serious, I couldn't help but laugh.

"This is the coolest cake ever. Thank you."

"You guys are awesome." Tanner winked, which set off fresh rounds of giggles.

"You want to help get ready for the party? I need someone to put all these chips into the big bowls on the table."

"We will! We will!" They grabbed the bags and scampered up onto the kitchen chairs to start filling the bowls.

"Thanks, man," I said, catching Sean's eyes.

He smiled. "Happy anniversary."

The lump in my throat was threatening to take up permanent residence if I didn't stop with all the sentimental shit. I gave a cough and grabbed my wallet off the counter. "I'm gonna run down and get the pizza and subs. I'll be back in a few."

"Need help?" Tanner asked.

"Nah, just make sure my brother doesn't eat all the chips before I get back."

I ran into Wendy in the stairwell on the way down to Gino's. Her boyfriend, Nate, looked nothing like I'd expected. She usually went for dark-haired guys like Tanner and Dex, but Nate was even blonder than me. I didn't really care what he looked like. What mattered was how he looked at Wendy, which was like someone who was totally fucking in love.

"Go on up, the door's open," I said after introductions had been made.

"See you up there." She pointed to the top of the stairs, giving Nate a little shove as she followed behind him, then turned to mouth "Isn't he hot?"

I chuckled and mouthed back "Very."

Wendy smiled so broadly, it made my jaw hurt.

Gino had our order ready to go. Five pizzas—two plain, two Gino's specials, one veggie—and a bunch of Italian subs on a party platter.

I tried to pay, but he pushed my hand away.

"It's on the house, kid. Go enjoy your party."

"I can't take all this for free."

"If it'll make you feel better, I'll give you shitty hours for the next two weeks."

I groaned. "Can't I just pay?"

"I'm kidding. Get outta here."

As I backed out of the door, balancing the tray atop the boxes, I heard a familiar voice.

"I see you've got Tanner's order. What are the rest of us supposed to eat?"

Bryan stood grinning and shaking his head as he held the door so I could step onto the street.

"You made it."

"Yep, came straight from the New Hampshire gig. I had the band drop me off. I'll just take a train to the city later."

He looked tired but still hot as hell in that effortless, shaggy-haired, "I'm a musician so it's cool that I always look like I just rolled out of bed" kind of way. "It's great to see you. I didn't tell Tanner or Wendy you were coming. They'll flip."

"Cool. I haven't seen anyone since the summer. You want help carrying that stuff?"

"Nah, I've got it. Can you just get the door? Our place is right up—" My mind stumbled over the rest of the thought as I noticed someone studying the Batmobile across the street.

Not just someone. My heart picked up speed. I'd know that blond hair anywhere—it was exactly like mine. "On second thought, can you take this? Our door's at the top of the stairs."

"Sure thing."

I handed everything to him.

"You okay? You look like you've seen a ghost."

"I think I did." His eyebrow rose. I tried a laugh. "It's okay, there's just someone I need to say hi to. I'll be up in a sec."

Bryan shrugged and headed up the stairs.

I made my way across the street, half expecting that when I got closer, I'd realize I was mistaken and it was some other tall blond dude checking out my car. As I approached he turned, eyes meeting mine.

No mistake.

"Hey, bro," Quinn said. "You're keeping her in good condition."

I tried not to gape at him. *You haven't said a word to me in six months, and now you want to talk about my car?* "Always have."

He smoothed his hand over the hood, nodding. "Yeah, I guess you have."

Silence hung in the air. "Look, uh, I've got company, so if you came to deliver another lecture, now's really not the time."

Quinn flinched, which surprised me and made me feel a little bad. *But, shit, what am I supposed to think with the way he's acted?*

He raked a hand through his hair, then met my eyes. "No lectures, I promise. And I know about the party."

"You do?"

"Sean told me."

And he came anyway. Great. All I needed was a scene to ruin this day. My stomach did the conga as I tried to figure out how to end this as quickly and painlessly as possible. "Quinn, I'm not in the mood—"

He raised a hand. "I came to apologize."

It's a good thing Bryan had taken the pizza boxes, because if I'd still been holding them, they'd have wound up all over the street.

Quinn kept talking. "I'm sorry for the way I've acted, toward you and toward Sean, and I'm sorry I left both of you to deal with Mom by yourselves. I was a dick."

I'd never heard him talk like that. But I couldn't really argue. "Okay."

He dragged a foot along the asphalt, looking down at his shoe. "I thought I was doing the right thing, you know? Following the laws of the church. I figured if I could get you to see that, both of you, then everything would get fixed for all of us. You. Sean. Mom. But it doesn't work that way, does it?"

"No, it doesn't."

"I should have been a better brother."

This time when he looked up, his blue eyes had clouded gray with a mist of tears. *Jesus.* I hadn't seen Quinn cry since Dad's funeral. "It's okay. I get it. You have higher priorities. You're a priest."

"Almost a priest."

"Close enough."

"Maybe," he said. "But that's no excuse. And, well, I'm here to tell you I'd like to give us a fresh start. If you want."

"You realize I'm still in love with Tanner, right? That's not changing." It felt amazing to say those words, out loud, in the middle of the street, with no fear.

"I know. And according to Sean, you've never been happier. Is that true?"

"Totally."

"Then I'm happy for you."

It was my turn to have cloudy eyes. I blinked rapidly to keep in control. "Thanks."

"You think maybe I can meet him?"

"You want to come to our anniversary party? There are other gay guys there. You're not going to start sprinkling holy water on anyone or anything, are you?"

Quinn gave a deep laugh. I'd missed that sound. "I think I can control myself. Besides, I left my holy water in my other pants."

For the first time, I noticed he wasn't dressed any way priestly today, just jeans and a T-shirt. "And you actually want to come?"

"I've missed you, Collie."

Sean still called me that, but Quinn hadn't said it since we were kids. My hesitation melted. "I've missed you too. Come on."

Quinn clapped his hand on my shoulder and followed me across the street, then up the stairs to our apartment. Even more people had shown up while I'd been out, and the place was buzzing with laugher and conversation.

Tanner caught my eye as soon as I walked in the door. He headed straight toward me, glancing between me and Quinn with a curious look on his face. I grabbed his hand and tugged him closer, leaning in for a quick kiss. If Quinn wanted to do this, he needed to show me he was serious.

When I pulled back from Tanner, I studied Quinn's face, looking for any shred of disapproval, ready to ask him to leave. All I saw was a smile directed at Tanner. He held out his hand. "You must be Tanner. I've heard a lot about you. I'm Collin's brother Quinn."

Tanner did his best to hide his reaction, but I could tell he was surprised. He shook Quinn's hand. "Welcome."

"Happy anniversary."

Tanner's eyes widened, but he smiled. "Thanks. Come on in. Can I get you a drink?"

"That would be great."

Tanner whispered in my ear. "You okay?"

"Yeah."

He held my eyes, studying them, then leaned in and gave me another kiss. This one lasted longer, sweet and steady, just what I needed. As he walked away, I looked around our apartment. My brothers, my friends, my boyfriend—almost everyone I cared about—all in one place, together, happy, celebrating that Tanner and I had made it. Celebrating our love.

I didn't know what the future might bring, but I knew what I had in that second, and it was more than I'd ever hoped for.

I'm happy.
I'm in love.
And I just want to savor every moment.

KAREN STIVALI is a prolific writer, compulsive baker, and chocoholic with a penchant for books, movies, and fictional British men. She's also the multiple-award-winning author of contemporary and erotic romances. Her lifelong fascination with people has led her to careers ranging from hand-drawn animator to party planner to marriage and family counselor, but writing has always been her passion. Karen enjoys nothing more than following her characters on their journey toward love. Whether the couples are m/f or m/m, it's guaranteed that Karen's novels are filled with food, friendship, love, and smoking hot sex—all the best things in life.

When Karen isn't writing (and often when she is), she can be found on Twitter attempting witty banter and detailing the antics of her fruit-loving cat, BadKitteh. She loves to hear from readers (and other writers), so don't hesitate to contact/follow/like her at:

Twitter: https://twitter.com/karenstivali
Facebook: https://www.facebook.com/KarenStivaliAuthor
Website: http://karenstivali.com
Pinterest: http://www.pinterest.com/karenstivali
Goodreads:
https://www.goodreads.com/author/show/5170527.Karen_Stivali
E-mail: karenstivali@gmail.com

Karen Stivali—Novels about love... like real life, only hotter.
RWA Passionate Plume Award winner 2012 and 2014
NEC-RWA Beanpot Readers' Choice Award winner 2013
RWA National Excellence in Romance Fiction Award double finalist 2014
PAN certified member of RWA and member of Rainbow Romance Writers

Cate Ashwood

THIRTY
Things

http://www.dreamspinnerpress.com

The Last Guy Breathing

SKYLAR M. CATES

http://www.dreamspinnerpress.com

Jacob Z. Flores
BEING TRUE

http://www.dreamspinnerpress.com

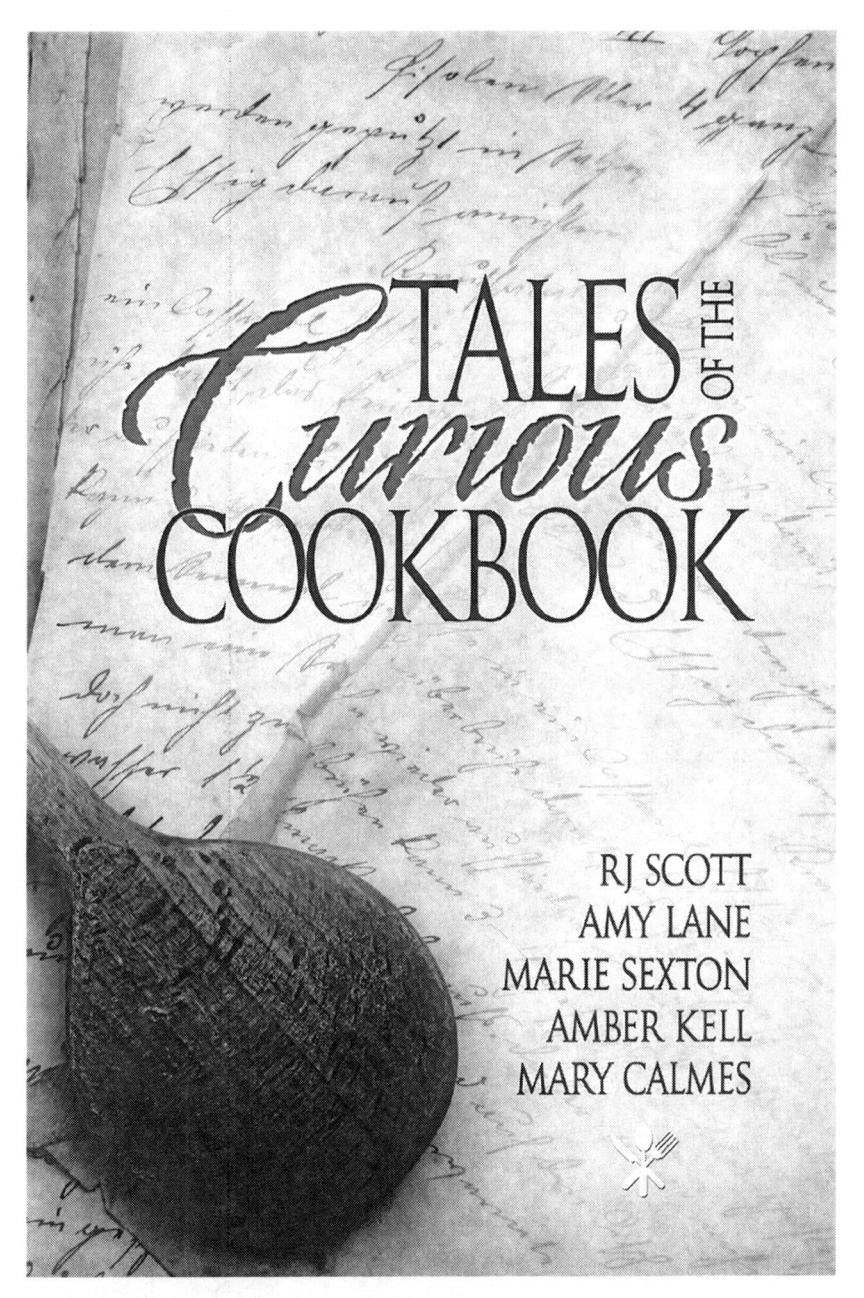

TALES OF THE Curious COOKBOOK

RJ SCOTT
AMY LANE
MARIE SEXTON
AMBER KELL
MARY CALMES

http://www.dreamspinnerpress.com

MICHELE FOGAL

KING OF
Snowflakes

WEST COAST BOYS

http://www.dreamspinnerpress.com

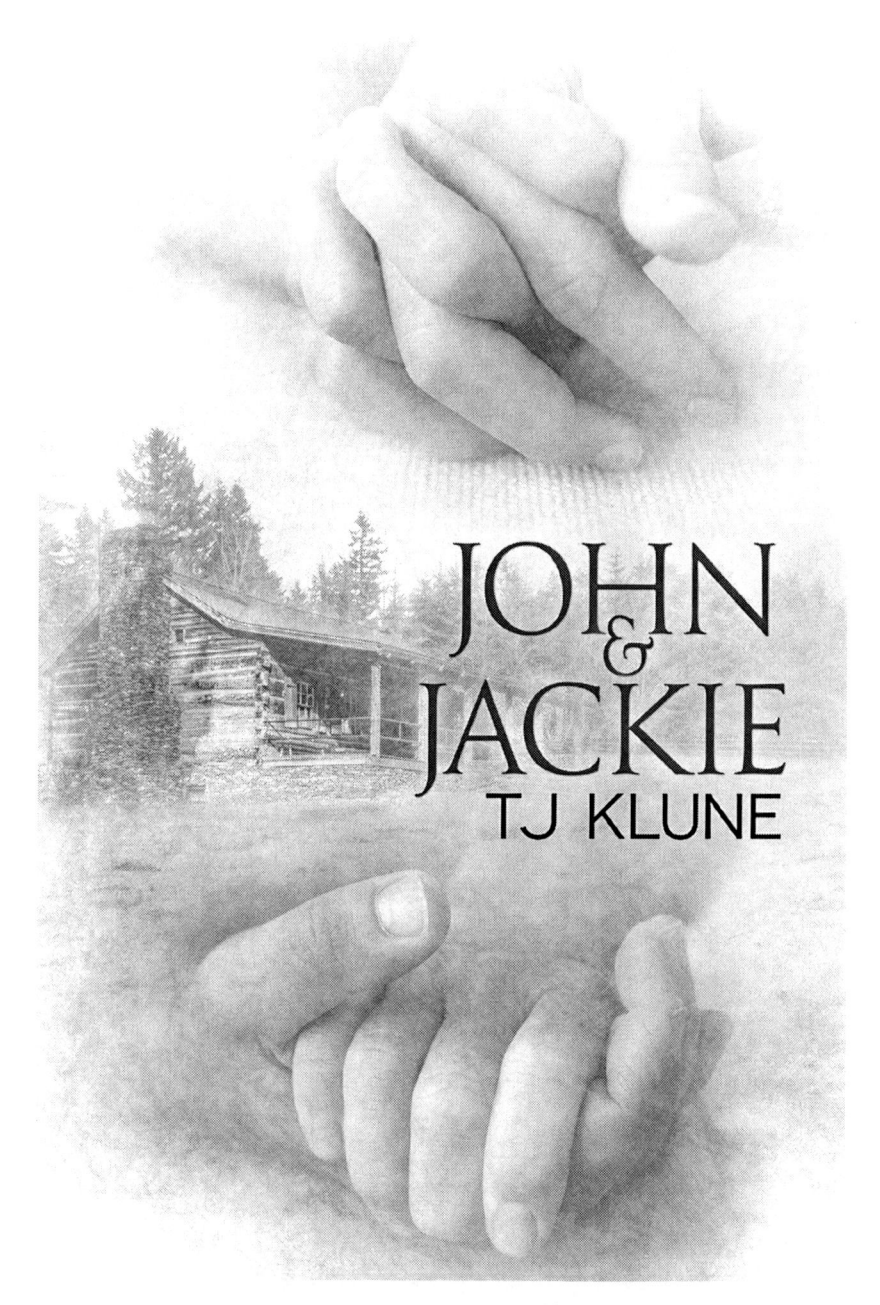

JOHN & JACKIE
TJ KLUNE

http://www.dreamspinnerpress.com

Before the FINAL ENCORE
Scotty Cade

http://www.dreamspinnerpress.com

MOST BEAUTIFUL Words

RAINE O'TIERNEY

http://www.dreamspinnerpress.com

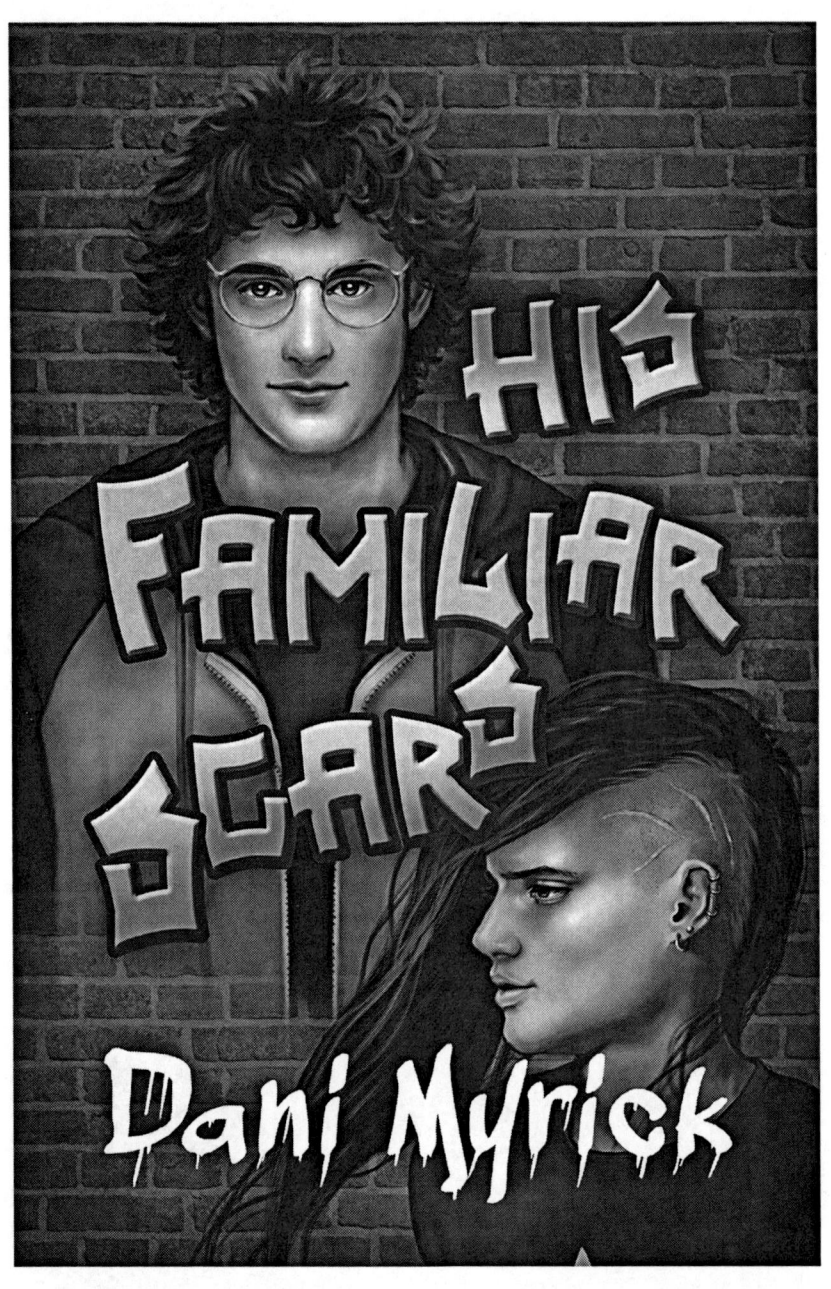

http://www.dreamspinnerpress.com

SERPENTINE SERIES

AIDAN'S JOURNEY

CJANE ELLIOTT

http://www.dreamspinnerpress.com

FOR MORE

OF THE
**BEST
GAY
ROMANCE**

DREAMSPINNER PRESS

dreamspinnerpress.com

CPSIA information can be obtained
at www.ICGtesting.com
Printed in the USA
FFOW03n2046250617
37107FF